BOUVARD AND PECUCHET

ALSO BY FLAUBERT

Dictionary of Accepted Ideas

Published by New Directions

Bouvard and Pécuchet

BY

GUSTAVE FLAUBERT

TRANSLATED BY

T. W. EARP AND G. W. STONIER

WITH AN INTRODUCTION BY

LIONEL TRILLING

A NEW DIRECTIONS BOOK

INTRODUCTION

by Lionel Trilling

I

FLAUBERT died suddenly in 1880, having brought close to its end but leaving unfinished and unrevised the novel that had occupied his thought for eight years. The entire dedication of himself with which Flaubert responded to the claims of art is of course the very essence of his legend, but to *Bouvard and Pécuchet* he gave a special and savage devotion which went beyond the call of literary duty as even he understood it. The book was to him more than a work of art; it was a deed. At the moment of what he conceived to be the ultimate defeat of true culture, it was an act of defiance and revenge. Flaubert was not unique in nineteenth-century France for his belief that bourgeois democracy was bringing about the death of mind, beauty, literature, and greatness; this opinion, among the distinguished writers of the century, was virtually a commonplace. But he was unique in the immediacy and simplicity with which he experienced the debacle—'I can no longer talk with anyone without growing angry; and whenever I read anything by one of my contemporaries I rage.' [1] He was unique too in the necessity he felt to see the crisis in all its possible specificity of detail. For him the modern barbarism was not

---

[1] All the quotations from Flaubert's letters are from the admirable *Selected Letters of Gustave Flaubert* edited and translated by Francis Steegmuller published by Farrar, Straus, and Young.

merely a large general tendency which could be comprehended by a large general emotion; he was constrained to watch it with a compulsive and obsessive awareness of its painful particularities. He was made rabid—to use his own word—by *this* book, *this* phrase, *this* solecism, *this* grossness of shape or form, *this* debasement of manners, *this* hollow imitation of thought. He was beyond believing that he could do anything to stem or divert the flood of swinishness, as he called it, that was sweeping away every hope of the good life—*Bouvard and Pécuchet* is a triumph of the critical mind, but if we suppose criticism to be characterised by the intention to correct and reform, the book cannot be called a work of criticism. In its intention it is less to be compared with any other literary work than with the stand of Roland at Roncesvalles. No less beset than the hero, no less hopeless, no less grim, and no less grimly glad, Flaubert resolves that while the breath of life is in him he will give blow for blow and pile up the corpses of his enemies as a monument to the virtues they despise and he adores.

His long fierce passion for the book was not matched by the expectation of certain of his friends who were most competent to estimate the chances of its success. 'I am preparing a book,' he wrote to Turgenev in November of 1872, 'in which I shall spit out my bile.' But Turgenev grew troubled, and so did Taine and Zola, because Flaubert was precisely not spitting out his bile. The new novel, as Flaubert said of it, was to be 'a kind of encyclopedia made into farce,' and he devoured libraries, his notebooks grew ever more numerous, and his pride in them grew with their number; he was to brag that he had read fifteen hundred books in preparation for the novel. Anyone who loved Flaubert must have been dismayed as he gave year after year of his life to gathering the materials for a massive joke which was no doubt very funny but surely not so funny as to need this sacrificial attention from a man of genius. His love of research, his insatiable craving for particularity, was said to have spoiled *Salammbô* by overloading it with antiquarian lumber. Now it threatened to defeat the new work. Turgenev and Taine believed that an intellectual satire such as Flaubert planned must be short if it was to be read; Turgenev pointed to Swift and Voltaire in support of his opinion that *Bouvard and Pécuchet* must be treated *presto*. But Flaubert persisted in his extravagance. What he wanted to do, he said, was nothing less than to take account of the whole intellectual life of France. 'If it were treated briefly, made concise and light, it would be a fantasy —more or less witty, but without weight or plausibility; whereas if I give it detail and development I will seem to be believing my own story, and it can be made into something serious and even frightening.' And he believed that it was exactly by an excess of evidence that he would avoid pedantry.

The misgivings of his friends seemed in part justified by the public response to the book when it was published in the year after Flaubert's death. At first it was accepted merely as a 'document,' that is, its interest seemed to derive less from itself than from its connection with its author. But as the years passed the first impression was corrected. With due allowance made for its unfinished, unrevised state, but quite in its own right, *Bouvard and Pécuchet* was given its place beside the great works of Flaubert's canon. Its pleasures are granted to be very different from those of *Madame Bovary* and *A Sentimental Education*, but French readers find in it a peculiar interest and charm consonant with its nature.

Its nature is singular. We cannot go so far as to say with Ezra Pound that the novel 'can be regarded as the inauguration of a new form which has no precedents,' and in any case, Mr. Pound, after having said that 'neither *Gargantua*, nor

Don Quixote, nor Sterne's *Tristram Shandy* had furnished the archetype,' goes on to show its clear connection with at least the first-named book. And if it can be argued that *Bouvard and Pécuchet,* in its character of 'a kind of encyclopedia made into farce,' has no specific literary genre except perhaps that which is comprised by *Gargantua,* it is still true that there are a sufficient number of works sufficiently analogous with it in one respect or another to constitute, if not a genre, then at least a tradition in which it may be placed. Yet its singularity must not be slighted.

If we try to say what was the characteristic accomplishment of the French novelists of the nineteenth century, we can scarcely help concluding that it was the full, explicit realisation of the idea of society as the definitive external circumstance, the main 'condition,' of the individual life. American literature of the great age was, as D. H. Lawrence was the first to see, more profound in this respect than the French, in that it went deeper into the unconscious life of society; and in England Dickens in his way and the later Trollope in his were more truly perceptive of social motives and movements. But the French achievement was more explicit than either the American or the English, it made itself available to more people. Almost, we might be moved to say, it made itself too available: it is the rare person who can receive the full news of the inherent social immorality without injury to his own morality, without injury, indeed, to his own intellect—nothing can be so stultifying as the simple, unelaborated belief that society is a fraud. Yet with the explicit social intelligence of the great French novels we dare not quarrel—it is a *given* of our culture, it is one of the ineluctable elements of our modern fate, and on the whole one of the nobler elements. What *Bouvard and Pécuchet* adds to this general fund of social intelligence is the awareness of the part that is played in our modern life by ideas—not merely by assumptions, which of course have always played their part in every society, but by ideas as they are formulated and developed in books. The originality of Flaubert's perception lies in its intensity; other novelists before Flaubert had been aware of the importance of ideas in shaping the lives of their heroes, and Flaubert himself, in *A Sentimental Education*, had shown Frédéric Moreau living in a kind of ideological zoo—Sénécal, Regimbart, Deslauriers, Pellerin, all have learned from books the roar or squeal or grunt by which they identify themselves. But in *Bouvard and Pécuchet* the books themselves are virtually the *dramatis personae*; it is they, even more than the actual people of the Norman village, that constitute reality for the two comic heroes. Through this extravagance Flaubert signalises the ideological nature of modern life.

No one has followed Flaubert in his enterprise. In the essay to which I have referred, Mr. Pound was bringing, in 1922, the first news of Joyce's *Ulysses* to the readers of the *Mercure de France*, and he spoke at some length of the connection that is to be found between *Ulysses* and *Bouvard and Pécuchet*. 'Between 1880 and the year *Ulysses* was begun,' he says, 'no one had the courage to make a gigantic collection of absurdities, nor the patience to seek out the man-type, the most general generalization,'—and he goes on to speak of Leopold Bloom as being, like Bouvard and Pécuchet, 'the basis of democracy, the man who believes what he reads in the papers.' The connection between the two novels is certainly worth remarking, but although *Ulysses* does indeed resemble *Bouvard and Pécuchet* in its encyclopedic effect, the use made of the absurdities they collect is very different in the one novel and in the other. The difference is defined by the dissimilar intellectual lives of Leopold Bloom and Bouvard and Pécuchet. To Bloom, ideas are the furniture or landscape of his mind, while to Bouvard and Pécuchet they exist, as I have suggested, as characters in the actual world. Bloom's ideas are notions; they are bits and pieces of fact and approximations and adumbrations of thought pieced together from newspapers and books carelessly read; Bloom means to look them up and get them straight but he never does. They are subordinate to his emotions, to which they lend substance and colour. If a judgment is passed upon them by the author, it is of an oblique sort and has to do with their tone, with their degree of vulgarity, not with their inner consistency or cogency. But Bouvard and Pécuchet are committed to ideas and confront them fully. They amass books and study them. Ideas are life and death to them.

There is no necessity to choose between the two conceptions of what Mr. Pound called 'the man-type, the most general generalization.' Leopold Bloom represents much of the modern mind from the lowest to the highest. His representativeness probably needs less to be insisted on than that of Bouvard and Pécuchet, who stand for the condition of life of any reader of this book, of any person who must decide by means of some sort of intellectual process what is the correct *theory* of raising his children; or what is the right *principle* of education; or whom he shall be psychoanalysed by, a Freudian, a Reichian, a Washingtonian; whether he 'needs' religion, and if so, which confession is most appropriate to his temperament and cultural background; what kind of architecture he shall adopt for his house, and what the true theory of the modern is; what kind of heating is best suited to his life-style; how he shall feel about the State; about the Church; about Labour; about China; about Russia; about India. If we try to say how the world has changed from, say, two hundred years ago, we must see that it is in the respect that the conscious mind has been brought to bear upon almost every aspect of life; that ideas, good, bad, indifferent, are of the essence of our existence. That is why Flaubert was made 'rabid' by his perception of stupidity. And if we look to see if anyone has matched Flaubert in the passion of his response to ideas, we will not discover that person in any art and only one in any other discipline—Nietzsche alone, I think, saw the modern world as Flaubert did, and with Flaubert's intensity of passion.

But when we have become aware of the singularity of *Bouvard and Pécuchet*, we must be no less aware of the tradition in which its singularity exists. As for the novel's connection with Rabelais, it may be observed even in certain aspects of the prose, not necessarily as a result of influence, perhaps only because of the effect of an analogous subject matter. 'He planted passion-flowers in the shade, pansies in the sun, covered hyacinths with manure, watered the lilies after they had flowered, destroyed the rhododendrons by cutting them back, stimulated the fuchsias with glue, and roasted the pomegranate tree by exposing it to the kitchen fire'—the errors of this catalogue are committed not by the infant Gargantua but by Pécuchet. Rabelais knew nothing of encyclopedias but he too wrote 'a sort of encyclopedia made into farce.' His intention was in part that of Flaubert—it was the intention of burlesque, the mockery of learning. But only in part: Rabelais also had the intention of which Flaubert's is the exact inversion. It is no doubt all too easy to reduce Rabelais to a classroom example of the high optimism of the early Renaissance, and to make more naïve than it really is his humanistic delight in the arts, sciences, crafts, and exercises which are available to man. Yet the optimism and the humanistic delight are certainly of the essence of Rabelais and they are specifically controverted in *Bouvard and Pécuchet*. We have but to look at the respective treatments of gymnastics to see how Flaubert stands Rabelais on his head—

Gargantua's friend Gymnast can make any demand upon his agility and strength, to Rabelais' great pleasure, but nothing is sadder than the middle-aged Bouvard and Pécuchet putting themselves to school to the regimen and apparatus of Amoros' Manual, which, absurd as it is, descends in a direct line from the Renaissance idea of the Whole Man, the vaunting mind in the vaulting body.

If we speak of encyclopedias, there is one actual encyclopedia which we must have in recollection—the great *Encyclopédie* itself. Flaubert never makes Diderot the object of his satire—one may well suppose that the author of *Rameau's Nephew* was the last man in the world with whom Flaubert would have sought a quarrel—but Diderot's great enterprise of the *Encyclopédie*, which derived its impulse as much from the spirit of Rabelais as from the spirit of Bacon, is the heroic and optimistic enterprise of which the researches of *Bouvard and Pécuchet* are the comic and pessimistic counterpart. To have thought of Diderot busily running about France, taking notes on this trade or that process, learning how spinning or weaving or smelting or brewing was done, so that all the world might have a healthy knowledge of the practical arts, would be to have the inspiration for those scenes in which Bouvard and Pécuchet undertake to deal with practical life, to grow their own food and to preserve it, to make their own cordial (*Bouvarine* it is to be called!). *Bouvard and Pécuchet* in its despair that anything at all can be done is the negation of the morning confidence and hope of the *Encyclopédie*.

Which brings us to the third book of *Gulliver's Travels*. The Voyage to Laputa, in which Swift satirises the scientific theories of his day, may be thought of as the ambivalent prolegomenon to the *Encyclopédie*—ambivalent because Swift was Baconian in his conception of the practical aim of science but anti-Baconian in his contempt for any kind of scientific method he knew of, even Bacon's positivism. In the expression of his scorn he provides a striking precedent for *Bouvard and Pécuchet*, which had for its explanatory subtitle, 'The failings of the methods of science.' The analogy that may be drawn between Flaubert's book and Swift's goes considerably beyond what is suggested merely by the Voyage to Laputa—it leads us, indeed, to the personal similarity between Flaubert and Swift. But this may better be observed in a later place.

Mr. Pound, having particularly in mind the encyclopedic nature of *Bouvard and Pécuchet*, finds *Don Quixote* to be a very different kind of thing—'Cervantes parodied but a single literary folly, the chivalric folly.' Yet it is not the parody of the chivalric idea that in itself makes *Don Quixote* what it is, but rather the complex drama that results from putting an elaborate idea to the test in the world of actuality. Flaubert said of Madame Bovary that she was the sister of Don Quixote; Bouvard and Pécuchet are at least consanguineous enough to be cousins. And their idea, despite its encyclopedic mutations, is, after all, as much a unity as Don Quixote's: they believe that the world yields to mind. And if *Don Quixote*, then certainly *Candide*, which also tests an idea in the laboratory of the world. The conclusion of *Bouvard and Pécuchet*, 'Let us return to copying,' has not become proverbial only because its proverbial possibilities have been pre-empted by 'Let us cultivate our garden.'

Then the second act of *The Bourgeois Gentleman*, in which Monsieur Jourdain receives instruction from the professors of the sciences, arts and graces, may be thought of as a small encyclopedia in the form of a farce and as the model for this history of the bourgeois savants. And the ingenious reader may amuse himself by discovering all the analogies that may be drawn between *Bouvard and Pécuchet* and *Faust*.

II

'*Bouvard et Pécuchet sont-ils des imbéciles?*' The blunt question is the title of an essay, notable in the history of Flaubert criticism, which was published in 1912 by the eminent scholar René Dumesnil. It is the question which lies at the heart of the ambiguity of *Bouvard and Pécuchet*.

It will perhaps seem strange that ambiguity should be imputed to the novel. In England and America more people know about *Bouvard and Pécuchet* than have read it. The author's purpose as stated in his famous correspondence, and also the outline of the story, are part of our general literary information. Neither the purpose nor the story suggests the possibility of ambiguity. Flaubert's avowed intention, that of pillorying the culture of bourgeois democracy, does not seem likely to induce or even permit more than one meaning to appear. As for his plan of having two simple copying clerks undertake to master seriatim all the sciences and disciplines and to come to grief or boredom with each one, it seems clear and schematic to a degree, even to a fault—it is hard to see why it should not be entirely within the control of the author's equally clear purpose. Yet it has been said by a French writer that of all the works of Flaubert, it is *Bouvard and Pécuchet* that gives the critics the most trouble; that it is a book which is intricate, complex, and difficult to analyse; that its meaning is hard to come at.[2]

Indeed, so great is the ambiguity of *Bouvard and Pécuchet* that it is possible to conclude that the book quite fails to be what Flaubert intended it to be. Which does not, of course, prevent it from being something else of a very good sort.

The trouble starts with the fact that Bouvard and Pécuchet,

[2] Claude Digeon, in his *Le Dernier Visage de Flaubert*, Paris, 1946, p. 94.

as Dumesnil demonstrated, are not imbeciles. Perhaps it is too much to say, as Dumesnil does say, that they have the souls of apostles, but imbeciles they certainly are not, and we shall be able to go considerably further in their praise than this mere negation. There can be no doubt that Flaubert began with the intention of making them as foolish and ridiculous as possible. We are surely not free to suppose that he had any inclination to show them mercy because they were poor clerks and lived very limited lives. When the word bourgeoisie came to be used in this country in a social-political sense, it was likely to be restricted in its reference to people of pretty solid establishment. For the social group more or less analogous to that to which Bouvard and Pécuchet belonged we used other words, choosing them according to our political disposition—'white collar worker,' 'office proletariat,' 'little people.' But Flaubert made no such distinction. For him the bourgeoisie was the bourgeoisie from top to bottom. He saw the characteristics and the power of the class as continuous from the wealthy to the poor. If he had thought to call the small bourgeoisie the 'little people,' he would have done so contemptuously, having reference to the size of their ideas and ideals and impulses. And he feared them exactly for this littleness, which he believed they wanted to impose upon the world. It was by no means the straitened lives that Bouvard and Pécuchet lived for forty-seven years until the great moment when they met each other that induced Flaubert to let them off from being imbeciles. No doubt in reference to just this hole-and-corner existence he had at one time cruelly planned to call the book 'The Memoirs of Two Cockroaches.'

But two cockroaches cannot be friends with each other. And François Denys Bartholomée Bouvard and Juste Romain Cyrille Pécuchet—their Christian names once mentioned in their history are forever forgotten and may as well be memorialised here—are truly friends. This fact is of decisive importance in the novel—it defeats whatever intention Flaubert may have had to make his protagonists contemptible. To Flaubert friendship was not merely a relation: it was a virtue, as it was for Montaigne, as it was for Swift.

Bouvard and Pécuchet are able to be friends because they are sufficiently different in their natures, although at one in their minds. Bouvard, as the sound of his name suggests, is the fleshier of the two, the more rotund, and the easier-going, the more sentimental, sensual, and worldly. Pécuchet, in accordance with his name, is lean and stringy; he is puritanical, passionate, pessimistic—a little more *sincere* than Bouvard. (Flaubert set great store by their names. When he overheard Zola say that he had found the perfect name for a character, Bouvard, he turned pale, and in the greatest agitation begged Zola not to use it. And he was much troubled when a banker named Pécuchet, a man he respected, played an important part in his financial life in 1875; the point of delicacy was settled by M. Pécuchet's death.)

Once in their life together, after many frustrations, at a moment when they are nervous and depressed, Bouvard and Pécuchet find that they can't stand the sight of each other; this is natural and transitory, and it but serves to emphasise the fullness and constancy of their devotion to each other. Their manner of life, we must recognise, has great charm. They are much harassed, much frustrated by practical as well as by intellectual matters, but their housekeeping, which is omnipresent in the story, is a pleasure to read about. Even when the economy falls quite to pieces and becomes sordid, it never quite belies the rich common poetry of their first meal, their first evening, their first morning in their own home. From their establishment we derive the pleasure which is afforded by the living arrangements of *Robinson Crusoe* or *The Swiss Family Robinson,* or Boffin's Bower, or Sherlock Holmes's rooms in Baker Street. Their enterprises are based on innocence and a pleasant sufficiency: they have a good deal in common with the respected author of 'Speculations on the Source of the Hempstead Ponds, with some Observations on the Theory of Tittlebats,' for Mr. Pickwick, another super-annuated bourgeois bachelor, was devoted to the life of the mind, and his scientific adventures, although more primitive than those of Bouvard and Pécuchet, are alike in kind. They have affinity with Tom Sawyer—they are consciously boyish in their dreams of glory, in their dreams of love; for a moment, in their hydrotherapeutic phase, they have their Jackson's Island and are seen naked as Red Indians and gleefully splashing each other from their adjoining baths. Their life, despite its disappointments, is a kind of idyll, and it approaches the pastoral convention—there is no reason not to think of them as two shepherds tending their woolly flocks of ideas. Who would not want to read Bouvard's 'Lament for Pécuchet,' or, for the matter of that, Pécuchet's 'Elegy for Bouvard,' whichever came first; and whose heart would not be wrung by the event either poem recorded and the loneliness of the survivor at the double copying desk, the contrivance of which had been the last ingenuity of the two friends?

Had they lived alone and pursued their studies and projects alone, it is possible that imbecility might have descended upon the mind of each. It is not until they meet each other that they really begin their intellectual life. Although they are always at one in their enthusiasm, they take sufficiently different views of questions to create between them a degree of dialectic; Flaubert, like Plato, conceived of friendship as one of the conditions of thought. Love and logic go together.

Not imbeciles, then, but certainly not without folly.

Wherein does the folly of Bouvard and Pécuchet lie? In part their error is the same as that of their prototype, Monsieur Jourdain—they want to learn too quickly. They do not know the true mode of thought, they have no patience. They would not understand what many of the great researchers meant when they said that they stared at the facts until the facts spoke to them. They are committed to the life of the mind in general, but not, in the way of the true scholar, in particular. They are perhaps too thoroughly Whole Men; they lack the degree of benign limitation which permits an intense preoccupation, making a single subject seem the satisfaction of the demands of a whole temperament. And then we must remember their age; they are forty-seven when they begin, they have no time for patience—they are about the same age as Faust was when he expressed his sense of the inadequacy of all the disciplines. They are Faustian; they must try everything, and to no intellectual moment are they able to say their 'Verweile doch!'

But their measure of folly is not what makes Bouvard and Pécuchet comic characters. They are comic through the operation of the censorship which the race exercises over those who address themselves to the large enterprises of the spirit. This censorship undertakes to say who may engage upon what high adventures. It decides who, by reason of age or degree of pulchritude or social class, may be permitted to fall in love, or have surpassing ambitions, or think great thoughts. Whether or not we are ourselves engaged in any of the great spiritual enterprises, we feel it our duty to protect their decorum and their décor by laughing at anyone who does not conform to the right image of the lover, the hero, or the thinker. This would be a more disagreeable human trait than in fact it is if we were not at the same time prepared to discover that some of the people whom we debar from their desires have their own special virtues. Leopold Bloom, although he has no ashplant and no irony and does not answer every question 'quietly' as Stephen Dedalus does, but, on the contrary, is without dignity in love or thought, is yet seen to be a proper object of our respect and affection. Don Quixote is too old, too stringy, too poor, as well as too late in the day, for chivalry and courtly love, but he is not too much or too little of anything to be wise with a new kind of wisdom. The ancient inscription that Mr. Pickwick discovers is deciphered to read 'Bill Stubbs, his mark,' which he believes to be nothing but the operation of malice—he really has no mind at all except what makes him defy Dodson & Fogg and become the saint of the Fleet.

So with Bouvard and Pécuchet. They are funny because they are what they are, because they are middle-aged, because one is fat and one is thin; because they wear strange garments; because they are unmarried and awkward in love; because they are innocent; because they are clumsy and things blow up in their faces, or fall on them, or trip them up; because they are gullible and think they are shrewd; because they are full of enthusiasm. Being funny in themselves, being comically *not* the men for high enterprises, they are therefore funny when they undertake the intellectual life. Their comicality is *a priori*, it does not grow out of their lack of intelligence. When it comes to intelligence, many a man has less who can command a better laboratory technique than theirs. Granted that they begin each adventure in stupidity, as they progress through the intellectual disciplines these 'simple, lucid, mediocre' minds (as Maupassant called them) are likely to see whatever absurdities are to be seen; they are the catalysts of the foolishness of others.

Then, whether or not they are properly to be called apostles, their degree of virtue and their generosity of spirit are unmistakable. Their hearts—and what is more, their minds—instinctively take the side of the insulted and injured. If they cannot stay long with one idea, they nevertheless live by the mind; the courage that this requires they abundantly have. It is not they who exemplify the vices of the bourgeoisie that Flaubert despised. For the bourgeoisie they have nothing but contempt. In their conflicts with the local priest, doctor, mayor, magnate, it is they who are in the right of things. They stand for intelligence: they are traitors to their class. And they suffer the consequences; they acquire the peculiar pathos of their dedication.

The evidence of their superiority gave umbrage. As they upheld immoral points of view, they were surely immoral themselves; slanders were invented about them.

Then a pitiable faculty developed in their spirit, that of perceiving stupidity and no longer tolerating it.

Insignificant things made them sad: advertisements in the newspapers, a smug profile, a foolish remark heard by chance.

Musing on what was said in the village, and on there existing as far as the Antipodes [other people like the members of the village bourgeoisie], they felt as though the heaviness of all the earth were weighing on them.

It is no wonder that more than one critic has wondered whether Bouvard and Pécuchet must not be taken as representatives of Flaubert himself, or of Flaubert and the good friend and neighbour of his later years, Laporte, who found pleasure in helping accumulate the material for *Bouvard and Pécuchet*.

III

Bouvard and Pécuchet, then, are not the objects of Flaubert's satire. At most they are the butts of his humour, which is strongly qualified by affection. They are never represented as doing anything in the least ignoble or mean. They are 'justified' characters. We therefore naturally suppose that the savageness which the book was intended to express is to be found in the exposition of the studies which the two friends undertake—this surely will constitute the fierce indictment of the bourgeois democracy.

But again our supposition is disappointed. The horrors of the culture of the bourgeois democracy play a considerably smaller part than we anticipate. They are less horrible than we had expected. And the animus with which they are exhibited turns out to be not nearly so savage as we had been led to hope.

As I have said, a good many of the misadventures of Bouvard and Pécuchet befall them simply because they are comic characters, or because life is as it is. If their tenant farmer cheats them, if their handyman diddles them, we cannot conclude that rural cupidity and the unreliability of rural labor have been brought about by the ascendancy of the bourgeoisie. If Bouvard, in two wonderful scenes, witnesses the terrible power of sexuality, in human beings and in peacocks, and cannot himself go much further in the direction of passion than a warm flush of inclination, or if Pécuchet contracts gonorrhea from his first sexual experience, we are not exactly being given examples of the effect of the bourgeois swinishness. When the hailstorm destroys the fruit which the two beginners have been almost successful in bringing to maturity, the phenomenon is not cultural but meteorological and, in its context, cosmological. That the agricultural treatises differ from each other, that 'as regards marl, Puvis recommends it, Ravet's handbook opposes it,' this cannot fairly be ascribed to the contemporary corruption of mind—it is of the immemorial nature of farming: since the time of Cain, farmers have exercised their moral faculties on just such differences of opinion. Pécuchet meditates on the inherent contradictions that seem to exist between fruit and branch: 'The authorities recommend stopping all the ducts. If not, the sap is injured, and the tree, of course, suffers. For it to flourish, it would have to bear no fruit at all. Yet those that are never pruned or manured yield fruit, smaller, indeed, but better flavoured' —this is not an indictment of the stupidity of bourgeois-democratic pomology but a profound consideration of the nature of life, cultural as well as arboricultural. In their true goodness of heart the two friends undertake to rear and educate a pair of brutalised waifs; they fail not because their educational methods are contemptible but because the human material has become intractable.

A considerable part of the intellectual criticism of the novel depends upon the inversion of the snobbish censorship to which I have referred. This is the mode of comedy which perceives that if any abstruse discipline is confronted with an actual human being, no matter how stupid—and, indeed, the stupider the better—it is the person who is justified as against the discipline. A draper should not be adept in arms nor study the arts of logic or language; still, when put in company of the fencing master who can kill a man by demonstrative reason, or the rhetorician who shows him that *A* is sounded with the mouth *so*, Monsieur Jourdain is not the greatest fool on the stage, nor would he be if he had secured Aristotle as his teacher. In any vaudeville dialectic the intellectual advantage always rests with the obtuse or primitive person; the straight man, the patient teacher who believes in the subject, is always discredited. No discipline which is confronted with the simplicity, the intellectual *innocence*, of Bouvard and Pécuchet can long maintain its pretence to value.

Then we must have in mind the large part that is played

in the book by the intellectual and quasi-intellectual absurdities which are as ridiculous as we want to call them, but about which it is impossible for a sensible man to be seriously troubled. Two of the amusing episodes of the novel concern themselves with Bouvard and Pécuchet training their memories by a compound of three mnemonic systems and hardening their bodies according to Amoros' Manual of gymnastics. René Descharmes, in his well known work, *Autour de Bouvard et Pécuchet,* devotes a long chapter to one of the mnemonic systems, the most famous one of all, that of Feinagle, and he gives another chapter to the gymnastic manual. In Descharmes, as in Flaubert, the books are very funny. But we can scarcely believe that these books, and the treatises on hygiene and diet, were the kind of thing that was making Flaubert 'rabid.' As long as there have been printed books there have been mnemonic systems and they have been absurd; there have always been professors of physical training and they have always had a grandiose solemnity which may still be observed. Quackery is pretty constant in culture, and it is the detritus of culture, not its essence.

An American scholar and critic, Mr. Hugh Kenner, recently described *Bouvard and Pécuchet* as 'the book into which Flaubert emptied his voluminous notes on human gullibility, groundless learning, *opinions chic,* contradictory authorities, ridiculous enthusiasms, the swill of the 19th century.' But we must think with a certain tenderness of some of 'the swill of the 19th century' because it has served as the intellectual aliment of certain of the best poets of our age, the men whom we must readily exempt from our general condemnation of our own culture and who have done most to make us aware of the awfulness of our culture and that of the nineteenth century. When Bouvard and Pécuchet involve themselves with the study of psychic and occult phenomena, their

xxiii

researches are no doubt less profound than those of William Butler Yeats, but not different in kind; and although they fall short of Yeats's degree of success in practice, still, on one occasion, they do startle themselves, their audience, and the reader by demonstrating an actual example of clairvoyance. Nothing that the delightful Robert Graves tells us about the Druids contradicts what Bouvard and Pécuchet discover in their study of the science of Celtic archaeology: 'Some uttered prophesies, others chanted, others taught botany, medicine, history and literature: in short, all the arts of their epoch. Pythagoras and Plato were their pupils. They instructed the Greeks in metaphysics, the Persians in sorcery, the Etruscans in augury, and the Romans in plating copper and trading in ham.' Then the passion of Bouvard and Pécuchet for antiquities, their lust for old documents, and the cultural conclusions they base on their investigations and accumulations are no different from those of Ezra Pound, about whom Mr. Kenner has written so well; and they have Mr. Pound's responsiveness to comprehensive schemes of social and economic reform. Their knowledge of the emotions of the Waste Land is no less intense than that of T. S. Eliot, and based on a not dissimilar experience; with them as with him despair arises from culture and leads to religion.[3]

Readers of literary bent, who have as an element of their pathos the belief that they are persecuted by science,[4] will set special store by those parts of the novel that have the effect of

---

[3] Mr. Kenner's remarks on *Bouvard and Pécuchet* appear in the essay 'Pound on Joyce' which serves to introduce Mr. Pound's essay 'James Joyce and Pécuchet' as it is reprinted in the Autumn, 1952, issue of *Shenandoah*.

[4] It is not sufficiently understood that men of science have an analogous —homologous?—pathos to support them in their own troubles: they believe that they are systematically persecuted by the humanities.

exposing the arrogance as well as the contradictions and absurdities of the physical science of the day. Everyone who has ever studied literature knows that physical science was the basis of the vulgar materialism of the nineteenth century. In this regard it is well to remember that Flaubert had no principled hostility to science as such—quite to the contrary, indeed. He takes note of the ridiculous statements that science can make, but much of the confusion that Bouvard and Pécuchet experience is the result of their own ineptitude or ignorance rather than of the inadequacy of science itself. It is not the fault of botany—although it may be the fault of a particular elementary text-book of botany—that they believe that all flowers have a pericarp, but look in vain for it when confronted by buttercups and wild strawberry.

Medicine, of course, is the natural prey of the comic—the treatment it receives in *Bouvard and Pécuchet* adds nothing in point of comic method to the classic one established by Molière. And this can serve to remind us of the extent to which the seventeenth and eighteenth centuries figure in the novel. These have become sacred eras, and persons of sensibility believe that either of them can show a virtue for every vice of the nineteenth century. Yet Flaubert represents them as being the seedground of literary stupidity.

> Think of devices which can captivate,

says Boileau.

By what means think of these devices?

> In all your speeches passion should be found,
> Go seek the heart, and warm it till it bound.

How 'warm the heart'?

The rules are not enough; genius is also necessary.

And genius is not enough. Corneille, according to the Académie Française, understands nothing of the theatre. Geoffroy depreciated

Voltaire. Racine was jeered at by Subligny. Laharpe bellowed at the name of Shakespeare.

What we may call the primary or elemental religious experience of Bouvard and Pécuchet is treated by Flaubert with considerable seriousness and sympathy; it is the theological developments which follow upon that experience that he mocks. This theology cannot be said to be peculiar to the nineteenth century or to the bourgeois democracy.

Again, when it comes to philosophy, it is not merely the philosophy of the nineteenth century that brings Bouvard and Pécuchet to their despair. It is philosophy in general, what anyone except a logical positivist would say were the genuine problems of philosophy. These take, it is true, a specifically modern form, in part because Flaubert had had his say about ancient philosophy in *The Temptation of St. Anthony*. But they go back at least as far as the seventeenth century. 'The famous *cogito* bores me,' says Bouvard, just like any truthful person who has read Descartes. He and Pécuchet attempt Spinoza. They feel that 'all this was like being in a balloon at night, in glacial coldness, carried on an endless voyage towards a bottomless abyss, and with nothing near but the unseizable, the motionless, the eternal. It was too much. They gave it up.' As who does not? Their response to the *Ethics* is not foolish, not trivial; they have caught most accurately the emotion that Spinoza enforces upon us, and they know that it is impossible to live with. Yet Flaubert, at the time of writing the novel, had a devoted admiration for Spinoza, as we all have.

What is being mocked? For even literature, the great palladium of Flaubert's life, is not proof against the corrosive action of the simple, lucid, mediocre minds of Bouvard and Pécuchet. It is not merely bad literature that bores them after their first afflatus of enthusiasm; it is literature itself.

The elements of each author that at first enchant them—the tone, the idiom, the system of distortion and extravagance—come to be the ground of their eventual boredom.

The more we consider *Bouvard and Pécuchet,* the less the novel can be thought of as nothing but an attack on the culture of the nineteenth century. Bourgeois democracy merely affords the setting for a situation in which it becomes possible to reject culture itself. The novel does nothing less than that: it rejects culture. The human mind experiences the massed accumulation of its own works, those that are traditionally held to be its greatest glories as well as those that are obviously of a contemptible sort, and arrives at the understanding that none will serve its purpose, that all are weariness and vanity, that the whole vast structure of human thought and creation is alien from the human person. Descharmes concludes his study of *Bouvard and Pécuchet* with the statement that the import of the novel is comprehended in a verse from *Ecclesiastes* which Flaubert might well have used as an epigraph: 'And I set my mind to search and to investigate through wisdom everything that is done beneath the heavens. It is an evil task that God has given the sons of men with which to occupy themselves.' The relevance of the pessimism of *Ecclesiastes* goes well beyond this single text.

The pessimism of *Bouvard and Pécuchet* is comparable with, although not the same as, that of *Gulliver's Travels.* Just as we may not lessen the depth of the pessimism of *Gulliver's Travels* by reading the book as if it were only the response to Swift's eighteenth century, so we may not lessen the depth of the pessimism of *Bouvard and Pécuchet* by reading it as if it were only the response to Flaubert's nineteenth century.

What does permit us to qualify the pessimism of *Bouvard and Pécuchet* is the comic mode in which it has its existence. The book is genuinely funny, and the comic nature of the two heroes invites us to stand at a certain distance from their woe. We are not dealing with, say, Musset's Octave, he who so advertised his self-pity by calling his history that of 'a child of the century,' by which he invites the reader to acknowledge a common paternity and thus approve his self-commiseration. Bouvard and Pécuchet permit us to laugh at ourselves in them and yet to remain detached from their plight. They are a *reductio ad absurdum* of our lives in culture, but we are not constrained to follow the reduction as far as it can take us.

They themselves qualify the pessimism of the book by their last act. Another famous copying clerk, an American, Melville's Bartleby the Scrivener, with the classic American pessimism which is more entire than any that the French have contrived, when he perceives the nothingness of society, simply curls up and wills to die, and dies. But when all is lost to Bouvard and Pécuchet, all is not lost: they procure the double copying desk, and the order of the day, which had come to them like a revelation, is 'Copier comme autrefois.' And so we last see them in the metamorphosis to which their lives entitle them, a sort of bachelor Baucis and Philemon, rustling their leaves at each other with a sweet papery sound. They have discovered the *'travailler sans raisonner,'* the virtue of work without philosophising, which *Candide* inculcates. Yet the abrogation of abstruse research does not mean the abrogation of mind, for what they copy from the old papers which they indiscriminately buy up are the absurdities they have learned to recognise. The results of their copying are to constitute, according to Flaubert's plan, the last part of the novel. Scholars have debated which of Flaubert's several collections of absurdities was to appear as the fruit of their efforts. The weight of the evidence seems to give that place to *The Dictionary of Accepted Ideas,* and most readers will be willing to accept this conclusion if only because of the pleasures of the *Dictionary* itself, which is the most elaborate of the collections.[5] But for the understanding of the novel itself it is almost enough to know that *something* was to follow, that, reduced as the two friends are, they have not lost their love of mind, to which they testify by recording the mind's failures.

IV

The pessimism of *Bouvard and Pécuchet* is qualified by certain other considerations. These are extraneous to the text, but our sense of the ambiguity of the novel justifies us in going beyond the text to see if we may gain further understanding from an awareness of the circumstances of its composition. Indeed, it is virtually impossible not to do something of this sort. In the time between his death and his centenary in 1921 the fame of Flaubert increased to the point where he was a classic of his language and the subject of an elaborate scholarship. His novels, which he had written according to his famous ideal of strict objectivity and stern impersonality, were read —and even when there was no excuse of ambiguity—more and more in the light of his personal legend, which seemed to grow ever greater in its power of appeal.

If there is such a thing as biographical success, Flaubert achieved it in its fullest measure, for the last period of his life is as interesting, both in event and thought, as the early years in which his mind was formed and the middle years of his decisive productions; and its pathos is irresistible. This pathos, I venture to suppose, is similar in the effect it has upon the French reader to that which moves the English

---

[5] Jacques Barzun's translation of the *Dictionary* is published by New Directions as a companion to this edition of *Bouvard and Pécuchet*.

reader in the life of Swift. It is the pathos of the man whose savage pride induces him to have always before his mind the idea of mankind as a whole, and to regard the human actuality with an angry disgust so intense that it seems to him—and sometimes to others—like a madness. Those individuals whom he exempts from his general contempt for the human kind he grapples to himself with hoops of steel. If he is incapable of marriage and even of sexual love in any conventional sense, he can give to a few women an extreme devotion; and to many men he can give a friendship of surpassing respect and loyalty.

It was in his remarkably deep affections that Flaubert was struck again and again in his last years. 'I am obsessed by the dead (my dead),' he wrote to Laure de Maupassant. 'Is this a sign of old age? I think so.' He was fifty-three. The year was 1873 and the necrology of the last four years had been long; it was to become longer. His mother, his dearest friends, his literary colleagues and comrades-in-arms—their deaths accumulated and were augmented by the passing of people whom he did not love as he loved his mother, or George Sand, or Louis Bouilhet, or whom he did not respect as he did Jules de Goncourt, or Gautier, or even Sainte-Beuve, but who nevertheless embodied his past, such as Louise Colet, his former mistress, and Maurice Schlesinger, the husband of the woman Flaubert had loved with a virtually mystic passion since his adolescence and whom he had enshrined as Mme. Arnoux.

He could make of his life an altar of the dead, as witness the time, effort, and passion he gave to keep alive the memory of the cherished Louis Bouilhet. But he could also make it an altar of the living. Perhaps he would not have said with Henry James that life is nothing unless it is sacrificial, but he acted as if he believed this to be so when he offered up his independence for the happiness of his niece Caroline.

xxx

Caroline Commanville was the only child of Flaubert's only sister, who had died in 1846, and she had been reared by her grandmother and her uncle. To Caro, as she was called, Flaubert gave the full of the devotion of which he was capable. His love, characteristically enough, expressed itself in his solicitude for the grace of her mind. Something of his yearning tenderness for her, which appears so unabashedly in the letters which she published after his death, was lent to Bouvard and-Pécuchet when, moved in part by belated parental impulses, they adopt the stray children to educate them for decorous and useful lives. Flaubert spent thirteen years on Caro's education, and the goal of his affectionate efforts was like that of Nature in Wordsworth's poem:

> This Child I to myself shall take;
> She shall be mine, and I will make
> A Lady of my own

—a Lady who in her own person should be the answer to the vulgarity and stupidity of the time.

How far he did indeed succeed in his best hopes for the intellectual grace of Caro may be judged by American readers from the description of her which Willa Cather gives after meeting her at a hotel at Aix in 1930, when she was a woman of eighty-four. And nothing can suggest better the moral limitations of Miss Cather and her feminised universe than the fact that although she renders the most intense and delicate homage to the charm of Mme. Franklin-Grout (as she had become), speaking at length of her manners, her command of many languages, the purity of her passion for art, her friendship with her uncle's great friends, her closeness to her uncle himself, she gives no intimation that for the sake of Caro, and at her behest, Flaubert had put himself into financial jeopardy, surrendering the fortune upon which he depended for his literary life, and with very little thanks from the beneficiary.

Up to 1875 the business affairs of Caroline's husband Commanville seemed to justify an elaborate establishment in Paris and a fashionable and expensive way of life. Then it became clear that Commanville was on the verge of bankruptcy. To save the Commanvilles from disgrace Flaubert pledged his entire fortune—when it came to the bourgeois pieties he was to be outdone by no one. He gave up his pleasant flat in Paris and took cheaper rooms, and in general greatly curtailed his expenses. He sold the property at Deauville from which he derived his income. At one time it seemed probable that he would have to give up the house at Croisset, where he had lived virtually all his life. This horrified him and wrung from him an agonized cry—without it, he said, using the English word, he would have no *home*. George Sand offered to buy it if possible and let him live in it all his life, but the sale proved unnecessary. In all, Flaubert put at the disposal of the Commanvilles 1,200,000 francs, in return for which he was to receive a small allowance.

The full extent of the sacrifice can be properly understood only if we feel the force of Gautier's remark that. Flaubert's bourgeois fortune was part of his creative endowment. The sacrifice being what it was, the Commanvilles' subsequent behavior gives the incident a Lear-like character. They did not pay the allowance promptly and Flaubert had to importune for it. They were angry when Flaubert, with much reluctance and humiliation, consented to allow his friends to procure a pension for him; they did not forgive the friends who had won his consent and campaigned for the pension. They felt he was a drain on their resources and called him 'the consumer'; their own way of life continued to be expensive. They required him to enlist his friends in further help to them. When the devoted Laporte, who himself had lost his fortune, refused to commit himself further, they insisted that Flaubert break with him, which he did in great sadness.

These events, interesting in themselves, are significant for our purpose as constituting the circumstance in which Flaubert wrote the *Three Tales* and as having a bearing upon their common theme of the sacrifice of the self; and the *Three Tales* must inevitably be read as a gloss upon *Bouvard and Pécuchet*. In September of 1875, with the Commanville affairs temporarily under control, Flaubert went to spend six weeks at Concarneau with his old friend, the naturalist Georges Pouchet. Flaubert's nerves were in a bad state, he was deeply distraught. He envied the calm with which his scientist friend went about his work. Unable to take up his own work on *Bouvard and Pécuchet*, he swam and walked to restore his equanimity and he began the story of 'St. Julian.' He took it with him when he left Concarneau and finished it in January. In February he began 'A Simple Heart,' which he completed in August. In August he began 'Herodias,' which he finished the following February. The stories appeared as a newspaper serial and then in a volume; they were greeted with almost universal admiration—Flaubert's first popular success since *Madame Bovary*.[6]

The part that these three stories play in Flaubert's artistic development cannot concern us here. Nor can we stop to consider all that they might be understood to say of Flaubert's inner life. What is of immediate consequence to us is the theme which they have in common and how that bears upon *Bouvard and Pécuchet*.

---

[6] The *Three Tales* have been translated by Arthur McDowell and published, with an introduction by Harry Levin, in The New Classics Series, New Directions, 1944.

The stories are well known and need be recalled but briefly. All are associated with Flaubert's native Rouen. The legend of St. Julian is the subject of a window of the Cathedral; the Herodias story is told on the tympanum of the Cathedral's south portal. The Félicité of 'A Simple Heart' was a servant-girl whom Flaubert had known in his boyhood. The story of St. Julian, a Christianised version of the Oedipus legend, tells of a young nobleman brought up to arms and the chase; his passion for killing is exorbitant (the catalogue of the beasts he slays reminds us of nothing so much as the fifteen hundred volumes Flaubert read for *Bouvard and Pécuchet*) until one day it is prophesied to him by a gigantic and invulnerable stag that he will kill his own mother and father. The prophecy comes true despite Julian's best efforts to circumvent it. Julian, shunned by all mankind, lives as a hermit. One cold night there comes to his hut a leper of extreme loathsomeness who asks for food, then for the warmth of Julian's embrace, then for a kiss upon his ghastly mouth. And as Julian's *caritas* extends to this last request, the leper appears as Christ and carries Julian off in glory. 'A Simple Heart' is a record of a life of religious piety and of entire devotion to others. Virtually the only events of Félicité's life are the deaths of those whom she loves and serves. (It has been remarked that Félicité has a seizure on the road very much like that which Flaubert suffered as the first episode of his illness; other possible connections with Flaubert are her cherishing of her nephew, her being exploited by her relatives, her being left destitute by the death of her mistress, and her continuing to live by sufferance in the stripped and empty house.) 'Herodias' is the story of John the Baptist imprisoned by the Tetrarch Antipas, of Salome's dance, and the severed head.

The religious elements of the three stories must not mislead us about the condition of Flaubert's belief. The *Tales* are not to be thought of as tentatives towards an avowal of faith. For this Flaubert's attitude towards religion was far too complex. Even in *Bouvard and Pécuchet*, as I have noted, Flaubert treats simple, primary religious faith, or impulse to faith, with great gentleness; what dismayed him were the intellectual extrapolations from this simplicity. Yet his response to religion is not comprised by the tenderness he could show to simple faith and his contempt for systematic theology. What his attitude to religion actually was in its considerable complexity has been well described by Philip Spencer: "He seems . . . to have regarded Christianity as a spent force. . . . The only two elements in Catholicism to which Flaubert responded were subordinate to the main tradition and divergent from it: the hatred of life, the negation of life's goodness, which he thought he discovered in Catholic philosophy, and, concomitant with it, the rigorous self-abasement of asceticism. But his own religious feeling, if such it can be called, was diffuse—a kind of creatureliness before the mystery of creation. 'What draws me above all things,' he wrote in 1857, 'is religion. I mean all religions, not one rather than another. Each dogma on its own repels me, but I consider the feeling that created them as the most natural and poetical in humanity. I don't like philosophers who find there only fraud and foolishness.' " [7] A man who can speak thus does not easily 'turn to religion,' and the *Three Tales* must not be thought of even as the tribute to religion of an unbeliever who perceives the charms and advantages of faith and who regrets his inability to believe. Flaubert was a very serious man.

But we shall not be wrong if we think of the stories as a tribute to what Flaubert took to be a characteristic mode of

---

[7] *Flaubert*, The Grove Press, 1953, p. 204.

Christianity, the 'negation of life's goodness'—life's goodness in general and specifically the goodness of man's life in culture. In each of the stories the protagonist exists beyond the life in culture and stands divested of every garment that culture weaves. Julian passes beyond parental love, beyond social rank, beyond heroism and fame, beyond the domestic affections, beyond all the things, persons, and institutions that bind us to the earth, and he reaches that moment of charity which is the surrender of what Flaubert believed to be the richest luxury of culture, the self in the separateness of sensibility and pride that define it. Félicité, endowed by nature and culture with no other gift than that of the power to love and serve, is deprived of every person upon whom her love has fixed, and is left with no other object to cherish save her poor stuffed parrot, the dumb effigy of the Speaking Bird, the Logos, the Holy Ghost. John the Baptist, naked and solitary, cries out from his prison-pit against the court of Antipas, and Flaubert is at his usual pains to specify not only the deeds but the artifacts—the garments and the food and the armament hidden beneath the palace—of which the Baptist's naked and solitary voice is the negation.

The *Tales*, that is, continue Flaubert's old despair of culture, which was, we may say, the prime condition of his art; it was a despair which was the more profound, we need scarcely say, because it was the issue of so great a hope. Emma Bovary had tried to live by the promises of selfhood which culture had seemed to make, and culture had destroyed her. Frédéric Moreau had ruined himself by never quite believing in the selfhood which culture cherishes as its dearest gift. Now Flaubert considers the condition of the spirit which puts itself as far as possible beyond the promises, the consolations, and the demands of culture; in each of the *Three Tales* he asks what remains when culture is rejected and transcended. The answer, given with a notable firmness and simplicity, is that something of highest value does remain—it is the self affirmed in self-denial: life's nothing unless sacrificial. And Bouvard and Pécuchet, sitting at their double copying desk, having a work and each other, but stripped of every idea, every theory, every shred of culture beyond what is necessary to keep men alive and still human, are, in their own mild negation of self, intended by Flaubert to be among the company of his saints.

BOUVARD AND PECUCHET

I

THERE was a temperature of ninety degrees, and the Boulevard Bourdon was completely deserted.

Lower down, the Canal St. Martin, enclosed by two locks, showed the straight line of its inky water. Midway, there was a boat filled with timber, and on the banks two rows of barrels.

Across the canal, between the houses separated by timber-yards, the clear expanse of sky was cut into segments of deep blue, and as the sun beat down, the white fronts, the slate roofs, the granite quays dazzled. A confused murmur rose far off in the sultry air; and everything seemed lulled in the Sunday quiet and the sadness of summer days.

Two men appeared.

One came from the Bastille, the other from the Jardin des Plantes. The taller, in a linen suit, walked with his hat tipped back, his waistcoat unbuttoned and tie in hand. The smaller, enveloped in a maroon frock-coat, bent forward under a peaked cap.

When they reached the middle of the boulevard they sat down at the same moment on the same bench.

In order to wipe their brows they removed their headgear, which each placed by his side; and the smaller man saw written in his neighbour's hat, 'Bouvard'; while the latter easily made out in the cap of the individual wearing the frock-coat the word 'Pécuchet.'

'Fancy that,' he said. 'We've both had the idea of writing our names in our hats.'

'Good heavens, yes; mine might be taken at the office.'

'The same with me; I work in an office too.'

Then they inspected one another.

Bouvard's pleasant appearance quite charmed Pécuchet.

His blue eyes, always half closed, smiled out of a rosy face. His trousers, buttoning at the side and wrinkling down over buckskin shoes, took the shape of his stomach, made his shirt bulge at the waist; and his fair hair, curling naturally in little coils, gave him a rather childish look. He kept up a sort of whistling with pouted lips.

Pécuchet's serious expression struck Bouvard.

One would have said he wore a wig, so flat and black were the locks that garnished his high skull. His face seemed all profile, on account of the nose, which came extremely low down. His legs, confined in tubes of lasting, were out of proportion to the length of his bust; and he had a deep, hollow voice.

This cry escaped from him: 'How pleasant it would be in the country!'

But according to Bouvard the suburbs were intolerable, from the din of the taverns. Pécuchet thought the same. Nevertheless, like Bouvard, he was beginning to feel tired of the capital.

And their eyes wandered over the heaps of builders' stones, the ugly water where a bundle of straw was floating, the foundry chimney rising into the horizon; a sewer discharged its stench. They turned the other way. Then they had in front of them the walls of the municipal granary.

Decidedly (and Pécuchet was surprised at this) it was even hotter in the street than at home! Bouvard advised him to take off his coat. Personally, he did not care a fig for convention!

Suddenly a drunken man zigzagged across the pavement; and they began a political discussion on the subject of the working classes. Their opinions were alike, except that Bouvard was perhaps more liberal-minded.

A clatter of wheels sounded on the road from amid a whirlwind of dust; it was three hackney carriages going towards Bercy, conveying a bride and her bouquet, men in white ties, ladies smothered up to the arms in petticoats, two or three little girls and a schoolboy. The sight of this wedding party led Bouvard and Pécuchet to talk of women, whom they declared flighty, perverse and obstinate. All the same they were often better than men; though at other times they were worse. In short, it was best to live without them; and Pécuchet had remained single.

'Well, I'm a widower,' said Bouvard, 'and without children!'

'Perhaps it's as well for you. But in the long run solitude is sad enough.'

Then, on the edge of the quay, there came into view a prostitute with a soldier. Pale, with black hair, and pitted with smallpox, she leaned on the arm of her escort, dragging her slippers and balancing her hips.

When she had passed, Bouvard indulged in a smutty remark. Pécuchet grew very red, and, doubtless to avoid replying, indicated with a glance that a priest was approaching.

The ecclesiastic stalked down the avenue of thin young elms that studded the pavement, and when the three-cornered hat was out of sight Bouvard expressed his relief, for he hated Jesuits. Pécuchet, without absolving them altogether, showed some respect for religion.

Meanwhile, twilight was falling, and in front of them the venetian blinds were being raised. The passers-by grew more frequent. Seven o'clock struck.

Their talk flowed on endlessly, comments following upon anecdotes, philosophical observations upon personal views. They ran down the municipal services, the tobacco monopoly, business, the theatre, the navy, and the entire human

19

race, like men who have suffered deep disappointments. Each, as he listened to the other, discovered forgotten corners in himself. And although they had passed the age of simple emotions, they experienced a new pleasure, a sort of blossoming, the charms of fresh tendernesses.

A score of times they had got up, had sat down again, had walked the length of the boulevard, from the top to the bottom lock, each time meaning to go, but not having the strength, detained by an enchantment.

However, they were saying good-bye, and were clasping hands, when Bouvard said suddenly: 'By Jove, suppose we have dinner together?'

'It had occurred to me,' replied Pécuchet, 'but I didn't like to suggest it.'

And he let himself be taken to a little restaurant facing the Hôtel de Ville, where there was good eating.

Bouvard ordered the meal.

Pécuchet was afraid of seasoned dishes, which heated the blood. This became the subject of a medical discussion. Next they celebrated the advantages of science: how many facts there were to be learnt, how much to go into—if only one had the time! Alas, their daily bread occupied them; and they raised their arms in astonishment, nearly embraced over the table, on discovering that they were both copying-clerks, Bouvard in a business house, Pécuchet at the Admiralty; which did not, however, prevent him from devoting a few moments each evening to study. He had noted some faults in the work of M. Thiers, and he spoke with the greatest respect of one Dumouchel, a professor.

Bouvard excelled in other directions. His hair watch-chain, and the way in which he whipped up the sharp sauce, proclaimed the experienced diner-out, and he ate with his napkin tucked under his arms, chattering of things which made Pécuchet laugh. It was peculiar laughter, on one very low note, always the same and coming out at intervals. Bouvard's was long and ringing, he bared his teeth and shook his shoulders, so that the diners by the door turned round.

When the meal was over, they went out to take a coffee in another establishment. Pécuchet, staring at the gas-jets, bewailed the growing evils of luxury, then with a disdainful gesture thrust the newspapers aside. Bouvard was more indulgent towards them. He liked writers in general, and as a youth had shown a disposition for the stage.

He wanted to try some balancing tricks with a cue and three ivory balls, as it had been done by Barberou, a friend of his. The balls invariably fell, and, rolling on the floor between people's legs, disappeared in the distance. The waiter, who had to come forward each time and fish for them on all fours under the benches, ended by complaining. Pécuchet had a row with him; and when the proprietor came on the scene, he would not listen to excuses and even quibbled over the bill.

Then he suggested that they should end the evening quietly at his lodgings, which were near by in the Rue Saint-Martin.

As soon as they had gone in, he put on a sort of print jacket and did the honours of the flat. A deal table, set exactly in the middle of the room, was always in the way with its corners; and round it, on the little tables, the three chairs, the old arm-chair, and in the corners, were scattered a number of volumes of the Roret Encyclopædia, the Mesmerist's Handbook, a Fénelon, and other old tomes, as well as a pile of papers, two coconuts, various medallions, a Turkish fez, and shells brought from Havre by Dumouchel. A layer of dust coated the walls, originally painted yellow. A shoe-brush lay beside the bed, the bedclothes hung down. On the ceiling one noticed a large black smudge produced by the smoke of the lamp.

Bouvard, no doubt on account of the smell, asked permission to open the window.

'The papers would fly away!' cried Pécuchet, who was afraid, moreover, of draughts.

Yet he was gasping in this little room heated since morning by the slates of the roof.

Bouvard said to him:

'If I were you, I'd take off that flannel!'

'What?'

And Pécuchet bowed his head, terrified at the thought of being without his protector.

'You must see me home,' continued Bouvard. 'The air outside will freshen you up.'

In the end Pécuchet put on his boots again, grumbling, 'I swear you've bewitched me!' and, despite the distance, he accompanied him all the way to his house at the corner of the Rue de Béthune, facing the Pont de la Tournelle.

Bouvard's room, with its polished floor, its muslin curtains and mahogany furniture, boasted a balcony overlooking the river. The two chief ornaments were a liqueur-stand in the middle of the sideboard, and along the mirror a row of daguerreotypes of his friends. An oil-painting occupied the alcove.

'My uncle!' said Bouvard.

And the taper in his hand lit up the features of a gentleman.

Red whiskers broadened the face surmounted by a tuft of hair curling at the ends. The high cravat, together with the triple collar of shirt, velvet waistcoat and black coat, gave him a stuffed appearance. Diamonds had been painted on the shirt-front. His eyes were fixed woodenly in their sockets, and he smiled with a little sly air.

Pécuchet could not help saying:

'One would take him for your father!'

'He is my godfather,' replied Bouvard carelessly, adding that at his christening he had been called after him François Denys Bartholomée. Pécuchet's names were Juste Romain Cyrille—and they were the same age: forty-seven. This coincidence gave them pleasure, but surprised them, each having thought the other much less young. Then they marvelled at Providence, which works in a mysterious way.

'For after all, if we had not taken a walk just now, we might have gone to our graves without meeting!'

And having exchanged their office addresses they wished each other good night.

'Don't go after the ladies!' cried Bouvard on the staircase.

Pécuchet descended the steps without replying to so coarse a remark.

Next day, in the courtyard of Descambos Bros., Alsatian Textiles, 92 Rue Hautefeuille, a voice called:

'Bouvard! Monsieur Bouvard!' He poked his head out of the window and recognised Pécuchet, who articulated more loudly:

'No I'm not ill. I have left it off.'

'Left what off?'

'This,' said Pécuchet, pointing to his chest.

The talk of the day before, along with the temperature of the room and the labours of digestion, had prevented him from sleeping, so much so that, unable to bear it any longer, he had thrown his protector to the other end of the room. In the morning he had remembered his action, luckily without ill-effects, and had come to tell Bouvard, who was thus raised in his esteem to a prodigious height.

He was the son of a small shopkeeper, and had not known his mother, who died very young. At fifteen he had been taken away from boarding-school and placed in a bailiff's office. The police came on the scene and his employer was sent to the galleys; a grim affair which haunted him still. Afterwards, he had tried several occupations: chemist's assistant, usher, purser on a steamer of the Upper Seine. Finally, the head of a department in the Admiralty, captivated by his handwriting, had engaged him as a copying-clerk; but the consciousness of an imperfect education, together with the spiritual needs engendered by it, had made him of an irritable humour; and he lived completely alone, without relatives, without a mistress. His distraction was to go out on Sundays and inspect the public works.

Bouvard's earliest recollections took him back to the banks of the Loire, to the courtyard of a farm. A man—it was his uncle—had brought him to Paris to teach him business. At his coming of age he was given a sum of several thousand francs. Then he had married and opened a confectioner's shop. Six months later his wife disappeared with the till. Friends, good living, and above all laziness, had soon ruined him. But he was smart enough to turn his handwriting to account; and for eleven years now he had kept his position with Descambos Bros., 92 Rue Hautefeuille. As for his uncle, who had previously sent him the famous portrait as a memento, Bouvard did not even know his address, and expected nothing more from him. An income of fifteen hundred francs and his salary as clerk enabled him to go out in the evenings and take a nap in a coffee-house.

So their meeting had assumed the importance of an adventure. At once they were drawn together by hidden sympathies. Besides, how explain these attachments? Why do the habits and limitations which we find unimportant or repugnant in one person enchant us in another? What we call love at first sight is true also of other passions. Before a week was over they were on terms of intimacy.

Often they would seek each other out at their offices. As

soon as one appeared, the other would close his desk, and they would go off together in the streets. Bouvard strode along, while Pécuchet quickening his pace, with his frock-coat flapping at his heels, seemed to glide on castors. Bouvard smoked a pipe, liked cheese, never missed his small black coffee. Pécuchet took snuff, ate only preserves at dessert, and with his coffee sucked a lump of sugar. The one was confident, irresponsible, open-handed; the other cautious, thoughtful, sparing.

Bouvard wanted to do Pécuchet a good turn by introducing him to Barberou. Once a commercial traveller he was now a stock-jobber; a good fellow, a patriot, a lady's man, who affected a common turn of speech. Pécuchet thought him disagreeable, and he took off Bouvard to see Dumouchel. That author (for he had published a little book on mnemonics) held literature classes at an academy for young ladies, had orthodox opinions and a grave manner. Bouvard was bored.

Neither concealed his opinion from the other, each respected the other's view. Their habits changed, and giving up their regular tables d'hôte, they ended by dining together every day.

They passed judgment on the latest plays, the government, the high price of living, business swindles. From time to time the story of the Diamond Necklace or the Fualdès trial would crop up in their conversation, and then they would go on to the causes of the Revolution.

They sauntered past the old curiosity shops. They visited the Conservatoire des Arts et Métiers, Saint Denis, the Gobelins, the Invalides and all the public collections.

When their papers were asked for, they made a show of having lost them, passing themselves off as two foreigners, two Englishmen.

In the galleries of the Museum they viewed the stuffed quadrupeds with astonishment, the butterflies with pleasure, the metals with indifference; fossils fired their imagination, conchology bored them. They peered into hot-houses, and shuddered at the thought of so many foliages distilling poison. What struck them most about the cedar was that it had been brought over in a hat.

They worked up an enthusiasm at the Louvre for Raphael. At the Central Library they would have liked to know the exact number of volumes.

Once they attended a lecture on Arabic at the Collège de France, and the professor was surprised by the sight of these two strangers trying to take notes. Thanks to Barberou, they got behind the scenes of a small theatre. Dumouchel gave them tickets for a meeting of the Academy. They kept abreast of discoveries, read the publishers' lists, and by such curiosity their intelligence. developed. Beyond a horizon which receded every day, they were aware of things bewildering and wonderful.

Admiring an old piece of furniture they lamented not having lived during the period when it was in use, although they were completely ignorant of that period. From the sound of certain names, they imagined as most beautiful the countries of which they knew least. Books whose titles were unintelligible to them seemed to contain some mystery.

And as their ideas grew they suffered more. When a mail-coach passed them in the street, they felt the need of going away in it. The Quai aux Fleurs made them sigh for the country.

One Sunday they started off early and walked all day through Meudon, Bellevue, Suresnes and Auteuil, wandering through the vineyards, plucking poppies at the edge of fields, sleeping on the turf, drinking milk, eating under the acacias of wayside inns; and they came back well in the night, dusty, weary, transfigured. They repeated these

26

walks a number of times. But the aftermath was so sad that they ended by giving them up.

The monotony of the office became hateful. Always the scratching penknife and the sand-sprinkler, the same inkpot, the same pens, and the same companions! Thinking the latter stupid, they spoke to them less and less. That brought them annoyances. Every day they arrived late and were reprimanded.

At one time they had been almost happy; but now they had a higher opinion of themselves, their work humiliated them, and they made common cause in this disgust, exciting and spoiling one another. Pécuchet acquired Bouvard's roughness; Bouvard took on something of Pécuchet's misanthropy.

'I'd rather be a street acrobat,' one would say.

'As well be a rag-picker,' the other would cry.

It was an abominable situation. And no way out! Not even a hope!

One afternoon (it was the twentieth of January 1839), when Bouvard was at his desk, a letter was brought by the postman.

He raised his arms, slowly his head tilted back, and he fell in a faint to the ground.

His fellow-clerks rushed forward, they loosened his tie. A doctor was sent for. He opened his eyes, and in answer to questions:

'Oh! . . . it's . . . it's . . . a little fresh air will do me good. Please leave me alone!'

And despite his corpulence he ran all the way without stopping to the Admiralty, pressing his hand to his brow, thinking he had gone mad, trying to be calm.

He asked them to fetch Pécuchet.

Pécuchet came.

'My uncle is dead! I'm his heir!'

'Impossible!'

Bouvard displayed the following lines:

MAÎTRE TARDIVEL, *Notary*,
Savigny-en-Septaine,
January 14*th*, 1839.

SIR,

I request your presence at my office to become acquainted with the will of your natural father, M. François Denys Bartholomée Bouvard, late merchant of the town of Nantes, deceased in this parish the 10th instant. This will contains an important bequest in your favour.

Yours faithfully,
TARDIVEL, *Notary*

Pécuchet had to sit down on a post in the courtyard. Then he handed back the paper, saying slowly:

'Provided . . . it's not . . . a practical joke!'

'You think it might be that!' replied Bouvard in a choking voice like a death-rattle.

But the postmark, the name of the firm in printed letters, the signature of the notary, all proved the authenticity of the news; and they looked at each other with mouths that twitched at the corner and a tear welling in their staring eyes.

They wanted room. They went as far as the Arc de Triomphe, came back by the water's edge, passed Notre Dame. Bouvard was very red. He clapped Pécuchet on the back, and for five minutes went off his head altogether.

They chuckled in spite of themselves. This inheritance, of course, would mount up. . . . 'Oh, it's too good to be true. Don't let's speak of it.' They spoke of it again. There was nothing in the way of their making inquiries at once. Bouvard wrote to the notary for details.

The notary sent a copy of the will, which ended thus:

'Therefore I bequeath to François Denys Bartholomée Bouvard, my acknowledged natural son, that portion of the estate legally at my disposal.'

28

The old fellow had begotten this son in his youth but had kept him well out of sight, passing him off as a nephew; and the nephew had always addressed him as uncle, though he knew well enough how the matter stood. Monsieur Bouvard had married in the forties, and then was left a widower. His two legitimate sons having turned out contrary to his hopes, he had felt remorse at having neglected his other child for so long. He would even have brought him into the house, but for the influence of his housekeeper. She left him, thanks to a conspiracy of the family, and in his isolation, near to death, he wished to repair his faults by leaving all of his fortune that he could to the fruit of his early love. It amounted to half a million, which meant a sum of two hundred and fifty thousand francs to the clerk. The elder brother, M. Etienne, had announced that he would not dispute the will.

Bouvard fell into a sort of stupor. He repeated in a low voice, smiling the slow smile of a drunken man: 'Fifteen thousand francs a year!' and even Pécuchet, whose head was stronger, could not get over this.

They were rudely shaken by a letter from Tardivel. The other son, M. Alexandre, had announced his intention of bringing the whole matter before the courts, and even of disputing the legacy, if that was possible; he would begin by demanding the formality of seals, an inventory, the nomination of a receiver, etc. Bouvard had a bilious attack over it. He was no sooner up again than he set off for Savigny, whence he returned without settlement of any kind and grumbling about the expense of the journey.

Then followed sleepless nights, alternations of rage and hope, ecstasy and despair. In the end, after six months, M. Alexandre calming down, Bouvard entered into possession of the estate.

His first exclamation had been, 'We'll retire to the country!' and this phrase, which linked his friend to his good fortune, had seemed to Pécuchet quite natural. For the union of these two men was indissoluble and profound.

But as he refused to hang on to Bouvard's coat-tails, he would not go away till his retirement. Two more years; no matter! He remained inflexible, and the thing was settled.

In order to decide where they should settle, they reviewed the various provinces. The North was fertile, but too cold; the Midi delightful in its climate, but plagued by mosquitoes; and the Centre, frankly, held no interest. Brittany would have suited them but for the bigoted nature of the inhabitants. As for the Eastern Districts, with their German dialect, they were unthinkable. Still there were other places. What, for example, of the districts of Forez, Bugey, Roums? Maps told one nothing. Besides, whether their house was here or there, the important thing was that they would have one.

Already they saw themselves in shirt-sleeves beside a grass border, pruning the roses, digging, hoeing and working the soil, planting out tulips. Waking with the lark, they would follow the plough, go out with a basket to gather apples, watch the butter being made, the corn threshed, the sheep sheared, the beehives tended, and they would revel in the mooing of cows and the scent of fresh-mown hay. No more copying! No more being ordered about! Not even the rent to pay! For they would have a house of their own, and they would eat the chickens of their farm-yard, the vegetables from the garden—and dine with their clogs on! 'We'll do just as we like! We'll grow beards!'

They purchased gardening implements and a mass of things 'which might come in useful,' such as a tool-box (every house should have one), followed by a pair of scales, a land-chain, a bath-tub in case of illness, a thermometer, and even a barometer, 'on the Gay-Lussac system,' for meteorological experiments, should the fancy take them. It would not be a bad idea either (for one cannot always toil out of doors) to have some good works of literature—and they went in search of them, puzzled sometimes to decide if a particular book was a real 'library book.' Bouvard cut short the discussion:

'Oh, we shan't need a library.'

'Besides, I have mine,' said Pécuchet.

They made plans ahead. Bouvard would bring his furniture, Pécuchet his big black table; the curtains would do, and with a few kitchen utensils that would be enough.

They had sworn secrecy about all this, but their faces beamed. Their colleagues thought they behaved queerly. Bouvard, who wrote sprawling over his desk, with elbows spread, the better to round his script, gave his peculiar whistle, half closing his heavy eyelids with a knowing look. Pécuchet, perched on a high stool with a straw seat, took every care with the pot-hooks of his large handwriting—but at the same time swelling his nostrils and compressing his lips as though afraid of letting out the secret.

After eighteen months' search they had found nothing. They made excursions to the parts round Paris, from Amiens to Evreux, and all the way from Fontainebleau to Havre. They wanted country that really was country, without exactly insisting on a beauty spot; but a shut-in horizon depressed them.

They fled the neighbourhood of other dwellings and yet dreaded solitude.

At times they would come to a decision, and then change their minds, afraid of repenting too late; the place having seemed to them unhealthy or exposed to the sea breezes or too near a factory or difficult of access.

Barberou saved them.

He knew their dreams, and one fine day he came to say that he had heard of a property at Chavignolles, between Caen and Falaise. It consisted of a farm of ninety-four acres, with a sort of manor-house and a garden in good trim.

They journeyed to Calvados, and were overjoyed. Only, for the farm and the house together (one was not for sale without the other), they were asked a hundred and forty-three thousand francs. Bouvard would not give more than a hundred and twenty thousand.

Pécuchet fought his obstinacy, begged him to give way, and finally offered to meet the difference himself. It was his whole fortune coming from his mother's money and his own savings. He had never breathed a word of it, reserving this capital for a special occasion.

Everything was paid towards the end of 1840, six months before his retirement.

Bouvard was no longer a clerk. At first, from distrust of the future, he had gone on with his work, but had given notice once he was certain of his estate. However, he willingly returned to Messrs. Descambos, and on the eve of departure gave a punch party to the whole staff.

Pécuchet, on the other hand, was disagreeable to his fellow-clerks, and went out on the last day slamming the door violently.

He had to look after the packing, go on a dozen errands, make several purchases, and take leave of Dumouchel.

The professor suggested that they should enter into a correspondence, whereby he would keep him in touch with the world of letters; and after congratulating him afresh, he wished him good luck.

Barberou was more touched by Bouvard's good-bye. He immediately gave up his game of dominoes, promised to come and see him in the wilds, ordered two anisettes and embraced him.

Bouvard, when he was home again, took in a great breath of air on his balcony, as he said: 'At last.' The lights on the quay were trembling in the water, the clatter of omnibuses died away in the distance. He recalled delightful days spent in this great town, happy-go-lucky meals in restaurants, evenings at the theatre, gossip with the porter's wife; and he felt a sinking of the heart, a sadness which he dared not confess.

Pécuchet walked up and down his room till two in the morning. He would never come back; so much the better! And yet, to leave something of himself behind, he cut his name in the plaster of the chimney-piece.

The heavier luggage had gone on the night before. The garden implements, bedsteads, mattresses, tables, chairs, a kitchen stove, the bath, and three casks of Burgundy would go down the Seine as far as Havre, and thence be dispatched to Caen, where Bouvard would be waiting to forward them to Chavignolles.

But the portrait of his father, the arm-chairs, the liqueur-stand, the books, the clock—all these valuables were placed in a removal van, to go by road through Nonancourt, Verneuil and Falaise.

Pécuchet decided to accompany them.

He sat himself by the driver's mate on his bench, and wrapped in his oldest coat, with scarf, mittens and his office foot-warmer, at daybreak on Sunday, March the twentieth, he left the capital.

The movement and the novelty of the journey occupied the first few hours. Then the horses slackened, which led to disputes with the driver and his mate. They chose abominable inns, and, although the full responsibility was theirs, Pécuchet from excess of caution slept in the same quarters.

The next day they set out at dawn, and the road ran on before them, always the same, ascending to the horizon.

The miles of rough stones stretched in front, the ditches were full of water, the country was spread out in great slabs of cold, monotonous green, clouds raced across the sky, and from time to time rain fell. On the third day it began to blow. The tarpaulin was loose and flapped in the wind like a ship's sail. Pécuchet hid his face under his cap, and each time he opened his snuff-box he had to turn right round so as to protect his eyes. During the jolts he heard all his luggage rattling behind, and shouted directions. Seeing that they had no effect, he changed his tactics: he became genial, even lent a hand; on the steep ascents he pushed at the wheel with the men; he went so far as to treat them to a tot after meals. Then they sped more briskly, so much so that near Gauburge the axle broke and the van tilted over. Pécuchet immediately went to look; the china cups lay in pieces. Raising his arms and grinding his teeth, he cursed the two idiots; the next day was lost because the driver was fuddled; but Pécuchet had not the strength to complain, his cup of bitterness had brimmed over.

Bouvard had not left Paris till a couple of days after, so that he might have a final dinner with Barberou. He reached the coachyard at the last moment, and woke up in front of Rouen Cathedral; he had taken the wrong diligence.

All the seats for Caen that evening had been booked; not knowing what to do he went to the Théâtre des Arts, and smiled at his neighbours, saying that he had retired from business and lately acquired an estate in the neighbourhood. When he got down at Caen on Friday, his packing-cases were not there. He received them on Sunday and sent them on by cart, after warning the farmer that he would follow in a few hours.

At Falaise, on the ninth day of his journey, Pécuchet hired an extra horse, and all went well until sunset. Beyond Bretteville, leaving the main road, he entered a lane, thinking each moment that he saw the gable of Chavignolles. But the track became fainter, then vanished, and they found themselves in the middle of ploughed fields. Night was falling. What were they to do? At last Pécuchet abandoned the van, and dabbling in the mud went ahead to reconnoitre. Whenever he neared a farm the dogs barked. He shouted at the top of his voice to ask the way. No one replied. He was frightened and got back to the open. Suddenly two lamps shone. He made out a carriage, and rushed forward to meet it. Bouvard was inside.

But where was the removal van? For an hour they hallooed in the darkness. At last it was found, and they arrived at Chavignolles.

A great fire of brushwood and fir cones was blazing in the dining-room. Places had been laid for two. The furniture which had come by cart cluttered the entrance. There was nothing missing. They sat down to table.

Onion soup, a fowl, fat bacon, and hard-boiled eggs had been got ready for them. The old woman who did the cooking came now and then to see if things were to their taste. They replied, 'Oh, excellent! excellent!' and the coarse bread hard to cut, the cream, the nuts, all delighted them. There were cracks between the tiles and the walls sweated. Still, they cast a glance of satisfaction round them as they ate at the little table on which a candle was burning. Their faces were flushed with the open air. As they leant back with bulging stomachs, their chairs creaked, and they kept saying to each other: 'Well, here we are! What luck! It's like a dream!'

Although it was midnight, Pécuchet fancied a turn in the garden. Bouvard had no objection. They took the candle, and shading it with an old newspaper walked round the borders. It was a pleasure to name the vegetables. 'Look— carrots! And cabbages!'

Then they inspected the espaliers. Pécuchet looked for shoots. Once or twice a spider fled suddenly along the wall, and their two shadows, in giant outline, repeated their gestures. The points of grass dripped dew. The night was pitch black, and everything stood still in a deep silence, at peace. Far off a cock crowed.

Between their two rooms was a small door which had been papered over. In bumping a chest of drawers against it, someone had managed to knock out the nails. They found it wide open. It was a surprise.

Undressed and in bed, they chatted for a while, then fell asleep, Bouvard on his back, his mouth open, bare-headed; Pécuchet on his right side, knees drawn up, decked in a cotton nightcap; and both snored away in the moonlight, which was flowing through the windows.

II

How delightful, waking next day! Bouvard took a puff at his pipe and Pécuchet took a pinch from his box, which they declared the best they had ever known. Then they went to the casement, to look at the view.

In front of them were fields, to the right a barn as well as the church tower, and to the left a screen of poplars.

Two main walks, forming a cross, divided the garden into four. The vegetables were edged with borders, where dwarf cypresses and cordons rose at intervals. On one side, an arbour led to an ornamental mound; on the other, a wall supported the espaliers; and at the bottom, a lattice gave on to the country. The other side of the wall there was an orchard; beyond the hedge a shrubbery; and behind the lattice a lane.

They were gazing at this scene when a man with grizzled hair and a heavy black overcoat came up the lane rattling his stick along the bars of the lattice. The old servant informed them that it was M. Vaucorbeil, a doctor well spoken of in the neighbourhood.

The other notabilities were: the Count de Faverges, a retired deputy, famous for his dairy-farm; the mayor, M. Foureau, who sold timber, plaster, all kinds of things; M. Marescot, the notary; the Abbé Jeufroy; and Mme Bordin, a widow with private means. As for herself, she was called Germaine after the late Germain, her husband. She worked by the day, but would like to take service with the gentlemen. They engaged her, and set off for the farm, half a mile away.

When they entered the yard, farmer Gouy was shouting at a lad, and his wife, seated on a stool, was gripping a turkey between her legs and cramming it with lumps of meal. The man had a low forehead, a sharp nose, eyes always on the ground, and broad shoulders. The woman was very fair, with freckled cheeks, and that simple expression one sees on the faces of peasants in stained-glass·windows.

In the kitchen, bundles of hemp hung from the ceiling. Three old flintlocks made a ladder on the tall chimney-piece. A dresser, loaded with flowered earthenware, occupied the middle of the wall; and the squares of bottle-glass in the window threw a pallid light on the tin and copper utensils.

The two Parisians wished to inspect everything, having viewed the property only once, and hastily at that. Farmer Gouy and his wife escorted them; and the litany of complaints began.

All the buildings, from the cart-shed to the distillery, needed repair. More room was wanted for the cheeses, new iron for the railings, the banks ought to be raised, the pond dug, and a number of fresh apple trees planted in the three enclosures.

After that they visited the crops, Farmer Gouy ran them down. They ate up too much manure, the cartage was expensive; impossible to clear the ground of stones; weeds choked the meadows; and this disparagement of his land diminished Bouvard's pleasure as he walked over it.

They came back by a sunk path under an avenue of beeches. From this side the house displayed its courtyard and front.

It was painted white, with yellow pointing. The barn and the still-room, the bakehouse and the woodshed projected at the back in two low wings. The kitchen communicated with a closet. Then came a hall, a second larger room, and the drawing-room. The four rooms on the first floor opened on to a corridor overlooking the courtyard. Pécuchet took one for his collections; the farthest was intended for the library; and, when they were opening cupboards, they found more old volumes, but had no fancy to read the titles. The important thing was the garden.

Bouvard, passing the hedge, discovered through the branches a plaster lady. With two fingers she was holding her skirt aside, knees bent and head resting on one shoulder, as though afraid of being surprised. 'Oh, excuse me! don't disturb yourself!' And this pleasantry so amused them that they repeated it a score of times each day for a month.

Meanwhile the gentry of Chavignolles wanted to make their acquaintance; people came to peep at them through the lattice. They boarded up the openings. The inhabitants were annoyed.

To keep off the sun, Bouvard wore on his head a handkerchief knotted in a turban, Pécuchet his cap; and he had a large apron with a pocket in front, in which were jumbled a pair of pruning-shears, his handkerchief and his snuff-box. Bare-armed and side by side they dug, weeded and pruned, setting themselves tasks, eating as quickly as possible; but they took their coffee sitting on the mound, so as to enjoy the view.

If they came across a snail, they drew near and squashed it, making a grimace as though cracking a nut. They never went without their spud, and chopped the grubs in half with such force that the iron of the tool sank three inches into the ground.

To get rid of caterpillars, they struck the trees furiously with long poles.

Bouvard planted a peony in the middle of the lawn, and tomatoes which would hang like lanterns under the arbour roof.

39

Pécuchet had a large pit dug in front of the kitchen and divided it into three compartments. There he could manufacture composts which would produce a heap of things whose decay would lead to other harvests providing other manures, on and on without end; and he used to dream on the edge of this pit, seeing, in the future, mountains of fruit, torrents of flowers, avalanches of vegetables. But the horse-dung so necessary for the hotbeds was lacking. Farmers did not sell it; innkeepers refused to give it. At last after much search, despite the prayers of Bouvard, and laying aside all modesty, he decided to go out with brush and pan himself.

It was in the midst of this occupation that Mme Bordin one day greeted him on the high road. When she had passed the compliments of the day with him, she asked after his friend. This lady's black eyes, very bright and small, her rich colouring, her self-possession (she even had a little moustache) intimidated Pécuchet. He answered shortly and turned his back—a piece of rudeness for which he was reproached by Bouvard.

Then the bad weather came, snow and hard frost. They installed themselves in the kitchen and constructed trellises; or else went through the rooms, chatted by the fire, watched the rain coming down.

After mid-Lent they looked forward to spring, and repeated every morning: 'The worst is over.' But the season was late in coming, and they tempered their impatience with: 'Things will soon be better.'

At last they saw the young peas coming up. There was a wealth of asparagus. The vine showed promise.

Now that they were skilled in gardening, they ought to succeed at agriculture—and they were taken with the ambition to develop the farm themselves. With good sense and application they would doubtless manage.

First, it was necessary to see how others went to work;

and they drew up a letter asking M. de Faverges the honour of investigating the system he employed. The count made an appointment at once.

After an hour's walk they reached the side of a hill overlooking the valley of the Orne. The river wound at their feet. Here and there rose blocks of red sandstone, and in the distance larger rocks formed a cliff overhanging the landscape covered with ripe corn. Trees, so thick that they hid the houses, divided the opposite hill into uneven squares, and stood out in darkened lines amid the grass.

Suddenly the whole of the estate came into view. Tiled roofs marked the farm. The white-fronted manor was to the right with a wood beyond, and a lawn sloped down to the river in which was reflected a row of plane trees.

The two friends entered a lucerne field which was being spread. Women with straw hats, handkerchiefs or paper caps, were lifting the hay from the ground with their long rakes; and at the end of the level, near the ricks, the stooks of hay were being quickly tossed into a long wagon to which three horses were harnessed. The count came forward, followed by his bailiff.

He was dressed in dimity; his stiff bearing and his mutton-chop whiskers gave him air at the once of a magistrate and a dandy. Even when he was speaking, his features did not stir.

After a brief exchange of courtesies he explained his system with regard to fodder; swathes should be turned without scattering them; stooks should be conical, and trusses made at once on the spot, then stacked by tens. As for the English mechanical rake, the land was too uneven for such an implement.

A small girl, her bare feet in slippers and wearing a dress which showed her body through the rents, was giving the women cider which she poured from a jug tilted on her hip. The count asked where the child came from; they knew nothing about her. The women had picked her up to wait on them during the harvest. He shrugged his shoulders, and walked away, uttering complaints against the immorality of the countryside.

Bouvard praised the lucerne. It was fairly good, despite the ravages of dodder; the budding agriculturists opened their eyes at the word 'dodder.' Owing to the number of his cattle he was going in for seed pastures; besides it made a good preparation for the other crops, which is not always the case with root-fodders.

'That at least seems to me incontestable.'

Bouvard and Pécuchet answered together:

'Oh, incontestable.'

They were on the edge of a field which had been well harrowed; a led horse was pulling a large box mounted on three wheels. Seven coulters, set underneath, were opening parallel ruts in the soil where the seed fell downwards through pipes. 'Here,' said the Count, 'I sow kohlrabi. Kohlrabi is the basis of my four years' rotation.'

And he began a demonstration of the sower. But a servant came to fetch him. He was wanted at the house.

The bailiff took his place, a weasel-faced man with an ingratiating manner.

He conducted 'the gentlemen' to another field, where fourteen mowers, bare-chested and legs apart, were cutting the rye with scythes. The blades hissed through the stalks which fell over to the right. Each man described a large semicircle in front of him, and they moved forward together in one line. The two Parisians were astonished at the strength of their arms and felt themselves possessed by an almost religious reverence for the wealth of the soil.

They proceeded to walk the length of several ploughed fields. Dusk was falling, rooks were swooping down to the furrows. Then they met the flock; the scattered sheep were grazing, and one could hear them as they browsed. The shepherd, sitting on a tree stump, was knitting a woollen sock, with his dog near him.

The bailiff helped Bouvard and Pécuchet over a stile, and they passed through two orchards where cows were chewing the cud under the apple trees.

All the farm buildings were contiguous and occupied three sides of the yard. The work was done mechanically by a turbine, harnessing the stream that had been turned for the purpose. Leather belts went from one roof into another, and an iron pump worked in the centre of the midden.

The bailiff drew their attention to small openings in the sheepfolds on a level with the ground, and ingenious doors in the pigsties which shut of themselves.

The barn was vaulted like a cathedral, with brick arches resting on stone walls.

To amuse the gentlemen, a woman threw handfuls of oats to the chickens. The shaft of the cider-press seemed to them enormous, and they ascended into the pigeon-loft. The dairy particularly astonished them. Taps in the corners gave enough water to swill the slabs; and on going in, the coolness took one by surprise. Brown jars along the windows were filled with milk to the brim. Earthenware pans held the cream. Then came the rounds of butter like slices of a copper pillar, and froth bubbled over the tin pails which had just been put down. But the gem of the farm was the cattle-shed. It was divided by wooden bars, reaching straight up to the ceiling, into two sections: one for the cattle, the other for those who tended them. It was hard to see in there, for all the shutters were closed. The oxen were eating, tethered by small chains, and their bodies exhaled a warmth which was pressed down by the low ceiling. But someone let in the light; suddenly a trickle of water ran along the gutter beside the racks. The sound of lowings was heard; horns rattled like sticks. All the oxen thrust their muzzles between the bars and slowly drank.

The big teams came into the yard and the foals neighed; near the ground two or three lanterns shone, then disappeared. The labourers went by, dragging their clogs over the stones, and the supper-bell rang.

The two visitors departed.

All they had seen enchanted them; their minds were made up. The same evening, they took from their shelves the four volumes of *The Country House*, had Gasparin's book on farming sent to them, and subscribed for an agricultural journal.

To go to market more easily they bought a trap which Bouvard drove.

Dressed in blue blouses, with wide-brimmed hats, gaiters up to their knees and horse-copers' sticks, they went prowling round the cattle, asking questions of the labourers, and put in an appearance at all the agricultural shows.

They very soon wearied farmer Gouy with advice, especially deploring his system of letting the land lie fallow. But the farmer stuck to his routine. He asked to be let off his rent, with the hail for an excuse. As to the ground rent, he paid none. His wife cried out at the most reasonable claims. In the end Bouvard declared his intention of not renewing the lease.

After that Gouy was stingy with the manure, let weeds grow, ruined the soil; and he went off with a scowl which hinted at revenge.

Bouvard had thought that twenty thousand francs, which was more than four times the rent of the farm, would be enough to start with. His notary sent the amount from Paris.

Their farm land comprised thirty-seven acres of orchard and meadow, fifty-seven of arable, and twelve in fallow situated on a stony hillock and called the Knoll.

They procured all the indispensable apparatus, four horses, a dozen cows, six pigs, a hundred and sixty sheep and, as hands, two carters, two women and a shepherd, not to mention a huge dog.

For the sake of ready money they sold their fodder. They were paid at their house; the gold napoleons counted over a chest of oats seemed to them more glittering than any others, more rare and valuable.

In November they brewed cider. It was Bouvard who whipped up the horse, and Pécuchet, standing in the trough, stirred the pulp with a spade.

They panted as they turned the vice; they strained the liquor into the vat, saw to the bungs, wore clogs, and thoroughly enjoyed themselves.

Starting from the principle that you cannot have too much corn, they got rid of about half their seed pasture; and as they had no compost, they used clods of manure, which they dug into the ground without breaking them, so that the crop was pitiable.

The next year they sowed very thickly. Storms followed. The grain was beaten down.

Nevertheless, they stuck to their wheat, and undertook to clear the Knoll of stones. A hamper was used to carry them away. All the year round, from morning till evening, through rain and sun, the eternal hamper was to be seen with the same man and the same horse clambering upwards, descending and remounting the little hill. Sometimes Bouvard walked behind, halting midway to wipe his brow.

Trusting no one, they themselves physicked their live-stock, administered purges and clysters.

Serious troubles occurred. The farmyard girl became pregnant. They engaged a married couple; children swarmed, male and female cousins, uncles, sisters-in-law;

a mob was living at their cost, and they resolved to sleep in turn at the farm.

But the evenings were sad. The dirtiness of the room offended them—and Germaine, who brought the meals, grumbled at every journey. They were swindled all round. The threshers hid corn in their pitchers. Pécuchet caught one, and bundling him outside by the shoulders, shouted:

'Wretch! You are a disgrace to the village that gave you birth!'

His appearance did not instil respect. Besides, he had misgivings about the garden. His whole attention would not have been enough to keep it trim—Bouvard was going to look after the farm. They had debated the matter, and come to this arrangement.

The first point was to have good hotbeds. Pécuchet had one built of brick. He painted the frames himself, and, fearing the blaze of the sun, whitewashed all the bell-glasses.

For his cuttings, he took the precaution of nipping off the tops along with the leaves. Then he devoted himself to layering. He tried all kinds of grafting: grafting in flute, in crown, in shield, herbaceous and English. With what care he adjusted the two libers! How he squeezed the ligatures! What a mass of paste to cover them!

Twice a day he would take his watering-can and swing it over the plants, as if he were censing them. When they turned green beneath the water falling in a fine rain, he seemed to slake his own thirst and to revive with them. Then, yielding to an intoxication, he tore off the rose of the can and poured a stream right out of the spout.

At the end of the hedge, next to the plaster lady, rose a sort of log-hut. Pécuchet kept his tools in it and spent delightful hours there unpodding the seeds, writing tickets, arranging his little pots. He used to rest on a box at the door and meditate improvements.

At the foot of the steps he had placed two bowls of geraniums; between the cypresses and cordons he planted sunflowers; and as the borders were covered with butter-cups, and all the walks with fresh sand, the garden dazzled with its profusion of yellow tints.

But the hotbed swarmed with grubs; despite the layers of leaves, under the painted frames and the daubed glasses there were only rachitic growths. The cuttings did not take, the grafts broke away, the sap of the runners dried up, the trees had the rot at the roots, the seed-plots were a desert. The wind threw down the bean props in its sport. Too much dung spoiled the strawberries, not enough topping the tomatoes.

There was a shortage of broccoli, aubergines, turnips and watercress, which he had meant to raise in a trough. After the thaw, all the artichokes perished. The cabbages con-soled him. One in particular filled him with hope. It spread out, still grew taller, and ended by being colossal and quite inedible. No matter, Pécuchet was happy to possess a prodigy.

Then he attempted what seemed to him the acme of this art: the culture of the melon.

He sowed several different kinds of seeds in pans with mould, which he buried in the hotbed. Then he prepared another hotbed; and when it had given off its heat, he planted out the finest growths, with bell-glasses above. He made all his cuttings according to the instructions of the gardening manual, left the flowers intact, allowed the fruit to form a cluster, chose one on each stem, picked off the others, and, when they were as big as a nut, he slid under the fruit a little board to prevent rotting from the dung. He warmed them, cooled them, wipe the mist off the glasses with

47

his handkerchief, and, when clouds came up, he hurriedly brought out straw-matting.

At night he could not sleep for them. He got up a number of times, and with bare feet in slippers, wearing a night-shirt, and shivering, he crossed the garden to lay his eiderdown on the frame.

The cantaloups ripened. Bouvard made a face at the first. The second was no better, nor the third. For each of them Pécuchet found a fresh excuse, up to the last which he threw out of the window, declaring that he could not understand it. Actually, as he had grown different species next to one another, the sweet variety got mixed with the bitter, the big Portuguese with the great Mongolian, and the presence of tomatoes completing the anarchy, there resulted abominable hybrids of a pumpkin flavour.

Then Pécuchet turned to his flowers. He wrote to Dumouchel for shrubs as well as seeds, bought a stock of heath-mould and resolutely set to work.

But he planted passion-flowers in the shade, pansies in the sun, covered hyacinths with manure, watered the lilies after they had flowered, destroyed the rhododendrons by cutting them back, stimulated the fuchsias with glue, and roasted a pomegranate tree by exposing it to the kitchen fire.

As the cold weather approached he sheltered the rose-bushes with domes of cardboard reinforced with candle-grease; they were like sugar-loaves held in the air by sticks.

The props of the dahlias were gigantic, and there could be seen, between their straight ranks, the twisted branches of a sophora japonica, which remained unalterable, without withering but without growing either.

However, since the rarest trees prospered in the parks of the capital they ought to succeed at Chavignolles; and

Pécuchet procured Indian lilac, Chinese roses and eucalyptus, then in the infancy of its fame. All his experiments collapsed. Each time he was most surprised.

Bouvard, like him, encountered obstacles. They consulted each other, opened one book, passed on to a second, then knew not what decision to make before the divergence of opinion.

Thus, as regards marl, Puvis recommends it, Roret's handbook opposes it.

As to plaster, despite Franklin's authority, Riéfel and M. Rigaud do not seem enthusiastic.

Fallow soil, according to Bouvard, was an antiquated prejudice, yet Leclerc gives cases where it is almost obligatory. Gasparin instances a farmer near Lyons who, for half a century, has cultivated cereals in the same field; that upsets the theory of rotation. Tull exalts ploughing to the detriment of manure; and here is Major Beetson who abolishes manure for ploughing!

In order to become weather-wise they studied the clouds according to Luke-Howard's classification. They gazed at clouds which stream out like manes, which resemble islands, which one would take for snowy mountains, trying to distinguish nimbus from cirrus, stratus from cumulus; the shapes changed before they could think of the names.

The barometer deceived them; the thermometer taught them nothing. They had recourse to the expedient devised by a priest of Touraine under Louis xv. A leech in a glass jar ought to climb up the side in case of rain, keep on the bottom for set fine weather, and move about at the threat of storm. But nearly always the atmosphere contradicted the leech: they put three others with it. All four behaved differently.

After much cogitation, Bouvard admitted that he had made a mistake. This property needed extensive farming by the intensive method, and he risked what remained of his loose capital, thirty thousand francs.

Egged on by Pécuchet, he had a frenzy for manure. In the compost-trench were flung together boughs, blood, entrails, feathers—everything that could be found. He employed Belgian dressing, Swiss fertiliser, lye, pickled herrings, seaweed, rags; he sent for guano, and tried to manufacture it; then, pushing his tenets to the extreme, would not let any urine be wasted. He suppressed the privies. Dead animals were brought into the yard with which he treated the soil. Their carcasses were scattered over the country in fragments. Bouvard smiled in the midst of the stench. A pump, installed in a tumbrel, spurted liquid manure over the crops. To those who put on airs of disgust he said: 'But it's gold! It's gold!'

And he regretted not having still more dung-heaps. Happy is the country where are natural grottoes filled with bird-droppings!

The rape was meagre, the oats poor, the corn sold badly because of its smell. A strange phenomenon was that the Knoll, now it was clear, yielded less than ever.

He thought it best to get new equipment. He bought one of Guillaume's hoeing-machines, a Valcourt weeder, an English sower, and Mathieu de Dombasle's large-sized swing-plough, though the ploughman sneered at it.

'Learn to use it!'

'Well, show me how!'

He tried to demonstrate it, but blundered, and the peasants chuckled. He could never discipline them to the call of the bell. Ceaselessly he shouted after them, ran from one place to another, noted observations in his diary, made appointments, and forgot them immediately. His head bubbled with industrial schemes. One day he would cultivate the poppy, with a view to opium, and, above all, milkvetch, which he would sell under the name of 'Family Coffee.'

In order to fatten his oxen more quickly he bled them every fortnight. He killed none of his pigs, but gorged them on salted oats. Soon the piggery was too small. They cluttered the yard, broke in the pailings, bit everybody.

During the hot weather twenty-five sheep began to sicken, and, a short while after, died. The same week three oxen were lost, in consequence of Bouvard's phlebotomy.

To destroy the locust-grubs he had the idea of shutting fowls in a wheeled cage, which two men would push behind the plough. This did not fail to break their claws.

He made beer with germander leaves, and gave it to the harvesters disguised as cider. Belly-aches broke out. The children cried, the women groaned, the men were furious. They all threatened to quit, and Bouvard gave way.

To convince them, however, that his beverage was harmless, he absorbed several bottles of it in front of them, felt queer, but hid his pains under an air of enjoyment. He even had the mixture taken into the house. He drank it the same evening with Pécuchet, and both did their best to enjoy it. Besides, it must not be wasted.

Bouvard's colic became very violent. Germaine went for the doctor.

He was a serious man, with a bulging forehead, who started by frightening his patient. The gentleman's queasiness must come from that beer of which people were talking. He wanted to know its composition, and condemned it in scientific terms, shrugging his shoulders. Pécuchet, who had provided the recipe, was abashed.

In spite of harmful liming, scanty hoeing and the weeding of the thistles at the wrong time, Bouvard, next year, had a fine crop of wheat before his eyes. He resolved to dry it by fermentation—the Dutch method, Clap-Mayer's system

—that is to say, he had it mown all together, and made into ricks which were to be pulled down when the gas began to escape from them, and then exposed to the open air; after which Bouvard went off without the least qualm.

The next day, while they were at dinner, they heard in the beech avenue the beating of a drum. Germaine went to see what was the matter, but the man was already a long way off. Almost at once the church bell rang violently.

Alarm gripped Bouvard and Pécuchet. They rose and, eager for news, went hatless towards Chavignolles.

An old woman passed. She knew nothing. They stopped a little boy, who answered:

'I think it's a fire.'

And the drum continued beating, the church bell ringing louder. Finally they reached the first houses of the village. The grocer shouted from a distance:

'Your farm is on fire!'

Pécuchet quickened to the double, and said to Bouvard, running in step beside him:

'One, two! One, two!' in rhythm, like the Chasseurs of Vincennes.

The road they were following was eternally up-hill; a slope of the ground hid the horizon. They reached the top near the Knoll, and at a single glance the disaster was apparent.

All the ricks, dotted here and there in the middle of the bare plain, were blazing like volcanoes in the evening stillness.

Round the biggest there were perhaps three hundred people; and under the orders of M. Foureau, the mayor, in his tricolour scarf, young lads with poles and draghooks were pulling the hay from the top in order to save the rest.

Bouvard, in his anxiety, almost knocked over Mme Bordin, who was standing by. Then, catching sight of one of his men, he overwhelmed him with abuse for not having given him warning. Whereas the man, with the greatest energy, had run first to the farmhouse and the church, then to the master's house, and come back the other way.

Bouvard lost his head. The labourers crowded round, all speaking at once, and he forbade them to pull down the ricks, imploring help, demanding water, calling for firemen.

'Where are they to come from?' cried the mayor.

'You ought to know!' replied Bouvard.

He stormed, made unpleasant remarks, and everybody admired M. Foureau's patience, for he was rough-natured, as was shown by his thick lips and bulldog jaw.

The heat of the ricks became so strong that no one dared go near. Beneath the greedy flames the hay twisted crackling, grains of corn peppered their faces like lead pellets. Then the stack fell to the ground, a great brazier, whence showered sparks. The red mass undulated with a sheen like watered silk, which showed in its changing lines parts that were vermilion red and others brown like clotted blood. The night had come, the wind whistled; wisps of smoke wrapped the crowd. Sputters of flame, from time to time, passed over the black sky.

Bouvard gazed at the fire, weeping quietly. His eyes had disappeared under their heavy lids, and his whole face seemed swollen by grief. Mme Bordin, toying with the fringe of her green shawl, called him 'Poor gentleman!' attempted to console him. Since nothing could be done he ought to be reasonable.

Pécuchet was not weeping. Very pale, or rather livid, with open mouth and hair plastered down by a cold sweat, he stood apart, lost in his thoughts. But the curé, suddenly arriving, murmured in a soothing tone:

'Ah! what a misfortune! most vexatious, to be sure! Please accept my wholehearted—'

53

The others pretended no regret. They chattered, smiling, with hands stretched to the blaze. One old man picked up the burning straws to light his pipe. Children began to dance. An urchin even called out that it was great fun.

'Yes, fine fun!' retorted Pécuchet, who had caught the remark.

The fire died away, the heaps sank, and an hour after nothing but ashes were left, making round black marks on the plain. Then all dispersed.

Mme Bordin and Abbé Jeufroy led MM. Bouvard and Pécuchet home.

On the way the widow addressed some very amiable reproaches to her neighbour on his bearishness, and the ecclesiastic expressed his great surprise at not yet having been able to make the acquaintance of so distinguished a parishioner.

Alone together, they sought the cause of the fire, and instead of recognising, like everybody else, that the damp straw had flamed up of itself, they suspected a revenge. It came no doubt from farmer Gouy, or perhaps from the mole-catcher. Six months before, Bouvard had refused his services, and even maintained, in a circle of listeners, that his activities were disastrous and should be stopped by the Government. Since then the fellow had roamed about the district. He had a big beard, and looked terrifying, especially in the evening, when he would appear outside people's yards, shaking his long pole decorated with pendent moles.

The damage was considerable, and, to find out where they stood, Pécuchet worked for a week at Bouvard's accounts, which struck him as a veritable labyrinth. After having checked up the day-book, the correspondence, and the ledger covered with pencil notes and references, he acknowledged the truth: no produce for sale, nothing to come in, zero in hand. The capital was conspicuous for a deficit of thirty-three thousand francs.

Bouvard would not credit this, and, more than a score of times, he began his calculations again. They always worked out the same. Two more years of such agriculture and their fortune would be lost! The only remedy was to sell.

At any rate they must consult a notary. It was a painful course, which Pécuchet undertook.

According to M. Marescot, it would be better not to put up bills of sale. He would speak of the farm to serious clients, and let the offers come.

'Very well,' said Bouvard. 'There's plenty of time.' He would engage a farmer, and then they would consider the matter. 'We shan't be any worse off than before; only it will mean having to economise.'

This vexed Pécuchet because of the garden, and some days later he said:

'We ought to devote ourselves exclusively to arbori-culture—not for pleasure, but as a speculation. A pear costing three sous sometimes fetches five or six francs in the capital! There are gardeners who make twenty-five thousand a year from apricots! In winter at St. Petersburg grapes cost a napoleon a bunch! It's a fine industry, you'll agree! And what's the price? Care, manure and the handling of a pruning-knife!'

He so spurred Bouvard's imagination that, at once, they looked in their books for plants to buy, and, having chosen names which to them seemed wonderful, they wrote to a market-gardener at Falaise, who eagerly undertook to send them three hundred saplings for which he had no market.

They called in a smith for the tree-props, an ironmonger for the wiring, and a carpenter for the stakes. The shape of the trees was designed in advance. Strips of lath on the wall made the pattern of candelabras. Two posts at each end of

55

the borders stretched horizontal wires; and, in the orchard, hoops indicated a structure of vases, thin sticks arranged conically, the shape of pyramids. Thus, on visiting them, one would seem to be viewing the pieces of an unknown machine, or the skeleton of a firework display.

Holes were dug; they cut the ends off roots, good as well as bad, and stuck them into a compost. Six months later the saplings were dead. New orders to the gardener followed, and new plantings in still deeper holes. But the rain soaking the soil, the graftings themselves took root and the trees rose up freely.

Spring came; Pécuchet set himself to prune the pear trees. He did not cut down the leaders, left the fruit spurs as they were, and persisting in his desire to have the Duchess pears in a square bed, whereas they should branch only sideways, he invariably snapped them or broke them down. As for the peaches, he got confused between the principal and the subsidiary branches. The barren ones and the bearers always showed up where they ought not to be, and it was impossible to obtain a perfect rectangle on the espaliers, with six branches on the right, and six on the left, not counting the chief ones, the whole to form a fine herring-bone pattern.

Bouvard tried to train the apricot trees; they rebelled. He forced their stems down to the level of the soil; none of them grew up again. The cherries, on which he had made notches, produced gum.

First they pruned a long way down, which did away with the buds near the base, then too little, which produced water shoots; and often they hesitated, unable to distinguish wood buds from fruit buds. They were delighted to have the blossoms, but, having perceived their mistake, they tore off three-quarters of them to strengthen the rest.

They talked ceaselessly of sap and cambium, nailing up,

56

hoeing and thinning. In the middle of the dining-room they had a framed list of their nurslings, with a number that tallied in the garden, marked on a little piece of wood at the foot of each tree.

Up at dawn, they laboured till nightfall, with bamboos in their belts. In the cold spring mornings Bouvard kept his knitted vest under his smock, Pécuchet his old coat under his apron, and people going along the lane heard them coughing through the mist.

Sometimes Pécuchet would draw his handbook from his pocket and study a paragraph, standing there, with his spade beside him, in the pose of the gardener who adorned the frontispiece. This resemblance greatly flattered him. It gave him a high opinion of the author.

Bouvard was for ever perched on a high ladder in front of the pyramids. One day he was taken dizzy, and, not daring to climb down, he had called to Pécuchet for help.

At last the pears came; and there were plums in the orchard. Then they employed all the usual devices against birds. But the bits of glass shone till they dazzled, the click of the windmill woke them in the night, and sparrows perched on the scarecrow. They made a second, and even a third, changing the costume, but without avail.

However, they could expect a certain amount of fruit. Pécuchet had just given the catalogue to Bouvard, when suddenly the thunder crashed and the rain poured—a heavy, beating rain. The wind, in gusts, shook the whole surface of the espalier. The props gave way one after another, and as the wretched cordons swayed, the pears were battered together.

Pécuchet, taken unawares by the downpour, had fled into the hut. Bouvard stayed in the kitchen. They saw splinters of wood, branches, tiles, whirling past them; and on the coast, twenty-five miles away, the sailors' wives who were watching the sea had not eyes more loving or hearts more anguished. Then suddenly the props and struts of the double espaliers, along with the trellises, collapsed on the borders.

What a sight when they went to look! Cherries and plums covered the grass among the melting hailstones. The Colmar pears were lost—the Bési-des-vétérans and the Jordoigne Triumphs. Of the apples there remained little more than a few Bons-papas; and a dozen Tetons-de-Vénus, the entire crop of peaches, rolled in the puddles beside the uprooted box-hedge.

After dinner, at which they ate little enough, Pécuchet said gently:

'Wouldn't it be as well to look at the farm, in case anything's happened?'

'Bah! To find fresh cause for misery!'

'Maybe! We're hardly favourites of fortune.'

And they grumbled at Providence and Nature.

Bouvard, elbow on table, uttered his little hiss, and, as one regret follows another, his old agricultural schemes came to mind again, above all, the starch and the new kind of cheese.

Pécuchet breathed noisily; and, stuffing pinches of snuff up his nose, dreamed that, if Fate had so willed, he would now have been active on an agricultural society, famous at the shows and mentioned in the newspapers.

Bouvard cast dismal glances round him.

'Damnation! I've a good mind to chuck all this. Let's go somewhere else!'

'Just as you like,' said Pécuchet.

And a moment later:

'The authorities recommend stopping all the ducts. If not, the sap is injured and the tree, of course, suffers. For it to flourish, it would have to bear no fruit at all. Yet those that are never pruned or manured yield fruit, smaller, indeed, but better flavoured. I insist on finding out why! And not only each kind requires particular care, but each tree as well, according to climate, temperature, and a heap of things! Where is the rule, then? And what hope have we of success or profits?'

Bouvard answered him:

'You'll see in Gasparin that profits can't exceed a tenth of the capital. Thus it would be better to deposit one's capital in a bank. At the end of fifteen years, as interest mounts up, one would have double without becoming a nervous wreck.'

Pécuchet drooped his head.

'Arboriculture is probably all humbug!'

'Like agriculture!' replied Bouvard.

Then they blamed themselves for having been too ambitious, and made up their minds henceforth to spare their toil and their money. Occasional pruning would be enough for the orchard. Double espaliers were banned; nor would they replace dead or fallen trees, though there were going to be ugly gaps unless they destroyed all those left standing. What should they decide?

Pécuchet made several rough sketches, using his box of compasses. Bouvard gave him advice. They arrived at nothing satisfactory. Happily they found in their library the work by Boitard entitled *The Architect of the Garden*.

The author divides gardens into an infinity of styles. There is, in the first place, the Melancholy or Romantic, which is distinguished by everlastings, ruins, tombs, and an 'ex-voto to the Virgin, indicating the spot where a cavalier, has fallen under an assassin's dagger.' The Terrible is constructed with overhanging rocks, shattered trees and burnt-out cabins; the Exotic, by planting Peruvian torch-thistles 'to bring back memories to a settler or traveller.' The Pensive must provide, like Ermenonville, a temple to philosophy. Obelisks and triumphal arches characterise the Majestic; moss and grottoes, the Mysterious; a lake, the Poetic. There is even the Fantastic, of which the finest specimen was lately to be seen in Württemberg, for there one encountered successively a wild boar, a hermit, several tombs, and a boat which left the bank of its own accord, in order to convey the visitor to a drawing-room where jets of water drenched him as he lay down on the sofa.

In the face of this wonderland, Bouvard and Pécuchet experienced a kind of vertigo. The Fantastic seemed to them reserved for royalty. The temple to philosophy would be a cumbrance. The ex-voto to the Madonna would lack significance, seeing there were no assassins, and, so much the worse for the settlers and travellers, American plants were too expensive. But rocks were possible, as well as shattered trees, everlastings and moss; and, with growing enthusiasm, after much experiment, helped by a single handyman and for a trifling sum, they made for themselves a residence that was unparalleled in the whole district.

The hedge, opening here and there, revealed the shrubbery, full of winding paths, like a maze. In the espalier-wall they would have liked to make an arch, under which a view would be discovered. As the keystone would not poise correctly, there resulted a huge breach, with scattered ruins.

They had sacrificed the asparagus to build an Etruscan tomb in its place—that is to say, a quadrilateral in black plaster, six feet high and resembling a kennel. Four young firs flanked this monument at each corner; it was crowned with an urn and embellished with an inscription.

In another part of the kitchen-garden a sort of Rialto spanned a pond, and they encrusted it with mussel-shells on the sides. The soil absorbed the water. Never mind, a cake would form at the bottom to keep it in.

The hut had been transformed into a rustic cabin, thanks to pieces of coloured glass.

At the top of the mound six trees, cut square, supported a tin gable with turned-up corners; this was meant for a Chinese pagoda.

They had gone to the banks of the Orne to select pieces of granite, had broken and numbered them, and brought them back in a cart, then joined the fragments with cement, piling them one on top of another; and thus in the middle of the lawn was a rock like an enormous potato.

Something was still wanting to complete the harmony. They cut down the biggest lime of the avenue (three-quarters dead already), and laid it full length in the garden, as though carried there by a torrent or struck by lightning.

The task ended, Bouvard, who was on the terrace, cried from a distance:

'Come here! There's a better view!'

'Better view!' was repeated on the air.

'I'm coming,' Pécuchet replied.

'Coming!'

'Hallo! an echo!'

'Echo!'

The lime tree, until then, had prevented its manifestation, and it was helped by the pagoda facing the barn, whose gable overtopped the avenue.

To try the echo, they amused themselves by yelling jokes; Bouvard howled out frisky ones, and obscenities.

He had been several times to Falaise, on the pretext of getting funds, and always returned with little parcels which he put in his chest of drawers. Pécuchet set off one morning for Bretteville, coming back very late with a basket which he hid under his bed.

Next day on waking, Bouvard had a surprise. The first two yews of the main walk, which the night before were still spherical, now had the form of peacocks, and a horn with two pot-buttons represented the beak and eyes. Pécuchet had been up since dawn and, trembling lest he be discovered, had clipped the two trees according to measurements by Dumouchel.

For six months the other trees behind them had been taking the shape, more or less, of pyramids, cubes, cylinders, stags or armchairs, but nothing equalled the peacocks. With generous praise, Bouvard admitted it.

Pretending to have forgotten his spade, he drew his companion into the maze, for he had taken advantage of Pécuchet's absence to furnish something staggering on his own account.

The gate to the fields was covered with a coating of plaster, on which were aligned in beautiful order five hundred heads of pipes, representing Abd-el-Kader, negroes, naked women, horseshoes and skulls.

'Now you see why I was so eager!'

'Indeed I do.'

And in their emotion they hugged each other.

Like all artists, they felt the need for applause, and Bouvard thought of giving a grand dinner-party.

'Take care!' said Pécuchet. 'You'll let yourself in for entertaining. There's no end to it!'

However, the matter was settled.

Since they had been living in the district they had kept to themselves. Everybody, in the wish to know them, accepted their invitation, except the Count de Faverges, who had been called to Paris on business. They fell back on M. Hurel, his factotum.

Beljambe, the innkeeper, once a chef at Lisieux, was to cook some of the courses. He would provide a waiter. Germaine had commandeered the farm-girl. Marianne, Mme Bordin's servant, would come too. At four o'clock the gates stood wide open, and the two proprietors, full of impatience, awaited their guests.

Hurel paused under the beech to put on his coat. Then the curé marched in, wearing a new cassock, and a moment after, M. Foureau, with a velvet waistcoat. The doctor was giving his arm to his wife, who walked with difficulty, sheltered under his umbrella. A wave of pink ribbon fluttered behind them: it was the bonnet of Mme Bordin, who was wearing a fine gown of shot-silk. Her gold watch-chain swung over her bosom, and the rings sparkled on her two hands that were covered with black mittens. Last came the notary, a panama on his head, a monocle in his eye, for the government official in him had not stifled the man of the world.

The drawing-room floor had been so waxed that you could not stand up. The eight Utrecht armchairs were back to the wall; a round table in the middle held the liqueur-stand, and, over the mantelpiece, was seen the portrait of Bouvard's father. The shadows, appearing in a false light, made the mouth grin, the eyes squint, and a slight mustiness on the cheeks gave a touch of reality to the whiskers. The guests found a likeness to his son, and Mme Bordin added, gazing at Bouvard, that he must have been an extremely good-looking man.

After an hour's waiting, Pécuchet announced that they could pass into the dining-room.

The white calico curtains with red fringes were, like those of the drawing-room, drawn right across the windows, and the sun, penetrating the material, threw a white light over the wainscoting, which had a barometer for its sole ornament.

Bouvard put the two ladies on either side of him; Pécuchet had the mayor on his left, the curé on his right, and a start was made with oysters. They tasted of mud. Bouvard was distressed, profusely apologetic, and Pécuchet got up and went to the kitchen to have it out with Beljambe.

All through the first course, consisting of a brill flanked by a *vol-au-vent* and stewed pigeons, the conversation turned on methods of making cider.

After that they discussed digestible and indigestible foods. The doctor, of course, was asked his opinion. He judged things sceptically, as a man who has seen to the bottom of knowledge, yet would not admit the slightest contradiction.

Along with the sirloin, Burgundy was served. It was cloudy. Bouvard, attributing this mishap to the rinsing of the bottle, made them try three others without success, then turned to Saint-Julien, obviously too young, and all the diners were silent. Hurel smiled without stopping; the waiter's heavy steps resounded on the tiled floor.

Mme Vaucorbeil, dumpy and grumbling in her manner (she was, moreover, near her confinement), had remained completely dumb. Not knowing what topic to set going, Bouvard mentioned the theatre at Caen.

'My wife never goes to the play,' replied the doctor.

M. Marescot, when he lived in Paris, only went to the Italiens.

'Well, I,' said Bouvard, 'used sometimes to treat myself to the pit at the Vaudeville for the farces.'

Foureau asked Mme Bordin if she liked farces.

'It depends what sort,' she said.

The mayor chaffed her. She answered back to his jokes. Then she gave a recipe for pickling gherkins. For her talents as a housewife were well known, and she had a little farm admirably looked after.

Foureau asked Bouvard:

'Do you intend to sell yours?'

'Goodness knows. At present I'm not sure—'

'What! Not even the Écalles slice?' replied the notary. 'That would suit you, Mme Bordin.'

The widow answered with a smirk:

'M. Bouvard's demands would be too high.'

'Perhaps one could soften him.'

'I shan't attempt it!'

'Nonsense, suppose you gave him a kiss!'

'Let's try at all events,' said Bouvard.

And he kissed her on both cheeks, to the applause of the company.

Almost at once they uncorked the champagne, whose popping led to further merriment. Pécuchet made a sign, the curtains opened and the garden lay revealed.

In the half-light it was somehow terrible. The rock, like a mountain, took up the lawn, the tomb made a cube in the midst of the spinach, the Venetian bridge a circumflex accent over the kidney beans—and the cabin beyond, a great black smudge, for they had fired the thatched roof to make it more poetical. The yews, in the shape of stags or armchairs, reached as far as the stricken tree, which extended from the elms to the arbour, where tomatoes hung like stalactites. A sunflower here and there showed its yellow disc. The Chinese pagoda, with its red paint, seemed like a lighthouse on the mound. The peacocks' beaks, caught by the sun, flashed fire, and behind the lattice, free of its boards, the dead level of the country bounded the horizon.

In the face of their visitors' astonishment, Bouvard and Pécuchet experienced veritable bliss.

Mme Bordin above all admired the peacocks; but the tomb was not understood, nor the burnt-out cabin, nor the wall in ruins. Then each passed in turn over the bridge. To fill the pond Bouvard and Pécuchet had been carting water all the morning. It had trickled away through the badly joined stones at the bottom which were covered with mud.

While they were walking about, the guests indulged in criticism: 'If I were you, I should have done that.—The green peas are late.—This corner, honestly, is all wrong.— With pruning like that you'll never get fruit.'

Bouvard was driven to answer that he did not care a hang for fruit.

As they were passing the row of elms, he said archly:

'Ah, here is someone we are disturbing; a thousand pardons!'

The joke was not taken up. Everyone knew the plaster lady.

At last, after several turns in the maze, they came to the gate with the pipes. Looks of stupefaction were exchanged. Bouvard noticed the faces of his visitors, and, impatient to hear their verdict—'What do you think of it?'

Mme Bordin burst out laughing. All did the same. M. le Curé gave a sort of clucking, Hurel coughed, the doctor laughed till he cried, his wife was taken with a nervous spasm; and Foureau, who never stood on ceremony, broke off an Abd-el-Kader, which he put in his pocket as a souvenir.

When they had emerged from the arbour, Bouvard, to surprise his party with the echo, yelled at the top of his voice: 'Your servant, ladies!'

Nothing, no echo. This was owing to repairs done to the barn, the gable and the roof having been demolished.

Coffee was served on the mound; and the gentlemen were going to start a game of bowls, when they saw in front of them a man watching through the lattice.

He was lean and swarthy, with tattered red trousers, a blue jacket, no shirt, his black beard cut like a brush; and he spoke in a hoarse voice:

'Give me a glass of wine!'

The mayor and Abbé Jeufroy had recognised him

immediately. He had once been a carpenter in Chavignolles.

'Now then, Gorju, move on!' said M. Foureau. 'Begging's not allowed.'

'Me! Begging!' cried the man furiously. 'I fought for seven years in Africa. I'm just out of hospital. No work to be had! Must I turn to murder? God Almighty!'

His rage fell of itself, and, with his two fists on his hips, he gazed at the gentry with a sad, mocking air. The weariness of bivouacks, absinthe and fever, a whole life of wretchedness and debauchery, showed in his troubled eyes. His pale lips trembled, exposing the gums. The vast purple of the sky wrapped him round with its blood-red light, and his obstinacy in staying there caused a sort of panic.

Bouvard, to end it, went for what was left in a bottle. The tramp swallowed greedily, then disappeared among the oats, gesticulating.

They reproved M. Bouvard. Such kindness encouraged disorder. But, annoyed at the ill-success of his garden, he took up the defence of the people: all talked at once.

Foureau extolled the Government, Hurel saw nothing in the world but landed property, Abbé Jeufroy lamented that religion was unprotected. Pécuchet railed against taxation. Mme Bordin cried from time to time: 'I must say I loathe the Republic!' And the doctor declared for progress. 'For after all, sir, we must have reforms.'—'Perhaps,' replied Foureau, 'but all those ideas are bad for business.'

'Damn business!' cried Pécuchet.

Vaucorbeil went on: 'You will at least admit our party's a practical one!' Bouvard would not go so far.

'If that's your view,' replied the doctor, 'we know where you stand! Good evening! And I hope the deluge comes, so that you can sail on your pond!'

'I'm going, too,' said M. Foureau a moment later; and

indicating the pocket where he had the Abd-el-Kader: 'If ever I want another, I'll come again.'

The curé, as he went, confided timidly to Pécuchet that he did not think the imitation tomb quite in place among the vegetables. Hurel, on leaving, made a low bow to the company. M. Marescot had disappeared after the dessert.

Mme Bordin repeated the details about her gherkins, promised a second recipe for brandy-plums, and took three more turns in the main walk; but as she was passing the lime tree the hem of her dress caught, and they heard her muttering: 'Good heavens! How idiotic this tree is!'

Till midnight the two Amphitryons breathed out their resentment under the arbour.

No doubt one could find fault with two or three little mishaps during the dinner; yet the guests had stodged like ogres, proof that it was not so bad. But as to the garden, such sneering arose from envy pure and simple—both of them became worked up.

'So water is needed for the pond! All right, they shall have a swan and fish as well!'

'They hardly noticed the pagoda!'

'It's imbecile to say the ruins are out of place!'

'And the tomb in bad taste! Why bad taste? Can't a man build one on his own property? I mean to be buried there myself.'

'Ah, don't talk of that,' said Pécuchet.

Then they passed the guests in review.

'The doctor seems to me a fine snob!'

'Did you catch Marescot grinning at the portrait?'

'What an ass the mayor is! When you go out to dinner, damn it all, you don't criticise the ornaments!'

'Mme Bordin?'

'There's a schemer for you! Leave me alone.'

Disgusted with the world they resolved to see no one, to live entirely by themselves and for themselves.

And they spent days in the cellar taking the tartar off the bottles, repolished all the furniture, distempered the rooms; every evening, watching the logs burn, they held forth on the best system of heating.

For the sake of economy they tried to smoke hams, to do their own washing. Germaine, whom they hindered, shrugged her shoulders. When the jam-making came round, she got into a temper, and they removed to the bakehouse.

It was an old laundry, where there was a large copper under the faggots, built in and admirably suited to their purpose, for they had been seized with an ambition to make preserves.

Fourteen glass jars were filled with tomatoes and green peas: they coated the stoppers with quicklime and cheese, wrapped them round with linen strips, then plunged them into boiling water. It steamed away; they poured in some cold: the difference of temperature made the jars explode. Only three were saved.

Then they procured some old sardine tins, laid veal cutlets inside and sank them in the copper. They came out round as balloons; the cold flattened them out again. To continue the experiment, they shut up, in other tins, eggs, chicory, lobster, a fish stew, a soup! and they congratulated themselves, like M. Appert, on having 'arrested the seasons'; such discoveries, according to Pécuchet, excelled the deeds of conquerors.

They improved on Mme Bordin's pickles, spicing the vinegar with pepper; and their brandy-plums were far superior! They obtained, by maceration, ratafias of raspberry and absinthe. With honey and angelica in a cask of Bagnols, they tried to make Malaga; and they also undertook the manufacture of champagne! The bottles of Chablis, mixed with must, burst of themselves. Then they no longer doubted their success.

As their researches widened, they came to suspect fraud in all articles of food.

They quarrelled with the baker over the colour of his bread. They made an enemy of the grocer by insisting that he adulterated his chocolates. They went to Falaise for lozenges, and under the chemist's very eye put his confection to the water test. It took on the appearance of bacon rind, which indicated gelatine.

After this triumph their pride knew no bounds. They bought the stock of a bankrupt distiller; and soon there arrived at the house strainers, kegs, funnels, skimmers, filters and scales, not counting a wooden bowl with a cannon ball and a Moorshead still, which required a reflecting furnace with a chimney.

They learnt how to refine sugar, and the different ways of boiling, large and small pearl, puffed, rolled, in drops, and caramel. But they were longing to use the still; and they applied themselves to liqueurs, starting with anisette. The fluid nearly always brought the solid bits with it, or else they stuck together at the bottom; at other times the quantities were wrong. Round them glistened the great copper pans, cucurbits advanced their pointed spouts, pipkins hung on the walls. Often one of them would be picking over herbs on the table while the other revolved the cannon-ball in the swinging bowl; they would stir the ladles, taste the mash.

Bouvard, always in a sweat, wore only a shirt and trousers drawn up to the pit of his stomach by short braces; but, featherheaded as a bird, he would forget the hole in the cucurbit, or make the fire too hot.

Pécuchet would mutter calculations, motionless in his long overall, a sort of child's pinafore with sleeves; and they looked on themselves as serious persons engaged in useful work.

Finally, they dreamed of a nectar which would surpass all others. They would put into it coriander as in Kümmel, kirsch as in Maraschino, hyssop as in Chartreuse, amberseed as in Vespetro, calamus aromaticus as in Krambambuly; and it was to be coloured red with sandalwood. But under what name should they launch it on the market? For they would want a name odd-sounding and easily remembered. After long research they decided to call it 'Bouvarine.'

Towards the end of autumn, spots appeared in the three jars of preserves. The tomatoes and the green peas were rotten. Could that result from the corking? And the problem of corking tormented them. They lacked the money to try new methods. The farm was eating them up.

On several occasions tenants had come forward; Bouvard would have none of them. But his head man did the farming after his orders, with a dangerous thrift, so that the crops fell off, everything was in jeopardy, and they were talking of their troubles, when farmer Gouy entered the laboratory, accompanied by his wife, who kept timidly in the background.

Thanks to all the preparation it had received, the land had been improved—and he was back to take the farm again. He disparaged it. Despite all their labour, the returns were doubtful; in short, if he wanted it at all, it was from love of the place and regret at leaving such good masters. They dismissed him coldly. He came back the same evening.

Pécuchet had lectured Bouvard; they were going to yield. Gouy demanded a lower rent, and when the others expostulated he started to bellow rather than talk, calling God to witness, enumerating his misfortunes, bragging of his merits. When they asked him to name a price, he hung his head without replying. Then the wife, who was sitting by the door, with a large basket on her knees, took up the same complaints, chirruping in a shrill voice like a wounded hen.

In the end the rent was fixed at three thousand francs a year, a third less than before.

Gouy made an offer for the equipment on the spot, and the debate began again.

The valuation of the items took a fortnight.

Bouvard was bored to death. He let everything go for so ridiculous a sum that Gouy first opened his eyes, and then crying, 'It's a bargain,' struck his palm against Bouvard's.

Afterwards the landlords, according to custom, suggested that they should have a bite indoors, and Pécuchet opened a bottle of his Malaga, less from generosity than from a wish to hear it commended.

But the farmer said ungraciously, 'It's like liquorice juice.'

And his wife, to 'take away the taste,' asked for a glass of brandy.

A more serious matter was occupying their thoughts. All the ingredients of 'Bouvarine' were at last collected.

They heaped them in the cucurbit, together with alcohol, lit the fire and waited.

In the meantime Pécuchet, worried by the mishap of the Malaga, took the tin boxes from the cupboard, whipped off the lid of the first, the second, the third. He threw them down in a fury and called Bouvard.

Bouvard turned off the tap of the worm and dashed towards the preserves. Disillusion was complete. The slices of veal were like boiled boot soles. A muddy liquid had replaced the lobster. The fish stew was unrecognisable. Toadstools had grown over the soup—and an intolerable stink infested the laboratory.

Suddenly, with the detonation of a shell, the still burst into a score of pieces which leapt to the ceiling, cracking the pots, knocking over the ladles, shivering the glasses; the coals were scattered, the stove demolished—and next day Germaine picked up a spatula in the yard.

The pressure of the steam had broken the apparatus—naturally so, as the cucurbit turned out to be blocked at the mouth.

Pécuchet had crouched at once behind the copper, and Bouvard had collapsed on a stool. For ten minutes they remained in this posture, white with fear, not daring to move an inch, amid the broken glass. When they recovered their speech, they asked themselves what could be the cause of so much ill-luck, especially the last? And they could make nothing of it, except that they had escaped death.

Finally, Pécuchet said:

'Perhaps it is because we never studied chemistry!'

III

So to study chemistry they procured Regnault's *Course*, and learnt in the first place 'that elements are perhaps compound.'

They are divided into metalloids and metals—a distinction that is 'by no means absolute,' says the author. Similarly, with regard to acids and bases, 'a substance may follow the law of acids or bases according to conditions.'

The notation seemed fantastic. The multiple proportions troubled Pécuchet.

'Since a molecule of A, for example, may combine with several particles of B, it seems to me that this molecule must resolve itself into the same number of particles; but if it is divided it ceases to be an entity, the original molecule. In fact, I don't understand it.'

'Nor do I,' said Bouvard.

And they had recourse to a less difficult work, that of Girardin, where they acquired the assurance that a hundred cubic inches of air weigh thirty-one grains, that there is no lead in pencils, that a diamond is only carbon.

What, above all, astounded them was that earth, as an element, does not exist.

They mastered the sections on the use of the blow-pipe, on gold, silver, washing linen, and plating saucepans; then, without more ado, Bouvard and Pécuchet hurled themselves upon organic chemistry.

How wonderful it was to discover in human beings the same substances as compose minerals! Yet they experienced a kind of shame at the thought that their own organism contained phosphorus like matches, albumen like the whites of eggs, hydrogen like gas lamps.

After pigments and fats, they came to fermentation. This led them to acids, and the law of valency worried them once more. They tried to make its meaning clear by way of atomic theory; and this completed their confusion.

To understand it all thoroughly, according to Bouvard, instruments were necessary.

This entailed great expense, and they had already spent too much.

But Dr. Vaucorbeil could no doubt throw light on the subject. They presented themselves during his consulting hours.

'Well, gentlemen, here I am! What's the matter with you?'

Pécuchet answered that they were not ill, and having revealed the object of their visit:

'First, we'd like to find out about atomic theory.'

The doctor turned very red, then reproved them for wanting to learn chemistry.

'I don't deny its importance, of course! But at the moment it's dragged into everything! That has a deplorable effect on medicine.'

And the surroundings added weight to his pronouncement.

Diachylum and bandages were trailing over the mantelpiece. The surgical case stood in the middle of the desk, probes filled a basin in the corner—and against the wall was a picture of a flayed man.

Pécuchet complimented the doctor on it.

'Anatomy must be a fascinating study.'

M. Vaucorbeil dilated on the pleasure he used formerly to take in dissection, and Bouvard asked what the relationship was of the female to the male internal organs.

To satisfy him, the doctor brought from his library a portfolio of anatomical plates.

'Take them with you! You can look over them more easily at home.'

The skeleton astonished them by the salience of its jaw, the eye-sockets, the frightful length of the hands. They lacked an explanatory work; so they went back to M. Vaucorbeil, and, thanks to his copy of Alexander Lauth's handbook, they learnt up the divisions of the bodily frame, marvelling at the dorsal spine, sixteen times stronger, it is said, than if the Creator had fashioned it in a straight line.

'Why exactly sixteen times?'

The metacarpals were Bouvard's despair; and Pécuchet, eagerly devoting himself to the cranium, lost heart at the sphenoid, although it is like 'a Turkish or Arabesque saddle.'

As to the joints, too many ligaments hid them, and they set to work on muscles.

But the insertions were not easy to find, and when they reached the vertebral grooves they gave up altogether.

Then Pécuchet said:

'If we went back to chemistry, wouldn't that be a chance to use the laboratory?'

Bouvard opposed this, and thought he recollected that lay-figures were manufactured for use in hot climates.

He wrote to Barberou, who gave information on the subject. For ten francs a month they could get one of M. Auzoux's models, and the week after, the carrier from Falaise deposited an oblong packing-case at their door.

They carried it into the washhouse, greatly excited. When the boards had been unnailed, the straw cleared away, and the tissue paper unwrapped, the mannequin appeared. It was brick-coloured, hairless, skinless, striped with numerous blue, red and white filaments. This was not so much a

76

corpse as a kind of toy, horrible-looking, very spick-and-span, and smelling of varnish.

Then they lifted the thorax and saw the two lungs, like two sponges; the heart like a large egg, a little to one side at the back; the diaphragm; the kidneys; a whole parcel of entrails.

'To work!' said Pécuchet.

The day and the evening passed.

They had put on blouses, like medical students in the operating-theatre, and by the light of three candles were busy with their pieces of cardboard, when a fist banged on the door. 'Come in!'

It was M. Foureau, followed by the village constable. Germaine's employers had amused themselves by showing her the dummy. She had rushed headlong to the grocer to give him an account of it, and the whole village thought by now that they were secreting a real corpse in their house. Foureau, yielding to public rumour, had come to investigate; curious neighbours were crowding in the yard.

When he entered, the model was lying on its side, and the muscles of the face being unhooked, the eye made an awful gap, and had a terrifying aspect.

'What brings you?' asked Pécuchet.

Foureau stammered.

'Nothing. Nothing at all!'

And, taking up one of the bits on the table:

'What's this?'

'The buccinator,' replied Bouvard.

Foureau was dumb, but smiled in an unpleasant way, jealous of their having a hobby beyond his understanding.

The two anatomists pretended to go on with their researches. The villagers, tired of kicking their heels outside, had invaded the washhouse, and as they were pushing each other the table shook.

77

'Ah! This is too much!' cried Pécuchet. 'Clear these people out!'

The policeman made the busybodies go away.

'Good!' said Bouvard. 'We don't need any help.'

Foureau took the hint, and asked him if they had the right, not being doctors, to own such an object. At any rate he would report it to the prefect.

'What a country!' No place could be more idiotic, savage and backward. The comparison they made between themselves and others consoled them; it was their ambition to be martyrs of science.

The doctor also came to see them. He scoffed at the model as too remote from reality, but profited by the occasion to deliver a lecture.

Bouvard and Pécuchet were delighted, and, at their request, M. Vaucorbeil lent them various tomes from his library, always asserting that they would never read them through.

They noted down, from the *Dictionary of Medical Science*, extraordinary instances of childbirth, longevity, obesity and constipation. They learnt all about the famous Canadian, De Beaumont; Tarare and Bijou, the polyphagists; the dropsical woman in the district of the Eure; the Piedmontese who went to stool every twenty days; Simon de Mirepoix, who died of ossification; and that one-time Mayor of Angoulême whose nose weighed three pounds!

The brain inspired them with philosophical reflections. In its interior they easily recognised the *septum lucidum*, composed of two lamellæ, and the pineal gland, like a small red pea; but there were also peduncles and ventricles, arches, columns, ganglions and all sorts of fibres, Pacchioni's foramen, and Paccini's glands—in fact, an inextricable mass, enough to last them a lifetime.

Sometimes, with swimming heads, they completely dismounted the model, then became muddled in trying to put the pieces back.

This was heavy work, especially after lunch, and soon they dozed off, Bouvard with sunken chin and protruding belly, Pécuchet with his head in his hands and elbows on the table.

Frequently, at such moments, M. Vaucorbeil, who was finishing his early round, would open the door.

'Well, colleagues, how's the anatomy going?'

'Admirably,' they would answer.

Then he put questions in order to trip them up.

When they were tired of one organ they passed on to another, thus touching and abandoning in turn the heart, the stomach, the ear, the intestines, for their cardboard friend wearied them to death, despite their efforts of enthusiasm. At last the doctor surprised them as they were nailing it down in its box.

'Good! Just what I was expecting.'

One could not embark on such studies at their age, and the smile which went with these words wounded them deeply.

What right had he to judge them incapable! Was science in this gentleman's keeping, as though he were a superior being?

Accepting his challenge, therefore, they went off to Bayeux to buy books. Physiology was their weak point, and a bookseller got them the treatises of Richerand and Adelon, well known in their day.

All the commonplaces on age, sex and temperament seemed to them of the utmost importance; they were delighted to learn that there are three kinds of animalculæ in the tartar of one's teeth, that the tongue is the seat of taste, and the feeling of hunger resides in the stomach.

In order to understand functionary processes better, they

regretted not having the faculty of ruminating like Montègre, M. Gosse, and Bérard's brother, and they masticated slowly, grinding and salivating, accompanying the morsel with their thoughts into the entrails, following it with scrupulous care and an almost religious attention down to its final consequences. To produce artificial digestion, they put meat in a phial containing a duck's gastric juice, and carried it under their armpits for a fortnight, without any result but making themselves malodorous.

They were to be seen racing along the high road in the fierce sunshine clad in wetted garments. This was to verify whether thirst is quenched by the application of water to the skin. They came back puffing, and both of them with colds.

Hearing, speech and vision were run through briskly; but Bouvard dallied over generation.

The reticence of Pécuchet on this matter had always surprised him. His ignorance appeared so complete that he pressed him for the reason, and Pécuchet, blushing, ended by making an avowal.

For a joke a band of friends had once dragged him to a brothel, whence he had fled, reserving himself for the woman he might love later on. A favourable opportunity had never presented itself, and thus, from false modesty, lack of money, fear of disease, obstinacy and habit, at the age of fifty-two, in spite of living in the capital, he still preserved his virginity.

Bouvard found this hard to credit, then roared with laughter, but stopped when he saw tears in Pécuchet's eyes; for he himself had never been wanting in the tender passion, having been captivated in turn by a tight-rope dancer, an architect's sister-in-law, a barmaid, and finally a little laundress, and the marriage was about to take place when he found out that she was with child by another.

Bouvard said: 'It's never too late to mend. Cheer up! I'll take you in hand—that is, if you'd like me to.'

Pécuchet answered, with a sigh, that it was to be thought of no more; and they resumed their physiology.

Is it true that the surface of our bodies is always giving off a subtle vapour? The proof is, that one's weight decreases every minute. If each day we could gain as much as we lose and divest ourselves of superfluity, a perfect balance of health would be maintained. Sanctorius, the discoverer of this law, spent half a century weighing his food and all his excreta daily, and himself as well, only taking a rest in order to write his calculations.

They tried to imitate Sanctorius. But as their scales would not support the weight of both, it was Pécuchet who began.

He took off his clothes, so as not to hinder perspiration, and stood on the weighing-plate, completely naked and exposing to view, despite his modesty, an elongated cylinder-like torso, short legs, flat feet and brown skin. In a chair by his side his friend was reading to him:

'Scientists assert that animal heat is developed by muscular contraction, and that it is possible, by the motion of the thorax and pelvic members, to increase the temperature of a tepid bath.'

Bouvard went to fetch their bath-tub, and, when all was ready, he plunged in, armed with a thermometer.

The ruins of the still, swept up towards the far end of the room, displayed their dim heap in the shadow. Now and then they could hear the mice nibbling; a faded smell of aromatic herbs exuded, and finding this agreeable, they chatted at their ease.

But Bouvard began to feel chilly. 'Move your limbs!' said Pécuchet.

He moved them, without any effect on the temperature. 'It's decidedly cold.'

'I'm not warm myself,' replied Pécuchet, also starting to shiver. 'But work your pelvic members! Make them stir!'

Bouvard opened his thighs and waggled his buttocks, rocked his stomach, puffed like a whale, then looked at the thermometer which all the time was falling.

'I can't make it out; yet my limbs are moving.'

'Not enough.'

And he went on with his gymnastics.

This had continued three hours, when once more he took hold of the thermometer.

'What! Fifty-three degrees! Good night! I'm getting out!'

A dog came in—a cross between a hound and a mastiff—yellow-haired, flea-bitten, with its tongue hanging out.

What were they to do? There were no bells, and their servant was deaf! They shivered, but dared not budge, for fear of being bitten.

Pécuchet thought it would help if he shouted threats and rolled his eyes. Then the dog barked and leaped round the scales, where Pécuchet, clinging to the ropes and drawing up his knees, tried to hoist himself as high as he could.

'That's no good,' said Bouvard; and he began coaxing the dog, making advances to it.

No doubt the dog understood. Bouvard resolutely patted it, and raised its paws on to his shoulders, tickling them with his fingers.

'Look here! It's got my trousers!'

It lay down on them and did not move.

Then, with the greatest care, one risked getting off the weighing-plate, the other leaving the bath; and when Pécuchet had dressed again, this remark escaped him:

'As for you, old fellow, you'll do for our experiments.'

What experiments?

They might inject phosphorus into it and shut it in a cellar to see if its nostrils would give out light. But how was an injection made? Besides, no one would sell them phosphorus.

They considered enclosing it in an air-bell, making it inhale gases, giving it poison to drink. But all that would not be very pleasant. At last they hit on magnetisation of steel by contact with the spinal marrow.

Bouvard, suppressing his excitement, held out some needles on a dish to Pécuchet, who planted them along the backbone. These broke, slid through his fingers and fell to the ground; he took others and pushed them in violently, anywhere. The dog burst its bonds, passed through the window like a cannon-ball, rushed across the courtyard and the lobby, and presented itself in the kitchen.

Germaine screamed when she saw it, bleeding, and with string round its paws. Just then her masters entered in pursuit. It made a leap and vanished. The old servant raged at them.

'Another of your stupidities, no doubt! and a nice mess it's made of my kitchen! Probably the creature will go mad! Good-for-nothings like you get put into jail!'

They returned to the laboratory to test the needles. Not one attracted any filings.

Germaine's prophecy began to trouble them. The dog might go mad, come back suddenly and fly at them. Next day they sought news everywhere. And for some years, as soon as one like it appeared in a field, they would turn from their path.

Other experiments failed. Contrary to the authorities, the pigeons that they bled, whether crammed or fasting, took the same time to die. Kittens plunged under water expired in five minutes, and a goose, which they had stuffed with madder-root, developed entirely white periostea.

The problem of nutrition tormented them.

How is it that the same juice produces bones, blood, lymph and excremental matter? But one cannot trace the metamorphoses of what one swallows. The man who only eats one kind of food is chemically identical with him who absorbs a variety. Vauquelin, after calculating all the lime contained in a hen's corn, found a larger quantity in its eggshells.

Thus a creation of a substance takes place. But how? Nobody knows.

Even the strength of the heart is not known. Borelli admits as much as is necessary to lift a weight of nearly two hundred thousand pounds, and Kiell estimates it at about eight ounces, whence they concluded that physiology is (as the old saying goes) the romance of medicine. Not having been able to understand, they did not believe in it.

A month slipped away in idleness. Then they thought of their garden.

The dead tree, lying in the middle, was an encumbrance; they sawed it up. This exercise fatigued them. Bouvard frequently needed to get his tools repaired at the smith's.

On his way there one day, he was stopped by a man carrying a canvas sack on his back, who wanted to sell him almanacs, tracts, medals that had been blessed, and, finally, François Raspail's *Guide to Health*. This pamphlet pleased him so much that he wrote to Barberou to send him the complete work. Barberou dispatched it, and mentioned in his letter a chemist to make up the prescriptions.

The clearness of the doctrine charmed them. All illnesses come from worms. They spoil the teeth, undermine the lungs, dilate the liver, work havoc in the intestines, and cause wind. Camphor is the best means for getting rid of them. Bouvard and Pécuchet adopted it. They used it for snuff, crumbled it and put it into cigarettes, bottles of sedative water and pills of aloes. They even undertook the cure of a hunchback.

It was a child whom they had come across one market day. His mother, a beggar, brought him to their house every morning. They rubbed his hump with camphorated oil, applied a mustard plaster to it for twenty minutes, then covered it with diachylum, and, to make sure of his return, gave him a meal.

With his mind turning on intestinal worms, Pécuchet noticed a curious patch on Mme Bordin's cheek. For a long time the doctor had been treating it with caustic. The size of a franc to start with, this patch had grown till it formed a red circle. They wanted to attempt its removal. She accepted, but on condition that Bouvard put on the ointment. She took up a pose by the window, unhooked the top of her bodice and remained with her cheek upturned, looking at him with an eye that would have been dangerous had it not been for Pécuchet's presence. Despite the fear of mercury, they administered calomel in the doses prescribed. A month later Mme Bordin was cured.

She sang their praises, and the collector of taxes, the mayor's clerk, the mayor himself—everyone in Chavignolles—inhaled it through quills.

But the hunchback did not grow straighter. The tax-collector abandoned his camphorated cigarette, it made him cough twice as much. Foureau complained of the pills of aloes, which gave him piles; Bouvard had colics and Pécuchet frightful headaches. They lost faith in Raspail, but took care not to say so, for fear of lowering their reputation.

And they displayed great zeal for vaccination, learnt to bleed over cabbage leaves, and even acquired a pair of lancets.

They went with the doctor to see his poorer patients, consulting their books afterwards.

The symptoms noted by the authors were not those that they had just seen. As for the names of diseases, Latin, Greek and French, they were a jumble of all tongues. They can be counted by the thousand, and the Linnæan classification is extremely convenient with its genera and species; but how could one be sure of the species? Then they lost their way in the philosophy of medicine.

They meditated on Van Helmont's archaeus, vitalism, Brownism, and organicism. They asked the doctor the origin of the scrofula germ, what becomes of contagious miasmas, and the methods, in all morbid cases, of distinguishing cause from effect.

'Cause and effect are interchangeable,' Vaucorbeil replied.

This want of logic disgusted them and they visited the patients by themselves, getting into their homes under the cloak of philanthropy.

In the corners of rooms, on dirty mattresses, lay people whose faces were lop-sided, while others' were swollen and crimson, or lemon-coloured, or even violet, with sharp nostrils, tremulous mouths, and gasps, hiccoughs, sweats, exhalations of leather and old cheese.

They read their doctors' prescriptions, and were astonished to see that sedatives are sometimes stimulants; emetics, purges; that the same remedy is applicable to various illnesses, and that an ailment disappears under opposite treatments.

Nevertheless, they gave advice, infused cheerfulness, and had the audacity to use a stethoscope.

Their imagination was getting to work. They wrote to the King, asking that a nursing home, of which they were to be the directors, should be established in Calvados.

They betook themselves to the chemist at Bayeux (the

one at Falaise still had a grudge against them on account of his lozenges) and engaged him to make *pila purgatoria* in the manner of the ancients—that is to say, medicinal pellets which can be absorbed by manipulation.

Following out the assertion that inflammations are checked by the lowering of temperature, they hung the armchair of a woman suffering from meningitis to the beams of the ceiling, and were swinging her with all their might, when her husband arrived and drove them out.

Finally, to the great scandal of the curé, they had taken up the new fashion of introducing thermometers into backsides.

Typhoid spread over the region; Bouvard declared that he would not meddle with it. But the wife of Gouy, their farmer, came moaning to them. Her husband had been ill for a fortnight and M. Vaucorbeil was neglecting him.

Pécuchet devoted himself to the case.

Lenticular patches on the chest, pains in the joints, a swollen stomach, a red tongue—all these were symptoms of dysentery. Remembering the phrase of Raspail, that fever is expelled by taking the patient off a diet, he ordered broths and a little meat. Suddenly the doctor appeared. The invalid, with two pillows at his back, was beginning a meal, between his wife and Pécuchet, who pressed food on him.

The doctor approached the bed and flung the plate out of the window, crying:

'It's sheer murder!'

'Why?'

'You're perforating the intestine, since typhoid brings weakening of the follicular membrane.'

'Not always.'

And a dispute took place on the nature of fevers. Pécuchet believed in their independent origin. Vaucorbeil made them derive from the organs. 'Thus I keep away all irritants.'

'But diet lowers vitality!'

'What's this rigmarole about vitality? What is it? Who's ever seen it?'

Pécuchet's arguments became confused.

'Besides,' said the doctor, 'Gouy doesn't want food.'

The invalid, under his cotton nightcap, gave a sign of agreement.

'Never mind, he needs it!'

'Rubbish! His pulse is ninety-eight.'

'What does the pulse matter?' And Pécuchet quoted his authority.

'We've had enough systems!' said the doctor.

Pécuchet folded his arms.

'You're an empiric, then?'

'Certainly not! But by observation—'

'And if the observation's wrong?'

Vaucorbeil took this remark for an allusion to Mme Bordin's herpes, whose history had been broadcast by the widow and whose remembrance vexed him.

'To begin with, one must have practised.'

'Those who have revolutionised the science didn't! Van Helmont, Boerhaave, Broussais himself.'

Vaucorbeil, without answering, bent towards Gouy, and, speaking more loudly:

'Which of us two do you want as your doctor?'

The sick man drowsily regarded the angry faces, and began to cry.

Neither did his wife know what to say, for the one was clever, but the other perhaps knew of a secret remedy.

'Very well,'' said Vaucorbeil, 'since you hesitate between someone with a diploma—' Pécuchet sneered. 'Why are you laughing?'

'Because a diploma isn't always an argument.'

The doctor was attacked in his livelihood, his privilege, his social position. He exploded furiously:

'We'll see about that when you go before the Court for illegal medical practice!'

Then, turning to the farmer's wife: 'Have him killed by this gentleman, if you like, and may I be hanged if ever I enter the house again.'

And he rushed into the avenue, brandishing his stick.

When Pécuchet returned, Bouvard was himself much worried. He had just had a visit from Foureau, exasperated about his piles. In vain Bouvard had insisted that they are a protection against all sorts of illnesses. Foureau flatly refused to listen, and threatened an action for damages. He had lost his head.

Pécuchet recounted his own history, which he considered more serious, and was slightly shocked at Bouvard's indifference.

Next day Gouy had a pain in his stomach. It might have come from the nourishment not digesting. Perhaps Vaucorbeil was right? After all, a doctor ought to know in such cases; and Pécuchet was assailed with regret. He was afraid of being a murderer.

Out of prudence, they got rid of the hunchback. But because of the meal that he thus lost, his mother raised a disturbance. It was not worth their coming every day from Barneval to Chavignolles.

Foureau calmed down and Gouy regained his strength. His cure now was certain. Such a success emboldened Pécuchet.

'Suppose we work at midwifery, with one of those models?'

'I've had enough of models!'

'But these are sectional figures in leather, invented for students of midwifery. I believe I could turn over a foetus!'

But Bouvard was tired of medicine.

'The springs of life are hidden from us, its ills are too many, their remedy doubtful, and one can't discover from authors any reasonable definition of health, illness, diathesis, or even pus!'

Indeed, all their reading had confused their minds.

Bouvard had a cold, and thought he was starting a fluxion of the chest. Leeches not having lessened the stitch in his side, he had recourse to a vesicatory, which acted on his kidneys. After that he thought he had the stone.

Pécuchet got cramp while trimming the hedge, and vomited after his dinner, which greatly alarmed him; then, noticing that his colour was somewhat yellow, he suspected a liver complaint, and wondered:

'Have I got jaundice?'

He ended by having it.

Mutually depressing each other, they looked at their tongues, felt their pulse, changed their mineral water, and purged. They were suspicious of cold, heat, wind, rain, flies and, above all, draughts.

Pécuchet imagined that the habit of snuff was dangerous. Besides, a sneeze sometimes brings about the rupture of an aneurism; and he deserted his snuff-box. From habit, he thrust his fingers in it; then, suddenly, recollected his unwisdom.

Since black coffee upsets the nerves, Bouvard wanted to give up his small cup; but he slept after his meals, and was alarmed on waking up, for prolonged sleep is a warning of apoplexy.

Their ideal was Cornaro, the Venetian who, as a result of dieting, reached an extreme old age. Without entirely copying him, it was possible to take the same precautions, and Pécuchet drew from the shelves a *Manual of Hygiene*, by Doctor Morin.

How had they managed to keep alive until then? The dishes they liked were forbidden. Germaine, in confusion, no longer knew what to give them.

Every sort of meat has its defects. Black puddings and pork, pickled herrings, lobster and game, are 'refractory.' The larger a fish is the more gelatine it contains, and therefore is heavy on the stomach. Vegetables cause acidity, macaroni brings dreams, cheese 'considered generally, is of difficult digestion.'

A glass of water in the morning is 'dangerous.' Every drink or food was followed by a similar warning, or else by these words: 'Bad! Beware of the abuse! Is not good for everybody!' Why bad? Where is the abuse? How tell if a thing is good for one?

What a problem was breakfast! They left off coffee and milk because of its shocking reputation, and then chocolate, for it is 'a mass of indigestible substances.' There remained tea. But 'nervous persons ought to avoid it altogether.' Yet Decker, in the seventeenth century, prescribed fifty gallons of it per day in order to swill the pancreas.

This information shook Morin in their esteem, all the more so because he condemned every kind of head-covering —hats, bonnets and caps—a severity that revolted Pécuchet.

Then they bought the treatise by Becquerel, where they saw that pork is in itself 'a good nutriment,' tobacco perfectly innocuous, and coffee 'indispensable for military men.'

Until then they had believed that damp localities were unhealthy. Not at all! Casper declares them less fatal than others. One cannot bathe in the sea without refreshing the skin; Bégin would have one dive into it while profusely sweating. Unwatered wine, after soup, is passed as admirable for the stomach; Lévy accuses it of harming the teeth. Finally, the flannel protector, that safeguard, that tutelary of health, that palladium cherished by Bouvard and second nature to Pécuchet—some authors, without ambiguity or fear of prejudice, condemn it for plethoric or sanguine people.

What, then, is hygiene?

'Truth on one side of the Pyrenees, falsehood on the other,' affirms M. Lévy; and Becquerel adds that it is not a science.

After that, they ordered for dinner oysters, a duck, pork and cabbage, cream, Pont-l'Évêque cheese, and a bottle of Burgundy. It was a liberation, almost a revenge; and they jeered at Cornaro! What an idiot one must be to bully oneself like that! What degradation always to think of prolonging one's existence! Life is only good so long as one enjoys it.

'A piece more?'

'Yes, please!'

'So will I!'

'Good health!'

'The same to you!'

'Let to-morrow look after itself!'

They egged each other on.

Bouvard proclaimed that he wanted three cups of coffee, although he was not a military man. Pécuchet, his cap down on his ears, took pinch after pinch, and sneezed without fear; and, feeling the need of a little champagne, they ordered Germaine to hie off to the tavern and buy a bottle. The village was too far. She refused. Pécuchet was indignant.

'I command you, d'you hear! Go at once!'

She obeyed, though grumbling, determined to leave her masters soon, to such a degree were they incomprehensible and fantastic.

Then, as formerly, they went to take a coffee with brandy on the mound. Harvest was just over, and the ricks in the middle of the fields lifted their dark masses against the calm, blue night. The farms were quiet. Even the crickets were heard no more. All the countryside was asleep. They digested, inhaling the breeze, which freshened their cheeks.

The sky, far above, was covered with stars, some sparkling in groups, others in a line, or else solitary and at distant intervals. A belt of shining dust, reaching from north to south, parted in two over their heads. Between these lights there were vast empty spaces, and the firmament appeared to be a sea of blue, with archipelagos and islands.

'What a lot of them!' cried Bouvard.

'We can't see them all!' answered Pécuchet. 'Behind the Milky Way are the nebulae; behind the nebulae yet more stars. The nearest is over two hundred million miles away.'

He had often gazed through the telescope in the Place Vendôme and remembered the figures.

'The sun is a million times bigger than the earth, Sirius twelve times bigger than the sun, and comets measure eighty-five million miles.'

'It's enough to drive one mad!' observed Bouvard.

He lamented his ignorance, and was even sorry not to have been at the École Polytechnique in his youth.

Then Pécuchet, turning towards the Great Bear, showed him the Pole Star, then Cassiopeia, whose constellation forms a Y, Vega in the Lyre, gleaming brightly, and on the far horizon red Aldebaran.

Bouvard, with head thrown back, laboriously followed the triangles, quadrilaterals and pentagons that have to be imagined, in order to find one's way about the heavens.

Pécuchet went on:

'The speed of light is two hundred thousand miles a second. A scintillation of the Milky Way takes six centuries to reach us. Thus a star, by the time we see it, may have disappeared. Several are intermittent, others never return. And they alter their positions; everything is in motion, everything passes.'

'Yet the sun is constant!'

'So it was thought at one time. But those who know nowadays declare that it's rushing towards the constellation of Hercules.'

This confused Bouvard's ideas, and, after a few minutes' reflection:

'Science is constructed according to the data given by a corner of the whole field. Perhaps it doesn't agree with the remainder, of which nothing is known, which is much bigger and can't be discovered.'

They spoke in this fashion, posted on the mound, in the starlight, and their conversation was divided by long silences.

Then they asked each other whether there were men in the stars. Why not? And since Creation is in harmony, the inhabitants of Sirius must be enormous; those of Mars of average size; those of Venus very small. Unless they are the same everywhere. Tradesmen and policemen exist up above; business is carried on; there are wars; kings are dethroned.

Some shooting stars fell suddenly, describing what seemed the parabola of a gigantic rocket on the sky.

'Look!' said Bouvard, 'there are worlds vanishing.'

Pécuchet replied:

'If ours in its turn made a plunge, the citizens of the stars would not be more moved than we are now. Such ideas check one's pride.'

'What's the object of it all?'

'Perhaps there's no object.'

'And yet—'

Pécuchet repeated: 'And yet—' two or three times, without finding anything else to say.

'All the same, I should greatly like to know how the universe came to be made.'

94

'It must be in Buffon,' replied Bouvard, whose eyes were closing. 'I can't keep it up any longer. I must go to bed.'

The *Epochs of Nature* taught them that a comet, striking the sun, had detached a portion of it which became the earth. First the poles cooled. All the waters had covered the globe; they shrank into caverns: then the continents were parted, animals and man appeared. The majesty of creation caused them a stupefaction as great as itself. Their heads swelled. They were proud to meditate on such great themes.

Minerals quickly tired them, and they had recourse, as a distraction, to *The Harmonies* of Bernardin de Saint-Pierre.

Harmonies vegetable and terrestrial, aerial, aquatic, human, fraternal and even conjugal—all were dealt with there, without omitting the invocations to Venus, the Zephyrs and the Loves. They were astonished that fish should have fins; birds, wings; seeds, a pod. They were filled with that philosophy which discovers virtuous intentions in Nature and looks on her as a kind of Saint Vincent de Paul, always busy scattering bounties.

Then they wondered at her prodigies—water-spouts, volcanoes, virgin forests—and bought M. Depping's work on *The Marvels and Beauties of Nature in France*. The Cantal region possesses three, Hérault five, Burgundy two —not more—while Dauphiné on its own account has as many as fifteen marvels. But soon there will be no more to discover. Grottoes containing stalactites are closing up, burning mountains are becoming extinct, natural glaciers are getting warmer, and the ancient trees, within which Mass used to be said, are falling under the levellers' stroke or are gradually dying.

Then their curiosity gradually turned towards animals.

They reopened their Buffon and were in ecstasies before the extraordinary inclinations of certain creatures.

But all the books in the world not being worth a personal

observation, they went into farmyards and asked the labourers whether they had seen bulls join with mares, pigs seek cows, and the males of partridges commit abominations with each other.

'Never in our lives!'

These questions were even found rather peculiar for gentlemen at their age.

They wanted to experiment with abnormal unions.

The least difficult is that of the he-goat and the sheep. Their farmer had no he-goat, so a neighbour lent his, and, the rutting season having come, they shut the two beasts in the press-house, hiding themselves behind the casks so that the operation could be accomplished without disturbance. Each animal first ate his little heap of hay, then they chewed the cud. The sheep lay down and baa'd without stopping, while the goat standing well on its knotty legs, dangling its great beard and ears, fixed on them eyes which shone through the darkness.

At last, on the evening of the third day, they judged it fitting to assist nature; but the goat, turning against Pécuchet, gave him a butt with his horns in the pit of his stomach. The sheep, seized with fright, ran round and round in the shed, as though in a circus-ring. Bouvard rushed after it, made a dive, and fell to the ground with handfuls of wool in his fists.

They resumed their experiments on some fowls and a duck, on a mastiff and a sow, in the hope that monsters would ensue, not understanding anything about the nature of species.

This word signifies a group of individuals whose descendants reproduce themselves; yet animals classified as of different species can reproduce themselves, and others, included in the same, have lost this faculty.

They flattered themselves that they could get a clear view

of the subject by studying the growth of cells, and Pécuchet wrote to Dumouchel for a microscope.

They placed on the glass slide in turn hairs, snuff, nails, a fly's foot; but they had forgotten the indispensable drop of water. At other times it was the little lamella, and they pushed each other, disarranging the instrument. Then, only perceiving a mist, they accused the optician and began to doubt the microscope. The discoveries attributed to it are perhaps not so positive?

Dumouchel, in sending them the parcel, had begged them to find him some ammonites and sea-urchins' cases, curiosities of which he had always been a collector, and frequent in their district. To incite them to geology, he sent the *Letters of Bertrand* and the *Discourse of Cuvier* on the revolutions of the earth.

After reading these, they pictured to themselves the following:

In the first place, a huge sheet of water, whence emerged lichen-stained promontories, and not a living being, not a sound. It was a silent, motionless and naked world; then long plants swayed in a mist like the vapour of a Turkish bath. A completely red sun warmed the damp atmosphere. Then volcanoes burst forth, igneous rocks sprang from the mountains, and the soft substance of porphyry and basalt became set. Third tableau: in shallow seas, islands of madrepores have risen; a group of palms, here and there, dominates them. There are shells like chariot-wheels, tortoises three yards and lizards sixty feet long: among the reeds, amphibians stretch their ostrich necks and crocodile jaws; winged serpents fly above. Finally, on the broad continents, the great mammals appeared, with limbs as shapeless as ill-hewn pieces of wood, hides more impenetrable than plates of bronze, or else shaggy and thick-lipped, with manes and contorted weapons of defence. Herds of mammoths pastured on the plains, where once was the Atlantic; the palaeotherium, half-horse, half-tapir, overturned with his snout the ant-hills of Montmartre, and the *cervus giganteus* trembled under the chestnut-trees at the voice of the cave bears, which made the dog of Beaugency, three times as high as a wolf, bay in his den.

All these ages have been separated from each other by cataclysms, of which our deluge was the last. It was like a fairy-tale in several acts, having man for the finale.

They were astonished to learn that imprints of dragon-flies and birds' claws exist on stones; and, after running through one of Roret's handbooks, they went in search of fossils.

One afternoon, as they were turning over the flints on the high road, the curé passed, and, greeting them in unctuous tones:

'So the gentlemen are busy with geology? Very good!'

For he respected this science. It confirms the authority of the Scriptures by giving proof of the deluge.

Bouvard spoke of coprolites, which are the petrified excrements of animals.

Abbé Jeufroy appeared surprised by the fact; after all, if it was true, it was one reason the more for admiring Providence.

Pécuchet admitted that their researches until then had not been fruitful; yet the region of Falaise, like all Jurassic districts, ought to abound in animal relics.

'I've heard tell,' replied Abbé Jeufroy, 'that an elephant's jaw was once found at Villers.' Besides, one of his friends, M. Larsoneur, a barrister at Lisieux, and an archaeologist, could perhaps furnish them with particulars. He had compiled a history of Port-en-Bessin, in which he noted the discovery of a crocodile.

Bouvard and Pécuchet exchanged a glance; the same

hope had come to them both, and, despite the heat, they remained standing for a long time, questioning the ecclesiastic, who sheltered under a blue cotton umbrella. The lower part of his face was rather heavy, his nose pointed, and he smiled continuously, or drooped his head and closed his eyes.

The church bell tolled the Angelus.

'Good evening, gentlemen! You'll excuse me, won't you?'

After his letter of introduction, they waited three weeks for Larsoneur's reply. At last it came.

The man at Villers who had unearthed the mastodon's tusk was Louis Bloche; details were lacking. As to his history, it comprised one of the volumes of the Lexovian Academy, and he would not lend his copy, for fear of spoiling the set. As regards the alligator, it had been discovered in the month of November, 1825, under the cliff of Les Hachettes at Sainte-Honorine, near Port-en-Bessin, in the Bayeux district. He presented his compliments, etc.

The obscurity which enveloped the mastodon stimulated Pécuchet's desire. He would have liked to go to Villers at once.

Bouvard objected that, to spare themselves a possibly useless and certainly expensive journey, it was best to collect information, and they wrote a letter to the mayor of the place asking what had become of a certain Louis Bloche. In the case of his being dead, could his children or relations give them an account of his valuable discovery? When was it made, and in what part of the parish had this document of primitive ages lain? Were there possibilities of finding similar ones? What was the hire, per day, of a man and a cart?

For all the trouble they took in applying to the deputy-mayor, then the chief town councillor, they got no news from Villers. No doubt the inhabitants were jealous of their fossils. Never mind, so long as they did not sell them to the English. The trip to Les Hachettes was decided on.

At Falaise, Bouvard and Pécuchet took the diligence for Caen. Then a trap conveyed them from Caen to Bayeux; from Bayeux they proceeded on foot to Port-en-Bessin.

They had not been deceived. Curious stones were to be found in the side of Les Hachettes, and by the innkeeper's direction they reached the shore.

The tide was out; it revealed all the shingle, and a field of seaweed down to the edge of the waves.

Grassy chines cut through the cliff, composed of soft brown soil, which, as it hardened, became a wall of grey stone in its lower strata. Thin trickles of water fell without ceasing, while the sea boomed in the distance. Sometimes it seemed to pause in its beating; and then only the little sound of streams was heard.

They slid about on the slippery vegetation, or else had to jump over holes. Bouvard sat near the water's edge and gazed at the waves, thinking of nothing, spellbound, motionless. Pécuchet led him towards the cliff to show him an ammonite encrusted in the rock, like a diamond in its matrix. They broke their nails on it, and would have needed tools; besides, night was falling. The sky was purple in the west and all the beach was overlaid with shadow. In the midst of the almost black seaweed, patches of water were spreading. The sea was mounting towards them; it was time to go back.

Next morning at dawn, with a bar and a pick, they attacked their fossil, whose envelope flew to pieces. It was an 'ammonites nodosus,' worn away at the end, but weighing quite sixteen pounds; and Pécuchet in his enthusiasm cried: 'We can't do less than give it to Dumouchel!'

Then they came across sponges, terebratulae, grampuses,

but no crocodile! Failing it, they hoped for the backbone of a hippopotamus or icthyosaurus—or any sort of bone contemporary with the deluge—when they saw, at a man's height, against the cliff, outlines which delineated the curve of a gigantic fish.

They consulted on the means of obtaining it.

Bouvard was to loosen it from the top, while Pécuchet, from below, would demolish the rock in order to get it down gently, without breaking.

As they were taking breath, they saw in the field above their heads a Customs officer in a cape, who was waving with an air of authority.

'Eh? What? Leave us alone!' And they went on with their task, Bouvard on tiptoe, tapping with his pick; Pécuchet, with bent back, mining with his bar.

But the officer reappeared in a valley lower down, redoubling his signals. They took but small notice. An oval form bulged under the thin soil, leant forward, and was about to slip down.

Another personage, with a sword, suddenly showed himself.

'Your papers?'

It was the local policeman on his round; and at the same time there arrived the Customs officer, who had hurried down a ravine.

'Arrest them, Morin, or they'll have the cliff down.'

'It is in the interests of science,' answered Pécuchet.

Then a mass fell, so nearly grazing all four of them that, a little closer, they would have been dead men.

When the dust cleared, they recognised a ship's mast, which crumbled under the Customs officer's boot.

Bouvard said with a sigh:

'We weren't doing much harm!'

'Nothing at all should be done on Admiralty ground,'

answered the policeman. 'Come on, who are you? I shall have to make out the summons.'

Pécuchet bridled, crying that it was an injustice.

'No arguments! Follow me!'

When they reached the harbour a crowd of urchins became their escort. Bouvard, red as a poppy, put on a dignified air; Pécuchet, very pale, darted furious glances; and these two strangers, carrying stones in their handkerchiefs, did not cut a good figure. For the time being they were shown into the inn, whose host kept guard at the door. Then the mason demanded his tools. They paid for them: a further expense, and the policeman had not come back. Why? At last a gentleman with the Cross of Honour set them free; and they departed, after giving their surnames, Christian names and address, on the undertaking to be more careful in future.

Besides their papers there were a good many other things that they needed, and, before attempting fresh exploration, they looked up Boné's *Guide for the Geological Traveller*. One must have, in the first place, a stout military haversack, then a land chain, a file, pincers, a compass and three hammers, stuck in a belt concealed by one's overcoat, and which thus 'saves an appearance of eccentricity, that should be avoided when travelling.' As a walking-stick Pécuchet boldly adopted an alpenstock six feet high, with a long iron point. Bouvard preferred an umbrella-stick, or compendium-umbrella, whose handle takes off to hook on the silk, contained separately in a little bag. They did not forget strong shoes and gaiters, 'two pairs of braces, on account of perspiration,' for each, and, although 'one cannot present oneself everywhere in a cap,' they recoiled before the expense of 'one of those collapsible hats, which bear the name of Gibus the hatter, their inventor.'

The same work gives maxims for behaviour: 'Acquaint

yourself with the language of the country you are visiting';
they were acquainted. 'Retain a modest bearing'; it was their
custom. 'Do not carry too much money'; nothing more
simple. Finally, to be spared all sorts of annoyance, it is a
good plan to adopt 'the status of an engineer.'

'Very well, we'll adopt it!'

Thus prepared, they began their expeditions, were sometimes away for a week, and spent their days in the open
air.

From time to time, on the banks of the Orne, they perceived in a cleft, masses of rock spreading their slanting
layers between the poplars and the heather, or else they were
disappointed at finding only beds of clay. Before a landscape, they admired neither the perspective nor the far
stretch of distance, but what was invisible, underground.
And every hill was for them one more proof of the deluge.
To the obsession for the deluge succeeded that for erratic
blocks. The big stones by themselves in the field must
derive from vanished glaciers; and they looked for moraines
and shell-marl.

Several times they were taken for pedlars, on account of
their equipment, and when they had answered that they were
'engineers,' a qualm seized them: the assumption of such a
title might bring them trouble.

At the end of the day they were panting under the weight
of their specimens, but courageously bore them back home.
They placed them along the steps, on the staircase, in the
bedroom, the dining-room, the kitchen, and Germaine
bewailed the amount of dust they made.

It was no light task, before sticking on the labels, to discover the names of the rocks. The diversity of colour and
graining made them confuse clay with marl, granite with
gneiss, quartz with limestone.

Also, the names vexed them. Why Devonian, Cambrian,

Jurassic, as if the soils denoted by these words existed only in Devon, in Wales and in the Jura. It was impossible to know one's way. What is a system for one is a stage for another; for a third merely an assise. The beds are lost in confusion; but Omalius d'Halloy warns you not to believe in geological classification.

This statement relieved them, and when they had seen polypous limestone in the plain of Caen, phyllades at Balleroy, kaolin at Saint-Blaise, oolite everywhere, and sought for coal at Cartigny, mercury at Chapelle-en-Juger, near Saint-Lô, they decided on a more distant expedition —a journey to Havre to study pyromanic quartz and Kimmeridge clay.

The moment they had left the packet-boat they asked the way that led under the lighthouses; falls of earth had blocked it; it was dangerous to adventure there.

A man with carriages for hire stopped them and offered excursions in the neighbourhood: Ingouville, Octeville, Fécamp, Lillebonne, 'Rome if need be.'

His prices were unreasonable, but the name of Fécamp had struck them. By making a little turn on the way they could see Étretat, and they took the Fécamp carrier to go the longer way round.

In the vehicle Bouvard and Pécuchet made conversation with three peasants, two housewives, a young priest, and did not hesitate to call themselves engineers.

It stopped before the harbour. They reached the cliff, and five minutes later were rubbing against it to avoid a great pool of water which penetrated like a gulf up the middle of the coast. Then they saw an arcade opening on a deep grotto; it echoed and was luminous like a church, with columns reaching from top to bottom and a carpet of sea-weed over its paving.

This work of nature astonished them, and, going on their

way and gathering shells, they rose to considerations on the beginning of the world.

Bouvard inclined to Neptunism; Pécuchet, on the contrary, was a Plutonian.

The central fire had split the earth's crust, raised the ground and made abysses. It was like an internal sea, having flux and reflux, and tempests. A thin coating separates us from it. We should not be able to sleep if we dreamed of all that there is beneath our feet. But the central fire diminishes and the sun grows weak, so that one day the earth will perish by cooling. It will become barren; all the wood and coal will be converted into carbonic acid, and no living creature will be able to exist.

'We aren't there yet,' said Bouvard.

'Let's hope not,' replied Pécuchet.

But in any case, this ending of the world, far off as it was, cast a gloom over them, and side by side they walked in silence over the shingle.

The cliff, perpendicular, clear white and streaked in places by veins of flint, stretched towards the horizon like the curve of a rampart five leagues long. An east wind, sharp and cold, was blowing. The sky was grey, the sea greenish and as though swollen. From the top of the crag birds were flying, wheeling, returning back swiftly to their crannies. Occasionally a loosened stone rebounded here and there before it fell down to them.

Pécuchet pursued his meditation aloud:

'Provided the earth isn't blotted out by a convulsion! We don't know the length of our period. The central fire only needs to boil over.'

'Yet it's growing less.'

'That hasn't prevented its explosions forming the Island of Julia, Monte Nuovo, and a lot of other places.' Bouvard remembered reading these particulars in Bertrand.

'But such turmoils don't occur in Europe.'

'I beg your pardon, indeed! Look at that at Lisbon. As to our own country, the coal mines and mines of martial pyrites are numerous, and can very well form craters as they fall in. Besides, volcanoes are always erupting by the sea.'

Bouvard turned his vision upon the waves, and thought he could perceive in the distance smoke rising to the sky.

'Since the Island of Julia,' Pécuchet went on, 'has disappeared, formations brought about by the same cause will perhaps meet the same fate. A little island of the Archipelago is as important as Normandy and even Europe.'

Bouvard pictured to himself Europe engulfed by an abyss.

'Suppose,' said Pécuchet, 'an earthquake takes place under the Channel. The waters rush into the Atlantic. The coasts of France and England, shaking on their foundations, lean towards each other, unite and, hey presto! everything in between is crushed.'

Instead of answering, Bouvard began to walk so fast that he was soon a hundred yards ahead of Pécuchet. Once by himself, the thought of an earthquake troubled him. He had not eaten since the morning; there was a throbbing at his temples. All at once, the ground seemed to tremble, and the cliff above him to tilt its head. Just then a shower of gravel scattered down.

Pécuchet saw him rush away violently, understood his fright, and called from a long way behind:

'Stop, stop! The period hasn't run its course yet,' and to catch him up he made enormous bounds with his alpenstock, bellowing, 'The period hasn't run its course yet!'

Bouvard, in a delirium, went on running. The compendium-umbrella dropped, the folds of his frock-coat were flapping, the haversack tossed about on his back. He was like a tortoise with wings, galloping among the rocks; one larger than the rest hid him.

Pécuchet arrived there out of breath, and saw no one. Then he turned back to reach the field by a ravine that Bouvard had no doubt ascended. This narrow short cut was hewn with great steps in the cliff, as wide as two people, and gleaming like polished alabaster.

Fifty steps up, Pécuchet wanted to go down again. The waves were beating with all their might, and he started to climb once more.

At the second bend, when he saw the void, he froze with terror. As he neared the third, his legs became a jelly. Air-currents vibrated round him, a cramp twisted his epigastrium. He sat on the ground with eyes closed, no longer aware of anything but the heart-beats that suffocated him. Then he cast away his alpenstock and resumed his ascent on hands and knees. But the three hammers, tucked in his belt, stuck into his stomach; the stones with which his pockets were stuffed beat his sides; the peak of his cap blinded him; the wind redoubled its force. At last he reached the plateau and there found Bouvard, who had made the ascent farther on, by a less difficult climb.

A cart gave them a lift. They forgot Étretat.

The next evening, at Havre, while waiting for the packet, they saw at the foot of the newspaper an article entitled, 'The Teaching of Geology.'

Full of facts, it displayed the subject as it was understood at the time.

There had never been a complete upheaval of the earth, but the same formations do not always endure the same length of time, and become extinct quicker in one place than another. Rocks of the same age contain different fossils, just as deposits, a long distance apart, contain similar ones. The ferns of past epochs are identical with those of the present day. Many modern zoophites are found in the most ancient strata. In short, actual modifications explain previous disturbances. The same causes are always at work, Nature does not proceed by leaps and bounds, and periods, says Brongniart, are, after all, only abstractions.

Cuvier, until then, had appeared to them in the brilliance of an aureole, on the peak of a science beyond dispute. This position was undermined. Creation had no longer the same discipline, and their respect for that great man decreased.

From biographies and extracts they learnt something of the doctrines of Lamarck and Geoffroy Saint-Hilaire.

All this went against recognised ideas and the authority of the Church.

Bouvard felt, as it were, disburdened of a broken yoke.

'I should like to see, now, what friend Jeufroy would reply about the deluge.'

They found him in his little garden, where he was waiting for the members of the vestry, who were meeting in order to buy a chasuble.

'What are you looking for, gentlemen?'

'Enlightenment, if you please.'

And Bouvard began:

'What is the meaning in Genesis of "the fountains of the great deep were broken up," and "the flood-gates of heaven?" For a fountain doesn't break, and there are no flood-gates in heaven.'

The abbé closed his eyes, then answered that it was always necessary to distinguish between the spirit and the letter. Some things which jar at first become clear by investigation.

'Quite so! but how can you explain the downpour that flooded over the tallest mountains, those five miles high? Just imagine—five miles! An expanse of water five miles deep!'

And the mayor, who had just arrived, added: 'By Jove, what a bath!'

'You'll admit,' said Bouvard, 'that Moses exaggerates like the deuce.'

The curé had read Bonald, and replied: 'I know nothing of his motives. No doubt it was to inspire the tribes he led with a salutary fear.'

'At any rate, where did this mass of water come from?'

'How do I know? The air was changed to rain, as often happens!'

By the garden door were to be seen entering M. Girbal the tax-collector, with Captain Heurtaux a land-owner. The innkeeper Beljambe came arm-in-arm with Langlois the grocer, who walked with difficulty on account of his catarrh.

Pécuchet, ignoring them, took up the discussion.

'Excuse me, Monsieur Jeufroy. The weight of the atmosphere, as science shows, is equal to that of a mass of water which would cover the earth to a depth of ten yards. Therefore, if all the air condensed and fell on it in a liquid state, it would increase the volume of existing water only very slightly.'

The churchwardens opened their eyes wide as they listened.

The curé lost patience.

'Will you deny that shells have been found on mountains? What has put them there if not the deluge? It's not usual, I presume, for them to grow in the soil by themselves, like carrots.' And this joke having made the assembly laugh, he added, pursing his lips: 'Unless that's another of your discoveries of science?'

Bouvard wanted to counter with the elevation of mountains, the theory of Élie de Beaumont.

'Don't know him,' replied the abbé.

Foureau hastened to say: 'He's from Caen! I saw him once at the prefecture there.'

'But if your deluge,' continued Bouvard, 'had carried the shells there, they would be found lying broken on the surface, not at depths of sometimes three hundred yards.'

The priest fell back on the truth of the Scriptures, the tradition of the human race, and the animals found in the ice in Siberia.

That does not prove that man was alive at the same time as they; the earth, according to Pécuchet, was considerably older.

'The Delta of the Mississippi goes back tens of thousands of years. The present period is at least a hundred thousand years old. The rolls of Mantho—'

The Count de Faverges advanced.

They were all silent at his approach.

'Pray continue; what were you saying?'

'These gentlemen were squabbling with me,' answered the abbé.

'About what?'

'About Holy Scripture, Monsieur le Comte.'

Bouvard thereupon asserted that they had the right as geologists to discuss religion.

'Take care,' said the count, you know the proverb, my dear sir: a little science takes us away from the Bible, a lot of it brings us back.' And in a tone at once haughty and paternal: 'Believe me, you'll come back!'

'Perhaps. But what can one think of a book which pretends that light was created before the sun, as if the sun wasn't the sole cause of light?'

'You forget what is called the Aurora Borealis,' said the priest.

Bouvard, without meeting the objection, strongly denied that there could be light on one side and darkness on the other; that there can have been an evening and a morning, when the stars did not exist; and that animals had appeared all of a sudden, instead of gradually evolving.

As the paths were too narrow they walked gesticulating on the borders. Langlois was seized with a paroxysm of coughing. The captain shouted: 'You're revolutionaries!'

Girbal: 'Peace! Peace!'

The priest: 'What materialism!'

Foureau: 'Let's get busy about the chasuble!'

'No, let me speak!' And Bouvard, becoming heated, went so far as to say that man descended from monkeys!

All the churchwardens looked at one another thunderstruck, and as if to reassure each other that they were not monkeys.

Bouvard went on: 'By comparing the foetus of a woman, of a bitch, a bird, a frog—'

'That's enough!'

'But I go still further,' cried Pécuchet. 'Man descends from fish!' There was an explosion of laughter, but, without heeding: 'The Telliamed, an Arab Book—'

'Come, gentlemen, the meeting!'

And they entered the sacristy.

The two friends had not bowled over the abbé as they had expected. So Pécuchet discovered in him 'the imprint of Jesuitry.'

Yet his aurora borealis was disturbing. They looked it up in Orbigny's manual.

It is an hypothesis to explain why the vegetable fossils of Baffin Bay resemble equatorial plants. We assume, in place of the sun, a great luminous source, now extinct, of which the aurora borealis is perhaps the only trace.

Then a doubt crept over them as to the origin of man, and in embarrassment they thought of Vaucorbeil.

His threats had come to nothing. As before, he passed

their lattice each morning, rattling the bars one after another with his stick.

Bouvard watched for him and, stopping him, said that he desired to submit a curious point of anthropology. 'Do you believe that the human race descends from fish?'

'What rubbish!'

'More likely from monkeys, don't you think?'

'Directly? It's impossible!'

Whom could one trust? For, after all, the doctor was not a Catholic.

They resumed their study, though without eagerness, tired of the Eocene and the Miocene, of Mount Jurillo, the Island of Julia, Siberian mammoths, and fossils invariably compared, by every author, to 'medals that are authentic witnesses'; so that one day Bouvard threw down his haversack, declaring that he would go no farther.

Geology is too restricted! We are hardly familiar with more than a few places in Europe. As for the rest, and the ocean-beds, we shall always be ignorant.

Finally, Pécuchet having used the phrase 'mineral kingdom':

'I don't believe in it, this mineral kingdom, for organic matter has taken part in the formation of flint, limestone, and possibly gold. Wasn't the diamond carbon once? and coal a conjunction of vegetables? for by heating it to I-don't-know-how-many degrees, one gets sawdust, so that everything passes, crumbles, is transformed. Creation takes place in an up-and-down and haphazard manner. We should do better to start on something else.'

He lay down on his back and began to doze, while Pécuchet, with bowed head and clasping his knee, gave himself over to his reflections. A skirt of moss bordered a deep lane, shaded by ash trees whose delicate tops were quivering; angelica, mint, lavender, exhaled their warm, spicy scents;

the air was heavy; and Pécuchet in a kind of stupor dreamed of the countless scattered existences round him, of buzzing insects, springs hidden under the grass, the sap of plants, birds in their nests, the wind, clouds, all nature, without endeavouring to solve its mysteries—carried away by its force, lost in its grandeur.

'I'm thirsty,' said Bouvard, waking.

'So am I; I'd be glad of a drink.'

'That's easy,' said a man in shirt-sleeves, who was passing with a plank on his shoulder.

They recognised the tramp to whom Bouvard had once given a glass of wine. With his hair curled, a waxed moustache, and swaying in a Parisian fashion he seemed ten years younger.

After about a hundred paces he opened the gate into a yard, threw his plank against a wall, and showed them into a high-ceilinged kitchen.

'Mélie! Are you there, Mélie?'

A young girl appeared; at his orders she went to draw the drink, and then stood by the table waiting on them.

Her coils of hair, the colour of corn, showed under a grey linen bonnet. Her mean garments fell along her body without a fold, and, with her straight nose and blue eyes, there was a certain delicacy about her that was both rustic and simple.

'She's nice, eh!' said the carpenter, while she was getting the glasses. 'You'd swear she was a lady disguised as a peasant—and good at her work, too. Poor little thing! Well, wait till I'm rich and marry you.'

'You always say such silly things, Monsieur Gorju,' she replied in a gentle tone, with a drawling accent.

A stableman came to take oats from an old chest, and let the lid fall back so clumsily that a piece of wood flew off.

Gorju flew into a rage at the awkwardness of all these

113

'country bumpkins,' then, on his knees in front of the chest, he looked for the place where the piece had come from. Pécuchet, offering his help, distinguished the shapes of human figures under the dust.

It was a Renaissance chest, with a spiral border at the bottom, clusters of grapes at the corners, and little columns divided the front into five compartments. In the middle, one saw Venus Anadyomene standing on a shell, then Hercules and Omphale, Samson and Delilah, Circe and her swine, and Lot's daughters making their father drunk; all this dilapidated, worm-eaten, and even with the right-hand panel missing. Gorju took a candle, so that Pécuchet could see more clearly the one on the left, which represented Adam and Eve under the tree of Paradise in an extremely indecent pose.

Bouvard also admired the chest.

'If you're keen on it, I'll let you have it cheap.'

They hesitated, thinking of the repairs.

Gorju could do them, being a cabinet-maker by trade.

'Very well! Come along!'

And he drew Pécuchet towards the orchard where Mme Castillon, the mistress, was spreading the washing.

Mélie, after cleaning her hands, took her lace-work from the window-ledge, and sat in the full sunlight, working.

She was framed in the lintel of the door. The bobbins disentangled beneath her fingers with a clatter of castanets. Her profile remained bent.

Bouvard asked about her parents, where she came from, what pay she received.

She was from Ouistreham, had no family, earned a pound a month. In fact, she pleased him so much that he wanted to take her into his service as a help for old Germaine.

Pécuchet reappeared with the farmer's wife, and while they went on haggling, Bouvard asked Gorju in a low voice if the girl would consent to come as their servant.

'I should say so.'

'But, of course,' said Bouvard, 'I must consult my friend.'

'Well, I'll arrange it. And speak low because of the missis.'

The bargain was struck at thirty-five francs. The repairs would be discussed later.

As soon as they were in the yard, Bouvard announced his intention with regard to Mélie.

Pécuchet halted (as an aid to reflection), opened his snuff-box, inhaled a pinch, and, having wiped his nose:

'Certainly, a good idea! Good lord, yes! Why not? Besides, you're the master.'

Ten minutes later Gorju appeared on the bank of a ditch and called to them:

'When shall I bring the piece of furniture?'

'To-morrow!'

'And that other little matter—have you decided?'

'Done!' replied Pécuchet.

IV

Six months later they had become archaeologists, and their house was like a museum.

An old wooden beam stood in the hall. Geological specimens blocked the staircase; and an enormous chain stretched on the floor along the corridor.

They had taken down the door between the two spare bedrooms and kept the outer door of the second locked, so as to make the two rooms into one.

After crossing the threshold, you stumbled against a stone trough (a Gallo-Roman sarcophagus), then a mass of ironmongery caught the eye.

On the wall opposite, a warming-pan hung above two andirons, and a fireback showed a monk caressing a shepherdess. On little tables all round were candlesticks, locks, bolts and screws. The floor could hardly be seen for fragments of red tiles. A table in the middle displayed the most choice pieces: the framework of a Normandy bonnet, two clay urns, medals, a phial of opaline glass. An upholstered armchair had a triangle of lace on its back. A bit of coat of mail adorned the partition of the right; and underneath, spikes supported a halberd horizontally—a unique piece.

The second room, to which two steps led down, contained the old books brought from Paris, and those they found in a cupboard when they arrived. The cupboard doors had been removed. This they called the library.

The genealogical tree of the Croixmare family took up all the back of the door. On the front panel, the figure in pastel of a lady in Louis Quinze costume made a pendant to the portrait of Bouvard's father. The overmantel to the mirror was adorned with a black felt sombrero, and a huge clog filled with leaves—the remains of a nest.

Two coconuts, which had belonged to Pécuchet since his youth, stood on the mantelpiece on either side of a cask in faience bestridden by a peasant. Near it, in a straw basket, was a farthing disgorged by a duck.

In front of the book-case stood a shellwork cabinet, with plush trimmings. Its lid supported a cat holding a mouse in her jaws—a petrification from Saint-Allyre—a work-box, also done in shells, and on this box a decanter of brandy containing a Bon-Chrétien pear.

But the finest piece was in the bow-window—a statue of Saint Peter. His right hand, gloved, grasped the key of Paradise, apple-green in colour. His chasuble, variegated by fleurs-de-lis, was sky-blue; and his tiara very yellow, pointed like a pagoda. He had tinted cheeks, large round eyes, a gaping mouth and a bottle-nose all on one side. Above hung a canopy made of an old carpet, whereon might be distinguished two Cupids in a circle of roses; and at his feet was a butter-jar, inscribed with these words in white letters on a chocolate ground: 'Fashioned before His Royal Highness Monseigneur the Duke of Angoulême, at Noron, October 3rd, 1817.'

Pécuchet, from his bed, could see all these objects stretching away in a long file, and sometimes he even went into Bouvard's room, to lengthen the perspective.

One place remained empty in front of the coat of mail—that of the Renaissance chest.

It was not finished; Gorju was still at work on it, planing the panels in the bakehouse, adjusting and detaching them.

At eleven o'clock he used to have lunch, then chat with Mélie, and often he did not appear again the rest of the day.

Bouvard and Pécuchet scoured the country in search of

new pieces to match the furniture. Their finds were unsuitable. But they came across a great number of curiosities. The taste for knick-knacks had come to them, then a love for the Middle Ages.

First they visited cathedrals; and the high naves reflected in the water of the fonts, the stained glass sparkling like a tapestry of jewels, the tombs at the far corners of chapels, the uncertain light of crypts—everything, even the coolness of the walls, caused them a quiver of delight, a religious emotion.

Soon they were able to distinguish periods, and, scorning vergers, they would say: 'Ah, a Romanesque apse! That's twelfth century; now we're dropping into the flamboyant.' They tried to understand the symbols carved on the capitals, such as the two griffins of Marigny nibbling a tree in blossom. Pécuchet read satire into the choristers with grotesque jowls which terminate the choir-stalls at Feugerolles. As for the exuberance of the obscene figure covering one of the mullions at Hérouville, it proved, according to Bouvard, that our ancestors relished a broad joke.

They ended by not tolerating the least sign of decadence. All was decadence, and they deplored vandalism, thundered against restorations.

But the style of a monument does not always correspond with its supposed date. The semicircular arch, of the thirteenth century, is still predominant in Provence. The ogive is perhaps extremely ancient, and some writers question whether the Romanesque was before the Gothic. This lack of certainty distressed them.

After the churches, they studied fortresses: those of Domfront and Falaise. They wondered at the grooves of the portcullis beneath the gate, and when they reached the top, they saw first the stretch of country, then the roofs of the town, the streets intersecting, carts in the square, women at the washhouse. The wall descended precipitately to the brambles in the moat, and they grew pale at the thought of men having climbed there, clinging to ladders. They would have risked themselves in the underground passages, but Bouvard was prevented by his stomach, and Pécuchet by his dread of vipers.

They wanted to see the old manor-houses of Curcy, Bully, Fontenay, Lemarmion, Argouge. Sometimes, at the corner of outhouses, behind the manure-heap, rises a Carlovingian tower. The kitchen, furnished with stone benches, brings memories of feudal festivities. Others have an altogether forbidding aspect, with their three walls still visible, loopholes under the stairs, high turrets with narrow sides. Then one comes to an apartment, where a window of the Valois period, carved like ivory, lets in the sun which warms rapeseed spread over the floor. Abbeys serve as barns. The inscriptions on gravestones are defaced. In the middle of the fields a gable remains standing, covered from top to bottom by ivy shaken in the wind.

A quantity of objects roused their desire of possession, a pewter pot, a paste buckle, printed calicoes with large flowerings. Lack of money restrained them.

By a providential chance, they brought to light at Balleroy, in a tinker's shop, a Gothic window, and it was big enough to cover, near the armchair, the right-hand part of the window as far as the second pane. The belfry of Chavignolles was visible in the distance, producing a superb effect.

With the bottom part of a cupboard Gorju made a praying-desk to put under the Gothic window, for he indulged their fad. It was so strong that they regretted monuments of which nothing at all was known, like the country-house of the bishops of Séez.

Bayeux, says M. de Caumont, must have possessed a theatre. They looked for the site without avail.

The village of Montrecy contains a field famous for the finds of medals that have been made there in the past. They counted on a rich harvest. The custodian refused them admittance.

They were no luckier with regard to the passage that connects a reservoir at Falaise with the outskirts of Caen. Ducks that had been introduced there emerged at Vaucelles, quacking, 'Can, Can, Can,' whence comes the name of the town.

No step, no sacrifice, was too great for them.

At the inn at Mesnil-Villement, in 1816, M. Galeron had a luncheon for the sum of four sols. They made the same meal and noted with surprise that things like that no longer occur.

Who is the founder of the Abbey of Sainte-Anne? Is there any relation between Marin Onfroy, who brought a new kind of apple into the country in the twelfth century, and Onfroy, Governor of Hastings at the time of the Conquest? How could they get hold of *The Cunning Fortune-Teller*, a comedy in verse by a certain Dutrezor, performed at Bayeux, and now exceedingly rare? Under Louis XIV, Hérambert Dupaty, or Dupastis Hérambert, compiled a work which has never appeared, full of anecdotes concerning Argentan; it was a question of finding these anecdotes. What have become of the autograph memoirs of Mme Dubois de la Pierre, consulted for the unpublished history of Laigle, by Louis Dasprès, officiating priest of Saint-Martin? Such were the problems, the doubtful points to be cleared up.

But often a slight clue leads to a vital discovery.

So they donned their blouses again, in order not to attract attention, and, looking like pedlars, presented themselves at house doors, offering to buy old papers. They had masses sold to them—school exercise-books, bills, old newspapers, nothing of any value.

Finally, Bouvard and Pécuchet applied to Larsoneur.

He was immersed in Celticism, and replied briefly to their questions, asking them others in return. Had they noticed on their rounds any traces of dog-worship such as is to be seen at Montargis; and specific details on the fires of St. John's Eve, marriages, popular sayings, etc.? He even requested them to select for him a few of those flint axe-heads, then called Celts, which the Druids employed in their 'criminal holocausts.'

Through Gorju they obtained a dozen and sent him the smallest, while the others went to enrich the museum.

They loved to walk there, swept it themselves, and had spoken of it to all their acquaintances.

One afternoon Mme Bordin and M. Marescot paid a visit of inspection.

Bouvard received them and began by showing them the hall.

The beam was no less than the ancient gibbet of Falaise— according to the carpenter who had sold it, who had this information from his grandfather.

The heavy chain in the passage came from the dungeons of the castle keep at Torteval. It resembled, according to the notary, the chains on the posts in courtyards. Bouvard was convinced that it had once been used to bind captives, and he opened the door of the first room.

'What are all these tiles for?' cried Mme Bordin.

'For warming bathrooms; but a little order, please. This is a tomb discovered at an inn, where it was used as a trough.'

Next, Bouvard took up the two urns filled with a soil that was human ashes, and raised the phial to his eyes in order to show by what method the Romans dropped their tears in it.

'But one only sees gloomy things in this house of yours!'

It was, in fact, rather solemn for a lady, and then he lifted from a piece of cardboard various copper coins and a silver farthing.

Mme Bordin asked the notary how much they would be worth nowadays.

The coat of mail, which he was examining, slipped through his fingers; some of its links broke. Bouvard disguised his vexation.

He was even obliging enough to unhook the halberd, and, bending down, raising his arms and stamping his heels, he pretended to hamstring a horse, make a bayonet thrust and beat down a foe. The widow, in her heart, found him a sturdy fellow.

She was enthusiastic over the shell-work cabinet. The cat from Saint-Allyre greatly surprised her, the pear in the decanter rather less so; then, arriving at the chimney-piece:

'Ah! there's a hat that needs mending.'

Three holes—bullet marks—pierced the brim.

It had belonged to a bandit chief under the Directory, David de la Bazoque, who was taken as a traitor and executed immediately afterwards.

'All the better. Quite right!' said Mme Bordin.

Marescot, in front of the collection, smiled disdainfully. He did not understand the clog that had been the sign for a shoe shop, nor the meaning of the cask in faience, a common cider mug; the Saint Peter, with his drunkard's countenance, was frankly deplorable.

Mme Bordin made this remark:

'It must have cost you a lot, all the same.'

'Oh! Not too much. Not too much.'

A tiler had surrendered it for fifteen francs.

Then she censured as improper the low neck of the lady in the powdered wig.

'Where's the harm,' answered Bouvard, 'when one has something to show?'

And he added in a lower tone:

'As you have, I'm sure.'

The notary turned his back on them, to study the branches of the Croixmare family. She made no reply, but started toying with her long watch-chain. Her breasts stretched the black taffeta of her bodice, and, drawing her eyelashes slightly together, she lowered her chin, like a pigeon showing off; then, with an innocent air:

'What was the lady's name?'

'There's no telling. She was a mistress of the Regent, you know—the one who was up to all those games.'

'I can quite believe it. The memoirs of the time—'

And the notary, without finishing his sentence, deplored this example of a prince carried away by his passions.

'But you're all like that!'

The two men protested, and a dialogue ensued on women and love. Marescot asserted that there are many happy unions; sometimes, even without our knowing it, the means to happiness is within our reach. It was a direct allusion. The widow's cheeks grew purple, but, recovering almost at once:

'We're no longer at the age of folly, are we, Monsieur Bouvard?'

'Eh, what? I shouldn't say that.'

And he offered his arm for the return to the other room.

'Mind the steps! That's right. Now, look at the window!'

They made out a scarlet cloak and two angels. All the rest was lost under the leadwork, which held together the numerous breaks in the glass. The light was failing, the shadows lengthened. Mme Bordin had become pensive.

Bouvard went off and reappeared muffled in a blanket, then knelt before the praying-desk, with elbows out, his face in his hands, the sunlight falling on his bald patch; and he was conscious of this effect, for he said:

'Don't I look like a monk of the Middle Ages?'

Then he raised his face in a slant, with swimming eyes, making it take on a mystical expression. In the corridor was heard the solemn voice of Pécuchet.

'Don't be alarmed! it's me."

And he came in with his head covered by a helmet—an iron pot with pointed handles.

Bouvard did not quit the praying-desk. The two others remained standing. A minute passed in stupefaction.

Mme Bordin seemed a little cold towards Pécuchet. However, he wanted to know if she had been shown all there was to see.

'I think so.'

Then, pointing to the wall:

'I must apologise; here we shall have an object that's being restored at present.'

The widow and Marescot departed.

The two friends had invented a game of rivals. They used to go on expeditions, one without the other, the second making offers higher than those of the first. Pécuchet had just acquired the helmet.

Bouvard congratulated him on it, and received commendation with regard to the blanket.

Mélie arranged it with cords like a monk's robe. They put it on by turn to receive visitors.

These included Girbal, Foureau, Captain Heurtaux, then others of a lower class—Langlois, Beljambe, their farmers, even the neighbours' servants; and each time they began their explanations afresh, showed the place where the chest was to be, affected modesty, and asked for indulgence because of the muddle.

On these occasions Pécuchet wore the zouave's cap

124

which he used to have in Paris, judging it more in keeping with the artistic surroundings. At a particular moment he would don the helmet, and tilt it back on his neck to free his face. Bouvard did not forget the halberd-drill; then, with a quick glance, they would ask each other whether the visitor was worthy of the 'Monk of the Middle Ages' being performed.

What excitement when the carriage of M. de Faverges stopped before their gate! He had only one word to say, this:

Hurel, his bailiff, had informed him that, in their ubiquitous search for documents, they had bought some old papers at the farm of Aubrye.

Quite true.

Had they not found the letters of the Baron de Gonneval, formerly aide-de-camp to the Duc d'Angoulême, who had made a sojourn at Aubrye? He wanted that correspondence for family reasons.

They had not got it, but possessed something that concerned him, if he would consent to follow them to the library.

Never had polished boots like his squeaked in the corridor. They stumbled against the sarcophagus, they even came within an inch of smashing several tiles. After going round the armchair and descending the two steps, he arrived in the second room, where they pointed out to him, under the canopy, in front of the Saint Peter, the butter-jar fashioned at Noron.

Bouvard and Pécuchet had thought that the date on it would come in useful some time.

Out of politeness the count inspected their museum. He repeated, 'Charming! very good!' at the same time giving himself little taps on the mouth with the knob of his riding-whip, and, speaking on his own account, he thanked them for having preserved these relics of the Middle Ages, an epoch of religious faith and chivalrous devotion. He had a love of progress, and was devoted, as were they, to these interesting studies; but politics, the local council, agriculture, a regular tornado of affairs distracted him.

'In any case, after you, one would only have leavings, for you'll soon have taken all the curiosities in the district.'

'Without conceit, we think so,' said Pécuchet.

However, there were still more to be discovered—at Chavignolles, for instance. In a lane by the cemetery wall was a font hidden under weeds from time immemorial.

They were delighted at this news, then exchanged a look signifying 'Is it worth the trouble?' But already the count was opening the door.

Mélie, who was behind it, swiftly took flight.

As he passed through the court, he noticed Gorju busy smoking his pipe, with arms folded.

'You employ that fellow? Hum! If a riot were to break out one day, I shouldn't trust him.'

And M. de Faverges mounted his tilbury.

Why had their maid seemed afraid of him?

They questioned her, and she said that she had been in service at his farm. She was the little girl who gave drink to the harvesters when they had first arrived two years before. She had been taken as help at the manor and dismissed 'owing to false reports.'

As for Gorju, what could there be against him? He was very handy and showed them great respect.

The next day, at dawn, they betook themselves to the cemetery.

Bouvard poked with his stick at the place mentioned. It had a hard sound. They pulled up some nettles and found a sandstone basin, a baptismal font in which weeds were growing.

Yet it is unusual to bury fonts outside churches.

Pécuchet made a drawing of it, Bouvard wrote a description, and they sent both to Larsoneur.

His reply came at once.

'Victory, my dear colleagues! It is undeniably a druidical bowl.'

Still, they must be cautious. The chisel marks were doubtful, and, as much for his own sake as theirs, he indicated a series of works to consult.

Larsoneur confessed in a postscript his eagerness to become acquainted with this bowl, which he could do in a few days' time, when he was making a journey to Brittany.

Thereupon Bouvard and Pécuchet dived into Celtic archaeology.

According to that science, the ancient Gauls, our ancestors, worshipped Kirk and Kron, Taranis Esus, Netalemnia, Heaven and Earth, the Wind and the Waters, and, above all, the great Teutates, who is the pagan Saturn. For Saturn, when he reigned in Phoenicia, married a nymph named Anobret, by whom he had a son named Jeüd, and Anobret had the characteristics of Sarah, while Jeüd was sacrificed (or very nearly so) like Isaac. Therefore Saturn is Abraham, whence it must be concluded that the religion of the Gauls had the same principles as that of the Jews.

Their society was very well organised. The first class of individuals comprised the people, the nobility and the King; the second class, law-givers; and in the third, the highest, were ranked, according to Taillepied, 'the various kinds of philosophers,' that is to say, the Druids or Saronides, who were themselves divided into Eubages, Bardes and Vates.

Some uttered prophesies, others chanted, others taught botany, medicine, history and literature: in short, 'all the arts of their epoch.' Pythagoras and Plato were their pupils. They instructed the Greeks in metaphysics, the Persians in sorcery, the Etruscans in augury, and the Romans in plating copper and trading in ham.

But of this people which dominated the ancient world, there remain only a few stones, either single or in groups of three, or arranged in galleries or forming circles.

Full of eagerness, Bouvard and Pécuchet studied successively the stone of the Post at Ussy, the twin stones at Guest, the Darier Stone near Laigle, and yet others.

All these blocks, equally insignificant, soon bored them; and one day, after they had viewed the menhir of Pessais, they were about to turn back when their guide led them into a beech-wood, encumbered with masses of granite like pedestals or gigantic tortoises.

The largest is hollowed out like a basin. One of its rims is raised, and from the bottom project two grooves going down to the ground. No doubt they were for blood to flow along! Chance does not fashion such shapes.

The roots of trees were intermingled with these jagged plinths. A thin rain was falling; in the distance, wisps of mist rose like tall ghosts. It was easy to picture, under the foliage, the priests in golden diadems and white robes, with their human victims, whose arms were bound behind them. And at the edge of the bowl, the Druidess watching the red stream, while the crowd shouted round her, to the noise of cymbals and trumpets made of aurochs' horns.

At once they decided upon a plan.

And one night, by the rays of the moon they made their way to the cemetery, treading like robbers in the shadow of the houses. Blinds were down, and the little buildings silent; not a dog barked.

Gorju had gone with them; they started work. Nothing was heard but the stones struck by the spade as it dug into the sod.

The neighbourhood of the dead was disagreeable to them; the church clock made a continuous rattle, and the rose-window of its spandrel was like an eye spying upon sacrilege. At last they carried off the bowl.

The next day they went to the cemetery to inspect the traces of the operation.

The abbé, who was taking the air at his door, begged them to do him the honour of coming in; and, having shown them into his little dining-room, he looked at them in a singular manner.

In the middle of the dresser, between the plates, was a soup bowl decorated with bunches of yellow flowers.

Pécuchet praised it, not knowing what to say.

'It's a piece of old Rouen ware,' the curé answered, 'an heirloom. Collectors think a lot of it, especially M. Marescot.'

As for him, he thanked God, he had no love of curios; and since they seemed not to understand, he declared that with his own eyes he had seen them making off with the font.

The two archaeologists were very shamefaced, and stammered. The object in question was no longer in use.

No matter, they must give it back.

Certainly, but at least they might be allowed to get an artist to come and draw it.

'Very well, gentlemen!'

'This is between ourselves, of course?' said Bouvard. 'Under the seal of the confessional!'

The ecclesiastic, smiling, reassured them with a gesture.

It was not he whom they feared, but rather Larsoneur. When the latter passed by Chavignolles, he would want to see the bowl, and his tattle would get to the ears of the Government. Out of prudence, they hid it in the bakehouse, then in the arbour, in the chest, in a cupboard. Gorju was tired of trundling it about.

The possession of such a piece engrossed them in the Celticism of Normandy.

Its origins are Egyptian. Séez, in the department of the Orne, was once written Saïs, like the town on the Delta. The Gauls swore by the bull, an importation of the ox Apis. The Latin name of Bellocastes, which was that of the people of Bayeux, comes from Beli Casa, dwelling or sanctuary of Belus. Belus and Osiris are the same divinity. 'Nothing is opposed,' says Mangou de la Londe, 'to there having been druidical monuments near Bayeux.' 'This region,' adds M. Roussel, 'resembles that in which the Egyptians built the temple of Jupiter-Ammon.' Thus there was a temple, and it contained treasure, as did all Celtic monuments.

In 1715, Dom Martin relates, a certain Héribel dug up, in the neighbourhood of Bayeux, several clay vases filled with bones; and he concludes (following tradition and authorities no longer extant) that this spot, a necropolis, was Mount Faunus, where the Golden Calf was buried.

But the Golden Calf was burned and swallowed—provided the Bible is not mistaken.

In the first place, where is Mount Faunus? The authors do not inform us. The natives know nothing about it. It would have been necessary to undertake excavations, and, with this in view, they sent a petition to the prefect, which met with no reply.

Perhaps Mount Faunus has disappeared, and was not a hill, but a tumulus? What does a tumulus signify?

Some contain skeletons placed like the foetus in the mother's womb. This means that the tomb was, as it were, a second gestation, to prepare them for another life. Thus the tumulus signifies the female, as the upright stone is the male organ.

Where there are menhirs, in fact, an obscene cult has

survived. Witness what took place at Guérande, Chiche-bouche, Croisic, Livarot. At one time towers, pyramids, candles, mile-posts, and even trees had the significance of phalluses—and for Bouvard and Pécuchet everything became a phallus. They collected the swing-bars of carriages, legs of armchairs, cellar bolts, chemists' pestles. When anyone came to see them, they asked: 'What do you think that's like?'—then confided the mystery; and if the visitor protested, they shrugged their shoulders pityingly.

One evening while they were meditating on druidical dogma, the abbé discreetly presented himself.

Immediately they showed him the museum, beginning with the stained-glass window; but they grudged the time before they would arrive at a new department, that of the phalluses. The ecclesiastic halted them, judging the exhibition indecent. He had come to demand his font.

Bouvard and Pécuchet begged a fortnight longer, enough time for making a cast.

'The sooner the better,' said the abbé.

Then he talked of unimportant matters.

Pécuchet, who had gone out of the room for a moment, slipped a napoleon into his hand.

The priest made a movement backwards.

'For your poor, of course.'

And M. Jeufroy, blushing, stuffed the gold piece into his cassock.

Give up the bowl, the sacrificial bowl—not as long as they lived! They even wished to learn Hebrew, which is the mother-language of Celtic, unless it is derived from it!—and were going to make the tour of Brittany—beginning at Rennes, where they had a meeting fixed with Larsoneur, to study the urn mentioned in the *Transactions* of the Celtic Academy, which seems to have contained the cinders of Queen Artemisia—when the mayor walked in, with his hat on his head, unceremoniously, like the brute that he was.

'Don't count your chickens before they're hatched! It must be given up!'

'What must?'

'That'll do! I know quite well you're hiding *it*.'

They had been betrayed.

They replied that they were keeping it with the curé's permission.

'We'll see.'

And Foureau went off.

An hour later he came back.

'The curé says not! Come on and explain.'

They stood firm.

First, no one had any use for the font—and it was not a font. They could prove this with a host of scientific reasons. Next, they offered to acknowledge, in their will, that it belonged to the parish.

They even offered to buy it.

'And besides, it's my property,' said Pécuchet. The twenty francs accepted by M. Jeufroy were a proof of contract; and if it was necessary to appear before a magistrate, so much the worse! The curé would be swearing what was false.

During these discussions, Pécuchet had several times seen the soup bowl again. And in his soul had increased the desire—the thirst—to possess that piece of faience. If the curé liked to make him a present of it, he would return the Druids' bowl. Otherwise, not.

From weariness or fear of scandal, M. Jeufroy yielded.

It was put in their collection, near the Normandy bonnet. The bowl adorned the church porch, and they consoled themselves for not having it with the reflection that the people of Chavignolles were ignorant of its value.

But the soup bowl inspired them with the taste for faience, a new subject for study and for exploration in the district.

It was the period when people of taste sought after old plates of Rouen ware. The notary possessed several, and had gained from them an artistic reputation, harmful to his profession, but which the seriousness of his nature compensated.

When he heard that Bouvard and Pécuchet had acquired the soup bowl, he came to propose an exchange with them.

Pécuchet refused.

'Don't let's speak of it any more,' and Marescot examined their pottery.

All the pieces fastened along the walls were blue on a dingy white ground; and some displayed their horns of abundance in green and reddish tints—shaving-basins, plates and saucers, articles long sought after, and brought back next to their hearts, in the folds of their overcoats.

Marescot sang their praises, spoke of other kinds of faience—the Hispano-Arabic, the Dutch, the English, the Italian—and, having dazzled them with his erudition: 'Suppose I have another look at your soup bowl?'

He made it ring with a tap of his finger, then inspected the two S's painted on the lid.

'The Rouen mark!' said Pécuchet.

'Ah well, a Rouen, properly speaking, had no mark. When we knew nothing about Moutiers, all the French faiences came from Nevers. It's the same with Rouen to-day. Besides, they imitate it perfectly at Elbeuf.'

'Impossible!'

'Majolicas can be very well imitated. Your piece has no value, and I was very near doing something silly!'

When the notary had disappeared, Pécuchet sank into the armchair, prostrated.

'We ought never to have given back the font,' said

Bouvard, 'but you get so excited, you always lose your head!'

'Yes, I lose my head,' and Pécuchet, seizing the bowl, hurled it away, against the sarcophagus.

Bouvard calmly picked up the pieces one by one, and, shortly afterwards, had this idea:

'Out of jealousy, Marescot might quite well have been making fun of us!'

'How?'

'There's nothing to prove that the bowl isn't genuine, while the other pieces that he pretended to admire are perhaps fakes?'

And the end of the day passed in uncertainty and regret.

It was no reason for abandoning the journey to Brittany. They even counted on taking Gorju with them, to help in excavating.

For some time he had been sleeping at the house, in order to finish mending the chest quicker. The prospect of going away upset him, and when they talked of the menhirs and tumuli they expected to see: 'I know better ones,' he said to them. 'In Algeria, in the south, near the sources of the Bou-Mursoug, one comes across any number.' He even described a tomb, that by chance had been opened before his eyes, which contained a skeleton squatting like a monkey, with its two arms round its legs.

Larsoneur, to whom they reported the fact, was quite unwilling to credit it.

Bouvard went into the matter, and started him off again.

How comes it that Gallic monuments are badly formed, when the same Gauls were civilised at the time of Julius Caesar? Doubtless the monuments dated from an earlier people.

Such an hypothesis, according to Larsoneur, was unpatriotic.

That did not matter. Nothing affirms that these monuments are the work of the Gauls. 'Show us a text!'

The academician was annoyed, and did not reply. And they were quite content, so much did the Druids bore them.

If they did not know what to go by with regard to ceramics and Celticism, it was because they were ignorant of history, particularly the history of France.

Anquetil's works happened to be in their library; but the succession of dronish kings gave them small amusement. The villainy of the Merovingian mayors did not shock them —and they gave up Anquetil, put off by the ineptitude of his comments.

Then they asked Dumouchel: 'What is the best history of France?'

Dumouchel, in their name, took out a subscription to a lending library, and sent them Augustin Thierry's *Letters*, along with two volumes by M. de Genoude.

According to that writer, royalty, religion and the national assemblies—those are the 'principles' of the French nation, which go back to the Merovingians. The Carlovingians acted contrary to them. The Capets, in conjunction with the people, strove to maintain them. Under Louis XIII, absolute power was established in order to conquer Protestantism, the last effort of feudality—and '89 is a return to the constitution of our ancestors.

Pécuchet admired his ideas.

They induced contempt in Bouvard, who had read Augustin Thierry first.

'Why are you making a song about the French nation, for there was no France, nor any national assembly! The Carlovingians usurped nothing at all. The kings didn't enfranchise the communes. Read for yourself!'

135

Pécuchet yielded to the evidence, and quickly went one better in scientific rigour. He would have considered it beneath him to say Charlemagne instead of Karl the Great, Clovis instead of Clodovic.

Nevertheless he was led away by Genoude, deeming it clever to make the two extremes of French history meet, so that the middle is all padding—and to be sure of this, they took out the collected works of Buchez and Roux.

But the sentimentality of the introductions, a jumble of Socialism and Catholicism, discouraged them. The multiplicity of details prevented their grasping the subject as a whole.

They had recourse to M. Thiers.

It was during the summer of 1845, and they were in the garden, under the arbour. Pécuchet, with a little stool beneath his feet, was reading aloud in his hollow voice, tirelessly, and only stopping to plunge his fingers in his snuff-box. Bouvard was listening to him with his pipe in his mouth, his legs apart, the top of his trousers unbuttoned.

Greybeards had told them of '93, and memories almost their own gave life to the flat descriptions of the author. In those days the highroads were covered with soldiers singing the Marseillaise. On the doorsteps sat women sewing the canvas for the tents. Sometimes there came a stream of men in red caps, carrying on the end of a slanted pike a bloodless head with hanging locks. The lofty tribune of the Convention towered above a cloud of dust, where enraged faces were howling cries of death. As one passed at midday near the lake of the Tuileries, one heard the shock of the guillotine, as though sheep were being axed.

And the breeze stirred the vine branches of the arbour, now and then the ripe heads of the barley swayed, a blackbird was whistling. As they cast their glances round, they savoured this calm.

What a pity that, at the beginning, no understanding had been possible! For if the Royalists had thought like the patriots, if the Court had behaved with more openness, and their adversaries with less violence, many misfortunes would not have come to pass.

By gossiping on these matters they became enthralled. Bouvard with his liberal spirit and tender heart was Constitutional, Girondin, Thermidorian. Pécuchet, bilious and of domineering temperament, declared himself Sansculotte and Robespierrist.

He approved the condemnation of the King, the most violent decrees, the cult of the Supreme Being; Bouvard preferred that of Nature. He would have saluted with pleasure the image of an enormous woman, pouring out of her breasts for her worshippers, not water, but Chambertin.

In order to have more facts to support their arguments they procured other works—Montgaillard, Prudhomme, Gallois, Lacretelle, etc.; and the contradictions in these books in no wise embarrassed them. Each took from them whatever would defend his cause.

Thus Bouvard did not doubt that Danton would have accepted three hundred thousand francs to bring forward motions that would destroy the Republic—and, according to Pécuchet, Vergniaud would have demanded six thousand francs per month.

'Not on your life! But tell me, why did Robespierre's sister accept a pension from Louis xviii?'

'She didn't! it was from Bonaparte, and since you look at it that way, who was it, a little before the death of Egalité, that had a secret conference with him? I insist that the suppressed paragraphs in the memoirs of la Campan be reprinted! The death of the Dauphin seems to me suspect.

The arsenal of Grenelle, when it blew up, killed two thousand people—cause unknown, so they say—what stupidity!' For Pécuchet thought he knew it, and attributed all the crimes of the period to the manœuvres of the aristocrats, or to foreign subsidies.

In Bouvard's mind, 'Ascend to Heaven, son of Saint Louis,' the virgins of Verdun and the breeches of human skin were undeniable facts. He accepted the numbers of Prudhomme—a million victims exactly.

But the Loire, red with blood from Saumur to Nantes, a length of forty-five miles, made him wonder. Pécuchet also doubted it, and they began to regard historians with suspicion.

The revolution is, for some, a satanic event. Others proclaim it a sublime exception. The vanquished on either side are, naturally, martyrs.

Thierry shows, with regard to the Barbarians, how absurd it is to inquire whether such and such a prince was good or bad. Why not follow this method in examining later epochs? But history must avenge morals; one is grateful to Tacitus for having lacerated Tiberius. After all, that the Queen may have had lovers, that Dumouriez after Valmy intended treachery, that it was the Mountain or the Gironde that began in Prairial, and the Jacobins or the Plain in Thermidor—what does it matter in the development of the Revolution, whose origins are deep-laid and whose results incalculable?

Thus it had to fulfil itself, to be what it was; but suppose the flight of the King unhindered, Robespierre escaping or Bonaparte assassinated—chances which depended on a less scrupulous innkeeper, an open door, a sleeping sentry—and the course of the world was changed.

They had no longer, on the men and deeds of the epoch, a single decided idea.

To judge it impartially, it would be necessary to have read all the histories, all the memoirs, all the newspapers and all the documents in manuscript, since from the least omission an error may ensue which will lead on to others *ad infinitum*. They renounced the undertaking.

But the taste for history had come to them, the need for truth on its own account.

Perhaps it is easier to find in bygone epochs? Authors, being far from the events, should speak of them without passion. And they started on the admirable Rollin.

'What a mass of nonsense!' cried Bouvard, after the first chapter.

'Wait a little!' said Pécuchet, rummaging in the depths of their library, where were huddled the books of the last proprietor, an old legist, eccentric and dilettante. And having displaced many novels and plays, with a Montesquieu and various translations of Horace, he reached what he was looking for—the work of Beaufort on Roman history.

Livy attributes the foundation of Rome to Romulus. Sallust gives the honour to the Trojans of Aeneas. Coriolanus died in exile according to Fabius Pictor, by the plots of Attius Tullus if one trusts to Dionysius; Seneca affirms that Horatius Cocles made a victorious return; Dion, that he was wounded in the leg. And La Mothe le Vayer expresses similar doubts, relative to other peoples.

There is no agreement on the antiquity of the Chaldeans, the date of Homer, the existence of Zoroaster, the two empires of Assyria. Quintus Curtius has written fairy-tales. Plutarch gives Herodotus the lie. We should have a different notion of Caesar if Vercingetorix had composed the Commentaries.

Ancient history is obscure from lack of documents. In the modern they abound; and Bouvard and Pécuchet returned to France and started on Sismondi.

The succession of so many men brought the desire to know them more intimately, to mingle with them. They wished to read the original documents: Gregory of Tours, Monstrelet, Commines—all whose names were odd or pleasant.

But the events became confused, through their ignorance of dates.

Happily they possessed Dumouchel's treatise on mnemonics, a duodecimo bound in boards, with this motto: 'Enjoy while learning.'

It combines the three systems of Allevy, Pâris and Fenaigle.

Allevy changes numbers into images, the figure 1 being denoted by a tower, 2 by a bird, 3 by a camel, and so on. Pâris strikes the imagination by means of the rebus; an armchair studded with screws will give: Clou, vis—Clovis; and as the sound of frying is 'ric, ric,' whitings in a frying-pan will recall Chilpéric. Fenaigle divides the universe into houses, which contain rooms, having each four walls with nine panels, each panel bearing an emblem. Thus, the first king of the first dynasty will occupy the first panel in the first room. A beacon on a hill will tell how he was named 'Phar-a-mond,' according to the system of Pâris. By Allevy's method, in placing above a mirror, which stands for 4, a bird 2 and a hoop o, one will obtain 420, the date of that prince's accession.

For greater clearness, they took, as a mnemonic base, their own house, where they were living, attaching to each one of its parts a distinct event—and the courtyard, the garden, the surroundings, the entire district, had no other meaning than to jog their memory. The boundary-posts in the country limited certain epochs, the apple trees were genealogical trees, the bushes were battles, the world became a symbol. They sought, on the walls, a quantity of things

140

that were not there, and ended by seeing them, but no longer knew the dates that they represented.

Besides, dates are not always authentic. They learnt, in a student's manual, that the date of the birth of Jesus must be put back five years earlier than is usual, that with the Greeks there were three ways of reckoning the Olympiads, and with the Romans eight ways of dating the beginning of the year. So many opportunities for mistakes, besides those that result from the signs of the zodiac, eras, and different sorts of calendars.

And from disregard of dates they passed to contempt for facts.

What is important is the philosophy of history.

Bouvard could not finish the famous discourse of Bossuet.

'The eagle of Meaux is a sham. He forgets China, India and America, but he takes care to tell us that Theodosius was "the joy of the universe," that Abraham "treated with kings as an equal," and that the philosophy of the Greeks descends from the Hebrews. This preoccupation with the Hebrews annoys me.'

Pécuchet shared this opinion, and wanted to make him read Vico.

'How can one admit,' objected Bouvard, 'that legends are truer than the truths of history?'

Pécuchet tried to give an explanation of myths, losing himself in the *Scienza Nuova*.

'Will you deny the plan of Providence?'

'I don't even know it!' said Bouvard.

They decided to refer the matter to Dumouchel.

The professor admitted that he was now out of the running as regards history.

'It changes every day. The kings of Rome and the travels of Pythagoras are contested. There are attacks on Belisarius, William Tell, and even the Cid, who has become, thanks to the latest discoveries, an ordinary bandit. It is to be hoped no more discoveries will be made, and the Institute might even establish a sort of canon laying down what must be believed!'

He sent as a postscript these rules of criticism noted down from Daunou's lectures:

'To quote as proof the witness of crowds is a bad proof; they are not there to answer to it.

'Reject impossibilities. Pausanias was shown the stone swallowed by Saturn.

'Architecture may lie—for example, the arch of the Forum, where Titus is named the first conqueror of Jerusalem, although it was taken by Pompey before him.

'Medals sometimes deceive. Under Charles ix, money was struck bearing the imprint of Henry ii.

'Allow for the skill of forgers, the interests of apologists and calumniators.'

Few historians have worked according to these rules, but all with a view to a particular cause, a religion, a nation, a party, or a system, or to flatter kings, give counsel to a people or provide moral examples.

Others, who pretend only to narrate, are not worth more; for one cannot tell everything; a choice is necessary. But in the selection of documents, a certain cast of mind will prevail; and as it varies according to the character of the writer, history will never be fixed.

'Regrettable!' they thought.

However, one can take a subject, exhaust the sources, analyse it well, then condense it in a narrative, which would be a summary of facts, reflecting the entire truth. Such a work seemed feasible to Pécuchet.

'Would you like us to try and write a history?'

'Nothing better! But what about?'

'Yes, indeed, what about?'

Bouvard was seated, Pécuchet walking up and down the museum. Then the butter-jar caught his eye, and halting suddenly:

'Suppose we wrote the life of the Duc d'Angoulême?'

'But he was an idiot!' replied Bouvard.

'Never mind! Persons of secondary rank sometimes have enormous importance, and he may have been at the hub of affairs.'

Books would give them data, and M. de Faverges no doubt possessed information on his own account, or from old gentlemen among his friends.

They meditated on this project, discussed it, and at last decided to spend a fortnight at the municipal library of Caen to carry out research.

The librarian put at their disposal general histories and pamphlets, with a coloured lithograph showing a three-quarter length of Monseigneur the Duc d'Angoulême.

The blue cloth of his uniform coat disappeared beneath epaulets, stars and the great red cordon of the Legion of Honour. An extremely high collar enclosed his long neck. His pear-shaped head was framed by wisps of hair and sparse whiskers; and heavy eyelids, a very pronounced nose and thick lips gave his face an expression of insignificant good nature.

When they had taken notes, they drew up a synopsis:

Birth and childhood, nothing remarkable. One of his tutors is the Abbé Guénée, the enemy of Voltaire. At Turin he is shown how to cast a cannon, and he studies the campaigns of Charles viii. Also, in spite of his youth, he is made colonel of a regiment of King's Levies.

1797. His marriage.

1814. The English take Bordeaux. He hastens up behind them and exhibits himself to the inhabitants. Description of the Duke's appearance.

1815. He is surprised by Bonaparte. Immediately he appeals to the King of Spain; and Toulon, but for Masséna, would have been delivered to the English.

Operations in the South of France. He is defeated, but released on his promise to surrender the crown jewels, carried off at full speed by the King, his uncle.

After the Hundred Days he returns with his parents and lives tranquilly. Several years pass.

The Spanish wars.—As soon as he has crossed the Pyrenees, victory everywhere follows the grandson of Henry IV. He carries the Trocadero, reaches the Pillars of Hercules, crushes faction, embraces Ferdinand, and returns.

Triumphal arches, flowers presented by young girls, dinners in prefectures, *Te Deums* in cathedrals. The Parisians are at the height of intoxication. The city offers him a banquet. Allusions to our hero sung in the theatres.

Enthusiasm wanes. For in 1827, at Cherbourg, a ball, got up by subscription, is a failure.

As he is Grand-Admiral of France he inspects the fleet about to set out for Algiers.

July 1830, Marmont tells him the state of affairs. Thereupon he gets into such a fury that he wounds his hand on the general's sword.

The King entrusts him with command of all the forces.

In the Bois de Boulogne he meets some detachments of the line and does not find a single word to address to them.

From Saint-Cloud he flies to the bridge of Sèvres. Coldness of the troops. That does not daunt him. The royal family leave Trianon. He seats himself at the foot of an oak, unfolds a map, meditates, mounts his horse again, passes before Saint-Cyr and sends words of hope to the cadets.

At Rambouillet, the bodyguard make their farewell.

He embarks, and is ill during the whole crossing. End of his career.

Draw attention to the importance of bridges. First, he

exposes himself uselessly on the bridge of L'Inn; he carries the Saint-Esprit bridge and the bridge of Lauriol; at Lyons the two bridges prove fatal, and his fortunes end in front of the bridge of Sèvres.

Picture of his virtues. Useless to vaunt his courage, to which he joined great political ability. For he offered every soldier sixty francs to desert the Emperor and in Spain he tried to bribe the Constitutionals.

His reserve was so profound that he consented to a marriage projected by his father and the Queen of Etruria, to the formation of a new cabinet after the Ordinances, to the abdication in favour of Chambord, to everything he was asked.

Yet he was not wanting in firmness. At Angers he broke the infantry of the National Guard, which, jealous of the cavalry and by means of a manœuvre, had arrived to escort him, so that His Highness was hemmed in by foot-soldiers and had his knees bruised. But he blamed the cavalry for the disorder and excused the infantry—a real judgment of Solomon.

His piety manifested by numerous acts of devotion, and his mercy by obtaining pardon for General Debelle, who had been in arms against him.

Intimate details, characteristics of the prince:

At the castle of Beauregard, in his childhood, he took pleasure, along with his brother, in digging a lake which is still to be seen. Once he visited the Chasseurs' barracks, asked for a glass of wine, and drank to the King's health.

To keep in step when walking he used to repeat to himself: 'One two, one two, one two!'

Some of his sayings have been preserved.

To a deputation from Bordeaux: 'What consoles me for not being at Bordeaux is to be in your midst!'

To the Protestants of Nîmes: 'I am a good Catholic, but I shall never forget that the most illustrious of my ancestors was a Protestant.'

To the cadets at Saint-Cyr, when all was lost:

'All is well, my friends! the news is good! All goes well, very well!'

After the abdication of Charles x: 'Since they don't want me, let them settle it themselves!'

And in 1814, on every occasion, even in the smallest village: 'No more war, no more conscription, no more united rights!'

His writings as good as his speeches. His proclamations unsurpassable.

The Comte d'Artois's first proclamation had begun thus: 'Frenchmen, the brother of your king is here!'

That of the Prince: 'I come. I am the son of your Kings. You are Frenchmen!'

Order of the day, dated from Bayonne: 'Soldiers, I come!'

Another, during the height of defection: 'Continue to sustain, with the vigour which is fitting to the soldiers of France, the struggle that you have begun. France expects it of you!'

The last, at Rambouillet: 'The King has reached an agreement with the Government established in Paris, and all conduces to the belief that this agreement is on the point of being concluded.'

'All conduces to the belief,' was sublime.

'One thing worries me,' said Bouvard, 'that is, there's no mention of his affairs of the heart.'

And they noted on the margin, 'Investigate the prince's love affairs.'

At the moment of leaving, the librarian showed them, as an afterthought, a second portrait of the Duc d'Angoulême.

Here he was a colonel of cuirassiers, in profile, with a still smaller eye, an open mouth, flat-haired, and on a prancing horse.

How could they reconcile the two portraits? Was his

hair flat or curly—unless he was so dandified as to have it curled?

A serious matter, according to Pécuchet, for the hair denotes temperament, and temperament the individual.

Bouvard thought that one knew nothing of a man while ignorant of his passions; and to clear up these two points, they called at the Faverges house. The count was not at home, and that held up their research. They went away vexed.

The door of their house was wide open, the kitchen empty. They mounted the staircase; and whom should they see in the middle of Bouvard's room but Mme Bordin, casting glances to right and left.

'Excuse me,' she said, forcing a laugh. 'I've been an hour here looking for your cook. I want her for my preserves.'

They found her fast asleep on a chair in the woodshed. They shook her. She opened her eyes.

'What is it now? You're always bothering me with your questions!'

Evidently Mme Bordin had been pumping her in their absence.

Germaine came out of her torpor, and declared that she had indigestion.

'I'll stay and look after you,' said the widow.

They saw a huge bonnet with flapping sides in the yard. It was Mme Castillon, the farmer's wife, who shouted: 'Gorju! Gorju!'

And from the barn the voice of their little servant answered shrilly:

'He's not there.'

Five minutes later she came down, with red cheeks, all in a flutter. Bouvard and Pécuchet reproached her for being so slow. She unbuckled their gaiters without a murmur.

Then they went to look at the chest.

It was scattered in pieces over the bakehouse; the carvings were chipped, the doors broken.

At this sight, in face of this new catastrophe, Bouvard could hardly keep back his tears, and Pécuchet was trembling.

Gorju, appearing almost at once, explained what had happened; he had just put the chest outside in order to varnish it, when a stray cow kicked it over.

'Whose cow?' asked Pécuchet.

'I don't know.'

'Ah, so you left the gate open, the same as you have now! It's your fault.'

They washed their hands of the whole business; he had been playing with them too long, and they were sick of him and his carpentry.

The gentlemen were making a mistake. The damage was not so great. In less than three weeks everything would be put right, and Gorju went with them to the kitchen, where Germaine arrived, dragging herself along, to cook the dinner.

On the table they noticed a bottle of Calvados, three-quarters empty.

'That's your doing, I suppose!' said Pécuchet to Gorju.

'Me? Certainly not!'

Bouvard pointed out: 'You're the only man in the house.'

'Well, what about the women?' answered the workman, with a knowing wink.

Germaine intercepted it:

'You might as well say it was me.'

'Of course it's you.'

'And perhaps it was me that smashed the chest?'

Gorju made a pirouette.

'Don't you see she's drunk?'

148

Then they blackguarded each other furiously, he pale and mocking, she purple and pulling out tufts of grey hair from under her cotton cap. Mme Bordin spoke up for Germaine, Mélie for Gorju.

The old woman burst out:

'It's an abomination! All day you spend together in the bushes, not to speak of the night! Filthy Parisian, preying on respectable people! You come to my masters and stuff them up with tales!'

Bouvard opened his eyes wide.

'What tales?'

'Don't you see he's making a fool of you?'

'No one can make a fool of me!' cried Pécuchet, and enraged at her insolence, exasperated by all these rebuffs, he gave her notice; she was to get out at once. Bouvard did not oppose the decision and they retired, leaving Germaine to heave with sobs at her misfortune, while Mme Bordin tried to console her.

In the evening, when they had calmed down, they went over these happenings, asking each other who had drunk the Calvados, how the chest had come to be broken, why Mme Castillon was calling Gorju—and whether he had dishonoured Mélie?

'We don't know,' said Bouvard, 'what's going on in our own house, yet we were pluming ourselves on finding out about the hair and the love affairs of the Duke of Angoulême!'

Pécuchet added:

'What a lot of other important and even more difficult questions there are!'

Whence they concluded that exterior facts are not everything. They must be supplemented by psychology. Without imagination, history is incomplete.

'Let's send for some historical novels!'

V

First they read Walter Scott.

It was the surprise of a new world.

The men of the past, who had been for them only phantoms or names, became living beings, kings, princes, wizards, footmen, gamekeepers, monks, gipsies, merchants and soldiers, who deliberate, fight, travel, do business, eat and drink, sing and pray, in the armories of castles, on the blackened benches of inns, along the winding streets of towns, under the awnings of booths, in the cloisters of monasteries. Landscapes, composed with artistry, group round scenes like a stage-setting. The eye follows a horseman galloping along the shore. You breathe the fresh wind amid the broom, the moon shines on lakes where a boat glides, the sun glitters on breast-plates, the rain falls on leafy cabins. Not knowing the originals, they found these pictures convincing, and the illusion was complete. So the winter was spent.

After lunch they would settle down in the morning-room on each side of the fireplace, and facing one another, book in hand, would read in silence. As the day wore on they would go for a walk along the main road, have a hasty dinner and continue their reading into the night. To shield his eyes from the lamp Bouvard wore blue spectacles; Pécuchet kept the peak of his cap drawn over his forehead.

Germaine had not left, and Gorju came, now and then, to dig the garden, for they had given in to them through indifference, heedless of practical things.

After Walter Scott, Alexandre Dumas amused them like

a magic lantern. His characters, active as monkeys, strong as bulls, gay as larks, enter and talk abruptly, jump off roofs on to the pavement, receive frightful wounds from which they recover, are reported dead and reappear. There are trapdoors under the boards, antidotes, disguises, and everything gets entangled, hurries along and is unravelled without a moment for reflection. Love observes the proprieties, fanaticism is light-hearted, massacres excite a smile.

Made critical by these two masters, they could not tolerate rubbish about Belisarius, foolery about Numa Pompilius, Marchangy, the Vicomte d'Arlincourt.

The colour in Frédéric Soulié (like that of the bibliophile Jacob) seemed to them thin, and M. Villemain scandalised them by producing, on page 85 of his *Lascaris*, a Spanish woman smoking a pipe, 'a long Arab pipe,' in the middle of the fifteenth century.

Pécuchet consulted the *Biographie Universelle* and undertook to revise Dumas from the historical point of view.

This author in *The Two Dianas* is wrong with his dates. The marriage of the Dauphin Francis took place on 15th October 1548 and not 20th March 1549. How does he know (see *The Page of the Duke of Savoy*) that Catharine de Médici, after the death of her husband, wished to resume war? It is very unlikely that the Duke of Anjou was crowned at night in a church—an episode which adds piquancy to the *Lady of Montsoreau*. In particular, *Queen Margot* swarms with errors. The Duke of Nevers was not absent. He gave his opinion at the Council before St. Bartholomew's Day, and Henry of Navarre did not follow the procession four days later. Henry III did not return from Poland so quickly. Besides, how many hackneyed stories! The miracle of the hawthorn, Charles IX's balcony, the poisoned gloves of Jeanne d'Albret—Pécuchet had no more confidence in Dumas.

He even lost all respect for Walter Scott because of the

blunders in *Quentin Durward*. The murder of the Bishop of Liège is put forward fifteen years. The wife of Robert de Lamarck was Jeanne d'Arschel and not Hameline de Croy. Far from being killed by a soldier, he was executed by Maximilian, and the face of Le Téméraire, when his body was found, did not wear a threatening expression, for it had been half eaten by wolves.

Still, Bouvard went on with Walter Scott, but ended by being bored with the repetition of the same effects. The heroine nearly always lives in the country with her father, and the lover, kidnapped as a child, is re-established in his rights and triumphs over his rivals. There is always a mendicant philosopher, a surly nobleman, pure young girls, facetious servitors, and interminable dialogues, stupid prudery, a complete lack of depth.

In disgust of such bric-à-brac, Bouvard took up George Sand.

He went into raptures over the wanton beauties and their noble lovers, would have liked to be Jacques, Simon, Bénédict, Lélio, and live in Venice! He uttered sighs, did not know what was the matter with him, felt himself changed.

Pécuchet, at work on historical literature, was studying plays.

He swallowed two Pharamonds, three Clovises, four Charlemagnes, several Philip Augustuses, a crowd of Joan of Arcs, and innumerable Marquises de Pompadours, and Conspiracies of Cellamare.

Nearly all seemed to him even more idiotic than the novels. For there exists on the stage a conventional history which nothing can destroy. Louis XI will not fail to kneel before the little images in his hat; Henry IV will be consistently jovial, Mary Stuart lachrymose, Richelieu cruel; in short, from love of simple ideas and respect for ignorance, all the characters have been cast in the same mould, so that the dramatist, far from elevating, degrades and, instead of instructing, stupefies.

As Bouvard had recommended George Sand, Pécuchet began to read *Consuelo, Horace, Mauprat,* was delighted by the author's defence of the oppressed, the social and republican side of her work, and the propaganda.

According to Bouvard, these spoilt the plot, and he asked at the library for love stories.

They took it in turns to read aloud *La Nouvelle Héloïse, Delphine, Adolphe, Ourika.* But the yawns of the one who was listening proved contagious to the other, who soon let the book slip from his hands to the floor.

They found fault with all these for saying nothing about the surroundings, the period, the dress of the characters. Only the heart is dealt with; always sentiment, as if there were nothing else in the world.

Then they nibbled at humorous novels, such as the *Journey Round My Room,* by Xavier de Maistre, *Under the Lime Trees,* by Alphonse Karr. In this class of book the author interrupts his narrative to talk of his dog, his slippers or his mistress.

Such flightiness at first charmed them, then seemed to them stupid, for the author, in displaying himself, obliterates his work.

Needing excitement, they plunged into adventure stories; the more involved, extraordinary and impossible the plot, the more they liked it. They tried hard to foresee the ending, became expert at it, and grew tired of a diversion unworthy of serious minds.

The works of Balzac amazed them, like a Babylon, and again like grains of dust under the microscope. In the most commonplace things new aspects emerged. They had not suspected such depths in modern life.

'What an observer!' cried Bouvard.

'I find him chimerical,' Pécuchet announced ultimately.

'He believes in the occult sciences, in monarchy and high society; he's dazzled by rogues, rakes up millions for you like centimes, and his middle-class people aren't ordinary people at all, but colossi. Why puff up what's flat and describe so much that's silly! He's written a novel on chemistry, another on the banks, another on the printing press; as a certain Richard has done *The Cabman, The Water-carrier, The Coconut Seller*. We shall have novels on every trade and every province, then on every town and the floors of every house and every individual, which will be no longer literature but statistics or ethnography.'

The vehicle mattered little to Bouvard. He wished to learn, to gain a deeper knowledge of human nature. He re-read Paul de Kock, and skimmed through *The Old Hermits of the Chaussée d'Antin*.

'How can you waste your time on such drivel,' said Pécuchet.

'But surely they'll be very interesting as documents.'

'You and your documents! I like something that lifts me up and sweeps me away from the sordidness of this world.'

And Pécuchet, drawn to the ideal, led Bouvard unconsciously towards tragedy.

The remoteness of the setting, the questions discussed and the high rank of the characters impressed them with a certain sense of grandeur.

One day Bouvard took up *Athalie* and recited the dream so well that Pécuchet wanted to try it himself. After the first phrase his voice became lost in a sort of mumbling. It was monotonous and, though loud, indistinct.

Bouvard, from experience, advised him to modulate his voice by letting it run from the bottom to the top note, and then back again—thus completing two scales, one rising and the other falling; and he himself went through this exercise every morning in bed, lying on his back, according to the precept of the Greeks. At the same time Pécuchet also practised; and their doors being shut, they bawled independently.

What pleased them in tragedy was the emphasis, the political speeches, the maxims on the perversity of fate.

They learnt by heart the most famous dialogues of Racine and Voltaire, and declaimed them in the corridor. Bouvard, as though at the Théâtre Français, walked with his hand on Pécuchet's shoulder; at intervals he halted and, rolling his eyes, with outstretched arms he arraigned Destiny. He had some good cries of grief from Laharpe's *Philoctetes*, a nice death-rattle from *Gabrielle de Vergy*, and, when he was playing Dionysius, the tyrant of Syracuse, a way of looking at his son while calling him 'Monster, worthy of me!' which was really terrible. Pécuchet forgot his part. He lacked, not the will, but the ability.

One day, in Marmontel's *Cleopatra*, he tried to reproduce the hissing of the asp as the machine invented for the purpose by Vaucanson might have done it. The failure of this effect made them laugh till evening. Tragedy fell in their esteem.

Bouvard was the first to grow tired and, without mincing matters, he showed how artificial and lame it was, the silliness of its machinery, the absurdity of confidants.

They went in for comedy, which is the school of fine shades. Every phrase must be pulled to pieces, every word underlined, every syllable weighed. Pécuchet could not manage it, and completely came to grief in *Célimène*.

Besides, he found the lovers too cold, the arguments a bore, the servants intolerable, Clitander and Sganarelle as false as Ægistheus and Agamemnon.

There remained serious comedy, or the tragedy of ordinary life, where we see the fathers of families afflicted, servants rescuing their masters, rich men giving away their fortunes, innocent sempstresses and villainous suborners: a type of drama which persists from Diderot to Pixérécourt. All these pieces preaching virtue offended them by their triviality.

The drama of 1830 charmed them by its movement, colour and youthfulness.

They made little distinction between Victor Hugo, Dumas or Bouchardy, and the diction must no longer be pompous or artful, but lyrical and distraught.

One day when Bouvard was trying to explain to Pécuchet the acting of Frédérick Lemaître, Mme Bordin suddenly appeared in her green shawl, bringing back a volume of Pigault-Lebrun, the gentlemen being so good as to lend her a novel now and then.

'Please go on,' for she had been there a moment, and enjoyed listening to them.

They made excuses. She insisted.

'Good lord,' said Bouvard, 'there's nothing to stop us—'

Pécuchet, from bashfulness, remarked that they could not perform extempore, without costume.

'Quite right! We shall have to dress up!'

And Bouvard looked for something to put on, but found only the Greek cap, which he took.

As the corridor was not wide enough they went down to the drawing-room.

Spiders ran along the walls, and the geological specimens, which encumbered the floor, had whitened the velvet of the armchairs with their dust. On the cleanest they spread a cloth so that Mme Bordin could sit down.

They must give her something good. Bouvard was in favour of *The Tower of Nesle*. But Pécuchet was afraid of parts requiring too much action.

'She'd prefer something classical! *Phèdre*, for instance!'

'Very well.'

Bouvard told the plot. 'It's a queen, whose husband has a

son by another woman. She's fallen madly in love with the young man—have you got it? Let's start, then!'

'Yes, prince! for Theseus I grow faint, I burn,
  I love him!'

And addressing Pécuchet's profile, he eulogised his bearing, his countenance—'that charming head'—lamented not having met him with the Greek fleet, would willingly have been lost with him in the labyrinth.

The tassel of the red cap inclined amorously, and his trembling voice and his good-natured face begged the cruel one to have pity on his flame. Pécuchet, turning away, panted to express emotion.

Mme Bordin, without moving, goggled her eyes, as though she were gazing at a pair of mountebanks; Mélie listened behind the door; Gorju, in shirt-sleeves, watched them through the window.

Bouvard began the second tirade. His acting expressed a fever of the senses, remorse, despair, and he threw himself on the imaginary sword of Pécuchet with such violence that, slipping among the stones, he nearly fell to the floor.

'Take no notice! Then Theseus arrives and she poisons herself.'

'Poor woman,' said Mme Bordin.

Then they begged her to choose a piece for them.

This embarrassed her. She had seen only three plays— *Robert the Devil*, in the capital; *The Young Husband*, at Rouen; and another at Falaise which was very amusing and was called *The Vinegar-Seller's Wheelbarrow*.

Finally Bouvard suggested the big scene from *Tartuffe*, in the third act.

Pécuchet thought an explanation necessary.

'You must know that Tartuffe—'

Mme Bordin interrupted: 'One knows what a Tartuffe is.'

Bouvard would have liked a skirt for a certain passage.

'There's only the monk's robe,' said Pécuchet.

'That will do! Put it on!'

He came back with it and a volume of Molière.

The beginning was poor. But when Tartuffe starts to caress Elmire's knees, Pécuchet assumed the voice of a policeman.

'*What does your hand there?*'

Bouvard immediately answered in sugary tones:

'*I feel your dress, the stuff is very soft!*' And he darted his eyes, stuck out his lips, sniffed the air, looked exceedingly lubricous, and even ended by addressing himself to Mme Bordin.

The man's glances embarrassed her, and when he stopped, humble and palpitating, she almost sought for a reply herself.

Pécuchet had recourse to the book:

'*The declaration is extremely gallant.*'

'Yes, indeed!' she cried. 'He's a fine coaxer.'

'Aren't I?' replied Bouvard proudly. 'But here's something else with a more modern touch.' And undoing his coat, he sat on a stone and, with head thrown back, declaimed:

'Your eyes' bright flames are flooding through my soul,
  Sing me a song, as oft at evening,
  With tears in your dark eyes, you used to sing.'

'That's like me,' she thought.

'Be happy! let us drink! full is the cup!
  Ours make this moment, and the world give up!'

'How funny you are!'

And she gave a giggle, which made her bosom rise, and exposed her teeth.

> 'Is it not sweet
> To love and see your lover at your feet?'

He knelt.
'Do leave off.'

> 'Oh let me sleep and dream upon thy breast,
> O Doña Sol, my beauty, my adored!'

'Here the bells are heard, and a mountaineer disturbs them.'

'Just as well! Otherwise—!' and, instead of finishing her phrase, Mme Bordin smiled. It was growing dark. She rose.

It had just been raining, and as the road by the beeches was difficult, it would be better to go back by the fields. Bouvard accompanied her down the garden to open the gate.

At first they walked past the cordons without speaking. He was still moved by his declaiming, and she, at the bottom of her heart, felt a sort of surprise, the charm that comes from literature. There are occasions when art excites commonplace natures, and whole worlds can be revealed by its clumsiest interpreters.

The sun had reappeared, making the leaves glitter, throwing luminous patches here and there in the thickets. Three sparrows with little chirps hopped on the trunk of an old lime tree that had been felled. A hawthorn in blossom showed its pink cluster, the heavy lilacs were drooping.

'Ah! that does one good!' said Bouvard, breathing in a lungful of air.

'Yes, but you work yourself up too much!'

'I may not have talent, but there's fire in me.'

'One can see . . .' she answered, pausing between her words, 'that . . . at one time you have . . . loved.'

'Only in the past, you think?'

She stopped.

'I know nothing about that.'

'What does she mean?' and Bouvard felt his heart beating.

A little pool in the middle of the gravel making them step aside, they walked up under the arbour.

Then they talked of the acting.

'What was the name of your last piece?'

'It was taken from a play, *Hernani*.'

'Oh,' then slowly, and speaking to herself, 'it must be nice to have a gentleman saying such things to you—and really meaning it.'

'I'm willing enough,' replied Bouvard.

'What, you?'

'Yes! Yes!'

'You're joking!'

'Not in the very least!'

And having glanced round, he took her by the waist from behind and kissed her vigorously on the neck.

She grew very pale, as though she were going to faint, and leaned with one hand against a tree, then opened her eyes and shook her head.

'It's over now.'

He gazed at her, astonished.

The grille being opened, she mounted the step of the little gate.

A runlet was flowing on the other side. She gathered up the folds of her petticoat and stood on the brink, hesitating.

'Will you let me help you?'

'No need.'

'Why?'

Oh, you're too dangerous!'

And she jumped, showing her white stocking.

Bouvard blamed himself for having missed an opportunity. Pooh, there would be another—and then, not all women are alike. Some like swift action, daring is fatal with others. In short, he was pleased with himself, and if he did not confide his hope to Pécuchet, it was from fear of comment, and not through delicacy.

From that day they used to recite in front of Mélie and Gorju, at the same time regretting that they had not a private theatre.

The little maid enjoyed it without understanding a word, amazed by the diction, fascinated by the purr of the verses. Gorju applauded the philosophical harangues in the tragedies and everything on the people's side in the melodramas; so that, delighted at his good taste, they thought of giving him lessons, with a view to making an actor of him later on. This prospect dazzled the workman.

The news of their performances had spread. Vaucorbeil made some sarcastic comments. Most people despised them.

Their pride mounted all the more. They dedicated themselves to art. Pécuchet wore moustaches, and Bouvard, with his round face and bald patch, could think of nothing better than to adopt 'a head like Béranger's.'

In the end they resolved to write a play.

The difficulty was to find a subject.

They hunted for it at lunch, and drank coffee—an indispensable stimulant for the mind—then two or three nips of spirit. They lay down on their beds for a doze; after which they descended into the orchard, took a turn, and finally went afield to seek inspiration, marching side by side, and returning exhausted.

Or again, they locked themselves in. Bouvard cleared the table, spread the paper in front of him, dipped his pen and fixed his eyes on the ceiling, while Pécuchet meditated in the armchair, with legs stretched out and head bowed.

At times they felt a tremor as though it were the waft of an idea; as they grasped at it, it vanished.

But there are ways of finding subjects. You take a title haphazard and something emerges from it; you elaborate a proverb, combine several adventures in one. None of these dodges worked. In vain they skimmed through collections of anecdotes, several volumes of famous trials, a mass of stories.

And they dreamed of being played at the Odéon, thought of the theatres, longed for Paris.

'I was meant for an author and not to be buried in the country!' said Bouvard.

'Same here,' replied Pécuchet.

He had an inspiration; if they were having so much trouble, it was because they did not know the rules.

They studied them in the *Practice of the Theatre*, by d'Aubignac, and in several less outmoded works.

There, important questions are debated: whether comedy should be written in verse; whether tragedy does not exceed its bounds in taking its plot from modern history; whether heroes should be virtuous; what kind of villains are appropriate; how far horrors are admissible. The details should all converge on a single point, the interest should grow, and the end should chime with the beginning—not a doubt of it!

> Think of devices which can captivate,

says Boileau.

By what means think of these devices?

> In all your speeches passion should be found,
> Go seek the heart, and warm it till it bound.

How 'warm the heart'?

Then rules are not enough; genius is also necessary.

And genius is not enough. Corneille, according to the Académie Francaise, understands nothing of the theatre. Geoffroy depreciated Voltaire. Racine was jeered at by Subligny. Laharpe bellowed at the name of Shakespeare.

Disgusted by the old criticism, they turned to the new, and sent for newspapers containing theatre notices.

What impudence! What obstinacy! What dishonesty! Insults to masterpieces, reverence paid to platitudes—and the ignorance of those who pass as learned, the stupidity of others who are called witty!

Perhaps it is to the public one should refer.

But sometimes they found popular works displeasing, and among those that had been hissed off there were some to their taste.

Thus, the opinion of men of taste is fallible, and the judgment of the mob inexplicable.

Bouvard put the conundrum to Barberou. Pécuchet, for his part, wrote to Dumouchel.

The ex-commercial traveller was astonished at their provincial flabbiness; old Bouvard was dithering, in short was 'out of things altogether.'

Plays are a commodity like anything else. They come under the head of fancy goods. One goes to the theatre for diversion. The best is what amuses.

'Oh, the fool!' cried Pécuchet. 'What amuses him is not the same as what amuses me, and others like him will grow tired of it later on. If plays are written only to be acted, how comes it that the best are always read?'

And he awaited Dumouchel's reply.

According to the professor, the immediate fate of a play proves nothing. *The Misanthrope* and *Athalie* failed. *Zaïre* is no longer understood. Who talks nowadays of

163

Ducange and Picard? And he recalled all the great contemporary successes, from *Fanchon the Organ-grinder* to *Gaspardo the Fisherman*, deploring the decadence of our stage. The cause of this is hatred of literature, or rather of style.

Then they asked themselves of what precisely style consists—and, thanks to the authors mentioned by Dumouchel, they learnt the secret of every kind: how to attain the sublime, the restrained, the simple; what turns of phrase are noble, the words that are low. *Dogs* is heightened by *devouring*. *Vomit* is only used figuratively. *Fever* applies to the passions. *Valour* is good in verse.

'Should we write verse?' said Pécuchet.

'Later on! First, let's work at prose!'

We are expressly advised to choose a classic and mould ourselves on him, but they all have their dangers, and have erred not only in style, but even more in language.

Such an assertion disconcerted Bouvard and Pécuchet, and they set themselves to study grammar.

Are there definite and indefinite articles in our idiom as in Latin? Some say yes, others no. They did not dare decide.

The subject always agrees with the verb, save on the occasions when it does not agree.

No distinction, again, between the verbal adjective and the present participle; but the Academy lays down one that is hard enough to grasp.

They were relieved to know that the pronoun *leur* is used not only for persons, but also for things, while *où* and *en* are used for things and sometimes for persons.

Should one say 'Cette femme a l'air bon' or 'l'air bonne'— 'une bouche de bois sec' or 'de bois sèche'—'ne pas laisser *de*' or '*que de*'—'une troupe de voleurs survint' or 'survinrent'?

164

Other difficulties: 'Autour' and 'à l'entour,' in which Racine and Boileau could see no difference; 'imposer' or 'en imposer,' synonyms with Massillon and Voltaire; 'croasser' and 'coasser,' confounded by La Fontaine, who yet could distinguish a crow from a frog.

Grammarians, it is true, disagree. Some see a beauty where others smell a fault. They admit principles whose consequences they reject, announce consequences whose principles they refute, lean on tradition, throw over the masters, and introduce strange refinements. Ménage, instead of *lentilles* and *cassonade* approves *nentilles* and *castonade*, Bouhours, *jérarchie* and not *hiérarchie*, and M. Chapsal *les œils de la soupe*.

Above all, Pécuchet was defeated by Jénin. What! *des z'hannetons* would be better than *des hannetons*, *des z'aricots* than *des haricots*—and under Louis XIV one pronounced *Roume* and Monsieur de *Lioune* instead of *Rome* and Monsieur de *Lionne*!

Littré dealt them the final blow by declaring that there had never been correct spelling and never would be.

From this they concluded that syntax is a fantasy and grammar an illusion.

At that time, too, a new rhetoric announced that one should write as one speaks, and that all will be well, provided one has felt and observed.

As they had felt and thought they had observed, they judged themselves capable of writing; a play is cramping by the narrowness of its form, but the novel allows more liberty. In order to write one they searched their memories.

Pécuchet remembered one of his office-chiefs, a very unpleasant fellow, and he hoped to get his revenge on him in a book.

Bouvard had known, at a wine shop, an old writing

master, who was a broken-down drunkard. Nothing could be more comic than he.

At the end of a week they decided to combine these two into one; they halted there, passed on to others: a woman who causes the ruin of her family—a woman, her husband and her lover—a woman who should be virtuous because of a physical malformation—an ambitious man, a wicked priest.

To these vague conceptions they tried to join things furnished by memory, trimmed and added to them.

Pécuchet was for sentiment and generalisation, Bouvard for imagery and colour; and they no longer saw eye to eye, each wondering that the other could be so narrow.

The philosophy known as aesthetics would perhaps settle their quarrels. A friend of Dumouchel's, a professor of philosophy, sent them a list of books on the subject. They worked separately and communicated their discoveries.

First, what is beauty?

For Schelling, it is the infinite expressing itself in the finite; for Reid, an occult quality; for Jouffroy, a fact incapable of analysis; for De Maistre, that which is pleasing to virtue; for Father André, that which gratifies reason.

And there exist several kinds of beauty: a beauty of science, geometry is beautiful; a beauty of behaviour, it cannot be denied that the death of Socrates was beautiful. A beauty of the animal kingdom: the beauty of the dog consists in its sense of smell. A pig could not be beautiful on account of its filthy habits; nor a snake, because it awakes in us ideas of baseness.

Flowers, butterflies, birds may be beautiful. In fact, the first condition of beauty is unity in variety; that is the root of the matter.

'Yet,' said Bouvard, 'two cross-eyes are more varied than two ordinary ones and produce a less good effect, as a rule.'

They entered upon the question of the sublime.

Certain objects are sublime in themselves, the thunder of a torrent, deep shadows, a storm-beaten tree. A character is beautiful when it triumphs, sublime when it struggles.

'I understand,' said Bouvard, 'beauty is beauty, the sublime is great beauty. How can they be distinguished?'

'By intuition,' replied Pécuchet.

'And where does intuition come from?'

'From taste.'

'And what's taste?'

It was defined as a special perception, swift judgment, the gift of perceiving certain relationships.

'So taste is taste; and all that says nothing about how to acquire it.'

It is necessary to observe the proper rules, but these rules vary; and however perfect a work may be, it will not be altogether free from reproach. Still, there is an indestructible beauty, whose laws we do not know, for its origin is a mystery.

Since one idea cannot be translated into all forms, we have to acknowledge boundaries between the arts, and, in each art, several kinds; but combinations occur where one style enters into another, or else fails in its object, and is no longer true.

Too exact an application of truth harms beauty, and a preoccupation with beauty hinders truth; yet without the ideal there is no truth. That is why types are of a more sustained reality than individual portraits. Besides, art deals only with illusion, but illusion depends on the observer, and is a relative, evanescent affair.

So they lost themselves in reasons. Bouvard believed in aesthetics less and less.

'If it isn't a joke its correctness will certainly be shown by examples. Listen, then.'

And he read some notes which had cost him much research.

'Bouhours accuses Tacitus of not having the simplicity that history demands. M. Droz, a professor, blames Shakespeare for his mixture of the serious and the farcical. Nisard, another professor, finds that André Chénier is, as a poet, inferior to the seventeenth century. Blair, an Englishman, deplores in Virgil the picture of the Harpies. Marmontel moans over the licence of Homer. Lamotte does not admit the immortality of his heroes. Vida is indignant at his metaphors. In a word, all constructors of a rhetoric, a poetic, or an aesthetic seem to me idiotic.'

'You're overdoing it,' said Pécuchet.

Doubts troubled him; for if second-rate intelligences (as Longinus remarks) cannot attain to faults, faults are the domain of the masters, and ought to be admired. That is going too far; yet the masters *are* the masters! He would have liked to make the doctrine agree with the works, the criticism with the poets, and capture the essential beauty; and these questions worried him so much that his bile was disturbed. He got jaundice.

It was at its worst when Marianne, Mme Bordin's cook, came to ask Bouvard to fix an appointment for her mistress.

The widow had not reappeared since the acting. Was this an advance? But why Marianne as intermediary? And Bouvard's imagination was roaming all night.

Next day at about two o'clock he was walking up and down the corridor, looking out of the window from time to time; there came a ring at the bell. It was the notary.

He crossed the court, mounted the staircase, placed himself in an armchair and, after exchanging preliminary courtesies, said that, tired of waiting for Mme Bordin, he had taken the initiative. She wanted to buy the Ecalles Farm.

Bouvard felt a sudden coldness and went into Pécuchet's room.

Pécuchet did not know what to reply. He was nervous, the doctor being due any minute.

At length Mme Bordin arrived. Her delay was explained by the elaboration of her toilet: a cashmere shawl, hat, kid gloves, the dress which accompanies important occasions.

After much circumlocution she asked whether three thousand francs would not be enough.

'An acre? Three thousand francs? Never!'

She blinked her eyelids: 'But for me!'

All three remained silent. M. de Faverges entered.

He carried under his arm, like a barrister, a morocco leather portfolio, and laying it on the table:

'They're pamphlets about reform—a burning question. But here's something that no doubt belongs to you,' and he held out to Bouvard the second volume of *Memoirs of the Devil*.

A moment ago Mélie had been reading it in the kitchen; and as one must keep an eye on such people's morals, he had thought proper to confiscate the work.

Bouvard had lent it to the maid. They talked about novels.

Mme Bordin liked them if they were not sad.

'Writers,' said M. de Faverges, 'depict life for us in flattering colours.'

'Well, they must depict,' Bouvard objected.

'In that case, it's only a matter of imitating life.'

'It's not a question of imitation.'

'At any rate, you'll admit that novels might fall into the hands of some young girl. I have a daughter myself.'

'A charming one!' said the notary, assuming his pose for the days when he drew up marriage contracts.

'Well, because of her, or, rather, the people about her, I forbid them in my house, for the common people, sir—'

'What about the common people?' asked Vaucorbeil, suddenly appearing at the door.

Pécuchet, who had recognised his voice, came to join the company.

'I maintain,' said the count, 'that some kinds of reading should be kept away from them.'

Vaucorbeil replied: 'Then you're not in favour of education?'

'Yes, I am. On the contrary.'

'While every day,' said Marescot, 'the Government's being attacked.'

'What's the harm?'

And the count and the doctor began to run down Louis-Philippe, recalling the Pritchard case, the September laws against the liberty of the press.

'And of the theatre,' added Pécuchet.

Marescot could contain himself no longer. 'It goes too far, your theatre.'

'There I agree with you,' said the count, 'plays that exalt suicide!'

'Suicide's a beautiful thing—witness Cato,' objected Pécuchet.

Without answering the argument, M. de Faverges condemned those works in which the most sacred things are mocked: family, property, and marriage.

'Well, what of Molière?' said Bouvard.

Marescot, a man of taste, retorted that Molière would not get by in these days, and was rather out of date too.

'At any rate,' said the count, 'Victor Hugo has been pitiless—yes, pitiless—to Marie-Antoinette, by pulling to pieces that type of queen under the disguise of Mary Tudor.'

'What!' cried Bouvard, 'an author like me hasn't the right—'

'No, sir, you haven't the right to show us crime without putting a corrective beside it, without giving us a lesson.'

Vaucorbeil, too, considered that art should have an aim: to try to improve the masses! 'Glorify science, our discoveries, patriotism!' and he praised Casimir Delavigne.

Mme Bordin eulogised the Marquis de Foudras. The notary replied:

'But what do you think of the language?'

'Language, what d'you mean?'

'He means style,' cried Pécuchet. 'Do you think his works are well written?'

'Certainly, most interesting.'

He shrugged his shoulders, and she coloured at the impertinence.

Several times Mme Bordin had tried to return to her business. It was too late to conclude it. She went out on Marescot's arm.

The count distributed his pamphlets, asking that they should be spread about.

Vaucorbeil was just going when Pécuchet stopped him.

'You're forgetting me, doctor.'

His yellow face was a lamentable sight, with his moustache and his black hair hanging down beneath a badly tied handkerchief.

'Purge yourself,' said the doctor, and giving him a couple of taps as though he were a child: 'Too many nerves; too artistic!'

This familiarity pleased Pécuchet. It reassured him, and when Bouvard and he were alone: 'You don't think it's serious?'

'No, of course not!'

They summed up what they had just heard. The morality

of art is confined for everyone within the limits which accommodate his interests. Literature is unpopular.

Then they turned over the count's pamphlets. All demanded universal suffrage.

'It seems to me,' said Pécuchet, 'that there will soon be an outbreak.' For he saw everything in black, perhaps because of his jaundice.

VI

On the morning of 25th February 1848 the news was brought to Chavignolles, by a wayfarer from Falaise, that Paris was under barricades, and the next day the proclamation of the Republic was posted up outside the town hall.

This great event astounded the inhabitants.

But when they learnt that the Supreme Court, the Court of Appeal, the Audit Office, the Chamber of Commerce, the Chamber of Notaries, the Order of Advocates, the Council of State, the University, the generals and M. de la Rochejacquelein himself were supporting the provisional government, they began to breathe more easily; and as trees of liberty were being planted in Paris, the municipal council decided they should have them in Chavignolles.

Bouvard made the offer of one, delighted as a patriot by the triumph of the people; as for Pécuchet, the fall of the royal house so exactly confirmed his predictions that he could not fail to be happy.

Gorju, zealously carrying out their orders, dug up one of the poplars that skirted the field over the Knoll, and transported it to 'Vaque's Walk,' at the entrance of the village, the place decided on.

At the hour of the ceremony all three were awaiting the procession.

There was a drum-beat, a silver cross appeared; then came two torches borne by choristers, and the curé with his stole, surplice, cope and biretta. Four choir boys accompanied him, a fifth carried the basin of holy water, and the sacristan followed.

He stepped up to the edge of the hole where the poplar stood with its trimming of tricolour ribbons. Opposite, could be seen the mayor and his two deputies, Beljambe and Marescot; then the notabilities, M. de Faverges, Vaucorbeil, Coulon the justice of the peace, an old fellow with a sleepy face; Heurtaux wore a forage cap, and Alexandre Petit, the new schoolmaster, had put on his frock-coat, a threadbare garment of green, his Sunday best. The firemen, commanded by Girbal, sword in hand, stood in single file; on the other side shone the white badges of several old shakos of the time of Lafayette—five or six, not more—the National Guard having fallen into disuse at Chavignolles. Peasants and their wives, workmen from neighbouring factories, children were huddled at the back; and the village policeman, Placquevent, five feet eight inches in height, kept an eye on them as he walked to and fro with folded arms.

The curé's address was like that of other priests on similar occasions. After thundering against kings, he glorified the Republic. Do we not say the Republic of letters, the Republic of Christ? What more innocent than the one, more beautiful than the other? Jesus Christ formulated our sublime symbol; the tree of the people was the tree of the cross. In order that Religion may bring forth fruits, she has need of charity, and in the name of charity the ecclesiastic implored his brothers not to commit any disorder, but to return home peaceably.

Then he sprinkled the tree, while he entreated the blessing of God—'May it grow, and recall to us our delivery from all servitude, and that brotherly love more gracious than the shade of its branches! Amen.'

Voices repeated *Amen*, and after a drum roll, the clergy,

singing a *Te Deum*, returned along the road to the church.

Their intervention had produced an excellent effect. The simple-minded saw in it a promise of happiness, the patriots a deference, a homage done to their principles.

Bouvard and Pécuchet thought they should have been thanked for their gift, or at least that it should have been alluded to; and they unbosomed themselves on the question to Faverges and the doctor.

What mattered such trifles! Vaucorbeil was delighted by the Revolution; the count, too. He execrated the Orleans family. They would see no more of them; good riddance! From now on, all for the people! And followed by Hurel, his factotum, he went to join the curé.

Foureau walked with his head down, between the notary and the innkeeper, irritated by the ceremony, afraid of a rising; and instinctively he turned to Placquevent, who, with the captain, was complaining of Girbal's inefficiency and the slack bearing of his men.

Some workmen passed along the road, singing the Marseillaise. In their midst Gorju brandished a stick; Petit accompanied them with eyes ablaze.

'I don't like that,' said Marescot. 'All the noise and excitement!'

'Oh, bless my soul,' replied Coulon, 'youth must have its fling!'

Foureau sighed.

'A queer sort of fun! and then the guillotine at the end!'

He had visions of the scaffold and was expecting atrocities.

Chavignolles felt the backwash of the agitation in Paris. The well-to-do took in newspapers. Every morning there was a crowd at the post office, and the postmistress would not have been able to get free of them but for the captain, who helped her on several occasions. Then they stood in the square, talking.

The first violent discussion was on the subject of Poland. Heurtaux and Bouvard called for its liberation.

M. de Faverges took a different view:

'What right have we to go there? It would bring the whole of Europe up in arms against us. No recklessness!'

And everyone being on his side, the two Poles kept silent.

On another occasion, Vaucorbeil defended Ledru-Rollin's circulars.

Foureau retorted with a reference to the forty-five centimes.

'But the Government,' said Pécuchet, 'has suppressed slavery.'

'What has slavery got to do with me?'

'Well, what about the abolition of the death penalty, in political cases?'

'Good God,' replied Foureau, 'you'd like to abolish everything. Still, who knows? Tenants are asking a good deal already.'

All the better! Landlords, according to Pécuchet, have been too much favoured. He that owns an estate . . .

Foureau and Marescot interrupted him, exclaiming that he was a communist.

'Me! A communist!'

And all talked at once. When Pécuchet proposed founding a club, Foureau had the hardihood to reply that they would never see one in Chavignolles.

Then Gorju demanded guns for the National Guard, the general vote having chosen him as instructor.

The only guns in the place were the firemen's. Girbal held on to them. Foureau was not anxious to give them up.

Gorju looked at him.

'They say, though, that I know how to handle one.'

For to his other occupations he added that of poaching, and often the mayor and the innkeeper would buy a hare or a rabbit from him.

'All right, take them!' said Foureau.

The same evening they began drilling.

It was on the green in front of the church. Gorju, in a blue smock, with a tie round his waist, went through the movements like clockwork. His voice, when he gave the commands, was rough.

'In with your bellies!'

And immediately Bouvard, holding his breath, drew in his abdomen, and stuck out his behind.

'Good God, I didn't tell you to make an arch!'

Pécuchet mixed up the files and the ranks, half-turn to the right, half-turn to the left. But the most pitiable figure was the schoolmaster. Weakly and thin, with a fringe of fair beard round his neck, he tottered under the weight of his gun, whose bayonet incommoded his neighbours.

They wore trousers of all colours, dirty baldricks, old regimentals that were too short, leaving their shirts visible at the waist; and each pretended to be 'too hard up to do anything else.' A subscription was opened to equip the poorer ones. Foureau was stingy, while the women played up well. Mme Bordin gave five francs, despite her hatred of the Republic. M. de Faverges equipped twelve men and never missed a parade. Afterwards he would take up his post at the grocer's and stand drinks to the first comers.

The Government's supporters began to flatter the lower orders; everything came after the working man. People intrigued for the advantage of a connection with them. They became lords.

The local workmen were, for the most part, weavers;

others were employed in the cotton mills or at a paper factory established recently.

Gorju fascinated them with his smart talk, taught them the back-kick, and took his cronies to drink at Mme Castillon's.

But the peasants were more numerous, and on market days M. de Faverges would walk round the market-place, inquiring into their wants, and trying to convert them to his ideas. They listened without answering, like old Gouy, ready to accept any government, provided the taxes came down.

By chattering, Gorju made a name for himself. Perhaps they would send him to the Assembly!

M. de Faverges was also thinking of it, while taking care not to give himself away. The conservatives were wavering between Foureau and Marescot. But as the notary kept to his office, Foureau was chosen; a bumpkin, an idiot. The doctor was furious.

Tired out by his routine, he longed for Paris, and it was his consciousness of a wasted life that gave him a melancholy air. A far greater career was going to open out for him; what a revenge! He drew up a declaration of faith, and went to read it to MM. Bouvard and Pécuchet.

They congratulated him; their doctrine was the same. However, they wrote better, knew more history, would cut as good a figure in the Chamber as he. Why not? But which of them should stand? And a tussle of modesty ensued.

Pécuchet would rather his friend than himself.

'No, it's your job; you've a better presence."

'Perhaps,' replied Bouvard, 'but you've more gumption,' and without solving the difficulty they drew up plans of campaign.

This vertigo of deputyship had seized others. The captain dreamed of it under his forage cap as he smoked his bulldog pipe, and the schoolmaster also in his form-room, and the curé between two prayers, so that at times he caught himself muttering, with his eyes towards heaven:

'Grant, O Lord, that I may be a deputy!'

The doctor, who had received encouragement, paid a visit to Heurtaux and explained his chances.

The captain did not stand on ceremony. Vaucorbeil was known, undoubtedly, but little cared for by his colleagues, and especially the chemists. Everyone would howl against him: the people did not want a gentleman; his best patients would leave him; and having weighed these arguments, the doctor regretted his foible.

As soon as he had gone, Heurtaux went to see Placquevent. Old soldiers oblige one another; but the policeman, although devoted to Foureau, bluntly refused to help him.

The curé satisfied M. de Faverges that the hour had not come. The Republic must be given time to settle down.

Bouvard and Pécuchet represented to Gorju that he would never be strong enough to overcome the coalition of peasants and shopkeepers, filled him with uncertainty, and robbed him of all confidence.

Through pride, Petit had made his ambition plain. Beljambe warned him that, if he failed, his dismissal was certain.

Finally the curé got orders from the bishop to keep quiet.

Then only Foureau remained.

Bouvard and Pécuchet were against him, recalling his bad grace over the guns, his opposition to the club, his reactionary views, his meanness—and they even persuaded Gouy that he wished to bring back the old regime.

Vague as the meaning of this word was in the peasant's mind, he detested it with a hatred that had accumulated in the hearts of his forefathers through ten centuries; and he turned against Foureau all his own and his wife's relatives, brothers-in-law, cousins, grand-nephews, a horde of people.

Gorju, Vaucorbeil and Petit continued the rout of the mayor; and the ground being thus cleared, Bouvard and Pécuchet, without anyone suspecting, were likely to succeed.

They drew lots as to who should stand. The draw achieved nothing, and they went to the doctor for advice.

He had some news for them: Flacardoux, editor of the *Calvados*, had announced his candidature. The disappointment of the two friends was complete; each resented it more on behalf of the other. But politics had warmed them. On election day they superintended the urns. Flacardoux got in.

The count had fallen back on the National Guard, without obtaining the epaulets of commander. The people of Chavignolles thought of naming Beljambe.

This bestowal of the public favour, always so whimsical and unpredictable, disturbed Heurtaux. He had neglected his duties, contenting himself with an occasional drill inspection and a few words of address. All the same, he thought it monstrous that people should prefer an innkeeper to an old captain of the Empire, and, after the invasion of the Chamber on 15th May, he said: 'If military ranks are given away like that in the capital, I shouldn't be surprised at anything!'

The reaction set in.

They believed in Louis Blanc's pineapple soup, Flocon's gold bed, the royal orgies of Ledru-Rollin, and as the provinces pretend to know all that goes on in Paris, the people of Chavignolles did not doubt these inventions, and believed the most absurd rumours.

One evening M. de Faverges came looking for the curé to tell him of the arrival in Normandy of the Comte de Chambord.

Joinville, according to Foureau, was getting ready with

his sailors to 'crush the Socialists.' Heurtaux maintained that soon Louis Bonaparte would be consul.

The factories were idle. Bands of destitute people wandered over the countryside.

One Sunday (it was in the early days of June) a policeman suddenly started off for Falaise. The workmen of Acqueville, Liffard, Pierre-Pont and St. Rémy were marching on Chavignolles.

The shutters were closed; the municipal council met and resolved, as a safeguard against catastrophes, to offer no resistance. The police were even kept in, with the injunction not to show themselves.

Soon there was heard a sound like the rumbling of a storm, then the song of the Girondins shook the windows; and men, arm-in-arm, passed along the road from Caen, dusty, sweating, and in rags. They filled the square. A great hubbub arose.

Gorju and two of his companions entered the hall. One, thin and wretched-looking, wore a knitted waistcoat, with the rosettes hanging down. The other, black as coal—a mechanic, no doubt—had stubbly hair, thick eyebrows and canvas shoes. Gorju carried his coat over his shoulder like a hussar.

All three remained standing, and the councillors, sitting round the table covered with a blue cloth, gazed at them, pale with anxiety.

'Citizens,' said Gorju, 'we must have work.'

The mayor trembled; his voice failed him.

Marescot answered in his place, that the council would consider the matter immediately; and when the comrades had gone out, they discussed several plans.

The first was to dig gravel.

In order to find a use for it, Girbal proposed a road from Angleville to Tournebu.

The Bayeux road served that very purpose.

They could clear out the pond; that was not a big enough job. (Or perhaps dig a second pond; but where?)

Langlois suggested making an embankment by Mortins in case of flood; according to Beljambe, it would be more useful to cut down the gorse. Impossible to reach a conclusion! With the object of appeasing the crowd, Coulon descended to the peristyle, and announced that they would prepare charity workshops.

'Charity? No thanks,' cried Gorju. 'Down with the aristos! We want the right to work!'

It was the question of the day, which he used as a means to popularity. They applauded.

In turning round, he elbowed Bouvard, whom Pécuchet had dragged there, and they entered into conversation. There was no hurry; the town hall was surrounded; the council could not escape them.

'Where'll you get money?' said Bouvard.

'From the rich! Besides, the Government will order public works.'

'And if there's no need for them?'

'They'll do for the future!'

'But wages will fall!' retorted Pécuchet. 'When there's a shortage of work, it means there are too many products already—and you're asking for more!'

Gorju bit his moustache. 'All the same . . . with the organisation of labour . . .'

'Then the Government will be master!'

Several men round them muttered: 'No! no! no more masters!'

Gorju grew angry. 'That doesn't matter! Workers should be given capital—or rather credit should be set up!'

'How?'

'Oh, I don't know, but credit ought to be set up!'

'That's enough,' said the mechanic, 'they're making fools of us, these fellows.'

And he climbed up the steps, threatening to break in the door.

There he was met by Placquevent, with right knee bent and clenched fists: 'Come one step nearer, and—'

The mechanic drew back. A hooting from the crowd penetrated the chamber; everyone rose with the desire to run away. No help had come from Falaise. They bewailed the count's absence. Marescot was twisting a quill, old Coulon groaned, Heurtaux worked himself up to make them send for the police.

'Order them to come!' said Foureau.

'I have no authority!'

Meanwhile, the noise grew louder, the square was covered with people; and everyone was looking at the first floor of the town hall when, at the middle window under the clock, Pécuchet appeared.

He had skipped up the back stairs, and aspiring to be a Lamartine, he started to harangue the people.

'Citizens!'

But his cap, his nose, his frock-coat, his whole person lacked distinction.

The man in the knitted waistcoat challenged him:

'Are you a workman?'

'No.'

'Employer, then?'

'Neither.'

'Be off then!'

'Why?' returned Pécuchet boldly.

And the next moment he disappeared, pinioned by the mechanic in the bay of the window. Gorju came to his assistance.

'Let him go! He's a decent chap!' They collared each other.

The door opened, and on the steps Marescot announced the decision of the council, suggested by Hurel.

The road from Tournebu should have a turning off to Angleville, leading to the Faverges manor.

It was a sacrifice which the parish took on itself in the interests of the working man.

They dispersed.

When Bouvard and Pécuchet got home, a sound of women's voices struck their ears. The servants and Mme Bordin were uttering cries, the widow loudest; and at sight of them:

'Oh, how lucky! I've been waiting for you for three hours! My poor garden hasn't a tulip left! filth all over the lawn! can't get rid of him!'

'Who?'

'Old Gouy.'

He had come with a cask of manure and dumped it in the middle of the lawn. 'He's digging now! Hurry up and stop him!'

'I'll come with you,' said Bouvard.

At the foot of the steps outside, a horse between the shafts of a tumbrel was nibbling at a spray of oleanders. The wheels, grazing the flower-beds, had crushed the box trees, broken a rhododendron, beaten down the dahlias— and clods of black dung, like molehills, embossed the lawn. Gouy was vigorously digging away.

One day Mme Bordin had said carelessly that she would like to have it turned up. Now he had set to work and, despite her orders, would not leave off. This was the way in which he understood the right to work, Gorju's speech having turned his head.

He went away only after violent threats from Bouvard.

Mme Bordin, by way of compensation, did not pay him for his labour and kept the manure. She was sagacious; the doctor's wife, and even the notary's, though of higher social rank, respected her.

The charity workshops lasted a week. No trouble occurred. Gorju had left the neighbourhood.

However, the National Guard was always about: parade on Sundays, several route marches, and patrols every night. They disturbed the village.

They rang front-door bells for fun; they made their way into bedrooms where married couples were snoring on the same pillow, then made broad jokes, and the husband would get up to bring them drinks. Afterwards they would return to the guard-room to play a hundred up at dominoes, would drink cider, eat cheese, and the man on duty at the door, bored to death, would peep in every moment. Thanks to Beljambe's slackness, indiscipline ruled.

When the disturbances of June broke out, everyone was in favour of 'flying to the relief of Paris,' but Foureau could not leave his duties, Marescot his office, the doctor his patients, Girbal his firemen. M. de Faverges was at Cherbourg. Beljambe kept his bed. The captain grumbled: 'They've no use for me, worse luck!' And Bouvard had the wisdom to restrain Pécuchet.

The patrols were extended in the country.

There were panics caused by the shadow of a rick or the shapes of branches. On one occasion the whole National Guard took to flight; in the moonlight they had seen a man under an apple tree with a gun, pointed straight at them.

Another time, on a dark night, the patrol, halting under a beech tree, heard someone in front.

'Who goes there?'

No answer.

They let him go on his way, following at a distance,

for he might have a pistol or a life-preserver; but when they reached the village within call of help, the dozen men of the platoon threw themselves on him all at once, shouting, 'Your papers!' He was hustled and covered with abuse. The men came out from the guard-room and dragged him in, and by the light of the candle burning on the stove they at last recognised Gorju.

A wretched greatcoat of lasting was thrown anyhow over his shoulder. His toes showed through the holes in his boots. Scratches and bruises were making his face bleed. He was terribly emaciated, and rolled his eyes like a wolf.

Foureau, arriving in a hurry, asked him how he came to be under the beech, what was his object in returning to Chavignolles, how he had spent his time during the past six weeks.

That was no business of theirs. He was a free man.

Placquevent searched him for cartridges. For the time being he would be locked up.

Bouvard intervened.

'It's no use,' said the mayor. 'We know your opinions.'

'All the same—'

'Be careful! I give you warning! Be careful!'

Bouvard did not persist.

Then Gorju turned to Pécuchet: 'And you, master, haven't you a word to say for me?'

Pécuchet hung his head, as though he had doubts of his innocence.

The poor devil smiled bitterly:

'I defended you, though.'

At daybreak, two policemen took him to Falaise.

He was not tried before a court martial, but sentenced by the magistrates to three months' imprisonment for the offence of uttering words tending to the subversion of society.

From Falaise he wrote to his old employers to send him quickly a good reference; and as their signature had to be witnessed by the mayor or his deputy, they preferred to ask this small service of Marescot.

They were shown into a dining-room decorated with plates in old faience; a buhl clock occupied the narrowest panel. On the mahogany table, which was without a cloth, there were two napkins, a tea-urn and cups. Mme Marescot crossed the room in a dressing-gown of blue cashmere. She was a Parisian, bored with the country. Then the notary came in, with a cap in one hand, a newspaper in the other; and at once, in the most friendly manner, affixed his seal—although their protégé was a dangerous character.

'Really,' said Bouvard, 'for a few words—'

'But words lead to crimes, my dear sir, I assure you!'

'And yet,' said Pécuchet, 'how can we draw a line between the innocence or guilt of a phrase? Something that's forbidden now will be commended later on,' and he censured the harshness with which the insurgents were being treated.

Marescot naturally advanced the protection of society, the public safety, the majesty of the law.

'Excuse me,' said Pécuchet, 'the rights of the individual are as respectworthy as those of the community, and you've nothing to oppose him with, except force—if he turns your maxim against you.'

Instead of answering, Marescot raised his eyebrows scornfully. So long as he continued to draw up his documents, and live among his plates in his pleasant little home, injustices of every kind could take place without moving him. He was busy and asked to be excused.

His doctrine of public safety had made them angry. Conservatives now talked like Robespierre.

Another matter for astonishment: Cavaignac was becoming unpopular. The Mobile Guard was open to suspicion.

Ledru-Rollin was done for, even in Vaucorbeil's estimation. The debates on the constitution interested no one, and on the 10th of December all the inhabitants of Chavignolles voted for Bonaparte.

The six million votes made Pécuchet feel coldly towards the people, and Bouvard and he studied the question of universal suffrage.

Since it belongs to everybody, it cannot possess intelligence. An ambitious man will always be leader, others will follow him like a flock, the electors not being required even to be literate; that is why according to Pécuchet there had been so many frauds in the presidential election.

'I don't agree,' replied Bouvard, 'rather I believe in the folly of the people. Think of all those who buy the Vitaliser, Dupuytren's hair restorer, lady's lotions, etc. These boobies form the mass of the electors and we submit to their will. Why can't one make an income of three thousand francs out of rabbits? Because too much overcrowding will make them die. In the same way, wherever there is a crowd, germs of stupidity, inherent there, will develop, and result in incalculable effects.'

'Your scepticism frightens me,' said Pécuchet.

Later on, in the spring, they met M. de Faverges, who informed them of the expedition to Rome. We should not attack the Italians, but should require guarantees. Otherwise our influence would be lost. Nothing was more legitimate than this intervention.

Bouvard stared. 'In connection with Poland, you maintained the opposite!'

'It's no longer the same.' Now it was a question of the Pope.

And when M. de Faverges said, 'We wish, we intend, we count on,' he represented a group.

Bouvard and Pécuchet were disgusted by the minority

quite as much as by the majority. The common people, in fact, were as bad as the aristocracy.

The right of intervention seemed a shabby trick. They sought for its principles in Calvo, Martens, Vatel—and Bouvard summed up:

'You intervene to put back a prince on the throne, to emancipate a people, or as a precaution, when there's danger ahead. In either case, it's an infringement of someone else's rights, an abuse of force, a hypocritical violence!'

'And yet,' said Pécuchet, 'nations, like men, are responsible.'

'Perhaps,' and Bouvard fell to dreaming.

Soon the expedition to Rome started.

At home, from hatred of subversive ideas, the leaders of the Parisian middle-class sacked two printing works. The great party of law and order had been formed.

Its chief members in the neighbourhood were the count, Foureau, Marescot, the curé. Every day, at about four o'clock, they stalked up and down the square, discussing the news. The main business was to distribute pamphlets. The titles were not without pungency: 'It is God's Will'— 'The Equal-sharer'—'An End to Muddle'—'Where are we going?' Best of all were the dialogues in rustic style, with oaths and bad French, to improve the minds of the peasants. Under a new law, the hawking of pamphlets was in the hands of the prefects; and Proudhon had just been clapped into the Sainte-Pélagie prison—a tremendous victory.

The trees of liberty were everywhere pulled down. Chavignolles obeyed the order. With his own eyes, Bouvard saw bits of his poplar on a wheelbarrow. They helped to keep the policemen warm—and the stump was offered to the curé, who had blessed it. What irony!

The schoolmaster did not hide his way of thinking.

Bouvard and Pécuchet congratulated him on it, one day as they were passing his door.

On the morrow he paid them a visit, which they returned at the end of the week.

Day was falling, the children had just left, and the schoolmaster in sleeve-guards was sweeping the yard. His wife, with a Madras handkerchief round her head, was giving suck to an infant. A little girl hid behind her petticoat; an ugly brat was playing at her feet; the water from the washing she had been doing in the kitchen flowed in front of the house.

'You see,' said the teacher, 'how the Government's treating us.' And at once he attacked the evil of capitalism. Wealth should be democratised, raw materials set free.

'I ask for nothing better,' said Pécuchet.

At least they ought to have recognised the right to public assistance.

'Yet another right!' said Bouvard.

Anyhow, the provisional government had been chicken-hearted in not insisting on fraternity.

'Then try to establish it!'

As it was no longer light, Petit roughly ordered his wife to bring a candle to the study.

Lithographs of radical orators were fastened with pins to the plaster walls. A bookshelf stood on a deal desk. There was a chair to sit on, a stool, an old soap-box; he affected to laugh at them. But poverty had stamped his cheeks, his narrow temples showed the stubbornness of a ram, an intractable pride. He would never yield.

'Besides, here's what keeps me going!'

It was a pile of newspapers on a shelf, and in feverish words he declared the articles of his faith: disarmament of the troops, abolition of the magistracy, equal wages, a levelling process by which the Golden Age should be reached under the form of the Republic, with a dictator at the head—a fellow who would get you there quickly!

Then he reached out for a bottle of anisette and three glasses, in order to propose the toast of the hero, the immortal victim, the great Robespierre!

At the doorway appeared the black cassock of the curé.

Having briskly saluted the company he addressed the teacher, and said in almost a whisper:

'How is our business about Saint Joseph getting on?'

'They have given nothing,' replied the schoolmaster.

'That's your fault!'

'I've done what I could!'

'Oh, really?'

Bouvard and Pécuchet discreetly rose. Petit made them sit down, and addressing the curé:

'Is that all?'

Abbé Jeufroy hesitated; then with a smile which softened the rebuke:

'It's said you are rather neglecting sacred history.'

'Oh, sacred history!' exclaimed Bouvard. 'What fault have you to find with it, sir?'

'Oh, none, none. Only there are perhaps more useful things to learn than the anecdotes of Jonah and the Kings of Israel!'

'You're not obliged to learn them,' replied the priest dryly.

And without regard for the strangers, or perhaps on their account:

'The catechism hour is too short.'

Petit shrugged his shoulders.

'Be careful. You'll lose your boarders!'

The ten francs per month for these pupils were the best part of his income. But the cassock exasperated him:

'So much the worse, have your revenge!'

'A man of my character does not think of revenge,' said the priest unmoved. 'Only I would remind you that the Act of the 15th of March gives us the supervision of primary education.'

'Don't I know it!' cried the teacher. 'It's even given to police inspectors. Why not to village constables? That would make it complete.'

And he sank on to the stool, biting his fingers, repressing his rage, stifled by a sense of impotence.

The ecclesiastic touched him lightly on the shoulder.

'I did not mean to annoy you, my friend. Keep calm. Have a little sense! Here is Easter coming; I hope you will set an example by going gladly to communion.'

'That's really too much! I—I submit to such mummeries?'

At this blasphemy the priest turned pale. His eyes flashed, his mouth trembled.

'Silence, unhappy man! Silence! . . . And it's his wife who looks after the church linen!'

'Well, what about it? What's she done?'

'She is never at Mass. Like yourself, for that matter!'

'Well, you can't dismiss a schoolmaster for that!'

'He can be transferred.'

The priest said no more. He was at the end of the room, in shadow. Petit sat musing, with his head on his chest.

They would arrive at the other end of France, their last sou eaten up by the journey, and there they would find again, under different names, the same curé, the same rector, the same prefect—all, even to the cabinet minister, were links in a chain dragging him down. He had already received one warning, others would follow. And then? In a sort of dream he saw himself walking along the highway, with a knapsack on his back, those he loved beside him, his hand stretched out towards a postchaise!

At that moment his wife was seized with a fit of coughing in the kitchen; the baby began to wail and the boy cried.

'Poor children!' said the priest in a soft voice.

The father thereupon burst into sobs.

'Yes, yes, I'll do anything you like!'

'I count on you,' replied the curé. And bowing to them: 'Good night, gentlemen!'

The schoolmaster remained with his face in his hands. He pushed Bouvard away.

'No, leave me alone! I wish I were dead! I'm a miserable wretch.'

The two friends reached home, congratulating themselves on their independence. The power of the clergy frightened them.

Now it was applied to strengthening the social order. The Republic would soon disappear.

Three million electors were excluded from universal suffrage. The caution-money required from newspapers was raised, the censorship re-established. There was talk of extending it to the serial stories. Classical philosophy was considered dangerous. The middle-classes preached the dogma of materialism; and the people seemed satisfied.

Those in the country returned to their old masters.

M. de Faverges, who had property in the Eure, was made a member of the Legislature, and his re-election to the General Council of Calvados was a foregone conclusion.

He was moved to give a luncheon to the notabilities of the district.

The hall where three servants were waiting to take their overcoats, the billiard-room and the two drawing-rooms opening into one another, the plants in china vases, the bronzes on the mantelpiece, the gilt wreaths on the plaster, the thick curtains, the big armchairs—all this luxury at once struck them as a politeness on their account; and when they entered the dining-room, at the sight of the table covered with viands in silver dishes, the array of glasses before each plate, the side-dishes here and there, and a salmon in the midst, every face brightened.

There were seventeen in the party, including two prosperous farmers, the sub-prefect of Bayeux, and a man from Cherbourg. M. de Faverges begged his guests to excuse the countess, who was prevented by a headache, and after some commendation of the pears and grapes which filled four baskets at the corners, they discussed the great news: the project of a descent on England by Changarnier.

Heurtaux wanted it as a soldier, the curé from hatred of Protestants, Foureau in the interests of trade.

'You're expressing,' said Pécuchet, 'the sentiments of the Middle Ages.'

'The Middle Ages had their good points,' replied Marescot. 'For instance, our cathedrals.'

'Still, sir, the abuses—'

'Never mind, the revolution would not have come—'

'Ah, the revolution! There's the root of all the evil,' said the ecclesiastic with a sigh.

'But everyone contributed to it, and (excuse me, M. le Comte) the nobility itself by its alliance with the philosophers!'

'What could you expect? Louis XVIII legalised robbery. Since then the parliamentary system has sapped our foundations—'

A joint of roast beef appeared, and for several minutes nothing was heard except the sound of forks and moving jaws, and the steps of the servants on the parquet floor, and these two words repeated: 'Madeira! Sauterne!'

The conversation was resumed by the gentleman from Cherbourg. How were they going to halt on the brink of the abyss?

'Among the Athenians,' said Marescot, 'among the Athenians, with whom we have much in common, Solon checkmated the democrats by raising the electoral census.'

'Better,' said Hurel, 'suppress the Chamber; all disorder comes from Paris.'

'We must decentralise,' said the notary.

'On a big scale,' added the count.

According to Foureau, the local authorities should have absolute control, even to the extent of refusing entrance to travellers, if they thought fit.

And while one dish followed another—chicken with sauce, crayfish, mushrooms, green salad, roast larks—many subjects were dealt with: the best system of taxes, the advantages of extensive farming, the abolition of the death penalty; the sub-prefect did not fail to cite the wit's charming saying: *Que Messieurs les Assassins commencent!*

Bouvard was surprised at the contrast between the surroundings and what had been said—for one always feels that words should correspond with environment, and that high ceilings are made for great thoughts. Nevertheless, he was flushed at dessert, and saw the fruit-dishes through a fog.

They had drunk Bordeaux, Burgundy and Malaga— M. de Faverges, who knew the people he was dealing with, had the champagne uncorked. The guests, touching glasses, drank to his success at the election, and it was after three when they moved into the smoking-room to take coffee.

A cartoon in the *Charivari* was spread out on a side-table between copies of the *Univers*; it showed a citizen, the flaps of whose frock-coat revealed a tail ending in an eye. Marescot explained it. There was a good deal of laughter. They consumed their liqueurs, and their cigar ash dropped on the silk upholstery of the furniture. The abbé, wishing to convince Girbal, attacked Voltaire. Coulon fell asleep. M. de Faverges declared his devotion to Chambord.

'The bees are an argument for monarchy.'

'But the ants for the Republic!'

However, the doctor was no longer a Republican.

'You're right,' said the sub-prefect, 'the form of government matters little.'

'So long as there's liberty,' objected Pécuchet.

'An honest man has no need of it,' replied Foureau. 'I don't make speeches myself! I'm not a journalist, and I tell you France wants to be governed with a mailed fist.'

They all called for a deliverer.

And going out, Bouvard and Pécuchet heard M. de Faverges say to the Abbé Jeufroy:

'We must re-establish obedience! Authority perishes if it becomes a matter for discussion. The Divine Right, that's the only thing!'

'Exactly, Monsieur le Comte.'

The pale rays of an October sun lengthened behind the woods, a moist wind was blowing; and as they walked over the dead leaves, they breathed like men who have been set free.

All they had been unable to say escaped them in exclamations.

'What idiots! what baseness! how can one believe in such obstinacy! To begin with, what is the meaning of Divine Right?'

Dumouchel's friend, the professor who had enlightened them on aesthetics, replied to their question in a learned letter.

The theory of divine right was formulated in the reign of Charles II by the Englishman Filmer.

Here it is:

'The Creator gave the first man sovereignty over the world. It was transmitted to his descendants, and the power of the King emanates from God. "He is his image," writes Bossuet. The paternal rule accustoms us to the domination of one man. Kings have been made after the model of fathers.

'Locke refuted this doctrine. The paternal is distinct from the monarchic power, every subject having the same right over his children as the monarch over his. Royalty exists only by the will of the people, and even election was evoked in the coronation ceremony at which two bishops, pointing to the King, asked the nobles and the peasants if they would accept him as such.

'Therefore authority comes from the people. They have the right "to do whatever they like," says Helvetius; "to change the constitution," says Vatel; "to revolt against injustice," argue Glafey, Hotman, Mably, etc.—and St. Thomas Aquinas authorises them to deliver themselves from a tyrant. They are even, says Jurieu, dispensed from the need of being in the right.'

Astonished at this axiom, they opened Rousseau's *Social Contract.*

Pécuchet went on to the end, then closing his eyes and throwing back his head, made an analysis of it.

'We assume an agreement whereby the individual forfeits his liberty.

'At the same time the people agreed to protect him against the inequalities of Nature, and gave him rights over his possessions.

'Where is the proof of the contract?

'Nowhere! and the community offers no guarantee. The citizens shall occupy themselves exclusively with politics. But since work must be done, Rousseau advocates slavery. The sciences have ruined the human race. The theatre corrupts, money is fatal, and the State should impose a religion under pain of death.'

'What!' they said to themselves, 'and this is the pontiff of democracy!'

All reformers have copied him—and they got hold of Morant's *Examination of Socialism*.

The first chapter expounds the doctrine of Saint-Simon.

At the top the Father, both Pope and Emperor. Abolition of inheritance, all personal and real estate forming a social base, which shall be exploited hierarchically. Manufacturers shall have charge of public funds. But there is nothing to be afraid of; we shall have as a ruler 'the one who loves us best.'

One thing is missing—Woman. On woman's liberation depends the safety of the world.

'I don't understand it.'

'Nor do I.'

And they tackled Fourierism.

All evils come from restraint. Let attraction be free, and harmony will be established.

The soul contains a dozen principal passions: five egoistic, four animal, three distributive. They belong—the first to the individual, the next to groups, the last to groups of groups, or series, the whole of which is a phalanx, a society of eighteen hundred persons, living in a palace. Each morning, carriages take the workmen into the country, and bring them back in the evening. There are banners, festivals, and cakes to eat. Every woman, if she likes, can have three men: a husband, a lover and the sire of her children. For bachelors, dancing-girls are provided.

'That would suit me!' said Bouvard. And he lost himself in dreams of the harmonised world.

By regulation of climate, the earth will become more beautiful; by inter-racial breeding, human life will be extended. We shall control the clouds as now we control lightning; at night it will rain on the towns to scour them. Ships will cross thawed polar seas beneath the aurora borealis. For everything is produced by the conjunction of two fluids, male and female, spouting from the poles, and the aurora borealis is a symptom of the planet in rut, a prolific emission.

'That's beyond me,' said Pécuchet.

After Saint-Simon and Fourier, the problem is narrowed down to questions of wages.

In the interests of the working classes Louis Blanc would abolish export trade; Lafarelle would introduce machines; another would take the tax off drink, or reform the system of guild masters, or distribute soup. Proudhon imagines a uniform tariff and claims for the State a monopoly of sugar.

'Your socialists,' said Bouvard, 'are always asking to tyrannise.'

'Oh no!'

'Yes, they are!'

'You're absurd!'

'And you're disgusting!'

They sent for the works which they knew only from extracts. Bouvard marked a number of passages, and showing them:

'Read for yourself! They offer us as examples the Essenes, the Moravian brotherhood, the Jesuits of Paraguay, and even the prison regime.

'Among the Icarians, lunch takes twenty minutes, women give birth in hospitals; as for books, printing is forbidden without the authority of the Republic.'

'But Cabet is a half-wit.'

'Now here we have Saint-Simon: publicists will have to submit their works to a committee of manufacturers. And from Pierre Leroux: the law will compel citizens to listen to an orator. And from Auguste Comte: priests will bring up the young, will have control of all spiritual matters, and possess the right to regulate procreation.'

These documents distressed Pécuchet. In the evening, at dinner, he replied.

'That there are some absurdities among Utopians, I agree; yet they deserve our love. The hideousness of the world appals them, and, in the hope of making it better, they have suffered all. Remember More decapitated, Campanella put seven times to torture, Buonarotti with a chain round his neck, Saint-Simon dying of want; many others. They could have lived in peace, but no, they walked along the chosen path with their heads among the stars, like heroes.'

'Do you believe that the world,' said Bouvard, 'will be changed, thanks to some gentleman's theories?'

'What does it matter?' answered Pécuchet. 'The time has come to leave off cowering in egoism. Let's look for a better system!'

'What, you think you'll find one?'

'Certainly!'

'You?'

And in the laughter that seized Bouvard, his shoulders and his stomach shook in concord. Redder than the preserves, with a napkin under his arm-pits, he repeated: 'Ho! Ho! Ho!' in an irritating manner.

Pécuchet left the room, banging the door.

Germaine called to him all over the house; and he was found in the depth of his room on an easy-chair, without fire or candle, his cap down over his eyes. He was not ill, but was giving himself up to his reflections.

The squabble was over; they recognised that their studies lacked a basis—political economy.

They inquired into supply and demand, capital and wages, imports, prohibitions.

One night Pécuchet was awakened by the squeaking of a boot in the corridor. In the evening, as usual, he had himself shot all the bolts. He called to Bouvard, who was sound asleep.

They remained rigid beneath the sheets. The noise did not begin again.

The servants, whom they questioned, had heard nothing.

But as they walked in the garden, they noticed a footprint in the middle of the border near the lattice, and two bars of the trellis were broken. Someone had evidently climbed over.

The policeman had to be notified.

As he was not at the town hall, Pécuchet proceeded to the grocer's.

Whom should he see at the back of the shop, by Placquevent's side, among the drinkers, but Gorju! Gorju dressed up like a gentleman and treating the company!

But there were other things more important.

They came to the question of progress.

Bouvard did not doubt its existence in the domain of science. But, in literature, it is less obvious; and, though prosperity may increase, the splendour of life disappears.

Pécuchet, to convince him, took a piece of paper. 'I trace an oblique undulating line. If you walked along it, you would lose sight of the horizon, each time it descends. But it rises again, and, in spite of its ups and downs, you will reach the peak. Such is the nature of progress.'

Mme Bordin entered.

It was the 3rd of December 1851. She was holding a newspaper.

Side by side, they swiftly read the appeal to the people, the dissolution of the Chamber, the imprisonment of the deputies.

Pécuchet became white. Bouvard looked at the widow.

'What? you don't say anything?'

'What do you expect me to do?' They had forgotten

to offer her a chair. 'I came here in the hope of doing you a pleasure. Ah, you're not very amiable to-day.' And she went off, shocked at their rudeness.

Surprise had struck them dumb. They went into the village to spread their indignation.

Marescot, who received them in the midst of his deeds, was of a different opinion. It was a good thing that an end had been put to the chattering of the Chamber. Henceforth they would have a business government.

Beljambe knew nothing of what had happened, and cared less.

In the market they found Vaucorbeil.

The doctor had finished with all such matters. 'You're wrong to worry about them.'

Foureau passed by, saying, with a sneer: 'The democrats are done for!' And the captain, on Girbal's arm, shouted in the distance: 'Long live the Emperor!'

But Petit would understand them, and, Bouvard having tapped on the window, the schoolmaster left his class.

He found it extremely amusing that Thiers should be in prison. That would give the people their revenge. 'Ah, my fine deputies, now it's your turn.'

Chavignolles approved of the fusillade on the boulevards. No mercy for the vanquished, no pity for the victims! The rebel is always a scoundrel!

'Let's thank Providence,' said the curé, 'and after that, Louis Bonaparte. He surrounds himself with the most distinguished men. The Count de Faverges will be made a senator.'

Next day they had a visit from Placquevent.

The gentlemen had been talking a great deal. He advised them to keep quiet.

'Do you want to know my opinion?' asked Pécuchet. 'Since the middle classes are hooligans, the workers jealous, the priests servile, and since, after all, the people accept every sort of tyrant, so long as he leaves their snouts in the trough, Napoleon is right! Let him gag the mob, stamp it under foot, crush it! That will never be too great a penalty for its hatred of the right, its cowardice, its ineptitude, its blindness!'

Bouvard was thinking: 'Progress—what a joke.' He added, 'And politics—a fine mess!'

'It's not a science,' replied Pécuchet. 'Military tactics is better: one can at least foresee what's going to happen. Suppose we start on it?'

'No, thanks!' answered Bouvard. 'I'm sick of everything. Let's sell this shanty and go, "to the sound of God's thunder, among the savages!"'

'As you please!'

Mélie, in the yard, was drawing water.

The wooden pump had a long handle. To lower it, she was bending her hips, and one could see her blue stockings up to the top of her calves. Then, with a quick gesture, she lifted her right arm, at the same time turning her head a little, and Pécuchet, as he watched her, was aware of something altogether fresh, a charm, a delight without bounds.

VII

Gloomy days began.

They no longer pursued their studies, for fear of disillusionment; the people of Chavignolles cold-shouldered them, the privileged newspapers gave them no information, and their loneliness was unbroken, their idleness complete.

Sometimes they opened a book, only to close it again—what was the use? On other days they resolved to tidy the garden, but at the end of a quarter of an hour they would be worn out; or to go and inspect their farm, but they came back disheartened; or to give an eye to the housekeeping, which set Germaine protesting, and they abandoned the idea.

Bouvard wanted to compile the catalogue of the museum, then condemned the curios as absurdities.

Pécuchet borrowed Langlois's duck rifle to shoot larks; the piece burst at the first shot, nearly killing him.

Then they existed in that monotony of country life, so heavy when the grey sky folds its languor about a spirit without hope. One hears the steps of a man in clogs passing along the wall, or the raindrops falling from the roof to the ground. From time to time a dead leaf grazes the windowpane, then twirls round and vanishes. The vague sound of bells is borne upon the wind. Deep within the shed a cow moos.

They yawned in each other's faces, consulted the calendar, gazed at the clock, waited for their meals; and the horizon was ever the same: fields in front, to the right the church, to the left a screen of poplars; their tops swayed in the mist unceasingly in mournful fashion.

Habits that they had tolerated became a burden. Pécuchet was irritating with his trick of placing his handkerchief on the tablecloth; Bouvard no longer quitted his pipe and swung his body as he talked. Disputes arose over the dishes, or the quality of the butter. While they sat together their thoughts went different ways.

Something had happened to upset Pécuchet.

Two days after the disturbance at Chavignolles, as he was taking his disappointed political ambitions for a walk, he came to a deep lane overarched with feathery elms, and heard behind him a voice crying, 'Stop!'

It was Mme Castillon. She was running by the hedge on the other side, without seeing him. A man, who was walking in front of her, turned round. It was Gorju; and they met about a yard from Pécuchet, the row of trees separating them from him.

'Is it true,' she asked, 'that you're going off to fight?'

Pécuchet shrank into the ditch in order to listen.

'Well yes,' said Gorju, 'I'm going off to fight. What's it matter to you?'

'How can you ask!' she cried, wringing her hands. 'Suppose you're killed, my darling! Stay here!' And her blue eyes, even more than her words, beseeched him.

'Leave me alone! I've got to go!'

She laughed in anger. 'So the other's given you permission?'

'Don't speak about her!' He raised his clenched fist.

'No, dear, all right. I'll be quiet, I won't say anything.' And the large tears rolled down her cheeks into the frill of her collar.

It was midday. The sun was shining over the country,

which was covered with yellow corn. Far away, the canopy of a wagon was slowly slipping out of sight. A torpor was abroad upon the air: not a bird's cry, not an insect's hum. Gorju had cut a switch, and was peeling the bark. Mme Castillon did not raise her head.

She was dreaming, poor woman, of her empty sacrifices, the debts she had paid, her pledges for the future on his account, her lost good fame. Instead of complaining she recalled to him the early days of their love, when she went, every night, to join him in the barn; and how once her husband, thinking that a robber was there, had let off a pistol-shot from the window. The bullet was still in the wall. 'The moment I saw you, I thought you were as handsome as a prince. I love your eyes, your voice, your walk, your smell!' She added, in a lower tone, 'I'm mad for your body!'

He smiled, flattered in his pride.

She held him, with her two hands pressed to his sides and her head thrown back, as if in worship.

'Dear heart! Dear heart! My angel! My darling! Tell me what you want? Money? I'll get you some. It was my fault. I loved you. Forgive me! Get yourself clothes at the tailor's, drink champagne, run after the girls—I'll let you do anything, anything!' With a final effort she murmured: 'Even her! So long as you'll come back to me!'

He bent over her mouth, with one arm round her hips to stop her falling, and she sobbed, 'My own! My love! How handsome you are! Oh, God, how handsome you are!'

Pécuchet, motionless, and up to his chin in the ditch, watched them, breathing hard.

'No fainting, now!' said Gorju. 'It would be maddening if I missed the diligence. There's a grand plot on foot, and I'm in it! Give me something to stand the conductor a drink.'

She took five francs from her purse. 'You can pay it back later on. But be patient. Just think what a time he's been paralysed! If you like, we could go to the Chapel of Croix-Janval, and there, my dearest, I'd swear, in front of the Holy Virgin, to marry you the moment he's dead.'

'Oh, that husband of yours will never die!'

Gorju had turned on his heels. She caught up with him, and, clinging to his shoulders:

'Let me go with you! I'll be your servant. You need someone. But don't go! Don't leave me! I'd rather be dead! Kill me!'

She dragged herself at his knees, trying to clutch his hands and kiss them; her bonnet fell off, then her comb, and her short locks tumbled. They were white at the temples, and as she gazed up, sobbing, red-eyed and swollen-lipped, fury possessed him, and he spurned her.

'Clear off, you old hag! Good-bye!'

She got up, snatched off the gold cross hanging from her neck, and, flinging it at him:

'Take it, then, you beast!'

Gorju went off, striking at the leaves on the trees with his switch.

Mme Castillon stopped weeping. With hanging jaw and dull eyes, she stood without moving, frozen in despair; no longer a human being, but a thing in ruin.

What he had just surprised was, for Pécuchet, the discovery of a new world—an entire new world—which contained dazzling radiances, riotous bursts of blossom, oceans, tempests, treasures, and abysses of infinite depth. What matter that it was charged with terror! He dreamed of love, was eager to feel it like her, like him to inspire it.

Still, he loathed Gorju, and in the guard-room found it difficult not to give his thoughts away.

Mme Castillon's lover humiliated him with his slender waist, his symmetrical side-whiskers, his glossy beard and conqueror's bearing. His own hair stuck to his scalp like a wet wig; his frame, in its overcoat, resembled a bolster, two of his canine teeth were missing, and his expression was hard. He considered Heaven unjust, felt himself an outcast, and his friend no longer loved him.

He was deserted every evening. Nothing had prevented Bouvard, since his wife died, from taking another, who would then have been pampering him and looking after his house. Now he was too old to think of it.

But he looked at himself in the glass. His cheeks still kept their colour, his hair was as curly as ever, not a tooth had gone, and, at the notion that he was yet capable of pleasing, he had a return of his youth. Mme Bordin rose in his memory. She had first made advances to him after the burning of the ricks, again at their dinner-party, then in the museum during the acting, and finally she had come, without bearing a grudge at their rudeness, on three Sundays running: so he went to pay her a call, then went again, and promised himself that he would seduce her.

After the day when Pécuchet had observed the little servant drawing water, he spoke to her more freely, and whether she was sweeping the corridor, spreading the washing, or cleaning saucepans, he could not get over his delight at seeing her, himself surprised at his emotion, as though still a boy. He suffered fevers and languors, and was tormented by the remembrance of Mme Castillon embracing Gorju.

He questioned Bouvard on the methods practised by libertines in order to capture women.

'They give them presents, and take them to restaurants.'

'Quite so; but after that?'

'Some pretend to faint, so as to be carried to the sofa, others drop their handkerchiefs on the floor. The best frankly arrange a meeting.' And Bouvard spread himself in descriptions which fired Pécuchet's imagination like obscene pictures.

'The first rule is not to believe a word they say. I've known women who, under the guise of saints, were absolute Messalinas! Above all, you must be bold!'

But boldness is not to be had for the asking. Every day Pécuchet put off his decision, intimidated further by the presence of Germaine.

Hoping that she would give notice, he set her more work to do, noted the times when she was fuddled, remarked loudly on her slovenliness, her laziness, and succeeded so well that they got rid of her.

Then Pécuchet was free!

With what impatience he awaited Bouvard's departure! What flutterings of the heart, when the door had closed!

Mélie was working at a small table near the window by the light of the candle; from time to time she broke the cotton with her teeth, then screwed up her eyes, to thread her needle.

First, he wanted to know what men pleased her. Was it, for example, Bouvard's sort? Not at all; she preferred them thin. He ventured to ask her if she had had lovers. 'Never!'

Then drawing near, he gazed at her small nose, her straight mouth, the mould of her face. He paid her some compliments, and exhorted her to prudence.

As he leant over her, he perceived in her bodice white forms whence emanated a warm scent which heated his cheek. One evening he touched with his lips the ringlets on her neck, and felt a commotion to his very marrow. Another time he kissed her on the chin, and could hardly refrain from biting her flesh, so savoury was it. She returned his kiss. The room whirled round. He saw no more.

He made her the present of a pair of boots, and frequently treated her to a glass of anisette. . . .

To save her trouble, he rose early, chopped wood, lit the fire, carried his attentions so far as to clean Bouvard's shoes.

Mélie did not faint or drop her handkerchief, and Pécuchet knew not what course to take, his desire increasing from the fear of satisfying it.

Bouvard assiduously paid court to Mme Bordin.

She received him, somewhat restricted in her shot-silk dress, which creaked like a horse's harness, and all the while playing with her long gold chain to keep herself in countenance.

Their conversation turned on the people of Chavignolles, or on her 'late departed,' once a bailiff at Livarot.

Then she asked Bouvard about his past, curious to hear about his youthful follies, and incidentally about his fortune, the interests which bound him to Pécuchet.

He admired the appearance of her house and, when he was dining there, the neatness of the service, the excellence of her table. A succession of exceedingly tasty dishes, interrupted at regular intervals by an old Pomard, brought them to dessert, at which they remained a long time over their coffee—and Mme. Bordin, swelling her nostrils, dipped her plump lip, lightly shaded with a black moustache, into her saucer.

One day she appeared in a low dress. Her shoulders fascinated Bouvard. As he was on a small chair in front of her, he began to pass his two hands along her arms. The widow bridled. He did not attempt it again, but saw in imagination curves of a marvellous amplitude and consistency.

One evening, when he had been disgusted by Mélie's cooking, he felt a joy in entering Mme Bordin's drawing-room. That was the place to live in!

The globe of the lamp, shaded with pink paper, cast a tranquil light. She was seated by the fire; and her foot showed beyond the hem of her skirt. After the first few words, conversation dropped.

Meanwhile, with half-closed eyes, she was looking at him languorously, and with persistence.

Bouvard could stand it no longer, and, kneeling on the floor, he stammered:

'I love you! Let's get married!'

Mme Bordin breathed hard, then, with an ingenuous air, said that he was joking; no doubt he was trying to make fun of her, which was not fair. His declaration had stunned her.

Bouvard retorted that they had no need of anyone's consent.

'What's to stop you? Your trousseau? Our linen bears the same mark—a B!—we'll unite our initials.'

The argument pleased her. But an important matter prevented her from deciding before the end of the month. And Bouvard groaned.

She was gracious enough to see him on his way, escorted by Marianne, who carried a lantern.

The two friends had kept their love affairs hidden from one another.

Pécuchet counted on always veiling his intrigue with the servant. If Bouvard objected, he would take her away to some other country, even Algeria, where living is not too dear! But he rarely indulged in these suppositions, full as he was of his love and reckless of the consequences.

Bouvard contemplated turning the museum into the bridal chamber, unless Pécuchet demurred; in which case he would live at his wife's house.

One afternoon of the following week—it was in her garden, the buds were beginning to open, and between the clouds there showed large patches of blue—she bent down to gather violets, and said as she presented them:

'Congratulate Madame Bouvard!'

'What! Do you mean it?'

'Yes, I mean it.'

He wished to clasp her in his arms, she pushed him away.

'What a man!'

Then growing, serious, she warned him that she would shortly be asking him a favour.

'It's granted.'

They fixed the coming Thursday for signing the marriage contract.

No one was to know about it until the last moment.

'All right.'

And off he went, looking up at the sky, sprightly as a gazelle.

The same morning, Pécuchet had sworn to die if he did not obtain the favours of the maid, and he had accompanied her down to the cellar, hoping that the darkness would give him courage.

She had tried to go away several times; but he detained her in order to count the bottles; to choose laths, or see what was left in the casks, which took up a good deal of time.

She stood facing him under a fanlight with her eyes cast down, the corner of her mouth raised a little.

'Do you love me?' said Pécuchet abruptly.

'Yes, I love you.'

'Well, then, prove it.'

And, putting his left arm round her, he began with the other hand to undo her bodice.

'You're going to hurt me?'

'No, my little angel, don't be afraid!'

'If M. Bouvard—'

'I won't tell him. You needn't worry!'

There was a pile of faggots behind her. She sank back on them with her breasts uncovered and her eyes averted;

then she hid her face under her arm, and anyone else would have understood that she did not lack experience.

Bouvard arrived soon after for dinner.

The meal passed in silence, each afraid of betraying himself; Mélie waited on them with her usual impassiveness; Pécuchet looked away to avoid meeting her eyes, while Bouvard stared at the wall, planning new decorations.

A week later, on the Thursday, he came back furious.

'The bloody bitch!'

'Who?'

'Mme Bordin.'

And he related how he had been lunatic enough to think of making her his wife; but a quarter of an hour ago, at Marescot's, it had all come to an end.

She had claimed as her dowry the Écalles estate, which he could not dispose of, having completed its purchase with a second party's money.

'That's so,' said Pécuchet.

'And I was fool enough to promise her any favour she asked—this was it!—while I kept insisting that, if she loved me, she would give way.'

Instead, the widow had fallen to abusing him, had disparaged his figure, his paunch.

'My paunch! I ask you!'

Meanwhile Pécuchet had left the room several times, walking with his legs apart.

'Are you in pain?' said Bouvard.

'Yes, yes—I'm in pain.'

And, having closed the door, Pécuchet, after much hesitation, confessed that he had just contracted a certain disease.

'You?'

'Me, of all people!'

'Oh, poor old chap—who's given it to you?'

He grew even redder, and said, in an even lower voice:

'It can only be Mélie.'

Bouvard sat dumbfounded.

The first thing was to get rid of the young woman.

She protested with an air of innocence.

Pécuchet's case, however, was serious; but, ashamed of his misconduct, he did not dare to see a physician.

Bouvard thought of appealing to Barberou.

They supplied him with the symptoms of the disease, so that he should consult a doctor who would treat it by correspondence. Barberou did so with relish, believing it was Bouvard's own case, and called him an old ram, at the same time offering his congratulations.

'It's a nice thing,' said Pécuchet, 'at my age; but why has she done this to me?'

'You pleased her.'

'She should have warned me.'

'Does love reason?'

And Bouvard began complaining of Mme Bordin.

He had often surprised her halted in front of Ecalles, with Marescot, talking to Germaine—so much manœuvring for a scrap of ground!

'She's a miser, that's what it is!'

So they ruminated over their misfortunes by the fireside in the morning-room, Pécuchet swallowing his medicines, Bouvard smoking pipes, and they discoursed on women.

'Strange need—if it is a need? They drive us to crime, to brutality and heroism. Hell under a petticoat, paradise in a kiss; the turtle's cooing, the serpent's coils, the cat's claws; treacherous as the sea, inconstant as the moon.'

They uttered all the well-known commonplaces.

It was the desire for women that had interrupted their friendship. They felt remorse.

'No more of them, eh? We can live without!'

And they embraced tenderly.

A new life must begin; and Bouvard thought that, when Pécuchet was cured, hydropathic treatment would do them good.

Germaine, who had come back since the other's departure, dragged the bath-tub into the corridor every morning.

The two good souls, naked as savages, flung great bucketfuls of water at each other, then ran back to their rooms. They were sighted through the lattice; and people were scandalised.

VIII

Satisfied with their regimen, they wished to strengthen their nerves by gymnastics. And taking up Amoros' Manual, they went through the diagrams.

All these young men, squatting, lying down, standing, bending their knees, stretching their arms, raising their fists, lifting weights, riding on blocks of wood, climbing ladders, capering on trapezes—such a display of strength and agility excited their envy.

However, they were saddened by the splendours of the gymnasium as described in the preface. For they would never be able to acquire a hall for the apparatus, a hippodrome for the races, a pool for swimming, or a 'Mount Olympus,' an artificial hillock a hundred feet in height.

A wooden vaulting-horse with the stuffing would have been expensive—they abandoned the idea; the fallen lime tree in the garden served as a horizontal bar; and when they were skilful enough to go along it from one end to the other, they set up a post from the espalier-props to serve as a vertical pole. Pécuchet used to climb to the top. Bouvard was always slipping back and gave it up.

The 'orthosomatic rods' appealed to him more, that is to say, two broomsticks bound by two cords, the first of which passes under the arm-pits, the second over the wrists; and for hours he would remain in this apparatus, with chin raised, chest expanded, and elbows close to the sides.

For want of clubs the wheelwright turned four pieces of ash resembling sugar loaves with bottle necks at the end.

These clubs were to be swung to right and left, forwards and backwards; but being too heavy, they slipped from their fingers at the risk of breaking their legs. No matter, they had set their hearts on Indian clubs and, fearing they might split, rubbed them every evening with wax and a piece of cloth.

Then they looked out for ditches. When they had found one which suited them, they put a long pole in the middle, jumped across off the left foot and back again. The country being flat they could be descried at a distance; and the villagers asked one another what could be these extraordinary objects bounding on the skyline.

When autumn came, they took to indoor exercises; these bored them. Why had they not a revolving chair, or the spring seat invented under Louis xiv by the Abbé de Saint Pierre? How was it made? Where could one obtain particulars? Dumouchel did not deign to reply.

Then they established in the bakehouse a see-saw, worked by hand. Over two pulleys attached to the ceiling a rope was passed, holding a crossbeam at each end. As soon as they had caught hold of it one pushed away from the ground with his toes, the other lowered his arms to the level of the floor; the first, by his weight, drew up the second who, slackening his rope a little, rose in his turn; in less than five minutes their limbs were dripping with perspiration.

In order to follow the directions of the Manual, they tried to become ambidextrous, even going so far as to deprive themselves temporarily of the use of the right hand. They did more; Amoros mentioned pieces of verse which should be chanted during the movements, and Bouvard and Pécuchet, as they walked, repeated hymn number nine:

'A king, a just king, is on earth a boon.'

When they beat their breasts:

'Friends, the crown and the glory,' etc.

While running:

'Ours the beast that flies in fear!
We're close behind the leaping deer!
The chase is almost done,
We'll run, and run, and run!'

and panting like dogs, they took heart at the sound of their own voices.

One branch of gymnastics fired them; its employment as a means of saving life.

But they would have needed children to practise carrying them in sacks, and requested the schoolmaster to provide them with some. Petit objected that the families would be annoyed. They fell back on first-aid to the wounded. One pretended to faint and the other, with the utmost precaution, trundled him away in a barrow.

As for military escalades, the author extols the ladder of Bois-Rosé, so named from the captain who once surprised Fécamp by climbing up the cliff.

In accordance with the illustration in the book they fitted a rope with little sticks and hung it in the cart-shed.

As soon as the climber has straddled the first stick and seized the third, he throws out his legs so that the second, which a moment before was against his chest, is now immediately under the thighs. He straightens himself, seizes the fourth, and so on. Despite prodigious writhings they found it impossible to reach the second stick.

Perhaps there is less difficulty in hanging on to rocks with one's hands, as did Bonaparte's soldiers at the attack on Fort Chambray? And to make one fit for such an exploit, Amoros has a tower in his establishment.

The ruined wall would serve the purpose. They attempted the assault on it.

But Bouvard, withdrawing his foot too suddenly from a hole, grew frightened, and was taken with a fit of giddiness.

Pécuchet found fault with their method; they had neglected to study the formation of the hand, and ought to return to first principles.

His exhortations were in vain; and in his pride and presumption, he took to stilts.

Nature seemed to have destined him for them, for he immediately used the large model, with treads four feet above the ground, and balancing on them, he stalked about the garden, like a gigantic crane out walking.

From the window Bouvard saw him reel, then fall flat into a mass of beans, whose props giving way broke his descent. He was picked up covered with earth, bleeding at the nose, livid, and he thought he had sprained himself.

Decidedly, gymnastics did not suit men of their age; they gave it up, no longer dared to move for fear of accidents, and remained all day long seated in the museum dreaming of other occupations.

This change of habits had its influence on Bouvard's health. He became very heavy, puffed like a whale after meals, wanted to get thin, ate less, and grew weak.

Pécuchet likewise felt himself 'undermined,' had itchings of the skin and lumps in the throat.

'Not so good,' he said. 'Not so good.'

Bouvard had thought of going to the inn to select several bottles of Spanish wine, with the object of tuning up his constitution.

As he was coming out Marescot's clerk and three other

men brought a walnut table for Beljambe; their master thanked him. It had answered admirably.

Bouvard thus learnt of the new fashion of table-turning. He joked about it to the clerk.

However, all over Europe, in America, in Australia, and India, millions of mortals spent their whole lives watching tables turn, and they had discovered the way to make prophets of canaries, to give concerts without instruments, to correspond by means of snails. The press, by seriously offering these impostures to the public, increased its credulity.

The spirits had begun by rapping out messages at the Faverges house, whence they had spread through the village; and in particular the notary questioned them.

Shocked by Bouvard's scepticism, he invited the two friends to an evening's table-turning.

Was it a trap? Mme Bordin would be there. Pécuchet went alone.

There were present the mayor, the tax-collector, the captain, other residents and their wives, Mme Vaucorbeil, Mme Bordin, of course; in addition, an old governess of Mme Marescot's, Mlle Laverrière, a rather squint-eyed lady with grey hair tumbling over her shoulders after the fashion of 1830. In an armchair sat a cousin from Paris wearing a blue suit and with an impertinent manner.

The two bronze lamps, the shelves containing curiosities, the ballads decorated with vignettes on the piano, and minute water-colours in huge frames, were the perpetual astonishment of Chavignolles. But this evening all eyes were directed towards the mahogany table. They would be testing it soon, and it had the importance of things that contain a mystery.

A dozen guests took their places round, their hands extended, their little fingers touching. Only the ticking of the clock was audible. The faces denoted a profound attention.

At the end of ten minutes, several complained of twitches in the arms. Pécuchet felt uncomfortable.

'You're pushing,' said the captain to Foureau.

'Not at all!'

'Yes, you are.'

'Really, sir!'

The notary pacified them.

Straining their ears, they thought they made out creakings in the wood. It was an illusion; nothing budged.

The other day, when the Auberts and Lormeaux came from Lisieux and they had specially borrowed Beljambe's table, everything had gone so well. But to-day this table was being obstinate. . . . Why?

No doubt the carpet was annoying it; and they went into the dining-room.

The chosen piece of furniture was a large round table at which Pécuchet, Girbal, Mme Marescot, and her cousin Alfred, installed themselves.

This one, which had castors, slid to the right; the operators, without moving their fingers, followed its movement, and of itself it gave two more turns. Everyone was amazed.

Then M. Alfred articulated in a high voice:

'Spirit! What do you think of my cousin?'

The table, swinging slowly, rapped nine times.

According to a card, where the number of raps was translated by letters, that signified 'charming.' Applause broke out.

Then Marescot, teasing Mme Bordin, called on the spirit to declare her exact age.

The foot of the table fell five times.

'What! five years?' cried Girbal.

'The tens don't count,' answered Foureau.

The widow smiled, secretly annoyed.

The replies to the other questions were a failure, owing to the alphabet being so complicated. Planchette was better, a quick method which Mlle Laverrière had utilised to note, in an album, the direct communications of Louis XII, Clémence Isaure, Franklin, Jean-Jacques Rousseau, etc. These contrivances were on sale in the Rue d'Aumale; M. Alfred promised to get one; then, addressing himself to the governess:

'But just for a quarter of an hour a little music, what? A mazurka!'

Two notes, struck on the piano, vibrated. He took his cousin by the waist, disappeared with her, returned. There was something refreshing in the breeze from her dress which swept the doors as she passed. She tilted back her head; he rounded his arm. The grace of the one was admired, the smart manners of the other; and, without waiting for the cakes, Pécuchet retired, astounded at the evening.

It was all very well for him to reiterate: 'But I saw it with my own eyes!' Bouvard denied the facts and yet consented to experiment himself.

For a fortnight they passed their afternoons facing each other, their hands on a table, then on a hat, a basket, plates. All these objects remained motionless.

The phenomenon of table-turning is none the less certain. The vulgar attribute it to spirits, Faraday to the projection of nervous action, Chevreul to unconscious efforts, or perhaps, as Ségouin admits, there extends from an assembly of people a magnetic current.

This hypothesis set Pécuchet musing. He took from the library *The Magnetiser's Guide*, by Montacabère, re-read it carefully, and initiated Bouvard into the theory.

All animate bodies receive and communicate the influence of the stars—a property analogous to the virtue of the loadstone. By directing this force, maladies can be cured; that is the principle. Since Mesmer, the science has developed, but it has always been a question of releasing the fluid and making passes which, in the first place, must produce sleep.

'Well, put me to sleep!' said Bouvard.

'Impossible!' replied Pécuchet. 'To undergo magnetic action and to transmit it, faith is indispensable.'

Then, gazing at Bouvard: 'Ah, what a pity!'

'What d'you mean?'

'Yes, if you liked, with a little practice, there could be no better magnetiser than you.'

For he possessed all that was needed—a dominating aspect, a robust constitution and strong character.

The discovery of this new faculty in himself flattered Bouvard. He plunged surreptitiously into Montacabère.

Then, as Germaine had buzzings in the ears which made her deaf, he said, in a careless tone:

'Suppose one tried magnetism?'

She had no objection. He sat facing her, took her two thumbs in his hands, and fixed her with a stare, as if he had done nothing else all his life.

The good woman, a foot-warmer under her heels, began by bending her neck; her eyes closed and, quite gently, she started to snore. At the end of an hour, during which they scrutinised her, Pécuchet said in a low voice:

'What do you feel?'

She woke up.

Later, no doubt, lucidity would come.

This success emboldened them and, taking up the exercise of medicine with assurance once more, they treated Chamberlan, the beadle, for his intercostal troubles; Migraine the mason, affected with a nervous disorder of the stomach, old mother Varin, whose encephaloid under the collar-bone demanded meat poultices for its nourishment; a gouty subject, old Lemoine, who dragged himself round the taverns; a consumptive, a paralytic, and many others. They also treated colds and chilblains.

After investigating a complaint, they questioned each other with a look, to know what passes to employ, whether they should be in strong or weak current, ascending or descending, longitudinal, transversal, bidigital, tridigital or even quinquidigital. When one was tired the other replaced him. Then, returned home, they noted their observations in a medical diary.

Their smooth manners captivated everyone. But Bouvard was the favourite, and his fame reached as far as Falaise when he cured La Barbée, the daughter of old Barbey, a retired sea-captain.

She felt as if she had a nail in the back of her head, spoke in a hoarse voice, often stayed several days without eating, then devoured plaster or coal. Her nervous fits, beginning with sobs, ended in a flood of tears, and every remedy had been tried, from infusions to moxas, so that through weariness she accepted Bouvard's offer.

When he had sent away the servant and bolted the door, he began to rub her abdomen, applying himself specially to the region of the ovaries. A feeling of comfort showed itself in her sighs and yawns. He placed a finger between her eyebrows, at the top of her nose; suddenly she became inert. If her arms were lifted, they fell back; her head kept whatever position he liked, and her eyelids, half closed and quivering spasmodically, revealed the eyeballs rolling slowly; they fixed themselves in the corners, convulsed.

Bouvard asked her if she felt any pain; she replied, 'No.' What were her sensations at the moment? She indicated her inside.

'What do you see there?'

'A worm.'

'What's to be done to kill it?'

She wrinkled her brow.

'I'm trying to think—no, I can't, I can't.'

At the second visit she prescribed nettle-broth for herself, at the third, catnip. The fits grew less, and disappeared. It was really like a miracle.

Nasal addigitation did not succeed with the others, and to induce somnambulism, they planned the construction of a mesmeric tank. Indeed Pécuchet had already collected filings and cleaned a score of bottles, when a scruple stopped him. Among the patients there would be females.

'And what shall we do if they are taken with an access of raging eroticism?'

That would not have worried Bouvard, but on account of gossip, and possibly blackmail, it was better to abstain. They contented themselves with a harmonica, which they took with them on their rounds, to the delight of the children.

One day when Migraine was worse they hurried to his bedside. The crystalline sounds exasperated him; but Deleuze says that one should not be intimidated by groans; the music went on.

'Enough, enough!' he cried.

'A little patience!' repeated Bouvard.

Pécuchet was tapping more quickly on the plates of glass, the instrument was vibrating, and the poor fellow howling, when the doctor appeared, attracted by the din.

'What, you again!' he cried, furious at always discovering them in his patients' houses. They explained their magnetic method. Then he fulminated against magnetism—a bag of tricks whose effects come from the imagination.

Yet animals can be magnetised—Montacabère says so, and M. Fontaine has succeeded in magnetising a lioness.

They had no lioness, but chance offered them another beast.

Next morning at six o'clock a ploughboy came to say that they were wanted at the farm for a cow whose life was despaired of.

They ran there.

The apple trees were in blossom, and the grass in the yard was steaming under the rising sun. At the edge of the pond, half covered with a cloth, a cow was mooing, shivering from the buckets of water that were being flung over it, and, swollen out of all proportion, it resembled a hippopotamus.

No doubt it had 'taken venom,' while pasturing in the clover. Farmer Gouy and his wife lamented, for the veterinary surgeon could not come, and a ploughman, who knew spells against the swelling, would not be bothered; but these gentlemen, whose library was famous, surely knew some secret.

Having turned up their sleeves they posted themselves, one in front of the horns, the other at the rump, and, with great internal efforts and frantic gesticulation, they parted their fingers to spread streams of fluid over the animal, while the farmer, his wife, their son, and the neighbours looked on almost in fear.

The rumblings, audible in the cow's belly, provoked flatulence in the depths of its entrails. It let wind. Then Pécuchet said:

'It's a doorway open to hope, an uncorking, perhaps.'

The uncorking took place, hope spurted up in a bundle of yellow matter bursting with the force of a shell. The hide relaxed, the cow deflated. An hour later there was no trace of swelling.

It was not the effect of imagination, assuredly. Then the fluid contains some particular virtue. It can be stored in objects from which it will afterwards be taken without loss of strength. Such a method saves the magnetiser a journey. They adopted it and sent their patients magnetised discs, magnetised handkerchiefs, magnetised water, magnetised bread.

Then, continuing their studies, they gave up the passes in favour of Puységur's system, which substitutes for the magnetiser an old tree with its trunk encircled by a cord.

A pear tree in their orchard seemed made for the very purpose. They prepared it by hugging it ardently at intervals. A bench was set up underneath. Their patients sat there in a row, and they obtained such wonderful results that, to confound Vaucorbeil, they summoned him to a seance, along with the gentry of the district.

Not one was absent.

Germaine received them in the morning-room, begging them to excuse her masters, who would come shortly.

From time to time there was a ring at the bell: it was the invalids, whom she conducted somewhere else. With nudgings of the elbow, the guests pointed out the dusty windows, the stains on the plaster, the paint peeling off; and the garden was deplorable. Dead wood everywhere! Two stakes in front of the breach in the wall barred the orchard.

Pécuchet presented himself.

'At your service, gentlemen.'

And at the end of the garden, under the tree of Edouin pears, they saw several persons seated.

Chamberlan, clean-shaven like a priest, in a short cassock of lasting and a leather skull-cap, was giving way to the twitchings caused by his intercostal complaint; near him Migraine, suffering as usual from his stomach, grimaced; Mother Varin, to hide her tumour, had a shawl wrapped round her several times; old Lemoine, his bare feet in slippers, sat with his crutches under him, and La Barbée, in her Sunday clothes, was looking extraordinarily pale.

On the other side of the tree were other persons: a woman with an albino's visage was wiping the suppurating glands on her neck; a little girl's face was half hidden by blue spectacles; an old man, whose spine was deformed by a contraction, knocked with involuntary movements against Marcel, a sort of half-wit, covered with a ragged blouse and patched trousers. His badly stitched hare-lip exposed his incisors, and bandages muffled his cheek, swollen by an enormous fluxion.

All held, in one hand, a string coming down from the tree, and the birds were singing; the smell of warm turf spread in the air. Sunlight passed between the branches. There was moss underfoot.

However, the patients, instead of sleeping, opened their eyes wide.

'Up to now it's not amusing,' said Foureau. 'Get started; I'm off for a moment.'

And he came back smoking an Abd-el-Kader, the last relic of the gate of pipes.

Pécuchet remembered an excellent method of magnetisation. He put all the patients' noses in his mouth and inhaled their breath, to attract the electricity to himself, while Bouvard embraced the tree with the object of strengthening the fluid.

The mason ceased his hiccoughs; the beadle was less agitated. The man with the contraction became motionless. They could now be approached, and made to undergo all the tests.

The doctor, with his lancet, pricked under the ear of Chamberlan, who trembled a little. The others' sensibility was evident; the gouty man uttered a cry. As to La Barbée, she smiled as though in a dream, and a thread of blood trickled under her chin. Foureau, to test her himself, wanted to seize the lancet and, on the doctor's refusal, he gave her a severe pinch. The captain tickled her nostrils with a feather, the tax-collector was about to stick a pin into her flesh.

'Let her be!' said Vaucorbeil. 'It's nothing remarkable after all. A case of hysteria. The devil would waste his Latin there.'

'That one,' said Pécuchet, pointing to Victoire, 'the scrofulous woman, is a doctor. She recognises illnesses and indicates the remedies.'

Langlois was agog to consult her on his catarrh; he did not dare: but Coulon, bolder, asked her for something for his rheumatism.

Pécuchet put his right hand into Victoire's left and, her eyes still closed, her cheeks slightly red, with quivering lips, the somnambulist, after muttering incoherently, prescribed *Valum Becum*.

She had served at an apothecary's in Bayeux. Vaucorbeil inferred that she wished to say *Album Graecum*, a phrase caught, perhaps, in the chemist's shop.

Then he went up to old Lemoine, who, according to Bouvard, could see objects through opaque bodies.

He was a former schoolmaster who had descended to drunkenness. White hairs clustered round his face, and, propped against the tree with open palms, he slept in the full sunlight with a majestic expression.

The doctor wound a cravat twice over his eyes, and Bouvard, putting a newspaper before him, said dictatorially:

'Read!'

He lowered his brow, moved his facial muscles, then threw back his head, and ended by spelling out:

'Cons—ti—tu—tion—al.'

'But with skill one can make any bandage slip.'

These doubts of the doctor's revolted Pécuchet. He went so far as to assert that La Barbée could describe what was actually happening at that moment in his house.

'Very well,' said the doctor.

And taking out his watch:

'What's my wife doing?'

La Barbée hesitated a long time, then with a sulky air:

'Eh, what? Ah yes, I've got it! She's sewing ribbons on a straw hat!'

Vaucorbeil tore a sheet from his memorandum book and pencilled a note, which Marescot's clerk hastened off with.

The seance was closed; the patients went away.

On the whole Bouvard and Pécuchet had not been successful. Was it because of the temperature or the smell of tobacco, or Abbé Jeufroy's umbrella, which had a copper ring, a metal hostile to the fluidic emission?

Vaucorbeil shrugged his shoulders.

Yet he could not question the good faith of MM. Deleuze, Bertrand, Morin, Jules Cloquet. Now, these professors assert that somnambulists have foretold events, and undergone painful operations without suffering.

The abbé told stories even more remarkable. A missionary had seen Brahmins run along an arch with their heads hanging down; the Grand Lama of Tibet rends his bowels in order to give out oracles.

'You're joking!' said the doctor.

'Not at all.'

'Come now. Confess!'

And the question taking a new turn, each produced anecdotes.

'Well,' said the grocer, 'I had a dog that was always ill when the month began with a Friday.'

'There were fourteen of us children,' said the justice of the peace. 'I was born on a fourteenth, my marriage took place on a fourteenth, and my Saint's-day falls on a fourteenth. Explain that if you can.'

Beljambe had often dreamt of the number of travellers he would have at his inn on the morrow, and Petit told the story of Cazotte's supper.

Then the curé uttered this reflection:

'Why not see in all that just simply—'

'Demons, you were going to say. Eh?' asked Vaucorbeil. Instead of replying the abbé nodded his head.

Marescot spoke of the Delphic oracle.

'Miasmas, no doubt.'

'If you're going to talk of miasmas—'

'I posit a fluid,' continued Bouvard.

'Nervoso-sidereal,' added Pécuchet.

'Prove it then! Show us it! Fluid, indeed! Besides, fluids are out of fashion. Listen to me.'

Vaucorbeil moved off into the shade, the others followed.

'If you say to a child, "I'm a wolf. I'm going to eat you," he imagines that you are a wolf and gets frightened; so it's a vision caused by words. In the same way, a sleep-walker accepts whatever fantasies you like. He does not imagine, but remembers; he's completely obedient; has only sensations when he believes he is thinking. In this way, crimes are committed through suggestion, and honest men can be transformed into wild beasts and involuntarily become cannibals.'

Glances were cast at Bouvard and Pécuchet. Their science was a danger to society.

Marescot's clerk reappeared in the garden, brandishing a letter from Mme Vaucorbeil.

The doctor tore it open, turned pale, and finally read out these words:

'I'm sewing ribbons on a straw hat.'

They were too astounded to laugh.

'A coincidence, damn it! That proves nothing.'

And as the two magnetisers had an air of triumph, he turned round at the door to say:

'You'd better not go on with it. These are dangerous amusements.'

The curé led away the beadle, rebuking him sharply.

'Are you mad? Without my permission! Practices forbidden by the Church!'

Everyone had just gone; Bouvard and Pécuchet were talking on the mound with the schoolmaster, when Marcel rushed out of the orchard with his chin-bandage undone, and stammered:

'Cured! cured! Oh, thank you, gentlemen!'

'All right, that'll do. Leave us alone!'

'How can I ever thank you? Good night, sirs.'

Petit, a man of advanced ideas, had found the doctor's explanation matter-of-fact, vulgar. Science is a monopoly in the hands of the rich, which excludes the people; to the old analytic method of the Middle Ages, it is time that a wide and spontaneous synthesis should succeed. Truth should obtain through the heart, and declaring himself a spiritualist, he referred to several works, which had their faults no doubt, but were a signal of the dawn.

They sent for them.

Spiritualism puts forward as a dogma the predestined betterment of our species. The earth will one day be heaven, and that is why this doctrine attracted the schoolmaster. Without being Catholic, it calls St. Augustine and St. Louis to witness; Allan-Kardec has even published fragments dictated by them, which are abreast of contemporary opinion. It is practical, beneficent, and reveals to us, like the telescope, superior worlds.

The spirits are transported there in an ecstasy after death. But sometimes they return to our globe, where they make furniture creak, join in our amusements, taste the beauties of nature and the pleasures of the arts.

Some of us, however, possess an aromal proboscis, that is to say, a long tube at the back of the head, which mounts from the hair up to the planets and allows us to converse with the spirits of Saturn; intangibilities are not the less real, and from the earth to the stars, from the stars to the earth, there is a to-and-fro, a transmission, a continual interchange.

Then Pécuchet's heart swelled with inordinate hope, and when night came, Bouvard surprised him at the window, gazing upon those luminous spaces which are peopled by spirits.

Swedenborg made long journeys there. In less than a year he explored Venus, Mars, Saturn and—twenty-three times—Jupiter. Moreover, he saw Jesus Christ in London, he saw St. Paul, he saw St. John, he saw Moses, and in 1736, he even saw the Last Judgment.

He also gave us descriptions of heaven.

You find there flowers, palaces, markets and churches, as with us.

The angels, who were once men, inscribe their thoughts on tablets, gossip about domestic or spiritual matters, and the office of priest belongs to those who, in their terrestrial life, have studied Holy Scripture.

As for hell, it is filled with a disgusting stench, with hovels, muck heaps, quagmires, persons shabbily dressed.

And Pécuchet racked his brain to discover what there is beautiful in these revelations. They seemed to Bouvard the ravings of a lunatic. All such matters transcend the bounds of nature! Besides, who knows anything about them? And they indulged in the following reflections:

Jugglers can delude a crowd; a man with violent passions will inflame others; but how can the will by itself affect inanimate matter? A Bavarian is said to have caused grapes to ripen, M. Gervais has revived a heliotrope; someone with greater powers, at Toulouse, can disperse the clouds.

Must we admit the existence of an intermediary substance between the world and ourselves? The od, a new imponderable, a sort of electricity, is nothing else perhaps. Its emissions explain the light which magnetised persons think they see, the wandering fires in cemeteries, supernatural forms.

These images, then, would not be an illusion, and the extraordinary gifts of persons who are possessed, like somnambulists, would have a physical cause.

Whatever its origin there is an essence, a secret and universal agent. If we could capture it, there would be no need of energy or prolonged effort. What now takes centuries would develop in a moment: every sort of miracle would be practicable, and the universe would be at our command.

Magic springs from this eternal desire of the human spirit. No doubt its value has been exaggerated, but it is not a fairy-tale. Orientals who understand it, perform prodigies. All travellers assert this, and at the Palais-Royal M. Dupotel disturbs the magnetic needle with a pass of his finger.

How become a magician? At first the idea seemed mad, but it recurred, tormented them, and they yielded, at the same time affecting to laugh at it.

Some preparation is necessary.

In order to reach a higher plane, they turned night into day, fasted and, wishing to convert Germaine into a more sensitive medium, rationed her food. She made up for it in drink, and consumed so much spirits that she very soon succeeded in soaking herself. Their promenades in the corridor woke her. She confused the sound of their steps with the buzzings in her ears and the imaginary voices which she heard coming from the walls. One day, when she had put a plaice that morning in the cellar, she was frightened to see it all covered with fire; from that time felt worse, and ended by believing that they had cast a spell over her.

Hoping to obtain visions, they squeezed one another's necks, made themselves sachets of belladonna, and finally adopted the magic box: a small box, from which rises a mushroom knob bristling with nails and which is carried over the heart by means of a ribbon attached round the chest. Everything failed; but they could still use Dupotet's circle.

Pécuchet scrawled a black circle on the floor with a piece of charcoal, to enclose the animal spirits which were to assist the ambient ones and, delighted at having the mastery over Bouvard, he addressed him with a pontifical air.

'I defy you to cross it!'

Bouvard considered the circle. Soon, his heart began to thud, his eyes swam.

'Let's get it over!'

And, to escape an inexpressible uneasiness, he jumped across.

Pécuchet, whose excitement was increasing, wished to make a dead man appear. Under the Directory, someone in the Rue de l'Échiquier used to exhibit the victims of the Terror. Instances of the dead returning are frequent. Even if it is only an illusion. . . . In any case, the question was to produce it.

The closer the dead are to us the more readily will they answer our call; but he had no relic of his family, neither ring nor miniature, not a hair, while Bouvard was in a position to invoke his father and, as he showed signs of repugnance, Pécuchet demanded:

'What are you afraid of?'

'I? Oh, of nothing! Do as you like!'

They bribed Chamberlan, who furnished them in secret with an old skull. A tailor cut out two black robes with hoods like a monk's habit. The Falaise coach brought them a long scroll, done up in paper. Then they set to work, the one eager of accomplishment, the other afraid of believing in it.

The museum was laid out like a catafalque. Three tapers shone on the edge of the table pushed against the wall, under the portrait of Bouvard's father, which was surmounted by the skull. They had even put a candle inside it, whose rays issued from the two eyeholes.

In the middle, incense was burning on a brazier. Bouvard remained behind it; and Pécuchet, turning his back on him, threw handfuls of sulphur into the grate.

Before invoking the dead it is necessary to get the consent of the demons. Now, it was Friday, a day which belongs to Béchet; they must deal first of all with Béchet. Bouvard, having bowed to right and left, with bent chin and outstretched arms, began:

'By Éthaniel, Anazin, Ischyros—'

He had forgotten the rest.

Pécuchet hastily breathed the words he had noted down on a card.

'Ischyros, Athanatos, Adonaï, Sadaï, Eloy, Messiasos' (the litany was long), 'I conjure you, I call upon you, I command you, O Béchet!'

Then, lowering his voice.

'Where are you, Béchet? Béchet! Béchet! Béchet!'

Bouvard sank into the armchair and was relieved not to see Béchet, his instinct condemning the attempt as sacrilegious. Where was his father's soul? Could it hear him? Suppose it were suddenly to appear?

The curtains slowly stirred in the wind, which was coming in through a broken pane, and the tapers threw wavering shadows on the death's-head and on the painted face. An earthy colour made them equally brown. The cheek-bones of the portrait were consumed by mould, the eyes had lost

236

their life, but a flame shone above in the sockets of the empty skull. It seemed at times to take the other's place, to rest on the collar of the frock-coat, to assume whiskers; and the canvas, half out of its frame, swayed and palpitated.

Little by little, as though a breath grazed them, they felt the approach of an impalpable being. Drops of sweat moistened Pécuchet's brow, and there was Bouvard with his teeth beginning to chatter, with a cramp gripping his stomach; the floor gave under his heels like a wave; the sulphur, burning in the chimney, came down in large spirals; at the same time bats were wheeling; a cry arose; who was it?

And under their hoods they had faces so distorted that their fear redoubled. They did not dare to make a gesture or even to speak, when behind the door they heard groans like those of a soul in pain.

At last they plucked up courage.

It was their old servant, who, spying them through a chink of the door, thought she had seen the devil and, on her knees in the corridor, she was frenziedly making signs of the cross.

Useless to reason. She left them the same evening, not wishing to remain a moment longer in the service of such masters.

Germaine gossiped. Chamberlan lost his place, and he formed a cabal against them with the Abbé Jeufroy, Mme Bordin and Foureau.

Their way of life, which was not other people's, caused displeasure. They became suspect, and even inspired a vague terror.

What above all ruined them in public opinion was their choice of a servant. For want of another, they had taken Marcel.

His hare-lip, his hideousness and gibbering made him shunned. A foundling, he had grown up wild in the fields

237

and, from those years of misery, retained an insatiable appetite. Animals dead of disease, rancid bacon, a battered dog, all came alike to him, provided the piece was big; and he was as gentle as a lamb, but completely stupid.

Gratitude had driven him to offer his services to Messieurs Bouvard and Pécuchet; and now, believing them sorcerers, he was hoping for extraordinary gains.

From the first he confided his secret to them. On the heath at Poligny a man had once found a gold ingot. The incident is reported by the historians of Falaise; they did not know its sequel: twelve brothers, before going a journey, had hidden twelve similar bars along the road from Chavignolles to Bretteville, and Marcel begged his masters to resume the search. These ingots, they told themselves, had perhaps been buried just before the emigration.

It was a case for the use of the divining rod. Its virtues are doubtful. However, they studied the question, and learnt that a certain Pierre Garnier brings scientific arguments in its support; springs and metals give out corpuscules, which have an affinity with wood.

That is hardly likely. But who knows? Let us try!

They cut a forked hazel twig, and went off one morning in search of the treasure.

'We'll have to give it up,' said Bouvard.

'No, dash it!'

After three hours' walking a thought arrested them. 'The road from Chavignolles to Bretteville!'—was it the old or the new? It must be the old!

They retraced their steps, and went over the neighbouring ground at random, the track of the old road not being easily recognised.

Marcel ran to right and left like a spaniel at a shoot. Every five minutes Bouvard was obliged to call him back; Pécuchet advanced step by step, holding the rod by its two branches, with the point upwards. Often it seemed to him that a force like a clamp was drawing it earthwards, and Marcel would quickly cut notches in the nearest trees so that they could find the place later on.

Pécuchet, however, slackened his pace. His mouth opened, the pupils of his eyes became fixed. Bouvard addressed him, shook him by the shoulders; he did not budge but remained inert, exactly like La Barbée.

Then he described how he had felt a sort of tearing round his heart, a strange condition arising no doubt from the rod; and he would not touch it again.

The next day they returned to the marked trees. Marcel dug holes with a spade; the excavation revealed nothing, and each time they looked sheepish. Pécuchet sat down beside a ditch; and while he was dreaming with his head raised, striving to hear the voices of the spirits through his aromal proboscis, wondering if he even had one, he fixed his gaze on the peak of his cap; the ecstasy of the previous evening once more seized him. It lasted a long time, and became dreadful.

Above the oats, in a by-path, appeared a felt hat; it was M. Vaucorbeil trotting on his mare. Bouvard and Marcel hailed him.

The crisis was ending when the doctor came up. To examine Pécuchet he lifted his cap—and perceiving a forehead covered with coppery marks:

'Ah, ha! *fructus belli*!—these are syphilitic spots, my dear fellow! Be careful! What! No trifling with love!'

Pécuchet, ashamed, replaced his cap, a sort of beret, bulging over a peak shaped like a half moon, and modelled on a diagram in Amoros.

The doctor's words disturbed him. He was reflecting with his eyes to the sky—and suddenly was seized again.

Vaucorbeil observed him, then, with a quick motion, knocked his cap off.

239

Pécuchet came to his senses.

'I thought so,' said the doctor. 'The glazed peak hypnotises you like a looking-glass, a fairly frequent phenomenon with people who gaze at a shining object too intently.'

He indicated a way of practising the experiment on fowls, bestrode his nag, and slowly passed out of sight.

About a mile off they noticed a pyramidal object standing on the horizon in a farmyard. One would have thought it a huge bunch of black grapes, spotted with red dots here and there. It was, according to the Normandy custom, a long pole fitted with cross-bars on which were settled turkeys, digesting in the sun.

'Let's go in,' and Pécuchet accosted the farmer, who agreed to their request.

They traced a line with whitewash in the middle of the press-house, tied a turkey's claws, then stretched it out flat on its breast, with its beak placed on the line. The bird closed its eyes, and soon appeared to be dead. It was the same with the others. Bouvard swiftly passed them on to Pécuchet, who laid them down side by side when they were hypnotised. The farm people gave signs of disquiet. The mistress cried out, a child burst into tears.

Bouvard untied all the birds. One after the other they revived, but there was no telling what might be the consequences. At a rather harsh answer by Pécuchet, the farmer seized his hay-fork.

'Get out, by God! or I'll slit your belly!'

They decamped.

Never mind, the problem was resolved: ecstasy depends on a material cause.

What, then, is matter? What spirit? Whence comes the influence of the one upon the other—and vice versa?

To find an explanation, they made researches in Voltaire,

in Bossuet, in Fénelon—and even renewed their subscription to a lending library.

The ancient writers were inaccessible because of the length of their works or the difficulty of the language, but Jouffroy and Damiron initiated them into modern philosophy, and they possessed authors dealing with the past century.

Bouvard drew his arguments from La Mettrie, Locke and Helvétius; Pécuchet from M. Cousin, Thomas Reid and Gérando. The first adhered to empiricism, idealism was all in all to the second. There was Aristotle in the one, and Plato in the other; they disputed.

'The soul is non-material,' said one.

'Certainly not!' said the other. 'Madness, chloroform, bleeding upset it; and since it does not think all the time, it is not a substance that does nothing but think.'

'Yet,' objected Pécuchet, 'I have within me something superior to my body, and which occasionally contradicts it.'

'A being within the being? The *homo duplex*! Absurd! Differing tendencies reveal opposite motives—that's all.'

'But this something, this soul, remains identical beneath external changes. Therefore it is simple, indivisible, and consequently spiritual.'

'If the soul were simple,' answered Bouvard, 'the newly-born would have memory and imagination like the fully grown. Thought, on the contrary, follows the development of the brain. As to being indivisible, the scent of a rose or a wolf's appetite can't be split in two any more than a wish or an affirmation.'

'That's got nothing to do with it,' said Pécuchet. 'The soul is exempt from the qualities of matter.'

'Do you admit weight?' replied Bouvard. 'Then, if matter can fall, it can also think. Having had a beginning, our soul must come to an end, and, dependent on the organs, disappear when they do.'

'Well, I maintain it's immortal. God cannot wish—'

'But if God doesn't exist?'

'What?'

And Pécuchet recited the three Cartesian proofs: *primo*, God is understood in the idea that we have of Him; *secundo*, existence is possible to Him; *tertio* and lastly, how can I have an idea of the infinite? And since we have this idea, it comes to us from God; therefore God exists.

He passed on to the testimony of experience, popular tradition, the need for there being a creator.

'When I see a clock—'

'Yes, yes! I know that one! But what about the clock-maker's father?'

'There must be a cause, though.'

Bouvard was doubtful of causes. 'Because one phenomenon succeeds another, we conclude that it derives from it. Prove it!'

'But the spectacle of the universe denotes an intention, a plan.'

'Why? Evil is as perfectly organised as good. The worm that grows in a sheep's head and makes it die is as good, anatomically, as the sheep itself. Abnormalities surpass normal functions. The human body could be better constructed. Three-quarters of the globe are sterile. The moon, that light-diffuser, does not always show itself. Do you think the sea was made for ships and the wood of trees for warming our houses?'

Pécuchet answered:

'Still, the stomach is made for digesting, the leg for walking, the eye for seeing, in spite of indigestions, fractures and cataracts. There are no structures without an object. Effects follow sooner or later. All depends on law. Therefore there are final causes.'

Bouvard thought that Spinoza would perhaps provide him with arguments, and wrote to Dumouchel for Saisset's translation.

Dumouchel sent him a copy, belonging to his friend Professor Varelot, exiled on the 2nd December.

The Ethics frightened them with its axioms and corollaries. They read only the places marked with pencil, and gathered this:

'Substance is that which is of itself and by itself, without cause or origin. That substance is God.

'He alone is its extension, and its extension is limitless. What could limit it?

'But, although infinite, it is not the absolute infinite, for it only contains one kind of perfection and the absolute contains them all.'

Often they stopped to reflect. Pécuchet absorbed pinches of snuff and Bouvard was red with attention.

'Does this interest you?'

'Yes, certainly. Go on!'

'God develops in an infinity of attributes, which express, each in its manner, the infinity of His being. We only know two of them—extension and thought.

'From thought and extension flow innumerable activities, which contain yet others.

'He who should embrace, at the same time, the whole of extension and the whole of thought, would not perceive any contingency there, anything accidental, but a geometric progression of terms, bound to each other by necessary laws.'

'Ah, that would be splendid!' said Pécuchet.

'Then, there is no liberty for man or God.' ('There, you see!' cried Bouvard.) 'If God had a will, an aim, if He acted for a purpose, it would be because He had a need, because He lacked perfection. He would not be God.

'Thus our world is only a speck in the totality of things,

and the universe is impenetrable to our consciousness, a portion of an infinity of universes displaying, in the neighbourhood of our own, infinite modifications. Extension envelops our universe, but is enveloped by God, who contains in His thought all possible universes, and His thought itself is enveloped in His substance.'

All this was like being in a balloon at night, in glacial coldness, carried on an endless voyage towards a bottomless abyss, and with nothing near but the unseizable, the motionless, the eternal. It was too much. They gave it up.

And wanting something less tough, they bought the *Course of Philosophy* for the use of schools, by M. Guesnier.

The author asks which is the best method, the ontological or the psychological.

The first is appropriate to the childhood of society, when man directed his attention towards the exterior world. But now that he has become introspective, 'we believe the second more scientific,' and Bouvard and Pécuchet decided in favour of it.

The aim of psychology is to study events that occur 'in one's own bosom'; these are discovered by observation.

'Let's observe!' And for a fortnight, after lunch, they made a habit of searching their consciousness, as chance dictated, in the hope of making great discoveries there, but made none, to their great astonishment.

A phenomenon occupies the ego, namely, the idea. What is its nature? It has been supposed that objects are mirrored in the brain and that the brain sends these images to our spirit, which causes consciousness.

But if the idea belongs to the spirit, how is matter to be represented? Thence comes scepticism regarding external perceptions. If it is material, spiritual things would not be represented. Thence comes scepticism concerning internal notions.

Besides, one must be careful. This hypothesis would lead to atheism.

For, an image being a finite object, it cannot possibly represent the infinite.

'Still,' objected Bouvard, 'when I dream of a forest, a person, a dog, I see that forest, person, or dog. Thus, ideas represent them.'

And they started on the origin of ideas.

According to Locke, there are two—sensation and reflection—and Condillac reduces all to sensation.

But in that case, reflection would lack a basis. It needs a subject, a sentient being; and it is powerless to furnish us with the great fundamental truths—God, merit and demerit, justice, beauty, etc.—notions that are called *innate*, that is to say, anterior to events, to experience, and that are universal.

'If they were universal, we should have them from our birth.'

'Only a disposition towards them is meant by that, and Descartes—'

'Your blessed Descartes is a flounderer, for he maintains that the foetus has them, and in another place avows that it's in an implicit manner.'

Pécuchet was surprised.

'Where did you find that?'

'In Gérando!' and Bouvard tapped him lightly on the stomach.

'Stop it!' said Pécuchet. Then, going on to Condillac: 'Our thoughts are not metamorphoses of sensation. Sensation occasions them and sets them going. To do so, a motive force is needed. For matter by itself cannot produce movement—and I found that in Voltaire,' added Pécuchet, making him a deep bow.

They kept churning out the same argument, each despising the other's opinion, without convincing him to the contrary.

But philosophy heightened them in their own esteem. They looked back with pity on their preoccupation with agriculture and politics.

At present the museum disgusted them. They would have asked nothing better than to sell their curios. And they passed on to Chapter Two: Of the Faculties of the Soul.

These amount to three—no more: that of feeling, that of knowing, that of willing.

In the faculty of feeling we must distinguish between physical and moral sensibility.

Physical sensations are naturally classified in five species, being controlled by the organs of the senses.

The actions of moral sensibility, on the contrary, owe nothing to the body. 'What is there in common between the pleasure of Archimedes at discovering the laws of weight, and the degraded rapture of Apicius devouring a boar's head?'

This moral sensibility has four kinds; its second kind, 'moral desires,' is divided into five species, and the phenomena of the fourth kind, 'affection,' are subdivided into two other species, among which is self-esteem, 'a legitimate tendency, doubtless, but one which, when exaggerated, takes the name of egoism.'

In the faculty of knowing is found perception, wherein one discovers two principal activities and four degrees.

Abstraction can hold out snares to perverse minds.

Memory permits of communication with the past as prevision with the future.

Imagination is rather a particular faculty *sui generis*.

So much labour to demonstrate so many platitudes, the author's pedantic tone, the monotony of the style—'We are prepared to recognise—Far be it from us—Let us ask ourselves'—the eternal praise of Dugald-Stewart, in fine, all this verbiage disheartened them to such a degree that, skipping the faculty of will, they entered upon logic.

It taught them what were analysis, synthesis, induction, deduction, and the chief causes of our errors.

They nearly all come from the misuse of words.

'The sun is setting, the day is growing dark, winter approaches'—vicious locutions and such as would make one believe they applied to personal entities, when it was only a matter of simple events. 'I remember such an object, axiom, truth'—illusion! Those are ideas, and not things at all, that remain in the ego, and correct speech demands, 'I remember such an act of my spirit by which I have perceived this object, by which I have deduced this axiom, by which I have admitted this truth.'

As the term which denotes an incident does not embrace all its activities, they tried to employ only abstract words; so that, instead of saying, 'Let's take a turn—it's time for dinner—I've got indigestion,' they gave out these phrases, 'A promenade would be salutary—this is the hour for absorbing nutriment—I feel the need of evacuation.'

Once masters of logic, they passed in review the different criteria, and firstly that of common sense.

If the individual cannot know anything, why should the sum of individuals know more? An error, were it even a hundred thousand years old, does not constitute a truth on account of its age. The mob invariably follows the beaten track. It is, on the contrary, the minority which achieves progress.

Is it better to trust to the testimony of the senses? They are sometimes deceptive, and only inform us of appearances. Reality escapes them.

Reason, being immutable and impersonal, offers more guarantees; but to manifest itself, it must be incarnate.

Then reason becomes my personal reason; a rule avails little if it is a false one. Nothing proves that it is correct.

We are recommended to check it by the senses; but they may heap shadow on shadow. From a confused sensation, a defective law will be induced, and one which, later, will prevent a clear view of things.

Morals remain. That is to make God descend to the level of the useful, as if our needs were the measure of the absolute.

As for evidence, attested by one and denied by another, it is a criterion of itself. M. Cousin has demonstrated this.

'I see only revelation,' said Bouvard. 'But, to believe in that, one must admit two previous things as known—the body that has felt and the intelligence that has perceived; one must admit sense and reason, which are human witnesses, and consequently suspect.'

Pécuchet reflected, folding his arms. 'But we're going to fall into the frightful abyss of scepticism.'

That frightened only weak minds, according to Bouvard.

'Thanks for the compliment,' replied Pécuchet. 'But there exist indisputable facts. One can attain truth within certain limitations.'

'What limitations? Do two and two always make four? Is the contained, in every case, less than the container? What does being near the truth mean, or a fraction of God, or a part of something indivisible?'

'Oh, you're only a sophist!' and Pécuchet, vexed, sulked for three days.

They employed them in running over the chapter-heads of several volumes. Bouvard smiled from time to time, and renewing the conversation:

'You see, it's difficult not to doubt. Thus, as for God, the proofs of Descartes, Kant, and Leibnitz are not the same, and mutually destroy each other. The creation of the world by atoms or by a spirit remains inconceivable.

'I feel myself at the same time matter and thought, while ignorant what either of them is.

'Impenetrability, solidity, weight, seem to me as much mysteries as my soul—all the more so, then, the union of soul and body.

'To explain it, Leibnitz has imagined his harmony; Malebranche, premonition; Cudworth, a mediator; and Bossuet sees in it a perpetual miracle, which is idiotic: a perpetual miracle would no longer be a miracle.'

'Quite so!' said Pécuchet.

And both avowed their weariness of philosophers. So many systems serve only to confuse. Metaphysics has no use. One can exist without it.

Besides, their money troubles were increasing. They owed for three barrels of wine to Beljambe, for twenty-five pounds of sugar to Langlois, a hundred and twenty francs to the tailor, sixty to the shoemaker. Expenses were always mounting and Gouy paid nothing.

They went to Marescot, in the hope of raising some money, either by selling the Ecalles, or mortgaging their farm, or transferring their house, which would be paid for by an annuity, and of which they would keep the use. An impracticable method, said Marescot, but a better plan was preparing, and they would be informed.

Then they thought of their wretched garden. Bouvard undertook to trim the arbour and Pécuchet to prune espaliers. Marcel was to dig the borders.

After a quarter of an hour they stopped; one closed his pruning-knife, the other laid down his scissors, and they began to stroll gently about—Bouvard in the shade of the limes, without a waistcoat, his chest stuck out, his arms bare; Pécuchet along the wall, with bent head, his hands clasped

249

behind him, the peak of his cap turned round over his neck as a protection; and so they walked parallel, without even seeing Marcel, who was resting on the step of the shed, eating a crust of bread.

During this meditation, thoughts had come bubbling up. They hailed each other, fearing to lose them; and metaphysics returned. It came back with the rain and sun, a pebble in their shoe, a flower on the lawn—with everything.

Watching a candle burn, they demanded whether the light was in the object or in our eye. Since stars may have perished by the time their beams reach us, we are perhaps admiring things that do not exist.

Having found one of Raspail's medicinal cigarettes in a waistcoat pocket, they crumbled it into water, and the camphor began to revolve.

Here is motion in matter! A superior degree of motion would lead to life.

But if matter in motion sufficed to create life, life would not be so various. For, in the beginning, there was neither earth, water, men, nor plants. What, then, is this primordial matter, which has never been seen, which has never been of the things of the earth, but has produced them all?

Sometimes they needed a book. Dumouchel, tired of helping them, did not answer, and they pursued the question passionately—Pécuchet especially.

His desire for truth became a burning thirst.

Moved by Bouvard's words, he abandoned spiritualism, soon took it up again, to leave it once more, and cried out, his head in his hands: 'Oh, doubt! doubt! I should like extinction better!'

Bouvard perceived the inadequacy of materialism and tried to hold to it, declaring, however, that he was playing a losing game.

They began reasoning on a solid basis; it crumbled away;

and suddenly an idea would vanish, as a fly darts off when one tries to catch it.

During the winter evenings they talked in the museum, by the fireside, gazing at the embers. The wind that whistled in the corridor made the panes shake, the black bulk of the trees swayed, and the sadness of the night increased the gravity of their thoughts.

Bouvard, from time to time, walked to the end of the room and back. The tapers and vases by the wall cast slanting shadows on the floor; and the Saint Peter, seen in profile, extended on the ceiling the silhouette of his nose, like a monstrous hunting-horn.

It was difficult to move freely among the objects, and often Bouvard bumped carelessly into the statue. With its great eyes, hanging underlip, and drunkard's expression, it annoyed Pécuchet as well. For a long time they had meant to get rid of it, but, from lack of effort, delayed from day to day.

One evening, in the midst of an argument on the monad, Bouvard stubbed his great toe against the point of Saint Peter's foot and, discharging his vexation on him:

'He annoys me, this clown! Let's throw him outside!'

This was difficult by way of the staircase. They opened the window and tilted him on the edge gently. Pécuchet, kneeling, tried to raise his heels, while Bouvard lowered his shoulders. The old image did not budge; they had to use the halberd as a lever, and at last managed to balance him evenly. Then, with a swing, he dived into the void, his tiara forward; a heavy sound echoed out, and next day they found him, broken in a dozen fragments, in the former manure-ditch.

An hour later the notary entered, bringing good news. A person in the locality would advance three thousand francs on a mortgage of their farm and, as they were rejoicing: 'By the by, there is one condition; that is, that you

251

sell the Ecalles for fifteen hundred francs. The loan will be settled this very day. The money's in my office at home.'

Both of them were eager to consent. Bouvard ended by answering: 'All right—agreed!'

'Agreed!' said Marescot. And he revealed the person's name; it was Mme Bordin.

'I guessed it,' cried Pécuchet.

Bouvard, humiliated, kept silent.

She or another, what was the difference? The chief thing was to be free of their difficulties.

The sum handed over (that for the Écalles would be paid later), they at once met all the bills, and were on their way home when, at the corner of the market, farmer Gouy stopped them.

He was going to their house to inform them of a misfortune. The wind the night before had blown down twenty apple trees in the yards, destroyed the distillery, and taken the roof off the barn. They passed the rest of the afternoon inspecting the damage, and the next day with the carpenter, the mason, and the tiler. The repairs would cost at least eighteen hundred francs.

Then, in the evening, Gouy arrived. Marianne herself had just told him of the sale of the Écalles—a piece of land that gave a splendid yield, and just suited him, that had no need of cultivation, the best bit of the whole farm! And he asked for a reduction in rent.

The gentlemen refused. The case was submitted to the magistrate, who decided in favour of the farmer. The loss of the Ecalles, worth two thousand francs an acre, would deprive him of seventy francs per year, and he would certainly win his case in the courts.

Their fortune was diminished. What was to be done? And soon, how were they to live?

They both sat down to table full of discouragement.

Marcel knew nothing about cooking; on this occasion the dinner was worse than ever. The soup was dish-water, the rabbit smelt bad, the beans were raw, the plates dirty, and, at dessert, Bouvard exploded, threatening to break everything over Marcel's head.

'Let's be philosophic,' said Pécuchet. 'A little less money, a woman's plots, a servant's awkwardness—what does it amount to? You are too embedded in matter.'

'But when it annoys me—' said Bouvard.

'I don't even admit its existence,' replied Pécuchet.

He had recently read a summary of Berkeley, and added:

I deny extension, time, space, substance even! For, true substance is spirit aware of its qualities.'

'Very well,' said Bouvard. 'But with the suppression of the world, proofs will be wanting for the existence of God.'

Pécuchet protested and at great length, although he had a cold in the head caused by iodide of potassium, and a permanent fever contributed to his excitement. Bouvard felt disturbed about this, and summoned the doctor.

Vaucorbeil prescribed orange juice with the iodide, and baths of sulphide of mercury later.

'What's the good?' answered Pécuchet. 'One day or another the form will disappear. The essence doesn't perish.'

'No doubt,' said the doctor, 'matter is indestructible. Still—'

'No, no! What is indestructible is Being. This body here in front of me—yours, doctor—prevents my knowing you yourself; it's only, so to speak, a garment, or rather, a mask.'

Vaucorbeil thought him mad.

'Good-bye! Take care of your mask!'

Pécuchet would not slow down. He got hold of an introduction to Hegelian philosophy and wanted to explain it to Bouvard.

'All that is rational is real. There is, indeed, nothing real but the idea. The laws of the spirit are the laws of the universe; man's reason is identical with God's.'

Bouvard pretended to understand.

'The absolute, therefore, is at once the subject and the object, the unity in which all differences are sunk. Thus contradictions are resolved. Darkness admits of light, cold mixed with warmth produces temperature; the organism is only maintained by the destruction of the organism. Everywhere there is a principle that divides, a principle that unites.'

They were on the mound, and the curé passed by the lattice, his breviary in his hand.

Pécuchet asked him in, to finish the explanation of Hegel for his benefit, and see what he thought of it.

The man in the cassock sat down with them, and Pécuchet started on Christianity.

'No religion has so well established this truth, that "Nature is only a moment of the idea!"'

'A moment of the idea!' murmured the priest, stupefied.

'Yes, indeed. God, by assuming a visible envelope, has shown His consubstantial union with it.'

'With nature? Oh! Oh!'

'By dying, He has rendered witness to the essence of death; therefore death was within Him. It made—it makes —a part of God.'

The ecclesiastic frowned.

'No blasphemy! It was for the salvation of the human race that He endured suffering.'

'Wrong! You are thinking of death in the individual, where doubtless it is an evil; but in relation to things outside, it is different. Don't separate spirit from matter.'

'But, sir, before the creation—'

'There never was a creation. It has always been there.

Otherwise new being would be added to the divine thought, which is absurd.'

The priest rose, having matters to see to elsewhere.

'I flatter myself that I've confounded him,' said Pécuchet. 'One more word. Since the earthly existence is only a continual passage from life to death, and from death to life, far from everything being, nothing is. But everything becomes, d'you understand?'

'Yes, I understand; or rather, I don't.'

Idealism at last exasperated Bouvard.

'I've had enough of it; the famous *cogito* bores me. One takes ideas of things for the things themselves. One explains what one knows very little about, by means of words that one doesn't understand at all. Substance, extent, energy, matter and soul. So much abstraction, imagination. As for God, impossible to know what He is, or even if He is. Once upon a time He caused the wind, the thunder, revolutions. Now He's diminishing. Besides, I don't see any use for Him.'

'And where are morals in all that?'

'Ah, goodness knows.'

'They lack a basis, definitely,' said Pécuchet to himself.

And he remained silent, cornered in a blind alley, the result of the premises that he had himself established. It was a surprise, a catastrophe.

Bouvard did not even any longer believe in matter.

The certainty that nothing exists (however much to be deplored) is not the less a certainty. Few people are capable of holding such a belief. This transcendentalism inspired them with pride, and they wished to display it. An occasion offered.

One morning, on their way to buy some tobacco, they saw a crowd in front of Langlois's door. It had gathered round the carrier's cart from Falaise, and there was a discussion concerning Touache, a convict who was at large in the neighbourhood. The conductor had seen him at the Croix-Verte between two policemen, and they were all heaving a sigh of relief.

Girbal and the captain remained in the square; then came the justice of the peace, curious to hear the news, and M. Marescot in velvet skull-cap and sheepskin slippers.

Langlois invited them to honour his shop with their presence. They would be more at their ease, and, despite customers and the ringing of the bell, the gentlemen went on discussing the misdeeds of Touache.

'Good God,' said Bouvard, 'he had bad instincts, that's all.'

'They can be curbed by virtue,' replied the notary.

'But if one hasn't any virtue?'

And Bouvard positively denied free-will.

'But,' said the captain, 'I can do what I wish. I'm free, for instance, to move my leg.'

'No, sir, because you've a motive for moving it.'

The captain sought a reply and did not find it. But Girbal fired this shot:

'A republican who speaks against liberties! That's comic.'

'What a joke!' said Langlois.

Bouvard took him up:

'Why don't you give your fortune to the poor?'

The grocer threw an anxious glance round his shop.

'What? I'm not such a fool. I keep it for myself.'

'If you were Saint Vincent de Paul you'd act otherwise, because you'd have his character. So you're not free.'

'A quibble,' answered the assembly in chorus.

Bouvard did not give way, and pointing to the scales on the counter:

'They'll keep without moving so long as one of them is empty. It's the same with the will; and the hesitation of scales, between two weights that seem equal, symbolises the labour of our spirit, when it's deciding on motives, until the moment when the stronger one wins and determines it.'

'All that,' said Girbal, 'doesn't help Touache in the least, and doesn't prevent him from being a thoroughly bad lot.'

Pécuchet put in a word:

'Vices are the properties of nature, like floods and storms.'

The notary stopped him, and, rising on tiptoe at each word:

'I find your system absolutely immoral. It gives free rein to every sort of excess, excuses crime and makes the guilty innocent.'

'Exactly,' said Bouvard. 'The unhappy creature who follows his appetite has every right to do so, the same as the honest man who listens to reason.'

'Don't stand up for scoundrels.'

'Why scoundrels? When a man's born blind, or an idiot, or a murderer, that seems disorder to us, as though order were known to us, as if Nature acted with a purpose.'

'Then you question Providence?'

'Yes, I question it.'

'Look at history, then,' cried Pécuchet. 'Remember the assassinations of kings, the massacres of peoples, dissensions in families, the plight of the individual.'

'And at the same time,' added Bouvard, for they egged each other on, 'this Providence looks after the little birds and makes the crayfish's claws grow a second time. Ah! if by Providence you mean a law that rules everything, I quite agree, I more than agree.'

'But, sir,' said the notary, 'there are principles.'

'What sort of a tale is that? A science, according to Condillac, is all the better for not needing any. They only summarise knowledge already acquired, and lead us to those very notions which are disputable.'

'Have you, like us,' pursued Pécuchet, 'scrutinised and dug down into the arcana of metaphysics?'

'That's what we've done, gentlemen; that's what we've done.'

And the gathering broke up.

But Coulon, drawing them aside, told them in a paternal tone that he was certainly not devout, and that he even detested the Jesuits. Yet he would not go so far as they. Oh, no, indeed not; and at the corner of the square they passed the captain, who was lighting his pipe and growling:

'Of course I do what I want to, good God!'

Bouvard and Pécuchet enunciated their abominable paradoxes on other occasions. They held up to doubt the probity of men, the chastity of women, the intelligence of the Government, the good sense of the people—in fact, they undermined all foundations.

Foureau became disturbed, and threatened them with prison if they continued such discourses.

The evidence of their superiority gave umbrage. As they upheld immoral points of view, they were surely immoral themselves; slanders were invented about them.

Then a pitiable faculty developed in their spirit, that of perceiving stupidity and no longer tolerating it.

Insignificant things made them sad: advertisements in the newspapers, a smug profile, a foolish remark heard by chance.

Musing on what was said in the village, and on there existing as far as the Antipodes other Coulons, Marescots, Foureaux, they felt as though the heaviness of all the earth were weighing on them.

They no longer went out, or received visits.

One afternoon, a conversation arose in the courtyard between Marcel and a gentleman in a wide-brimmed hat and dark eyeglasses. It was the academician Larsoneur.

He could not help noticing a parted curtain and doors closing. His call had been an overture of reconciliation, and he went off raging, instructing the servant to tell his masters that he regarded them as boors.

Bouvard and Pécuchet did not care. The world was diminishing in importance; they saw it as through a cloud, come down from their brains, over their eyes.

Besides, is it not an illusion, a bad dream? Perhaps, after all, prosperity and misfortune are balanced. But this welfare of the species does not console the individual.

'And what do other people matter to me?' said Pécuchet.

His despair afflicted Bouvard. It was he who had pushed Pécuchet so far, and the dilapidation of their dwelling sharpened their gloom with daily irritations.

To induce cheerfulness they reasoned with each other, set themselves tasks, and quickly fell back into greater laziness, into a profound depression.

When meals were over they remained with their elbows on the table, groaning lugubriously. Marcel stared, then returned to his kitchen and stuffed himself in solitude.

In the middle of the summer they received a formal announcement of Dumouchel's marriage with Mme Olympe-Zulma Poulet, a widow.

'May God bless him!'

Then they remembered the time when they were happy.

Why did they no longer go out with the harvesters? Where were the days when they went into the farms, looking for antiques? Nothing, now, brought those delightful hours that distilling or literature had filled. They were separated from them by an abyss. Something irrevocable had befallen.

They wanted to take a walk in the fields as they used to, went a long way, and got lost. Little clouds were like wool in the sky, the wind swayed the heads of oats, a brook murmured by a meadow, when suddenly a horrible smell stopped them, and they saw, on the stones between the briers, the corpse of a dog.

The four legs were dried up. The grinning jaw revealed ivory fangs beneath blue chops; instead of the belly there was an earth-coloured mass that seemed to quiver, so thickly did it pullulate with vermin. It stirred, beaten by the sun, under the buzzing of flies, in that intolerable stench—a fierce, and as it were, devouring odour.

But Bouvard wrinkled his brow and tears damped his eyes.

Pécuchet said stoically: 'One day we shall be like that.'

The thought of death had taken possession of them. They talked of it as they went back.

After all, it does not exist. We depart in the dew, in the breeze, in the stars. We become part of the sap of the trees, the sparkle of jewels, the plumage of birds. We give back to Nature what she has lent us, and the void before us holds nothing more awful than the void behind us.

They tried to imagine death in the form of a very dark night, a bottomless pit, a never-ending swoon—anything at all was better than this monotonous, absurd and hopeless existence.

They recited their unsatisfied desires. Bouvard had always wanted horses, carriages, the best Burgundies, and beautiful yielding women in a splendid mansion. Pécuchet's ambition was philosophic knowledge. With that, the most vast of problems, that which contains all others, would be resolved in a twinkling. When would he get so far?

'As well finish at once.'

'As you like,' said Bouvard.

And they examined the question of suicide.

Where is the evil in rejecting a burden that crushes you, in performing an act that harms nobody? If it offended God, should we have the power to accomplish it? It is not a cowardice, in spite of what is said; rather a noble insolence, to flout, even to one's own hurt, what men most prize.

They deliberated on the kind of death to choose.

Poison is painful. It needs too much courage to cut one's throat. Suffocation is frequently unsuccessful.

Finally, Pécuchet took two of the ropes used in their gymnastics up to the loft. Then, having tied them round the same roof-beam, he let a noose hang down and placed two chairs underneath, in order to reach the ropes.

It was the method decided on.

They wondered what impression would be made in the neighbourhood, whither their library, their papers, their collections, would find their way. The thought of death made them affectionate. But they did not give up their project, and, by dint of talking about it, grew used to it.

On the evening of the 24th December, between ten and eleven, they were meditating in the museum, each dressed in his own fashion. Bouvard had a blouse over his knitted waistcoat; and Pécuchet, to save expense, had not left off his monk's robe for three months.

Since they were extremely hungry (for Marcel, who had gone out early, had not come back), Bouvard thought it would do them good to take a nip of brandy, and Pécuchet to have some tea.

As he was lifting the kettle, he spilt the water on the floor.

'Clumsy!' cried Bouvard, and finding the brew weak, he wanted to strengthen it with two more spoonfuls.

'It'll be awful,' said Pécuchet.

'Not a bit.'

And, each pulling the caddy towards him, the tray fell; one of the cups was broken, the last of their beautiful china service.

Bouvard turned pale—'Go on! Wreck everything! Take your time!'

'Quite a catastrophe, in fact.'

'Yes, a catastrophe! It was my father's.'

'Your natural father,' added Pécuchet, sneering.

'Ah, now you're insulting.'

'No, but you're sick of me. I can see it. Own up!'

And Pécuchet was seized with anger—or rather, madness. Bouvard too. They both shouted at once, one irritated by hunger, the other by alcohol. Pécuchet's throat only gave out a croak.

'It's hell, this existence; I'd rather be dead. Good-bye!'

He grabbed the taper, turned on his heels, and banged the door.

Bouvard, in the dark, had difficulty in opening it, ran after him, and reached the attic.

The candle was on the floor, and Pécuchet standing on one of the chairs, with the rope in his hand.

Bouvard wanted to follow suit.

'Wait for me!'

And he was climbing on the other chair, when suddenly stopping:

'But . . . we've not made our wills.'

'My word! That's true.'

Sobs swelled their breasts. They went to the little window to breathe.

The air was cold and many stars were shining in a sky black as ink.

The whiteness of the snow that covered the earth was lost in the mist on the horizon.

They perceived, close to the ground, little lights which, approaching and growing larger, were all moving towards the church.

Curiosity impelled them there.

It was the midnight Mass. The lights came from the lanterns of the shepherds, some of whom were shaking their capes in the porch.

The serpent was wheezing, the incense smoked. Glasses, hanging along the nave, outlined three crowns of multi-coloured fire, and in the far distance, on either side of the tabernacle, enormous candles erected their red flames. Above the heads of the crowd and the women's hoods, beyond the choristers, one could make out the priest in his golden chasuble; to his high-pitched voice answered the strong tones of the men filling the roodloft, and the wooden vault trembled on its stone arches. Pictures representing the Stations of the Cross decorated the walls. In the middle of the choir, before the altar, a lamb was lying with its feet tucked under it and ears pricked up.

The warmth gave them a queer feeling of comfort, and their thoughts, lately so agitated, became calm like waves appeased.

They heard the Lesson and the Creed, observed the movements of the priest. Meanwhile the old and the young, the poor women in rags, the farmers' wives in their high bonnets, the sturdy young men with fair whiskers—all were praying, absorbed in the same deep joy, and, on the straw of a stable, they saw the infant Christ shining like a sun. This faith of others touched Bouvard despite his reason, and Pécuchet notwithstanding the hardness of his heart.

There was silence: all backs were bent, and, on the tinkling of a bell, the little lamb baa'd.

The priest lifted up the host as high as he could reach. Then burst out a song of joy that called the world to the feet of the King of the Angels. Bouvard and Pécuchet involuntarily joined in, and felt as though a dawn were rising in their souls.

IX

At three o'clock the next day Marcel reappeared with green face, bloodshot eyes, a lump on his forehead, trousers torn, dirty and stinking of spirits.

After his annual custom, he had been to a place named Iqueville, fifteen miles off, to celebrate Christmas Eve with a friend; and, stuttering more than ever, weeping, wanting to strike himself, he begged forgiveness, as though he had committed a crime. His masters pardoned him. A singular calm persuaded them to mercy.

The snow had melted suddenly, and they were walking in their garden sniffing the warm air, happy to be alive.

Was it only chance that had turned them from death? Bouvard felt moved. Pécuchet called to mind his first communion; and, full of gratitude to the Power, the Cause on which they depended, the idea came to them of reading books of devotion.

The New Testament dilated their souls, dazzled them like a sun. They saw Jesus standing on the mount, one arm raised, with the crowd listening below; or again on the edge of the lake, amid the Apostles hauling at their nets; then on the ass, to the clamour of *Alleluias*, His locks fanned by the waving palms; and at last high on the cross, bowing His head whence a dew falls eternally upon the world. What won them, what gave them pleasure, was the tenderness towards the humble, the defence of the poor, the exaltation of the oppressed. And in this book where Heaven is displayed, there is nothing theological amid so many precepts, no dogma; nothing demanded but purity of heart.

As for miracles, their reason was not surprised by them; they had known them from childhood. The nobility of Saint John delighted Pécuchet and prepared him to understand the Imitation better.

Here were no more parables, flowers, birds; but groans, and a shrinking of the soul within itself. Bouvard grew sad as he turned these pages, which seemed written when the day was overcast, deep within a cloister between a belfry and a tomb. There our mortal life appears so lamentable that we have to forget it and turn to God; and the two cronies, after all their disappointments, felt the need of simplicity, of loving something, of finding rest for their souls.

They made a start with Ecclesiastes, Isaiah, Jeremiah.

But the Old Testament frightened them, with its lion-voiced prophets, the commotion of thunder in the sky, all the sobs of Gehenna, and its God who scatters empires as the wind does clouds.

They read it on Sundays, at vesper-time, while the church bell was tolling.

One day they attended Mass, then went again. It was a distraction at the end of the week. The Count and Countess de Faverges greeted them from a distance—which caused remark. The justice of the peace said, with a wink, 'Splendid. I commend you!'

All the ladies of the neighbourhood now sent them consecrated bread.

Abbé Jeufroy paid them a call; they returned it and continued on visiting terms, and the priest did not talk about religion.

They were astonished at this reserve; so Pécuchet, in a negligent manner, asked him how one should set about acquiring faith.

'Practise first.'

They began to practise, the one hopefully, the other

defiantly, Bouvard convinced that he would never become devout. For a month he followed all the offices regularly, but, unlike Pécuchet, did not wish to constrain himself to fasting.

Was it a matter of hygiene? One knows what hygiene is worth! A question of decorum? Hang decorum! A mark of submission to the Church? Little he cared for that! In short, he declared the rule absurd, pharisaical, and opposed to the spirit of the New Testament.

On previous Good Fridays they had eaten what Germaine provided.

But on this occasion Bouvard had ordered a steak. He seated himself, cut the meat, and Marcel looked at him scandalised, while Pécuchet gravely skinned his slice of cod.

Bouvard remained with his fork in one hand, his knife in the other. At last, plucking up courage, he raised a morsel to his lips. Suddenly his hands trembled, his ruddy countenance grew pale, his head fell back.

'Are you ill?'

'No, but—' and he made an admission. As a result of his upbringing (it was stronger than himself), he could not eat meat on that day, for fear of dying.

Pécuchet, without abusing his victory, profited by it to live as he chose.

One evening he came home with his countenance filled with sober joy, and, letting the word escape, said he had just confessed.

Then they discussed the importance of confession.

Bouvard admitted that of the early Christians, which was made in public; the modern form is too easy. Yet he did not deny that this investigation of ourselves might be an element of progress, a spur to morality.

Pécuchet, eager for perfection, sought out his vices: the

gusts of pride had long since departed. His taste for work acquitted him of sloth; as to greed, no one was more temperate. Sometimes anger got the better of him.

He swore to cease from it.

After that, it would be necessary to acquire the virtues, humility first—that is to say, to believe himself incapable of all merit, unworthy of the least reward; to mortify his spirit and put himself so low as to be trodden under foot with the mire on the highways. He was still far from this disposition.

He lacked another virtue—chastity. For, secretly, he missed Mélie, and the pastel portrait of the lady in the Louis xv dress disturbed him with its low-cut bodice.

He shut it up in a cupboard, pushed his modesty to the extent of fearing to regard his own body, and went to bed in a pair of drawers.

So much precaution against lust set it aflame. In the morning especially he had to undergo terrific struggles, like Saint Paul, Saint Benedict, and Saint Jerome at a very advanced age; as a result they had recourse to ferocious penances. Pain is an expiation, a remedy and a means, a homage to Jesus Christ. All love demands sacrifice—and what kind is more painful than that of our own body?

In order to mortify himself, Pécuchet gave up his glass of brandy after meals, reduced himself to four pinches of snuff a day, and no longer wore his cap during the extreme cold.

One day Bouvard, who was nailing up the vine, placed a ladder by the wall of the terrace near the house, and unintentionally found himself looking into Pécuchet's room.

His friend, stripped to the waist, was gently lashing his shoulders with the clothes-beater; next, in more lively fashion, took off his trousers and flogged his rump; and then fell on a chair, out of breath.

Bouvard was embarrassed as by the revelation of a mystery which ought not to have been discovered.

For some time he had noticed less dirt on the windows, fewer holes in the napkins, better food—changes that were due to the intervention of Reine, the curé's servant.

Mingling church affairs with those of the kitchen, as strong as a ploughman, and faithful although disrespectful, she invaded households, gave advice, and took possession. Pécuchet trusted implicitly to her experience.

On one occasion she brought with her a corpulent individual, with little eyes like a Chinaman's, and a nose like a vulture's beak. It was M. Gouttman, dealer in church goods. He unpacked some from their boxes in the shed: crosses, medals and chaplets of all sizes, candelabra for oratories, portable altars, bouquets of tinsel, sacred hearts of blue cardboard, Saint Josephs with red beards, porcelain Calvaries. Pécuchet coveted them. Only the price gave him pause.

Gouttman did not ask for money. He preferred making exchanges, and, going up to the museum, he offered a supply of his wares for some of the old iron-work and all the lead.

They appeared hideous to Bouvard. But Pécuchet's look, Reine's persuasiveness and the merchant's patter, ended by winning him round. When he saw him so malleable, Gouttman wanted the halberd as well; Bouvard, tired of displaying his exercises with it, let it go. The total valuation was made; the gentlemen still owed a hundred francs. They agreed to an arrangement on the condition of four bills at three months' interval, and congratulated themselves on a good bargain.

Their purchases were scattered through all the rooms. A manger filled with hay and a cathedral in cork adorned the museum.

On Pécuchet's mantelpiece was a Saint John the Baptist

in wax; along the corridor were portraits of episcopal celebrities, and at the foot of the stairs, under a lamp that hung by chains, a Holy Virgin in sky-blue mantle and crowned with stars. Marcel kept these splendours clean, imagining that paradise contained nothing more beautiful.

What a pity the Saint Peter was broken, he would have looked so well in the hall! Pécuchet sometimes halted by the old manure-trench, where could be seen the tiara, a sandal, the tip of an ear. He sighed, then went on with his gardening, for he now joined manual labour to religious exercises, and dug the soil, clad in his monk's robe and comparing himself with Saint Bruno. This masquerade was perhaps a sacrilege; he renounced it.

But he took on an ecclesiastical manner, no doubt because of his contact with the curé. He had the appropriate smile and the voice, and, with a chilly gesture, slid his two hands into his sleeves up to the wrists. There came a time when the crowing of the cock importuned him, the roses sickened him; he no longer went out of doors, or else threw angry glances over the countryside.

Bouvard let himself be taken to the Feast of the Annunciation. The children singing hymns, the clusters of lilac, the festoons of greenery gave him, as it were, the sense of an imperishable youthfulness. God was manifested in his heart by the pattern of nests, the clearness of springs, the bounty of the sun; and his friend's devoutness seemed to him extravagant, overnice.

'Why do you groan during meals?'

'We must eat with groans,' replied Pécuchet, 'because by eating, man lost his innocence'—a phrase he had read in the *Seminarist's Manual*, two duodecimo volumes borrowed from M. Jeufroy; and he drank water from the shrine at La Salette, gave himself up, behind closed doors, to ejaculatory prayers, and hoped to enter the brotherhood of Saint Francis.

To obtain the gift of perseverance, he resolved to make a pilgrimage to the Blessed Virgin.

The choice of localities embarrassed him. Should it be to Our Lady of Fourvières, of Chartres, of Embrun, of Marseilles, or of Auray? Our Lady of La Délivrande was the nearest and as suitable as any.

'You'll go with me.'

'I should look like a ninny,' said Bouvard.

After all, he might come back a believer, to which he had no objection, and yielded out of good nature.

Pilgrimages should be made on foot. But twenty-seven miles would be hard going; and carriers' carts not being congruous with meditation, they hired an old cab, which, after twelve hours on the road, put them down in front of the inn.

They had a double-bedded room with two washstands supporting two water-jugs in little round basins, and the proprietor told them that it had been the 'Monks' room' during the Revolution. Our Lady of La Délivrande had been carefully hidden there, so that the good fathers could say Mass secretly.

This gave pleasure to Pécuchet, and he read aloud an account of the chapel, which he had picked up in the kitchen below.

It was founded at the beginning of the second century by Saint Régnobert, first bishop of Lisieux, or by Saint Ragnebert, who lived in the seventh, or by Robert the Magnificent, in the middle of the eleventh.

The Danes, the Normans, and, most of all, the Protestants have burnt and ravaged it at different times.

About 1112, the original statue was discovered by a sheep, which, striking with its foot in a pasture-ground, showed the place where it lay, and on that spot Count Baldwin built a sanctuary.

Her miracles were innumerable. A merchant of Bayeux, captive of the Saracens, invoked her; his irons fell off and he escaped. A miser finds in his attic a troop of rats, calls her to his aid, and the rats disappear. The contact of a medal, that had touched her effigy, made an old materialist of Versailles repent on his deathbed. She restored the power of speech to a man named Adeline, who had lost it for blaspheming; and, by her protection, M. and Mme de Becqueville had enough strength to live chastely in the married state.

Among those she has healed of incurable affections are cited Mlle de Palfresne, Anne Lirieux, Marie Duchemin, François Dufai, and Mme de Jumillac, whose maiden name was d'Osseville.

Famous people have paid her visits—Louis XI, Louis XIII, two daughters of Gaston d'Orléans, Cardinal Wiseman, Samirrhi, Patriarch of Antioch; Mgr Véroles, Vicar Apostolic of Manchuria—and the Archbishop of Quélen came to give thanks for the conversion of Prince Talleyrand.

'She will be able,' said Pécuchet, 'to convert you too.'

Bouvard, already in bed, gave a kind of grunt, and fell sound asleep.

At six o'clock next morning they entered the chapel.

A new one was being built; tarpaulins and planks encumbered the nave, and the rococo monument displeased Bouvard, especially the altar in red marble, with Corinthian pilasters.

The miracle-working statue, in a niche to the left of the choir, is draped in a spangled robe. The sacristan arrived, with a candle for each of them. These he stuck on a sort of triangular candlestick overtopping the balustrade, demanded three francs, made a bow, and went off.

Then they examined the ex-votos.

Inscribed tablets bore witness to the gratitude of the

faithful. There were two swords placed crosswise, given by a former scholar of the École Polytechnique, brides' bouquets, soldiers' medals, silver hearts, and on the ground, in the corner, a forest of crutches.

From the sacristy issued a priest carrying the pyx.

After halting a few minutes at the foot of the altar he went up three steps, and recited the *Oremus*, the *Introit* and the *Kyrie*, which the kneeling chorister reeled off in a single breath.

The congregation was small, twelve or fifteen old women. One heard the clicking of their rosaries and the sound of a hammer striking the stones. Pécuchet, leaning over his prayer-stool, answered the *Amens*. During the elevation, he prayed Our Lady to send him a constant and indestructible faith.

Bouvard, on a chair by his side, took his prayer book from him and paused at the Litanies to the Virgin.

'Most pure, most chaste, venerable, gentle, powerful, merciful, tower of ivory, house of gold, gate of the dawn.'

These words of adoration, these hyperboles, drew him towards her to whom so much homage is paid.

He imagined her as she is represented in church paintings, on a pile of clouds, with cherubim at her feet, the Infant Christ at her breast—mother of tenderness that heals all the sorrows of the earth—apotheosis of womanhood; for man, the fruit of her womb, exalts her love and seeks only to rest upon her heart.

When the Mass was over, they strolled past the shops that are built against the wall on one side of the square. There you see a display of statues, basins for holy water, urns with gold bands, Jesus Christs of coconut, ivory chaplets; and the sun, catching the glass of the cases, dazzled their eyes, and emphasised the crudity of the paintings, the ugliness of the designs. Bouvard, who at home would have considered these objects horrible, was indulgent. He bought a little Virgin in blue clay. Pécuchet was content with a rosary as a memento.

The salesmen were shouting:

'Come on! Come on! For five francs, three francs, sixty centimes, two sous—don't refuse Our Lady!'

The two pilgrims loitered without choosing anything. Rough comments were passed.

'What are those johnnies up to?'

'Probably they're Turks.'

'Protestants, more likely.'

A big young woman pulled Pécuchet by his coat; an old man in spectacles laid a hand on his shoulder; everybody yelled at once; then, leaving their stalls, hemmed them in, plaguing and insulting them more than ever.

Bouvard could stand it no longer.

'Leave us alone, damn you!'

The mob fell apart.

But a fat woman followed them for some distance across the square and shouted that they would be sorry for it.

Re-entering the inn, they found Gouttman in the café. Business had brought him to the district, and he was talking to a man examining accounts on the table in front of them.

This man had a leather cap, very wide trousers, a red face and a supple carriage despite his white hair; he looked at once like a retired officer and an old actor.

Occasionally he dropped an oath; then, on a word spoken in low tones by Gouttman, he immediately grew calm and went on to another paper.

Bouvard, after staring at him for a quarter of an hour, went over.

'Barberou, surely?'

'Bouvard!' cried the man in the cap, and they embraced.

In twenty years Barberou had met with every kind of fortune.

Newspaper editor, insurance agent, manager of an oyster-bed—'I'll tell you about that.' At last, returning to his earliest profession, he had become a traveller for a Bordeaux firm, and Gouttman, who 'worked the diocese,' placed his wine orders with the clergy. 'But excuse me; I'll be with you in a minute!'

He had resumed his accounts, when, starting from the bench:

'What? Two thousand?'

'Certainly!'

'But that's far too much!'

'What d'you mean?'

'I mean I've seen Hérambert myself,' answered Barberou furiously. 'The bill says four thousand: no tricks, now!'

The salesman did not lose countenance. 'Well, that lets you out. What then?'

Barberou rose, and from his face, at first pale and then purple, Bouvard and Pécuchet thought he was going to strangle Gouttman.

He sat down again and folded his arms. 'You must admit you're a rare scoundrel!'

'No insults, Monsieur Barberou; there are witnesses: take care!'

'I'll bring an action.'

'Tut, tut!' Then, closing his case, Gouttman raised his hat slightly: 'Till next time,' and went out.

Barberou explained the business. For a credit of a thousand francs, doubled as a result of Gouttman's methods of usury, he had delivered him three thousand francs' worth of wine. That should have paid his debt, with a thousand francs to spare; but he still owed three thousand. His employers would dismiss or prosecute him—'Swine!

Robber! Dirty Jew! And to think that he dines in priests' houses! Besides, everything that touches the cloth—' And he stormed against the priests, banging on the table with so much violence that the statuette nearly fell.

'Gently!' said Bouvard.

'Hullo, what's this?' and Barberou undid the wrapping of the little Virgin. 'A souvenir of the pilgrimage! Yours?'

Bouvard smiled non-committally instead of replying.

'It's mine,' said Pécuchet.

'I'm shocked at you,' answered Barberou. 'But I'll cure you of that, don't you worry.' And as one should be philosophic, and there's no use in moping, he invited them to lunch.

All three sat down to table.

Barberou was in good form—reminded them of the old days, put an arm round the waitress, wanted to measure Bouvard's paunch. He would soon be visiting them, and would bring a book that would make them sit up.

The thought of his visit gave them only a moderate pleasure. They talked of it for an hour in the cab, to the horse's trot. Then Pécuchet closed his eyes. Bouvard, too, fell silent; he was inwardly tending towards religion.

M. Marescot had called the evening before on an important matter. Marcel knew nothing more.

The notary could not receive them till three days later, and then explained the business at once. For an annual payment of seven thousand five hundred francs Mme Bordin proposed to buy the farm from Bouvard.

She had had an eye on it since she was a girl, knew all its ins and outs, its faults and advantages; and this passion was like a gnawing cancer. For the good lady, in true Normandy fashion, cherished property above everything, less for the safety of her capital than for the happiness of feeling the soil that belonged to her under her feet. In that hope she had made inquiries, had kept a daily watch and saved up for years, and now she was waiting impatiently for Bouvard's answer.

He felt awkward, not wishing that Pécuchet should one day find himself penniless. But the opportunity must be seized; it was the fruit of the pilgrimage. Providence a second time had manifested itself in their favour.

They offered these conditions: an annual payment, not of seven thousand five hundred francs, but of six thousand to pass on to the survivor. Marescot pointed out that one of them was in poor health. The other's constitution tended towards apoplexy. Mme Bordin signed the contract in a fever of longing.

Bouvard remained depressed. Someone wanted his death, and this reflection inspired him with solemn thoughts, ideas of God and eternity.

Three days after, M. Jeufroy invited them to a formal banquet that he gave once a year to his colleagues.

The dinner began about two o'clock in the afternoon and went on till eleven at night.

They drank perry, fired off puns. Abbé Pruneau composed an acrostic on the spot, M. Bougon did card tricks, and Cerpet, a young curate, sang a little ballad that had a flavour of gallantry. Such company amused Bouvard. He was less gloomy the next day.

The curé often came to see him, and displayed religion in its most gracious aspect. After all, what risk is there? And Bouvard soon consented to approach the holy table. Pécuchet was to participate in the sacrament at the same time.

The great day arrived.

The church was crowded, because of the first communions. The gentry and their wives overflowed the benches, the poorer folk stood at the back, or in the gallery over the door.

What was shortly to happen was unaccountable, thought Bouvard, but reason was not enough for the comprehension of certain matters. Very great men have admitted this. As well do as they, and in a kind of torpor he gazed at the altar, the censer, the tapers, with a slight blankness in his mind, for he had eaten nothing and felt a strange weakness.

Pécuchet, by meditating on Christ's passion, stimulated himself to transports of love. He would have liked to offer up his soul, and the souls of others—and the delights, the ecstasies, the illuminations of the saints, all beings, the whole universe. Although he prayed with fervour, the different parts of the Mass seemed to him rather long.

At last the little boys knelt on the first step of the altar, their clothes making a black strip, above which the fair or dark heads rose unevenly. Their places were taken by the girls, who wore flowing veils under their crowns; from a distance, one would have thought them a line of white clouds at the end of the nave.

Then it was the turn of the grown-ups.

The first on the north side was Pécuchet, but too much moved, no doubt, he was rocking his head to left and right. The curé could hardly put the host into his mouth, and he received it with rolling eyes.

Bouvard, on the other hand, opened his jaws so wide that his tongue hung over his lip like a flag. Rising, he bumped Mme Bordin. Their eyes met. She was smiling; without knowing why, he blushed.

After Mme Bordin, Mlle de Faverges, the countess, their lady companion, and a gentleman who was a stranger to Chavignolles, went up to the altar together.

The last two were Placquevent and Petit the schoolmaster, when suddenly Gorju was seen approaching.

He no longer had a beard; and he resumed his place,

with his arms crossed over his chest, in a highly edifying manner.

The curé harangued the little boys. They must take care, later on, not to act like Judas who betrayed his Lord, and must keep spotless their robe of innocence. Pécuchet sighed for his own. But chairs were being scraped, mothers were hurrying to embrace their children.

The parishioners exchanged greetings at the door. A few were weeping. Mme de Faverges, while she was waiting for her carriage, turned to Bouvard and Pécuchet and presented her future son-in-law.

'The Baron de Mahurot, engineer!'

The count had complained of never seeing them. He would be back next week.

'Make a note of it, I beg.'

The barouche having arrived, the ladies of the mansion went off and the crowd dispersed.

In their courtyard they found a parcel in the middle of the lawn. Since the house was shut up, the postman had thrown it over the wall. It was the work which Barberou had promised them: *Examination of Christianity*, by Louis Hervieu, an old pupil of the Ecole Normale. Pécuchet thrust it aside. Bouvard did not want to look at it.

He had been frequently told that the sacrament would transform him; for several days he awaited its flowering in his soul. He remained unaltered, and a doleful astonishment invaded him.

What! God's flesh mingles with our flesh and produces no effect! The thought that governs worlds does not enlighten our spirit! The supreme power abandons us to impotence!

M. Jeufroy reassured him, prescribing the *Catechism* of Abbé Gaume.

Pécuchet's devotion, on the other hand, had increased.

He would have liked to communicate in both kinds, sang psalms as he walked down the corridor, stopped his neighbours to argue and convert them. Vaucorbeil laughed in his face, Girbal shrugged his shoulders, and the captain called him Tartuffe. It was thought now that they were going too far.

It is an excellent habit to consider things as symbols. If the thunder growls, picture to yourself the Last Judgment; before a cloudless sky, contemplate the abode of the blessed; say to yourself on your walks that each step brings you nearer to death. Pécuchet observed this method. When he picked up his clothes he thought of the carnal envelope in which the second person of the Trinity is arrayed, the ticking of the clock recalled to him the beating of His heart, a pin-prick the nails of the cross; but in vain did he stay on his knees for hours, multiplying his prayers and straining his imagination; self-abasement did not come: impossible to attain to perfect contemplation.

He had recourse to mystic authors: Saint Theresa, John of the Cross, Louis of Granada, Simpoli, and in more recent times Monsignor Chaillot. Instead of the sublimities which he expected, he found only platitudes, a slipshod style, frigid imagery, and a wealth of comparisons taken from the jeweller's shop.

However, he learnt that there is an active and a passive purgation, an internal and an external vision, four kinds of prayer, nine excellencies in love, six degrees of humility, and that the wounding of a soul does not differ much from spiritual theft.

Several points embarrassed him.

Since the flesh is damned, why must we thank God for the boon of existence? What proportion must be observed between the fear indispensable to salvation and the hope which is no less so? Where is the sign of grace? etc.

M. Jeufroy's replies were simple.

'Don't torment yourself. By wishing to understand everything you run down a dangerous slope.'

The *Catechism of Perseverance* by Gaume had so disgusted Bouvard that he took to Louis Hervieu. It was a summary of the modern exegesis forbidden by the Government. As a republican Barberou had bought a copy.

It raised doubts in Bouvard's mind, and first on the question of original sin.

'If God created man sinful, He ought not to punish him; and evil is anterior to the fall, since there were already volcanoes and wild animals. In a word, this dogma upsets my notions of justice.'

'What do you expect?' asked the curé. 'It is one of those truths which everybody accepts, without our being able to furnish proofs; and we ourselves visit the sins of the fathers on the children. Thus morality and the law justify this decree of Providence, which one finds in Nature, too.'

Bouvard shook his head. Also he had doubts of hell.

'For all punishment should aim at reforming the guilty, which becomes impossible when it is everlasting. And how many endure it! Only think: all the ancients, the Jews, the Mohammedans, idolaters, heretics, and children who have died unbaptized—the children created by God and with what object?—to punish them for a crime they have never committed!'

'Such is the opinion of Saint Augustine,' added the curé, 'and Saint Fulgentius involves even the foetus in damnation. The Church, it is true, has come to no decision on this point. Remember, though, it is not God but the sinner who damns himself, and the offence being infinite, since God is infinite, the punishment also must be infinite. Is that all, sir?'

'Explain the Trinity,' said Bouvard.

'With pleasure. Let's take a comparison: the three sides of a triangle. Or, better still, our soul, which contains being, knowing and willing; so that what we call faculty with man is person with God. There's all the mystery.'

'But the three sides of a triangle are not each a triangle; these three faculties of the soul do not make three souls, and your persons of the Trinity are three Gods.'

'Blasphemy!'

'Then there's only one person, one God, a substance affected in three ways.'

'Let us worship without understanding,' said the curé.

'Very well,' said Bouvard.

He was afraid of passing for an unbeliever, of being badly received at the manor.

It was winter and they were visiting there three times a week, about five o'clock, and the cup of tea warmed them. The count by his demeanour 'recalled the style of the Old Court'; the countess, fat and placid, showed a fine discrimination in everything. Mlle Yolande, their daughter, was 'the type of our girlhood,' the angel of Keepsakes, and Mme de Noares, their companion, resembled Pécuchet, having a pointed nose.

The first time they entered the drawing-room she was championing somebody.

'I assure you he's changed! His present proves it.'

This somebody was Gorju. He had just offered the betrothed couple a Gothic praying-desk. It was brought along. The arms of the two houses had been inscribed in coloured relief. M. de Mahurot seemed pleased with it, and Mme de Noares said to him:

'You remember my protégés?'

Forthwith she led in two children, an urchin of some twelve years, and his sister, who was perhaps ten. Through the holes in their rags, their limbs were red with cold. The one was wearing old slippers, the other had only a single clog. Their hair came down over their foreheads, and they looked about them with burning eyes like frightened wolf cubs.

Mme de Noares related how she had met them one day on the main road. Placquevent could not account for them.

They were asked their names.

Victor, Victorine.

Where was their father?

In prison.

And what was he doing before that?

Nothing.

Their part of the country?

Saint-Pierre.

But which Saint-Pierre?

The two children, for reply, only snivelled, saying: 'Don't know, don't know.'

Their mother was dead and they were begging.

Mme de Noares explained how dangerous it would be to abandon them; she softened the countess, touched the count's pride, was supported by mademoiselle, persisted, succeeded. The gamekeeper's wife would take care of them. Afterwards, work would be found, and since they could neither read nor write, Mme de Noares would give them lessons herself, in order to prepare them for their catechism.

When M. Jeufroy came to the manor, the two youngsters were sent for; he would question them, then deliver a lecture in which was a certain ostentation on account of the audience.

Once when he had discoursed on the patriarchs, Bouvard, as he came away with him and Pécuchet, vigorously ran them down.

Jacob was conspicuous for his frauds, David for his murders, Solomon for his debaucheries.

The abbé replied that they must have a wider vision. Abraham's sacrifice is a figure of the Passion; Jacob another figure of the Messiah, like Joseph, and the bronze serpent, and Moses.

'Do you believe he wrote the Pentateuch?'

'Yes, undoubtedly.'

'Yet it records his death. The same holds for Joshua; and as for Judges, the author informs us that at the time of which he is writing, Israel did not yet have kings. The book then was written under the Kings. The prophets astonish me too.'

'Now he's going to deny the prophets!'

'Not at all! But in their exaltation they saw Jehovah under so many forms—as a fire, a bush, an old man, a dove —and they weren't certain of the revelation because they always asked for a sign.'

'Oh, and you discovered these fine things . . .'?

'In Spinoza.'

At this word the curé leapt.

'Have you read him?' asked Bouvard.

'God forbid!'

'Still, sir, science . . .'

'Sir, one can't be learned unless one's a Christian.'

Science moved him to sarcasm.

'Can your science make an ear of corn grow? After all, what do we know?' he said.

But he himself knew that the world was created for us; that the archangels are above the angels; that the human body will rise again as it was at the age of thirty.

His clerical self-confidence irritated Bouvard who, from distrust of Louis Hervieu, wrote to Varlot, and Pécuchet, better informed, demanded explanations of scripture from M. Jeufroy.

The six days of Genesis represent six great epochs. The precious vases, stolen by the Jews from the Egyptians, must be understood as intellectual riches, the arts whose secret they had pillaged. Isaiah did not strip himself completely, *nudus* in Latin signifying naked to the waist; thus Virgil advises people to go naked to work, and this writer would not have given a precept contrary to decency! There is nothing extraordinary about Ezekiel devouring a book; do we not speak of devouring a pamphlet or a newspaper?

But if one sees metaphor everywhere, what becomes of fact? The abbé maintained nevertheless that all these things had happened.

This manner of interpretation seemed to Pécuchet disloyal. He went on with his researches, and brought a note on the contradictions in the Bible.

Exodus informs us that for forty years sacrifices were made in the desert; if we are to believe Amos and Jeremiah, there were none. Chronicles and the book of Esdras do not agree about the numbering of the people. In Deuteronomy, Moses sees the Lord face to face; according to Exodus, he never saw Him. Where then is inspiration?

'The more reason for accepting it,' replied M. Jeufroy, smiling. 'Deception has need of connivance, genuineness doesn't care! When in difficulty, we come back to the Church. She is always infallible!'

On what does infallibility depend? The Councils of Basle and Constance refer it to the Councils. But often the Councils differ: witness what happened to Athanasius and Arius; those of Florence and Lateran confer it on the Pope. But Hadrian vi declares that the Pope, like anyone else, can err.

Quibbling! All that does not affect the permanence of dogma.

Louis Hervieu's work instances these divergencies: baptism was at one time reserved for adults; extreme unction did not become a sacrament until the ninth century;

the real presence was decreed in the eighth, purgatory recognised in the fifteenth, the Immaculate Conception dates from yesterday.

And Pécuchet reached a state in which he no longer knew what to think of Jesus. Three of the Evangelists make Him out a man. In one passage from St. John He appears to equal Himself to God; in another from the same gospel, to acknowledge Himself inferior.

The abbé rejoined by citing the letter of King Abgar, the actions of Pilate, and the testimony of the Sibyls, 'the foundation of which is genuine.' He traced the Virgin among the Gauls, the annunciation of a redeemer in China, the Trinity everywhere, the Cross on the cap of the Grand Lama, in Egypt grasped by the hands of the gods; and he even produced a drawing, showing a gnostic cross, which according to Pécuchet was a phallus.

M. Jeufroy secretly consulted his friend Pruneau, who looked out authors to support him. A conflict of erudition began; and spurred on by self-conceit, Pécuchet became transcendental, mythological.

He compared the Virgin to Isis, the Eucharist to the *homa* of the Persians, Bacchus to Moses, Noah's ark to the ship of Xithuros; these resemblances demonstrated in his view the identity of religions.

But there cannot be several religions, since there is only one God; and when he was at the end of his arguments, the man in the cassock exclaimed:

'It is a mystery!'

What is the meaning of this word? Lack of knowledge; very well. But if it denotes something of which the mere statement implies contradiction, it is a stupidity; and now Pécuchet would not let M. Jeufroy alone. He surprised him in his garden, awaited him at the confessional, pursued him in the sacristy.

The priest devised plans of escaping him.

One day, when he had set off for Sassetot to administer the sacrament, Pécuchet planted himself on the road in front of him, in such a manner as to make conversation inevitable.

It was an evening towards the end of August. The red sky was darkening and a large cloud had formed, regular at the base and with scrolls on top.

Pécuchet began by talking casually; then having slipped out the word 'martyr'—'How many of them do you think there were?'

'A score of millions at least.'

'Their number is not so great according to Origen.'

'Origen is suspect, you know.'

A big gust of wind swept by, bending the grass of the ditches and the two rows of elms stretching to the horizon.

Pécuchet resumed:

'Among the martyrs are included a number of Gallic bishops, killed while resisting the barbarians, which is another matter altogether.'

'Are you going to defend the Emperors?'

According to Pécuchet they had been maligned.

'The history of the Theban legion is a fable. In the same way I contest Symphorosa and her seven sons, Felicitas and her seven daughters, and the seven virgins of Ancyra condemned, though septuagenarians, to violation, and the eleven thousand virgins of Saint Ursula, who had a companion called *Undecemilla*—a name taken for a number; still more I doubt the ten martyrs of Alexandria!'

'All the same—all the same, they're found in authors worthy of belief.'

Some raindrops fell. The curé opened his umbrella; and Pécuchet, when he was underneath, went so far as to pretend that the Catholics had made more martyrs among the Jews, the Mohammedans, the Protestants and the free-thinkers than all the Romans in classical times.

The ecclesiastic exclaimed:

'But we find ten persecutions from Nero to Caesar Galba!'

'Well, and the massacres of the Albigenses? and Saint Bartholomew's Eve? and the revocation of the Edict of Nantes?'

'Deplorable excesses, no doubt, but you aren't going to compare these people with Saint Stephen, Saint Lawrence, Cyprian, Polycarp, a host of missionaries?'

'Excuse me—I'd remind you of Hypatia, Jerome of Prague, John Huss, Bruno, Vanini, Anne Dubourg!'

The rain increased, and its lines darted with such force that they rebounded from the ground like little white crackers. Pécuchet and M. Jeufroy walked slowly, pressed close to one another, and the curé said:

'After abominable tortures, they were flung into boiling coppers.'

'The Inquisition employed torture in the same way, and burnt one very daintily.'

'Illustrious women were exhibited in the *lupanars*!'

'Do you think Louis xiv's dragoons were sticklers for decency?'

'And mark you, the Christians had done nothing against the State!'

'No more had the Huguenots!'

The wind blew, sweeping the rain through the air. It pattered on the leaves, trickled along the side of the road, and the mud-coloured sky intermingled with the fields which lay bare after the harvest. Not a roof. Only in the distance a shepherd's hut.

Pécuchet's thin overcoat no longer had a dry stitch. The water ran down his spine, got into his boots, into his ears and eyes, despite the Amoros cap; the curé, holding up the tail of his cassock with one hand, exposed his legs, and the three corners of his clerical hat spat water on his shoulders like the gargoyles of a cathedral.

They had to stop, and, turning away from the storm, they remained face to face, belly to belly, their four hands gripping the swaying umbrella.

M. Jeufroy had not ceased defending the Catholics.

'Did they crucify your Protestants, as was done to Saint Simeon, or have a man devoured by two tigers, as happened to Saint Ignatius?'

'But you must make allowance for the number of women separated from their husbands, for the children snatched from their mothers! And the exile of the poor over snows and amid precipices! They were jammed into prisons; dragged, nearly dying, on the hurdle to execution.'

The abbé sneered.

'You will forgive me for not believing a word of it. And our own martyrs are less dubious. Saint Blandina was delivered naked in a net to a mad cow. Saint Julia perished overwhelmed with blows. Saint Tarachus, Saint Probus and Saint Andronicus had their teeth smashed by a hammer, their sides broken by iron combs, their hands pierced by red-hot nails, their skin torn off their skulls.'

'You're exaggerating,' said Pécuchet. 'The deaths of martyrs in those days were an amplification of rhetoric.'

'What! Of rhetoric?'

'Yes! while I, sir, I'm telling you history. The Catholics in Ireland disembowelled pregnant women to take their children.'

'Never.'

'And gave them to the pigs.'

'Come, come.'

'In Belgium, women were buried alive.'

'What nonsense!'

'We've got their names.'

'But all the same,' objected the priest, angrily shaking his umbrella, 'one can't call them martyrs. There are none outside the Church.'

'Excuse me. If the value of the martyr depends on the doctrine, how can he serve to prove its excellence?'

The rain had left off; not a word was spoken till they reached the village.

But on the threshold of the presbytery the abbé said:

'I'm sorry for you, really I'm sorry for you!'

Pécuchet at once related his altercation to Bouvard. It had roused in him a feeling against the Church, and an hour later, seated before a fire of brushwood, they read *The Curé Meslier*. These clumsy negations shocked them, then reproaching themselves for having perhaps misunderstood heroes, they perused the history of the most illustrious martyrs in the *Biographie Universelle*.

What a shouting of the mob when they came into the arena; and if the lions and jaguars were too mild, they were urged on with cries and gestures. The martyrs were seen all covered in blood, yet smiling, looking up to heaven; St. Perpetua tied up her hair so as not to appear in the least distressed. Pécuchet began to reflect. The window was open, the night calm, many stars were glittering. In martyrs' souls there must have passed something of which we have no idea, a joy, a divine spasm! And Pécuchet, by dwelling on it, said that he could understand, that he would have done as they.

'You?'

'Certainly.'

'Seriously—do you believe, or don't you?'

'I don't know.'

He lit a candle; then his eyes falling on the crucifix in

the alcove—'How many people in their misery have turned to Him!'

And after a silence—'They've spoilt Him; it's the fault of Rome, the trickery of the Vatican!'

But Bouvard admired the Church for its magnificence, and would have liked to be a cardinal in the Middle Ages.

'I'd have looked grand in the purple, don't you think?'

Pécuchet's cap, warming by the fire, was not yet dry. While he was stretching it he felt something in the lining, and a medal of St. Joseph fell out. They were perplexed, the incident seemed inexplicable.

Mme de Noares asked Pécuchet if he had not experienced, as it were, a change, a happiness, and betrayed herself by her questions. One day when he was playing billiards she had sewn the medal into his cap.

Evidently she was in love with him—they could have married, she was a widow—and he did not suspect this love, which might perhaps have brought happiness into her life.

Although he showed more devoutness than M. Bouvard, she had dedicated him to St. Joseph whose help is invaluable for conversions.

No one knew as well as she all the beads and the indulgences they procure, the efficacy of relics, the properties of holy waters. Her watch was held by a chain which had touched the bonds of St. Peter.

Among her charms there shone a pearl of gold, an imitation of the one in the church of Allouagne which contains a tear of Our Lord; a ring on her little finger enclosed some hair of the Curé of Ars, and as she used to gather herbs for the sick, her room resembled a sacristy and a dispensary.

She spent her time writing letters, visiting the poor, breaking up clandestine alliances, spreading photographs of the Sacred Heart. A gentleman was going to send her some 'martyrs' paste,' a mixture of paschal wax and human dust from the Catacombs which is employed, for desperate cases, in the form of plasters or pills. She promised some to Pécuchet.

He seemed shocked by such materialism.

In the evening a man from the count's brought him a basketful of tracts reporting the pious sayings of the great Napoleon, the witticisms of priests in wineshops, the terrifying deaths in store for unbelievers. Mme de Noarès knew it all off by heart, together with any number of miracles.

Some that she related were stupid, miracles without any object, as if God had performed them to dumbfound the world. Her own grandmother had stowed away some plums covered with a cloth in a cupboard, and when it was opened a year later, thirteen of them could be seen on the cloth making the shape of the cross.

'Explain that if you can.'

It was her favourite remark at the end of her stories, which she upheld with the stubbornness of a mule; otherwise she was a harmless soul, of lively disposition.

But on one occasion she lost her temper. Bouvard was disputing with her the miracle of Pezilla; a fruit-stand in which wafers were hidden during the Revolution had become gilded of itself.

'Perhaps there was a little yellow at the bottom coming from the damp.'

'No, no! I tell you there wasn't! The cause of the gilding was contact with the Eucharist.'

And she gave, as proof, the testimony of the bishops.

'It is, they say, like a shield, a—a palladium over the diocese of Perpignan. You can ask M. Jeufroy.'

Bouvard could stand it no longer, and having taken another look at his Louis Hervieu, he set off with Pécuchet.

The ecclesiastic had finished dinner. Reine offered them chairs, and at a sign fetched two small glasses which she filled with *Rosolio*.

After which Bouvard disclosed what had brought him.

The abbé did not give a direct reply.

'With God everything is possible, and miracles are a proof of religion.'

'Yet there are laws.'

'That's got nothing to do with it. He interferes with them to instruct, to correct.'

'How do you know that He interferes?' replied Bouvard. 'So long as nature follows its course, we don't think of it; but when anything extraordinary happens, we see the hand of God.'

'It may be there,' said the ecclesiastic. 'And when an event is certified by witnesses?'

'Witnesses will swallow anything, for there are false miracles.'

The priest reddened.

'No doubt . . . sometimes.'

'How are they distinguished from genuine ones? And if the genuine miracles, which are held as proof, are themselves in need of proof, why perform them?'

Reine interrupted and, preaching like her master, said that we must submit.

'Life is transitory, but death is eternal.'

'In other words,' said Bouvard, tossing off the *Rosolio*, 'the miracles of the past are no more proof than the miracles of to-day; similar arguments support those of the Christians and of the pagans.'

The curé threw his fork on the table.

'The others were false, must I say it again! There are no miracles outside the Church!'

'Why,' said Pécuchet to himself, 'it's the same argument

as for the martyrs; the doctrine depends on the facts and the facts on the doctrine.'

M. Jeufroy, after drinking a glass of water, continued:

'At the very moment you deny them, you believe. A world that has been converted by twelve fishermen, there is a grand miracle, if you like!'

'Not a bit.'

Pécuchet had another explanation.

'Monotheism comes from the Hebrews, the Trinity from the Indians, the Logos from Plato, the Virgin Mother from Asia.'

No matter! M. Jeufroy held to the supernatural, did not wish that Christianity should have the least human justification, although he saw, among all peoples, premonitions or distortions of it. The cynical ungodliness of the eighteenth century he would have tolerated; but modern criticism, with its politeness, exasperated him.

'I prefer the atheist who blasphemes, to the sceptic who quibbles!'

Then he looked at them with an air of triumph, as if to dismiss them.

Pécuchet returned home in a state of melancholy. He had hoped for a reconciliation between faith and reason.

Bouvard made him read this passage from Louis Hervieu:

'To know the abyss that separates them, oppose these maxims:

'Reason says to you: The whole includes the part, and faith replies: By transubstantiation Jesus, when He took communion with His apostles, had His body in His hand and His head in His mouth.

'Reason says to you: No one is responsible for the crimes of others, and faith replies: By original sin.

'Reason says to you: Three makes three; and faith declares: Three makes one.'

They ceased to visit the abbé.

It was the period of the war with Italy.

Honest men trembled for the Pope, thundered against Victor Emmanuel. Mme de Noares went so far as to wish for his death.

Bouvard and Pécuchet protested only mildly. When the door of the drawing-room opened before them and they admired their reflections passing the tall mirrors, while from the windows could be seen walks where the red waist-coat of a servant stood out against the green, they felt a delight; and the luxury of their surroundings made them indulgent towards the words that were spoken there.

The count lent them all the works of M. de Maistre. He elaborated these principles before a circle of intimates: Hurel, the curé, the justice of the peace, the notary and the baron, his future son-in-law, who used now and then to spend a night at the house.

'What is abominable,' the count would say, 'is the spirit of '89! First they question God; then they dispute about government; then comes liberty—liberty of insult, of revolt, of enjoyment, or rather of pillage—so that religion and authority ought to proscribe all independents and heretics. There would be an outcry no doubt about persecution, as though executioners persecuted criminals. I sum it up thus: there can be no State without God! The law can't be respected unless it comes from above, and in fact it's not a question of the Italians, but of knowing which will win, revolution or the Pope, Satan or Jesus Christ.'

M. Jeufroy showed his approval in monosyllables, Hurel with a smile, the justice of the peace by nodding his head. Bouvard and Pécuchet stared at the ceiling; Mme de Noares, the countess and Yolande were making garments for the poor; and M. de Mahurot, beside his fiancée, was turning over the leaves of a book.

Then there were periods of silence when everyone seemed plunged in the solution of some problem. Napoleon III was no longer saviour, and he had even set a deplorable example by letting stone-masons work at the Tuileries on Sunday.

'It oughtn't to be allowed,' was the count's usual phrase.

Social economy, the fine arts, literature, history, scientific doctrine—he laid down the law on everything in his position as Christian and father of a family; and would to God that the Government, in this respect, exercised the same severity which he showed in his household! Authority alone is judge of the dangers of knowledge; spread too widely, it excites the people to fatal ambitions. They were happier, these unfortunate people, when the nobles and the bishops tempered the absolutism of the king. Now they were being exploited by manufacturers. They would fall into slavery.

And all looked back regretfully to the old regime: Hurel through meanness, Coulon through ignorance, Marescot as an artist.

As soon as he got home, Bouvard fortified himself with La Mettrie, d'Holbach, etc.; and Pécuchet had drifted away from a religion which had become the tool of government. M. de Mahurot attended communion to please 'the Faverges ladies,' and, if he went regularly, it was on account of the servants.

A mathematician and dilettante, who played waltzes on the piano and admired Topffer, he was distinguished by a scepticism in the best of taste. The reports of feudal abuses, of the Inquisition or the Jesuits, were prejudiced; and he stood for progress, though distrusting everyone who was not a gentleman or had not come out of the École Polytechnique.

M. Jeufroy also displeased them. He believed in sorcery, but made jokes about idolatry; maintained that all languages are derived from the Hebrew; his rhetoric lacked spontaneity; it was invariably the stag at bay, honey and worm-wood, gold and lead, perfumes, urns, and the Christian soul compared with the soldier who ought to say in the face of sin: 'Stand and deliver!'

To escape his discourses, they arrived at the house as late as possible.

One day, however, they found him there. He had been waiting an hour for his two pupils. Suddenly Mme de Noares came in.

'The little girl has disappeared. I'm bringing Victor. Oh, the wretched boy!'

She had found, in his pocket, a silver thimble which had been missing for three days; then stifled with sobs:

'That's not all! No! While I was scolding him he showed me his bottom!'

And before the count or the countess could say anything: 'But it's really my fault; forgive me.'

She had concealed from them the fact that the two orphans were the children of Touache, who was now in prison.

What was to be done?

If the count sent them away they were lost, and his charitable act would be taken for a caprice.

M. Jeufroy was not surprised. Man being by nature corrupt, he must be punished for his own good.

Bouvard protested. Leniency was better.

But the count once more expatiated on the rod of iron which was as necessary for children as for peoples. These two were full of vices: the little girl was a liar, the boy a brute. After all, the theft might have been excused, the insolence never; education should be the school of respect.

So the keeper, Sorel, was to give the young man a good hiding at once.

M. de Mahurot, who had something to say to him, under-took the commission. He fetched a gun from the wall and called Victor, who had stayed in the middle of the courtyard, hanging his head.

'Follow me,' said the baron.

Since the road to the gamekeeper's did not go far out of the way to Chavignolles, M. Jeufroy, Bouvard and Pécuchet accompanied them.

A hundred yards from the house he asked them not to talk while they were going through the wood.

The ground sloped down to the river, where there were large blocks of stones. Under the setting sun, the water was glittering with gold discs. The green of the hills opposite was in shadow. A keen wind was blowing.

Some rabbits came out of their burrows, and nibbled the grass. There was a gun-shot, a second and yet another, and the rabbits jumped, then rolled over. Victor threw himself forward to seize them, and panted, dripping with sweat.

'You'll make a fine mess of your togs,' said the baron.

There was blood on his ragged smock.

The sight of blood was repugnant to Bouvard. He would not admit that it should ever be shed.

M. Jeufroy replied:

'Circumstances sometimes justify it. If the guilty person does not give his own blood, someone else must—a truth taught us by the Redemption.'

According to Bouvard, the Redemption had been almost useless, nearly all men being damned, despite Our Lord's sacrifice.

'But He renews it every day in the Eucharist.'

'And whatever the priest's unworthiness,' said Pécuchet, 'the miracle is accomplished by the words.'

'There is the mystery, sir.'

Meanwhile, Victor had riveted his eyes on the gun, and even tried to touch it.

'Down with your paws!'

And M. de Mahurot took a path through the wood.

The ecclesiastic had Pécuchet on one side and Bouvard on the other, and he said:

'Come now, you know *Debetur pueris*.'

Bouvard assured him that he humbled himself before his Creator, but was indignant that people had made Him into a man. We fear His vengeance, we work for His glory, He has all the virtues, arms, eyes, a policy, a habitation. Our Father which art in heaven, what does that mean?

And Pécuchet added:

'The universe has expanded, the earth is no longer its centre. It revolves among an infinitude of other worlds, many of which surpass it in size, and this shrinkage of our world shows us a more sublime ideal of God.

'So religion should be changed. Paradise, with its blest always in a state of contemplation, always singing and looking down on the tortures of the damned, is a piece of childishness. When one thinks that the basis of Christianity is an apple!'

The curé was annoyed.

'Deny Revelation, that'd be simplest.'

'How do you expect God to have spoken?' asked Bouvard.

'Prove that He hasn't!' said Jeufroy.

'Once more, who says so?'

'The Church!'

'Fine witness!'

The conversation bored M. de Mahurot, and as they were walking along:

'I advise you to listen to the curé, he knows more about it than you do!'

Bouvard and Pécuchet indicated that they were going to take another road, then at the Croix-Verte:

'Good evening to you.'

'Good evening,' said the baron.

All this would be retailed to M. de Faverges, and perhaps a breach would follow. So much the worse. They felt that they were despised by the grand folk, who never asked them to dinner, and they were tired of Mme de Noares with her continual remonstrances.

They could not, however, keep the De Maistre, and a fortnight later they returned to the manor, not expecting to be received.

Yet they were.

All the family were in the boudoir, besides Hurel and, surprisingly, Foureau.

Correction had failed to correct Victor. He refused to learn his catechism, and Victorine used gutter-words. In short, the boy should go to a reformatory and the girl to a convent.

Foureau undertook to carry out these instructions, and he was leaving when the countess called him back.

They were waiting for M. Jeufroy so that, with all present, they could fix the date of the marriage, which was to take place at the town hall in plenty of time before the church ceremony—to show their contempt for civil marriage.

Foureau tried to defend it. The count and Hurel attacked it. What was a municipal function compared with an ecclesiastical one! And the baron would not have considered himself married had it been only in front of a tricolour scarf.

'Bravo!' said M. Jeufroy, coming in. 'Marriage having been established by Jesus Christ—'

Pécuchet stopped him.

'In which gospel? At the time of the apostles it was so little thought of that Tertullian compares it to adultery.'

'Oh, what next!'

'Yes! And it's not a sacrament! A sacrament must have a sign. Show me the sign for marriage!'

In vain did the curé reply that it represented the union of Christ with the Church.

'You don't understand Christianity either! And the law. . . .'

'The law bears the imprint of Christianity,' said M. de Faverges; 'without that it would authorise polygamy!'

A voice replied:

'Where would be the harm?'

It was Bouvard, half hidden by a curtain.

'One can have a number of wives, like the patriarchs, the Mormons, the Mohammedans, and yet be an honest man!'

'Never!' cried the priest. 'Honesty consists in rendering what is due. We owe homage to God. So he who is not a Christian is not honest!'

'As honest as anyone else,' said Bouvard.

The count seemed to discern in this retort an attack on religion. He extolled Christianity: it had freed the slaves.

Bouvard gave references which proved the contrary.

'Saint Paul exhorts them to obey their masters, as they would Jesus. Saint Ambrose calls slavery a gift from God.

'Leviticus, Exodus and the Councils have sanctioned it. Bossuet classes it among the rights of man. And Monsignor Bouvier approves it.'

The count objected that Christianity, all the same, had developed civilisation.

'Yes, and idleness, by making poverty a virtue.'

'Still, sir, the morality of the Gospels?'

'Ha, ha, not so moral! Those who labour only for the last hour are paid as much as those who began with the first. To him that hath shall be given, and from him that hath not shall be taken away. As for the precept of receiving blows without returning them and allowing oneself to be robbed, it encourages bullies, cowards and scoundrels.'

They were doubly scandalised when Pécuchet declared that he had as much liking for Buddhism.

The priest burst out laughing:

'Ha, ha, ha! Buddhism!'

Mme de Noares raised her arms.

'Buddhism!'

'What . . . Buddhism!' repeated the count.

'Do you know anything about it?' said Pécuchet to M. Jeufroy, who grew confused. 'Well then, learn something! Better than Christianity, and earlier, it recognised the emptiness of worldly things. Its practices are austere, its followers more numerous than all the Christians put together, and as for incarnation, Vishnu has, not one, but nine! So now you know.'

'Travellers' tales,' said Mme de Noares.

'Backed up by freemasons,' added the curé.

And all speaking at once—'Go on, won't you?'—'A nice thing!'—'I think it's rather funny!'—'Impossible!'

So that Pécuchet, in exasperation, declared that he would become a Buddhist!

'You are insulting Christian ladies,' said the baron.

Mme de Noares sank into an armchair. The countess and Yolande were silent. The count rolled his eyes. Hurel was waiting for orders. The abbé, to contain himself, was reading his breviary.

This sight calmed M. de Faverges, and looking at the two friends:

'Before finding fault with the Gospels, and when one has made slips in one's life, there are certain debts to be paid. . . .'

'Debts?'

'Slips?'

'Enough, gentlemen. You should understand me!'

Then addressing Foureau:

'Sorel knows what to do. Go and see him.'

And Bouvard and Pécuchet withdrew without taking leave.

At the end of the avenue they gave vent, all three, to their resentment.

'I'm treated like a servant,' grumbled Foureau.

And the others agreeing with him, he felt almost sympathetic towards them, despite the remembrance of his piles.

Road-menders were at work in the neighbourhood. The foreman came up, it was Gorju. They began to talk. He had been given charge of making the road, voted in 1848, and owed his place to M. de Mahurot, the engineer. 'The one who is going to marry Mlle de Faverges! You've just come from there, I suppose.'

'For the last time!' said Pécuchet savagely.

Gorju assumed an innocent expression:

'A quarrel! Dear, dear!'

And if they could have seen his face when they turned on their heels, they would have observed that he had scented the cause of it.

A little farther on they stopped before a trellised enclosure, in which there were dog-kennels and a red-tiled cottage.

Victorine was on the doorstep. They could hear dogs barking. The gamekeeper's wife came out.

Knowing the reason of the mayor's visit, she called Victor.

Everything was prepared already, and their belongings in two handkerchiefs, fastened with pins.

'Good-bye,' she said to them. 'What a comfort to be rid of such vermin!'

Was it their fault that they were born of a convict father? On the contrary, they seemed quiet enough, and did not even worry where they were being taken.

Bouvard and Pécuchet watched them as they walked on in front.

Victorine was humming some indistinguishable words with her bundle on her arm, like a milliner carrying a band-box. From time to time she turned round, and Pécuchet, at the sight of her fair curls and pretty figure, regretted not having such a child of his own. Brought up in other surroundings, she would be charming later on. What a happiness to see her growing, to hear every day her bird-like chatter, to kiss her when he wanted; and a feeling of tenderness in his heart rose to his lips, making his eyes moist, oppressing him a little.

Victor, like a soldier, had slung his bundle over his shoulder. He whistled, threw stones at the crows in the furrows, and darted under the trees to cut switches. Foureau called him back; and Bouvard, holding him by the hand, enjoyed feeling the strong, vigorous fingers of the lad within his own. The poor little devil asked for nothing but to be allowed to grow freely, like a flower in the open; and he would wither up between walls, with lessons, punishments, a heap of idiocies! Bouvard was seized with an impulse of pity, an indignation against fate, one of those rages in which one wants to down the Government.

'Frisk about!' he said. 'Enjoy yourself! Play while you can!'

The youngster ran off.

His sister and he were to sleep at the inn, and at daybreak the messenger from Falaise would take Victor and set him down at the reformatory of Beaubourg; a sister from the orphanage at Grand-Camp would come to fetch Victorine.

Foureau, after giving these details, plunged back into his own reflections. But Bouvard wished to know how much the maintenance of these two children would cost.

'Pooh . . . somewhere about three hundred francs, I'd

say! The count has given me twenty-five to go on with. What a skinflint!'

And stung to the quick by the contempt shown to his scarf, Foureau sharpened his pace in silence.

Bouvard murmured: 'They make me feel sorry for them. I'd be glad to take charge of them.'

'So would I,' said Pécuchet, the same idea having occurred to both.

No doubt there were difficulties in the way?

'None,' replied Foureau.

Besides, he had the right, as mayor, to entrust deserted children to anyone he liked. And after long hesitation:

'Very well then, yes, take them! that'll rile him.'

Bouvard and Pécuchet led them away.

When they got home they found Marcel kneeling under the Madonna at the foot of the stairs, praying fervently. With his head flung back, his eyes half closed and his hare-lip gaping, he had the appearance of a fakir in ecstasy.

'What a beast!' said Bouvard.

'Why? Perhaps he's sharing in things of which you'd be jealous if you could see them. Aren't there two worlds quite apart? The object of one's thought has less value than the manner of thinking. What does the belief count? The important thing is to believe at all.'

Such were Pécuchet's objections to this remark of Bouvard.

X

THEY obtained a number of works relating to education, and their system was decided on. It would be necessary to banish all metaphysical ideas and, after the experimental method, to follow the lead of Nature. There was no hurry, for the two pupils would have to forget what they had learnt already.

Although they had strong constitutions, Pécuchet wished, Spartan-like, to harden them yet more, to accustom them to hunger, thirst, bad weather, and even that they should wear shoes with holes in them so as to prevent catching cold. Bouvard opposed this.

The dark closet at the end of the corridor was to be their bedroom. Its furniture consisted of two camp beds to sleep on, a jug; a round window opened over their heads, and spiders ran along the plaster.

Often they remembered the inside of a hut where quarrels were frequent.

Their father had returned one night with blood on his hands. Some time after, the police came. Then they had lived in a wood. Men who made clogs used to embrace their mother. She died; a cart had taken them away. They were always being beaten; they got lost. After that they could see once more the policeman, Mme de Noares, Sorel, and, without wondering why, this house in which they were happy. But they were disagreeably astonished when, at the end of eight months, their lessons began again. Bouvard took charge of the girl, Pécuchet of the boy.

Victor made out his letters, but did not succeed in forming

syllables. He stuttered over them, stopped suddenly and looked idiotic. Victorine asked questions. How comes it that the 'ch' in orchestra has the sound of a 'k,' and that of 'tch' in 'church'? Sometimes two vowels must be joined, at other times separated. All this does not seem right. She grew indignant.

The masters gave their lessons at the same hour in their respective rooms, and the partition being thin, these four voices, one fluty, one deep, and two sharp, made a frightful hubbub. To end it, and to spur the youngsters on by competition, they decided to have them working together in the museum, and began with writing.

The two pupils, at each end of the table, made copies; but the position of their bodies was bad; they had to be straightened. Their pages fell down, their pens broke, the ink was overturned.

On certain days Victorine got on well for three minutes, then began scribbling, and, seized with discouragement, would sit staring at the ceiling. It was not long before Victor fell asleep, lolling over the middle of the desk.

Perhaps they were ill? Too great a strain is bad for young minds.

'Let's stop,' said Bouvard.

Nothing is more stupid than to make children learn by heart; yet if the memory is not exercised it will atrophy, and they made them recite, over and over, the first fables of La Fontaine. The children approved of the ant that piles up treasure, the wolf that devours the lamb, the lion that takes all the shares.

Growing bolder, they wrecked the garden. But what recreation could be found for them?

Jean-Jacques Rousseau in *Emile* counsels the teacher to encourage his pupil in making his own toys, surreptitiously helping him a little. Bouvard could not succeed in constructing a hoop, or Pécuchet in sewing up a ball. They passed on to instructive games, such as cutting paper patterns. Pécuchet showed them his microscope. A candle having been lit, Bouvard would outline on the wall, with the shadow of his fingers, the profile of a hare or a pig. His audience tired.

Some authors extol the pleasures of the picnic, or a trip on the water; but, frankly, was it practicable? And Fénelon recommends from time to time 'a harmless conversation.' Impossible to think of a single one!

They returned to lessons; and the alphabetical blocks, the copy-books, the toy printing press, all had failed when they devised a stratagem.

Since Victor was inclined to gluttony, they showed him the name of a dish; soon he was reading in the cookery book with ease. Victorine, being coquettish, was promised a new dress if she would write a letter, ordering it from the dress-maker. In less than three weeks she had accomplished this prodigy. It was pandering to their faults, a pernicious method no doubt, but successful.

Now that they could read and write, what should they be taught next? It was a further puzzle.

Girls have no need of learning, as have boys. All the same they are brought up usually as mere animals, their only intellectual equipment being confined to mystical trash.

Is it expedient to teach them languages? 'Spanish and Italian,' insists the Swan of Cambray, 'serve no purpose except for reading dangerous books.' Such a motive seemed to them silly. However, Victorine would have no use for these languages, while English is more widely used. Pécu-chet studied its rules; he demonstrated, with some solemnity, the way to pronounce *th*.

'See, it's like this—*the, the, the*!'

But before instructing a child, we must know its aptitudes. These may be discovered by phrenology. They plunged into it, then wanted to verify its assertions by practising on one another. Bouvard exhibited the bumps of benevolence, imagination, veneration, and amorous energy—*vulgo*, eroticism.

On Pécuchet's temporals were found philosophy and enthusiasm, joined to a crafty disposition.

Such in fact were their characters. What surprised them more was to recognise in one, as in the other, a propensity for friendship and, charmed by this discovery, they embraced tenderly.

Next, they examined Marcel. His greatest fault, of which they were not ignorant, was an excessive appetite. Nevertheless, Bouvard and Pécuchet were dismayed when they found, above the ear, on a level with the eye, his organ of alimentivity. As the years went on, their servant, perhaps, would grow like that woman in the Salpêtrière hospital who ate eight pounds of bread a day, swallowed on one occasion fourteen plates of soup and, on another, sixty bowls of coffee. They would not have enough to keep him.

Their pupils' heads showed nothing extraordinary; no doubt they had gone about things the wrong way. A very simple expedient enabled them to develop their experience.

On market days they glided amid the peasants in the square, between the sacks of oats, the baskets of cheeses, the calves, the horses, indifferent to jostling; and when they had found a young boy with his father, they would ask if they might feel his skull for a scientific purpose.

The majority did not even reply; others, thinking it had to do with an ointment for ringworm, were angry, and refused; a few, from indifference, let themselves be taken to the church porch, where they would be undisturbed.

One morning, when Bouvard and Pécuchet were beginning operations there, the curé suddenly appeared and, seeing what they were doing, denounced phrenology as leading to materialism and fatalism.

The thief, the murderer, and the adulterer have only to cast the blame of their crimes on their bumps.

Bouvard objected that the organ predisposes towards the act without, however, compelling it. From a man having in him the germ of a vice, there is nothing to prove that he will be vicious.

'Besides, I wonder at the orthodox, for they uphold innate ideas, and reject propensities. What a contradiction!'

But according to M. Jeufroy, phrenology denied the divine omnipotence, and it was unseemly to practise it under the shadow of the sacred building, in the very face of the altar.

'Be off, be off!'

They established themselves at Ganot's the barber's. To conquer any hesitation, Bouvard and Pécuchet went so far as to stand the parents a shave or a trimming.

One afternoon the doctor came in to get his hair cut. As he was sitting down in the chair, he saw in the glass the reflection of the two phrenologists passing their fingers over a child's head.

'So you're up to those tricks?' he said.

'How do you mean—tricks?'

Vaucorbeil smiled contemptuously; then declared that there could not be a variety of organs in the brain.

Thus one man can digest food which another cannot. Are we to assume that, in the stomach, there are as many stomachs as we find tastes? However, one kind of work is a relaxation from another; an intellectual effort does not extend to all the faculties, each has its distinct seat.

'Anatomists have not come across it,' said Vaucorbeil.

'That's because they have dissected badly,' replied Pécuchet.

310

'What?'

'Oh, yes! They cut off sections without regard to the connection between the parts'—a phrase he remembered from a book.

'What drivel!' cried the physician. 'The cranium is not moulded on the brain, the exterior over the interior. Gall is wrong, and I defy you to substantiate his doctrine by taking three people at random in the shop.'

The first was a peasant woman with large blue eyes.

Pécuchet looked at her and said:

'She has a good memory.'

Her husband attested the fact, and offered himself for examination.

'Well, as for you, my man, you're a difficult person to persuade.'

According to the others, there was no more stubborn fellow in the world.

The third experiment was made on a boy, who was accompanied by his grandmother.

Pécuchet asserted that he must be fond of music.

'I should say he is,' said the old lady. 'Show them. Let the gentlemen see.'

He drew, from his smock, a jew's harp and began to puff at it.

There was a crash, it was the door violently slammed by the doctor as he went out.

They no longer doubted themselves and, calling their pupils, they resumed the analysis of their skulls.

Victorine's was even all round—a sign of balance—but her brother had a deplorable cranium; a very large protuberance, in the mastoid angle of the parietals, indicated the organ of destruction, or assassination, and a swelling lower down was the sign of covetousness or theft. Bouvard and Pécuchet were depressed for a week.

But it was necessary to understand the exact meaning of the words. What we call combativeness implies a contempt for death. If it produces homicides, it can also cause the saving of life. Acquisitiveness includes the pickpockets' knack and the keenness of business men. Irreverence has its parallel in the spirit of criticism, cunning in circumspection. An instinct is always divided into two parts, a bad and a good. The second will be destroyed by cultivating the first, and, according to this system, a daring child, so far from being a bandit, will become a general. A lazy man will be only prudent, the miser economical, the reckless generous.

A magnificent dream filled their minds: if they carried the education of their pupils to a successful end, later on they would found an establishment having as its object the discipline of the intellect, the curbing of strong impulses, the ennoblement of the heart. Already they were talking of subscriptions and building.

Their triumph at Ganot's had made them famous, and people came to consult them, hoping to have their fortunes told.

There was a procession of skulls of all kinds: round as balls, pear-shaped, like sugar-loaves, heads square, high, narrow and flat, with bulls' jaws, birds' faces, pigs' eyes; but such a crowd interfered with the hairdresser's work. Their elbows rubbed against the glass case containing the perfumery; they disturbed the combs; the wash-basin was broken; and he bundled out all the amateurs, begging Bouvard and Pécuchet to follow them, an ultimatum which they accepted without a murmur, for they were a trifle weary of cranioscopy.

The next day, as they were passing the captain's patch of garden, they saw him talking to Girbal, Coulon, and the local policeman with his youngest son Zéphyrin, dressed as a choir-boy. His surplice was quite new; he was parading in it before returning it to the sacristy, and they were complimenting him.

Curious to know what they thought of him, Placquevent asked the gentlemen to feel his little boy's head.

The skin of the forehead looked as though it had been stretched; a thin nose, very gristly at the end, fell obliquely over pinched lips; the chin was pointed, the eyes furtive, the right shoulder too high.

'Take off your cap,' his father said to him.

Bouvard slid his hands through the straw-coloured hair, then it was Pécuchet's turn, and they communicated their observations to each other in low tones.

'*Biophily* very plain. Ah, ha! *Approbativeness! Conscientiousness* absent! *Amativeness* nil!'

'Well?' said the policeman.

Pécuchet opened his snuff-box and took a pinch.

''Pon my word,' said Bouvard, 'he's hardly brilliant.'

Placquevent blushed with humiliation.

'All the same, he'll do as he's told.'

'Indeed!'

'But I'm his father, by God! and I've surely the right—'

'To some extent,' replied Pécuchet.

Girbal joined in: 'A father's authority is unquestionable.'

'But supposing he's an idiot?'

'No matter,' said the captain, 'his power's no less absolute.'

'It's in the children's interest,' added Coulon.

According to Bouvard and Pécuchet they owed nothing to the authors of their days, while parents, on the other hand, owe them sustenance, instruction, attention—everything, in fact.

The villagers cried out upon this immoral opinion. Placquevent resented it as an insult.

'They're a fine pair, I must say, that you pick up on the road. They'll go far! Take care.'

'Care of what?' asked Pécuchet sharply.

'Oh, I'm not afraid of you!'

'Nor I!'

Coulon intervened, calmed the policeman and persuaded him to go.

For some moments there was silence. Then it was a question of the captain's dahlias, for he would not let them depart without viewing them one by one.

Bouvard and Pécuchet were on their way home when a hundred yards in front they perceived Placquevent; and beside him Zéphyrin was raising his elbow to shield off the blows.

What they had just heard expressed under other forms were the ideas of the count; but the example of their pupils witnessed to the superiority of liberty over restraint. A little discipline, however, was necessary.

Pécuchet nailed up a blackboard in the museum for lessons; a daily record was to be kept, from which the child's acts, noted down each evening, would be read out the next day. All was to be done to the sound of a bell. Like Dupont de Nemours, they would begin with fatherly injunctions, then pass on to military commands, and all familiarity was forbidden.

Bouvard tried to teach Victorine arithmetic. Sometimes they made a mistake; when they had laughed over it together, she used to kiss him on the neck where there was no beard, and ask for a holiday: he let her go off.

In vain did Pécuchet ring the bell for lessons and shout the military command from the window; the boy did not come. His socks always hung down over his ankles; at table even, he thrust his fingers into his nose and did not restrain his wind. Broussais with regard to such behaviour, vetoes rebukes, for 'one must obey the solicitations of the instinct of self-preservation.'

Victorine and he used terrible language, saying *Oi* for *I*, *summat* for *something*, *'er* for *her*, *winders* for *windows*, *rine* for *rain*. But since grammar cannot be understood by children, and since they will get to learn it if they hear others speaking correctly, the two companions kept an eye on their own utterances until it became painful.

They differed in their opinions as to geography. Bouvard thought it more logical to start from the parish; Pécuchet from the world as a whole.

With a watering-can and some sand he endeavoured to demonstrate what was meant by a river, an island, a gulf, and even sacrificed three flower-beds for the three continents; but the cardinal points did not penetrate Victor's skull.

On a January night, Pécuchet took him out into the bare country. As they went along, he sang the praises of astronomy: sailors employ it on their voyages; without it Christopher Columbus would not have made his discovery. We should be grateful to Copernicus, Galileo and Newton.

It was freezing hard, and, on the blue-black sky, an infinity of lights were sparkling. Pécuchet raised his eyes.

'What! No Great Bear!'

The last time he had seen it, it was turned the other way; finally he discovered it, then pointed out the pole star, always in the north, by which we set the compass.

The next day he placed an armchair in the middle of the drawing-room and started to waltz round it.

'Imagine that this chair's the sun, and that I'm the earth; this is the way it moves.'

Victor gazed at him wonderingly.

Then he took an orange, thrust a piece of wood through it to denote the poles, and made a charcoal ring round it to mark the Equator. After which he turned it about a lighted candle, showing that all the parts of its surface were not illuminated at the same time, which causes the variation of climates; while for the changes of the seasons, he tilted the orange, since the earth does not keep upright, which accounts for equinoxes and solstices.

Victor had understood nothing. He believed that the earth twirls on a long needle, and that the Equator is a ring embracing its circumference.

Pécuchet explained Europe to him with an atlas; but, confused by so many lines and colours, he could no longer find the names. The basins and mountains no longer tallied with the countries, the political divisions muddled the physical. All this, perhaps, would be made clear by the study of history.

It might have been more practical to start with the village, then the district, the county, the province; but Chavignolles possessing no chronicle, it was best after all to stick to world-history. So many events encumber it, that only its finest flowers should be selected.

For Greece there is, 'We will fight in the shade,' the envy that banished Aristeides, and Alexander's trust in his physician. For Rome, the geese on the Capitol, the tripod of Scaevola, the barrel of Regulus. Guatimozin's bed of roses bulks largely for America. As for France, it includes the vase of Soissons, the oak of St. Louis, the death of Joan of Arc, the boiled chicken of Henry IV; there is an embarrassment of choice, without counting, 'To me, Auvergne!' and the sinking of the *Vengeur*.

Victor mixed up men, centuries and countries. Yet Pécuchet was determined not to engulf him in subtleties, and the mass of fact is a veritable labyrinth.

He fell back on the catalogue of the kings of France. Victor forgot them, for want of knowing the dates. But if Dumouchel's *memoria technica* had been inadequate for them, what would it be for him? To sum up: history can only be learnt by reading much. This he would have to do.

Drawing is useful on all sorts of occasions; hence Pécuchet had the temerity to teach it himself, from nature, by beginning at once on landscape.

A bookseller at Bayeux sent him paper, india-rubber, two drawing-boards, chalks and fixative for their works, which, enclosed in glass and frame, were to adorn the museum.

Rising at dawn, they set forth with a chunk of bread in their pockets; and some while was spent in finding a point of view. Pécuchet wanted to reproduce at the same time what lay under his feet, the far horizon, and the clouds, but the distances always took a lion's share of the first sketch; the river toppled from the sky, the shepherd marched upon his flock, a sleeping dog seemed to run. For his part he gave it up, remembering having read this definition: 'Drawing is composed of three elements—line, shading, fine shading, not to mention the sweeping stroke. But only a master is able to furnish the latter.' Pécuchet rectified his pupil's line, collaborated with him over the shading, kept watch over his fine shading and waited for a chance of providing the sweeping stroke. It never came, for the whole landscape was incomprehensible.

The sister, as lazy as the boy, yawned over the multiplication table. Mlle Reine showed her how to sew, and when she marked the linen, she raised her fingers so prettily that Bouvard, in the end, had not the heart to torment her with sums. They would go back to them another time. No doubt, arithmetic and sewing are necessary for housekeeping, but it is cruel, as Pécuchet objected, to bring

317

girls up with a view only to their future husband. All are not destined for marriage; and if one wants them to do without men in the future, there is much that they must learn.

Science may be taught by examples from the most ordinary objects, such as explaining what wine is made of; and this having been done, Victor and Victorine had to say it over again. The same course was followed with spices, furniture and light; but for them light was the lamp, which had nothing in common with the spark from a flint, the flame of a candle or moonlight.

One day Victorine asked: 'Why does wood burn?' Her teachers looked at each other in a quandary, the theory of combustion being beyond them.

Another time Bouvard talked, from the soup to the cheese, about nutritious elements, and staggered the two little beings with fibrin, casein, fat and gluten.

Then Pécuchet wanted to explain how blood is renewed, and floundered about in the circulation.

It is not an easy dilemma—if one starts from facts, the simplest demand over-complicated explanations; and by going straight to theories, one begins with the absolute, with faith.

Where was the solution? To combine the two ways of instruction, the rational and the empirical; but a double means to a single end is the opposite of a method. Well, so much the worse!'

To introduce them to natural history, they tried scientific promenades.

'Look,' they said, pointing to a donkey, a horse, or an ox, 'those animals with four feet are called quadrupeds. In general, you can tell birds by their feathers, reptiles by their scales, and butterflies belong to the insect class.' They had a net to catch them with, and Pécuchet, holding the little creature gingerly, made them remark the four wings, the six feet, the two antennae, and the bony trunk that inhales the nectar of the flowers.

He plucked herbs by the side of the ditches, told their names, and, when he did not know them, invented them, in order to preserve his authority. In any case, nomenclature is the least important part of botany.

He wrote this axiom on the blackboard: 'Every plant has leaves, a calyx, and a corolla enclosing an ovary or pericarp, which contains the seed.' Then he ordered his pupils to botanise in the country and pick the first specimens they came upon.

Victor brought him buttercups, Victorine, a wild strawberry plant; in vain he sought for the pericarp.

Bouvard, suspicious of his lore, looked in the library, and found, in the *Lady's Monitor*, a drawing of an iris where the ovaries were situated not in the corolla, but below the petals, in the stalk.

Flowering in their garden were goose-grass and lilies of the valley; these plants of the madder family were without a calyx: thus the principle written on the blackboard was incorrect.

'It's an exception,' said Pécuchet.

But by chance they came upon a field-madder in the grass, and it had a calyx.

'Here's a pretty problem. If the exceptions themselves aren't true, what's to be relied on?'

One day, when they were on a walk, they heard peacocks crying, and casting their glances over the wall, at first sight failed to recognise their farm. The barn had slate tiles, the fences were new, the paths freshly paved. Old Gouy appeared.

'Impossible! Is it really you?'

How much had happened in three years; among other

things, the death of his wife. But he was still as strong as an oak—'Come in a moment!'

It was the beginning of April, and through the three orchards the apple trees in blossom extended the ranks of their pink and white clusters; the sky, of a satin-blue colour, was cloudless; table-cloths, sheets and towels were dangling, held by clothes-pegs to the taut washing-lines. Gouy raised them so that they could pass, and suddenly they came face to face with Mme Bordin, bareheaded, in a loose pinafore, with Marianne lifting armfuls of linen up to her.

'Good morning, gentlemen! Make yourselves at home. I'm going to sit down, I'm quite exhausted.'

The farmer proposed a little drink all round.

'Not now,' she said, 'I'm too hot.'

Pécuchet accepted, and disappeared towards the cellar with Gouy, Marianne and Victor.

Bouvard sat on the ground beside Mme Bordin. He received his payments punctually, had nothing to complain of, and was no longer angry with her.

The strong daylight played over her profile; one of her black coils had come down, and the little wisps of hair on her neck stuck to the skin, which was sunburnt and damp with perspiration. At each breath her bosom rose. The perfume of the grass mingled with the healthy aroma of her solid flesh, and Bouvard had a revival of sentiment that overwhelmed him with joy. Then he complimented her on her property.

She was delighted with it, and spoke of her projects.

To enlarge the orchards she was going to level the high bank.

At that moment, Victorine was climbing the slope and picking primroses, hyacinths and violets, without a fear of the old horse that was grazing below.

'Isn't she a nice little thing?' asked Bouvard.

'Yes, they're nice—little girls.'

And the widow heaved a sigh that seemed to express the disappointment of a lifetime.

'You could have had one.'

She bowed her head.

'It only depended on you.'

'What?'

He gave her such a look that she turned a deep red, it was so like a crude embrace; but immediately after, fanning herself with her handkerchief:

'You've missed the coach, my dear.'

'I don't understand.'

And without rising, he moved nearer.

She looked him up and down for a long time, then, smiling and with moist eyes: 'Yes, it's your fault.'

The sheets enclosed them all round like bed curtains. He leant over on his elbow, brushing her knees with his face.

'Why? Why, though?'

And as she did not speak, and he was in a state when vows count for nothing, he tried to justify himself, accused himself of folly and pride.

'Forgive me! Everything will be as it used to be, won't it?'

And he had seized her hand, which she left within his own.

A sudden gust of wind set the sheets flapping, and they saw two peacocks, a male and a female. The female stood motionless, her legs apart, her rump in the air. The male circled about her, spread his tail in a fan, strutted, clucked, then leapt upon her, bending his feathers forward so that they covered her like a bower, and the two large birds trembled in a single shudder.

Bouvard felt a quiver in Mme Bordin's hand. She

quickly freed herself. In front of them, open-mouthed and as though petrified, was young Victor, staring hard; and a little farther off, Victorine, stretched on her back in the bright sunshine, was smelling all the flowers that she had plucked.

The old horse, frightened by the peacocks, broke one of the lines in his rush, entangled his legs in it, and galloped through the three orchards, dragging the washing after him.

At Mme Bordin's furious cries, Marianne ran up. Gouy swore at his horse: 'Bloody hack! Screw! Thief!' kicked it in the belly, struck it over the ears with the handle of a whip.

Bouvard was angry to see an animal beaten.

The peasant answered:

'I've got the right. It's mine.'

That was not a good reason.

And Pécuchet, arriving, added that animals also had their rights, for like us they have a soul, if indeed ours exists.

'You're an unbeliever,' cried Mme Bordin.

Three things had exasperated her: the washing, to be done again; her religion, which had been insulted; and the fear that she had just been caught in a compromising attitude.

'I thought you were made of sterner stuff,' said Bouvard.

She replied severely: 'I don't like scoffers.'

And Gouy blamed them for having damaged his horse, whose nostrils were bleeding. He growled in a low tone:

'These bloody fools spoil everything! I was going to shut him up when they came.'

The two companions retreated, shrugging their shoulders.

Victor asked them why they had been annoyed with Gouy.

'He abuses his strength, which is wrong.'

'Why is it wrong?'

Would the children ever have any idea of justice? It might be.

And that very evening Pécuchet, with Bouvard on his right, a few notes under his hand, and the two pupils in front of him, began a course of morals.

This science teaches us to control our actions.

It has two motives—pleasure and interest; and a third more imperious—duty.

Duties are divided into two classes. First, duties towards ourselves, which consist in taking care of our bodies, preserving ourselves from all kinds of harm. They understood that perfectly. Second, duties towards others; that is to say, to be always loyal, cheerful and even brotherly, the human race being only a single family. Often a thing that suits us hurts our fellows; interest differs from good, for good is irreducible from itself. The children did not understand. He postponed the sanctions of duty till the next time.

In all that, according to Bouvard, he had nowhere defined good.

'Why do you want it defined? It's something we feel.'

In that case, lessons on morals would only be suitable to moral people, and Pécuchet's course went no further.

They read their pupils stories tending to inspire a love of virtue. These sent Victor to sleep.

To strike his imagination, Pécuchet hung on the walls of his room pictures depicting the life of the good and the bad character. The first, Adolphe, embraced his mother, learnt German, helped a blind man, and was admitted to the École Polytechnique.

The bad one, Eugène, began by disobeying his father, had a dispute in a café, beat his wife, fell down dead-drunk, broke into a safe; and a final picture showed him in the convict prison where a gentleman accompanied by a little boy was saying, as he pointed him out: 'You behold, my son, the dangers of misconduct.'

But for children the future does not exist. It was all very well to soak them in this maxim, 'that work is honourable, and the rich are sometimes unhappy'; they had known workers who were in no wise honoured, and called to mind the big house where life seemed enjoyable.

The torments of remorse were portrayed to them with so much exaggeration that they smelt a rat, and distrusted the rest of what they were told.

An attempt was made to control them by appealing to the sense of honour, the idea of public opinion and the sentiment of glory, by singing the praises of great men, and above all, useful citizens like Belzunce, Franklin and Jacquard. Victor evidenced no eagerness to resemble them.

One day when he had done a sum without making a mistake, Bouvard sewed on his jacket a ribbon that stood for merit. He was very proud of it; but having forgotten the date of Henry IV's death, Pécuchet crowned him with a donkey's cap. Victor began to bray so violently and for so long, that his cardboard ears had to be removed.

His sister, like him, showed herself proud of commendation, and indifferent to blame.

To increase their sensibility, they were given a black cat which they were to look after, and a few coppers were counted out to them, to give as alms. They considered it an unjust stipulation, since the money was theirs.

In conformity with a wish of their tutors, they called Bouvard 'Uncle' and Pécuchet 'Cousin'; but they addressed them familiarly, and half the lessons were taken up, as a rule, by disputes.

Victorine abused Marcel, climbed on his back and pulled his hair; to mock his hare-lip, she spoke through her nose like him, and the poor man dared not complain, because he loved the little girl so much. One evening his raucous voice was raised in an extraordinary manner. Bouvard and

324

Pécuchet went down to the kitchen. The two pupils were staring into the fireplace, and Marcel, with clasped hands, was crying:

'Take him out! It's too much! It's too much!'

The cover of the cooking-pot blew off like a bursting shell. A greyish mass jumped up to the ceiling, then turned madly round and round, screeching horribly. They recognised the cat, as thin as a rail, without hair, its tail like a piece of cord, its huge eyes starting from its head. They were the colour of milk, as though blank, and yet were gazing.

The hideous beast kept on howling, hurled itself into the fireplace, disappeared, then fell down amid the cinders, motionless.

It was Victor who had committed this atrocity, and the two old companions recoiled, pale with stupefaction and horror. To the reproaches addressed to him, he answered, like the policeman for his son, and the farmer for his horse: 'Why, it's mine!' without awkwardness, naïvely, with the calm of a gratified instinct.

The boiling water from the pot had spread over the ground; saucepans, tongs and cinders were strewn over the flags.

It took Marcel some time to clean the kitchen, and his masters and he buried the poor cat in the garden, under the pagoda.

Afterwards, Bouvard and Pécuchet had a long discussion about Victor. The paternal strain was beginning to show. What should they do? Giving him back to M. de Faverges or entrusting him to others would be a confession of failure. Perhaps he would improve.

But they no longer cared, their hope was shaken and tenderness had vanished. Yet what a pleasure it would have been to have by one's side a boy curious of one's ideas, whose progress one could observe, who would afterwards be like a brother; but Victor lacked sense, and heart still more. And Pécuchet sighed, his hands clasped round his knee.

'The sister's no better,' said Bouvard. He dreamed of a girl of about fifteen, of delicate nature and sprightly humour, adorning the house with elegance and youth; and, as though he had been her father and she had just died, the good old fellow wept.

Then, seeking to excuse Victor, he brought forward Rousseau's opinion: 'A child has no responsibility; it cannot be moral or immoral.'

These two, according to Pécuchet, had arrived at the age of discernment, and they studied ways of correcting them. For a punishment to do good, says Bentham, it must be proportionate to the fault and its natural consequence. If a child breaks a window-pane, the pane should not be replaced; let him suffer from the cold: if, no longer hungry, he asks for more, give it him; indigestion will soon make him sorry. If he is lazy, let him stay without work; boredom will bring him back to it.

But Victor did not feel the cold, his constitution could endure excesses, and idleness suited him.

They adopted the opposite method, corrective punishment. Extra tasks were set him, he became lazier; they took away his jam, his greediness was doubled. Perhaps irony would be effective? Once, when he had come to lunch with dirty hands, Bouvard chaffed him, called him a handsome cavalier, a muscadin, a dandy. Victor listened glowering, suddenly grew livid, and threw his plate at Bouvard's head; then, furious at having missed his aim, hurled himself at him. It would have taken three men to master him. He rolled on the ground, trying to bite. Pécuchet doused him from a distance with a jug of water; immediately he became calm, but had a cold for two days. It was the wrong method.

They tried another. At the least sign of anger, they treated him as though he were ill, and put him to bed. Victor felt comfortable there, and burst into song. One day he had stolen an old coconut from the library and set about splitting it, when Pécuchet arrived.

'My coconut!'

It was a souvenir of Dumouchel, which Pécuchet had brought from Paris to Chavignolles; and he raised his arms with indignation to see it treated thus. Victor began to laugh. 'Cousin' could stand it no longer, and with a lusty smack sent him rolling to the far end of the room, then, quivering with emotion, went off to complain to Bouvard.

Bouvard reproached him.

'How stupid you are, with your coconut. Blows only brutalise, and terror is bad for the nerves. You are degrading yourself.'

Pécuchet objected that corporal punishment is sometimes indispensable. Pestalozzi employed it, and the famous Melanchthon confesses that, without it, he would have learnt nothing. But savage punishment has impelled children to suicide; one can read of instances. Victor had barricaded himself in his room. Bouvard conducted negotiations through the door, and to make him open, promised him a plum tart.

After that Victor grew worse.

There remained a method advocated by Monsignor Dupanloup: 'the look of severity.' They tried to imprint a frightening aspect on their countenances, and produced no effect.

'We have only religion left to try,' said Bouvard.

Pécuchet protested; they had banished it from their programme.

But reasoning does not satisfy every need. The heart

and the imagination desire something else. For many souls, the supernatural cannot be left out, and they decided to send the children to catechism.

Reine offered to take them. She was back in their house again, and knew how to make herself liked with her caressing ways.

Victorine suddenly changed, became reserved and good as gold, knelt before the Madonna, admired the sacrifice of Abraham, and sniggered disdainfully at the name of Protestant.

She declared that fasting has been prescribed for her; they inquired about it, and it was not true. On Corpus Christi Day some of the rockets disappeared from their bed in the garden, to decorate the altar; she impudently denied cutting them. Another time she abstracted from Bouvard a franc, which she put in the sacristan's plate at vespers.

Hence they concluded that morality is distinct from religion; when it has no other basis its importance is secondary.

One evening, while they were at dinner, M. Marescot entered. Victor took to flight at once.

The notary, having refused to sit down, related what brought him; young Touache had been fighting with his son and had almost killed him.

As Victor's origin was known, and as he was disagreeable, the other urchins called him 'Convict,' and just recently he had had the insolence to give M. Arnold Marescot a hiding. Dear Arnold bore traces of it all over his body. 'His mother's in despair, his clothes are in tatters, his health endangered. What are we coming to?'

The notary demanded vigorous chastisement, and that Victor should no more go to catechism with the others, to prevent fresh disturbances. Bouvard and Pécuchet, although wounded by his bullying manner, promised all that he asked, and completely surrendered.

Had Victor obeyed the sentiment of honour or of revenge? In either case, he was not a coward.

But his brutishness alarmed them. Music soothes the savage breast; Pécuchet conceived the idea of teaching it to him.

Victor had a great deal of trouble in reading the notes fluently, and not confusing the terms *adagio*, *presto* and *sforzando*.

His master exerted himself to teach him scales, the common chord, the diatonic, the chromatic, and the two kinds of intervals, known as major and minor.

He made him sit upright with chest out, shoulders well back, mouth wide open, and, to set him an example, he intoned in a forced voice; Victor's issued painfully from his larynx, so much did he contract it. When the bar began with a crotchet-rest, he either started off at once or too late.

Nevertheless Pécuchet embarked on part-singing for two voices. He took a stick to hold instead of a baton, and waved his arms authoritatively, as though he had an orchestra behind him; but occupied with two labours at once, he got the time wrong. His mistakes led to others on the part of his pupil, and wrinkling their brows and craning their necks, they ploughed on haphazard to the foot of the page.

At last Pécuchet said to Victor: 'You'll never shine in a choral society.' And the teaching of music was abandoned.

Besides, perhaps Locke is right—'it is pursued in such dissolute company that one is better busied otherwise.'

Without wanting to make a writer of him, it would be a good thing if Victor knew how to put a letter together. A reflection stopped them: the epistolary style cannot be learnt, for it is an exclusively feminine attribute.

They dreamed, then, of embedding a few chunks of

literature in his memory, and, with too great a wealth to choose from, consulted the work by Mme Campan. She recommends Éliacin's scene in *Athalie*, the choruses of *Esther*, and the whole of Jean-Baptiste Rousseau.

This is rather old-fashioned. As for novels, she forbids them, since they portray the world in too rosy a light.

Still, she allows *Clarissa Harlowe* and the *Father of the Family* by Mrs. Opie. Who is Mrs. Opie?

They could not find her name in the *Biographie Universelle*. There remained fairy-tales. 'They'll begin wanting diamond palaces,' said Pécuchet. Literature develops the mind, but excites the passions.

Because of her passions, Victorine was expelled from the catechism class. She had been surprised kissing the notary's son, and Reine was not to be trifled with; her face was grim under her bonnet with its big frame. After such a scandal, how could they keep so depraved a little girl?

Bouvard and Pécuchet dubbed the curé an old woman. His servant defended him, grumbling: 'We know all about you! We know all about you!' They retorted, and she went off, rolling terrible eyes.

Victorine, indeed, was seized with affection for Arnold, so handsome did she think him, with his lace collar, his velvet jacket, and nice-smelling hair; she took him nosegays until the moment when she was denounced by Zéphyrin.

How absurd it was, the two children being perfectly innocent!

Ought they to be taught the mystery of procreation?

'I don't see any harm in it,' said Bouvard. 'The philosopher, Basedow, explained it to his pupils, though he only dealt with pregnancy and birth.'

Pécuchet thought differently. He was beginning to be uneasy about Victor.

He suspected him of a bad habit. Why not? Some

grave men continue it all their lives, and it is said that the Duc d'Angoulême was addicted to it.

Pécuchet questioned his pupil in such a way that his eyes were opened to these ideas, and soon there was no doubt about it.

Then he called him criminal, and wanted, as a treatment, to make him read Tissot. This masterpiece, according to Bouvard, was more pernicious than useful. It would be better to inspire him with poetic sentiment. Aimé Martin records that, in a similar case, a mother lent the *Nouvelle Héloïse* to her son, and that, to render himself worthy of love, the young man eagerly adopted the path of virtue.

But Victor was incapable of imagining a Sophie.

'Suppose we took him to a brothel instead?'

Pécuchet expressed his horror of prostitutes.

Bouvard thought it a foolish reserve, and even spoke of making a special journey to Havre.

'What are you thinking about? We should be seen going in.'

'Well, buy him an apparatus!'

'But the truss-maker would perhaps think it was for me,' said Pécuchet.

The boy should have had some active sport, like hunting; but that would have meant the expense of a horse and a gun. They preferred to tire him out, and undertook long tramps in the country.

The urchin escaped them, although they kept an eye on him in turns; they were worn out, and in the evening had no strength to write the day's record.

While they waited for Victor they talked to the passers-by, and in their zeal for education tried to teach them the rules of health, deplored the wastage of water, the prodigality of the manure-heaps, thundered against superstitions —the blackbird's skeleton in the barn, the blest sprig of box-wood in the stable, or the bag of worms on the fever patient's toes.

From that they turned their attention to nurses, and fumed against the way babies were looked after: some keep them short of gruel, which makes them perish of weakness; others stodge them with meat before they are six months old, and they die of indigestion; many wash them with spittle; all handle them roughly.

Whenever they saw an owl nailed on a door, they used to enter the farm, and say: 'You're making a mistake. Those creatures live on rats and field-mice. A mass of caterpillars' grubs has been found in an owl's stomach.'

The villagers knew them from having seen them, first as doctors, then in quest of old furniture, then looking for stones, and they answered:

'Rubbish. Don't try to teach us!'

Their conviction was shaken, for sparrows clean the vegetables of insects, but gobble the cherries; owls devour vermin, but also bats, which are useful creatures—and if moles eat slugs, they also throw up the soil. Of one thing they were sure, that all game should be destroyed, as ruinous to agriculture.

One evening, as they were going through the Faverges wood, they came in front of the house where Sorel, at the side of the road, was gesticulating to three other people.

The first was one Dauphin, a cobbler, small, thin and with a sulky expression. The second, old Aubain, odd-job man in the villages, wore a shiny yellow coat and blue canvas trousers. The third, Eugène, M. Marescot's servant, was conspicuous for his beard, trimmed like a magistrate's.

Sorel was showing them a noose of copper wire, which was joined to a silk thread held down by a brick—what is called a collar—and he had caught Dauphin laying it down.

'You're witnesses, aren't you?'

Eugène bent his chin approvingly, and old Aubain replied:

'If you say so.'

What enraged Sorel was the impudence of setting a snare outside his very house, the scamp having thought that no one would have the idea of suspecting its presence in such a place.

Dauphin adopted the tearful manner.

'I stepped on it as I was walking; I even tried to break it.' He was always being accused, people had a grudge against him; he was really unlucky!

Sorel, without replying, had taken from his pocket a notebook, and pen and ink, to write out a summons.

'Stop!' said Pécuchet.

Bouvard added: 'Let him go! He's all right.'

'He's a poacher.'

'Well, what does that matter?' And they began to defend poaching: it is known, in the first place, that rabbits eat the young shoots, hares destroy corn; indeed, with the exception of the woodcock perhaps . . .

'Let me be!' And the gamekeeper wrote away, with clenched teeth.

'What obstinacy!' murmured Bouvard.

'Another word and I'll call the police.'

'You're a clumsy brute,' said Pécuchet.

'You're not much yourself,' replied Sorel.

Bouvard, forgetting himself, called him a blockhead and a flunkey, and Eugène kept repeating, 'Peace! peace! the law must be respected,' while three yards away old Aubain was groaning on a heap of stones.

Stirred by these voices, all the dogs of the pack left their kennels; their blazing eyeballs and black muzzles were to be seen through the bars, and as they darted about they barked terribly.

'Don't bother me any more!' cried their master, 'or I'll set them on your heels.'

The two friends departed, content, however, to have upheld progress and civilisation.

Next day they received a summons to appear in the magistrate's court for insults to the gamekeeper, and in default to be sentenced to a fine of one hundred francs damages, 'not counting the expenses of prosecution, in view of the contraventions by them committed; cost, six francs seventy-five centimes, Tiercelin, bailiff.'

Why prosecution? Their heads turned, then, growing calmer, they prepared their defence.

On the day appointed, Bouvard and Pécuchet went to the town hall, an hour too soon. Nobody! Seats and three armchairs surrounded an oval table covered with a cloth, a niche had been hollowed out of the wall to hold a stove, and the bust of the emperor, set on a little pedestal, commanded the scene.

To kill time they went up to the attic, where there were a fire-pump and a few banners, and in a corner on the ground, more plaster busts: the great Napoleon without his crown, Louis xviii in a dress-coat with epaulets, Charles x recognisable by his hanging lip, Louis-Philippe with his arched eyebrows and hair trimmed in a pyramid; the slope of the roof grazed his neck, and all the busts were fly-blown and dusty. This spectacle disturbed Bouvard and Pécuchet. They felt a contempt for governments as they returned to the main hall.

There they found Sorel and the policeman, the one with his badge on his arm, the other in a peaked cap. A dozen people stood chatting, summoned for neglecting pavements, letting their dogs stray, having no lamps on their carts, or keeping a wineshop open during Mass.

At last Coulon appeared, dressed in a robe of black serge

334

and a round toque with velvet border. His clerk placed himself on the left, the mayor in his scarf on the right, and, shortly after, the case of Sorel versus Bouvard and Pécuchet was called.

Louis Martial Eugène Lenepveur, footman at Chavignolles (Calvados), took advantage of his privilege as witness to dilate on what he knew of a crowd of subjects foreign to the dispute.

Nicolas Juste Aubain, labourer, was afraid of displeasing Sorel and injuring the defendants; he had heard high words, but could not swear to them, and pleaded his deafness as the reason.

The magistrate made him sit down again, then, addressing the gamekeeper:

'Do you persist in your charges?'

'Of course.'

Coulon then asked the two accused what they had to say.

Bouvard maintained that he had not insulted Sorel, but that in taking the poacher's side he had acted in the interest of our country tradition; he recalled feudal abuses, and the ruinous hunting parties of the nobles.

'No matter, the contravention—'

'Wait!' cried Pécuchet. 'The words contravention, crime and offence mean nothing. To want thus to classify punishable actions is to establish an arbitrary basis. One might as well say to citizens, "Do not trouble about the value of your actions; that is only determined by the punishment of authority." The Penal Code, too, seems to me a foolish work, without principles.'

'That may be,' replied Coulon.

And he was about to pronounce judgment, but Foureau, who was public prosecutor, rose.

The keeper had been interfered with in the execution of his duty. If property is not respected, all is lost.

'In brief, may it please Your Worship to award the maximum penalty.'

It was the sum of ten francs in the form of damages for Sorel.

'Bravo!' cried Bouvard.

Coulon had not finished.

'The Court condemns them, in addition, to a fine of five francs as guilty of the contravention referred to by the public prosecutor.'

Pécuchet turned to those present. 'A fine is a trifle to the rich but a disaster to the poor. I don't care one way or the other.'

And he seemed to snap his fingers at the Court.

'Really,' said Coulon, 'I'm surprised at people of intelligence—'

'The law excuses you from having any,' answered Pécuchet. 'A magistrate holds office for an indefinite period, while a judge of the Supreme Court is considered capable till he is seventy-five years old, and one of the Primary Court no longer so at the age of seventy.'

But, on a gesture of Foureau, Placquevent came forward. They protested.

'It would be different if you were nominated by vote!'

'Or by the Council General.'

'Or by a board of arbitrators from a respectable list.'

Placquevent pushed them out, and they departed under the hisses of the rest of the accused, who thought to curry favour by such meanness.

To give play to their indignation they went to Beljambe's in the evening. His café was empty, the regular customers being accustomed to leave at about ten. The lamp was turned low, the walls and bar appeared through a mist; a woman came forward. It was Mélie.

336

She did not seem put out, but drew them two beers, with a smile. Pécuchet, ill at ease, quickly took his departure.

Bouvard went back there by himself, amused some of the villagers by his sarcasms on the mayor, and henceforth frequented the tavern.

Six weeks later Dauphin was acquitted for lack of evidence. It was shameful. The same witnesses, whose testimony against them had been accepted, were now suspect.

And their rage knew no bounds when the registrar's office sent them notice to pay the fine. Bouvard attacked the registration system as a danger to property.

'You're mistaken,' said the collector.

'Well, it handles a third of the public revenue. I'd like to see a less vexatious process of taxation, a better land assessment, a change in the mortgage system, and the abolition of the Bank of France, which enjoys the privilege of usury.'

Girbal, unequal to the discussion, became confused in his argument, and did not reappear.

Bouvard, however, pleased the innkeeper; he attracted customers, and while waiting for the place to fill, chatted familiarly with the barmaid.

He enunciated quaint ideas on primary education. On leaving school one should be able to nurse the sick, understand scientific discoveries, and take an interest in the arts. The demands of his programme embroiled him with Petit, and he offended the captain by asserting that soldiers, instead of wasting their time at drill, would do better growing vegetables.

When the question of free trade cropped up, he brought Pécuchet with him, and all through the winter there were angry glances in the café, airs of scorn, insults and shouting, with bangs of the fist on the tables, making the bottles jump.

337

Langlois and the other tradesmen defended protection; Oudot of the spinning factory and Mathieu the goldsmith, nationalism in industry; the landlords and farmers the same in agriculture; everybody wanting concessions for himself, to the detriment of the majority. The discourses of Bouvard and Pécuchet spread alarm.

As they were accused of ignoring 'the practical side of things,' and of a tendency to communism and immorality, they developed these three conceptions: the replacement of the family name by a matriculation number; the institution of a French hierarchy, in which, to keep one's rank, it would be necessary at intervals to enter for an examination; no more punishments or rewards, but in every village a record of each inhabitant, to be transmitted to posterity.

Scorn was poured on their system. They embodied it in an article for a Bayeux newspaper, drew up a memorandum for the prefect, a petition to Parliament and a memorial to the emperor.

The newspaper did not publish their article.

The prefect did not deign to answer.

Parliament was silent, and for a long time they awaited a letter from the Tuileries.

What could be occupying the emperor? Women, of course!

Foureau, on behalf of the sub-prefect, advised them to be more circumspect.

They cared not a jot for the sub-prefect, the prefect, the councillors of the prefecture, even the Council of State. Administrative justice was a monstrosity, for the administration governs its servants unjustly by threats and favours. In short, they became nuisances, and the leading townspeople enjoined Beljambe not to admit these two individuals.

Thereupon Bouvard and Pécuchet burned to distinguish themselves by an achievement which would dazzle their fellow-citizens, and could evolve nothing better than plans for the embellishment of Chavignolles.

Three-quarters of the houses were to be demolished, in the middle of the village a spacious square would be built, an infirmary on the Falaise side, slaughter-houses on the road to Caen, and, at Vaque's Walk, a polychromatic romanesque church.

Pécuchet sketched out a colour-wash in Chinese ink, not forgetting to tint the woods in yellow, the buildings in red and the fields in green, for pictures of an ideal Chavignolles pursued him in his dreams; he tossed on his mattress.

One night this awoke Bouvard.

'Are you ill?'

Pécuchet stammered: 'I can't sleep for Haussmann.'

About this time he received a letter from Dumouchel asking the price of sea-bathing on the Normandy coast.

'He can go to the deuce with his sea-bathing! What time have we got for writing letters?'

And when they had procured a land-chain, a grapho-meter, a spirit-level and a compass, other studies began.

They invaded people's property; often the villagers were surprised to see the two men planting surveying staves in the ground.

With a quiet air Bouvard and Pécuchet announced their project and its probable consequences.

The inhabitants were disturbed, for the authorities might adopt their point of view.

Sometimes they were roughly bundled off.

Victor used to clamber up walls and mount roofs to fix signals for them; he showed willingness, and even ardour, for the job.

They were also more content with Victorine.

When she ironed the washing she pushed her iron over the board humming a tune in a low voice; she busied herself with the housekeeping, made Bouvard a smoking-cap, and her quilted work earned her compliments from Romiche.

This was one of those tailors who go round the farms mending clothes. He stayed at the house for a fortnight.

A hunchback with blood-shot eyes, he made up for his physical defects by his broad humour. While the masters were out, he amused Marcel and Victorine by telling them funny stories, protruded his tongue till it reached his chin, imitated the cuckoo, played the ventriloquist, and in the evening, to save the expense of an inn, slept in the bakehouse.

Then very early one morning, Bouvard, who was feeling cold, went there for some sticks to light his fire.

He was struck motionless by what he saw.

Behind the remains of the chest, on a pallet, Romiche and Victorine were sleeping together.

He had an arm round her waist, and his other hand, as long as an ape's, was clasping her by the knee; his eyes were half closed, and his face still convulsed with a spasm of pleasure. She smiled, extended on her back. The gap in her chemise left her young bosom uncovered, marked with the red imprints of the hunchback's caresses; her fair hair streamed out, and the clearness of dawn cast its pale light over them.

Bouvard felt for a moment as though he had been struck over the heart. Then modesty prevented him from making a single gesture, and he was assailed by painful thoughts.

'So young! Lost, lost!'

Thereupon he went off to wake Pécuchet, and, in a word, told him all.

'Ah, the scoundrel!'

'We can do nothing. Be calm.'

For a long time they sighed together, Bouvard coatless and with arms folded, Pécuchet on the edge of the bed, barefooted and in a cotton nightcap.

340

Romiche was going that day, having finished his work. They paid him disdainfully, in silence.

But fate was against them.

Not long afterwards Marcel took them to Victor's room and showed them a twenty-franc piece at the bottom of his drawer. The boy had asked him to change it.

How had it come there? By a theft, of course! And one committed during their surveying expeditions. But to give it back they would have needed to know whose it was, and if it was claimed they would look like accomplices.

So, after calling Victor, they ordered him to open the drawer; the napoleon was no longer there. He pretended not to understand.

A moment ago, however, they had seen the coin, and Marcel was incapable of lying. The incident had so overwhelmed him that he had kept in his pocket since the morning a letter for Bouvard.

'SIR,
'Fearing that M. Pécuchet may be ill, I ask you to be kind enough—'

'Who is it from?'
'Olympe Dumouchel, *née* Charpeau.'

She and her husband wanted to know at what bathing-place—Courseulles, Langrune or Lucques—they would find the best and most select visitors, the way to get there, the price of laundry, etc.

This insistence made them angry with Dumouchel; then lassitude plunged them into still heavier discouragement.

They went over all the trouble that they had taken—so many lessons, precautions, worries!

'And to think,' they said, 'that once we wanted to make her a schoolmistress, and, only the other day, to get him a job as a foreman.'

'Ah, what a disappointment!'

'If she's vicious, it's not the result of her reading.'

'And I taught the boy Cartouche's biography to make him honest.'

'Perhaps they felt the want of a family and a mother's care?'

'I was a mother to them,' said Bouvard.

'Alas!' answered Pécuchet, 'but some natures have no moral sense, and education can do nothing for them.'

'Ha, a fine thing—education!'

As the orphans knew no other calling, two places would be found for them as servants, and after that, thank God! they could wash their hands of them. And from that day, 'Uncle' and 'Cousin' made them take their meals in the kitchen.

But they soon grew bored, their minds needing occupation, their life an object.

Besides, what does an occasional failure prove? What had been disastrous with children might be less difficult with grown-ups. And they thought of starting an adult class.

A lecture would be necessary to make their ideas public. The large room at the inn would do admirably for that purpose.

Beljambe who, as deputy-mayor, was afraid of compromising himself, at first refused, then, thinking that he would profit by it, changed his mind and sent them word by his servant. Quite overjoyed, Bouvard kissed her on both cheeks.

The mayor was away; the other deputy, M. Marescot, taken up with legal business, would pay little notice to the lecture; so it would be given, and the crier announced it for the following Sunday at three o'clock.

Only on the evening before did they think of their clothes.

Pécuchet, luckily, had kept an old dress-coat with a velvet collar, two white ties, and black gloves. Bouvard donned his blue frock-coat, a nankeen waistcoat and buckskin shoes; and they were very excited as they walked through the village and arrived at the Golden Cross. . . .

(Here Gustave Flaubert's manuscript ends. We publish an extract of the synopsis, found among his papers, which indicates the conclusion of the work.)

LECTURE

THE Golden Cross inn—two wooden galleries at the sides on the first floor with projecting balcony—main building at the end—café on the ground floor, dining-room, billiard saloon; the doors and windows are open.

Crowd: gentry, poorer folk.

Bouvard: 'The first thing is to demonstrate the utility of our project, our studies give us the right to speak.'

Speech by Pécuchet, pedantic style.

Follies of the government and the administration—excess of taxes, two economies to be made: suppression of the Church budget, and also the Army's.

He is accused of atheism.

'On the contrary; but we need a religious revival.'

Foureau comes in and wants to dissolve the meeting.

Bouvard raises a laugh at the mayor's expense by recalling his imbecile rewards for owls.—Objections.

'If it is necessary to destroy the animals that injure plants, it would be necessary also to destroy cattle which feed on grass.'

Foureau retires.

Speech by Bouvard—familiar style.

Prejudices: celibacy of priests, futility of adultery—female emancipation:

'A woman's earrings are the badge of her former servitude.'

Breeding-studs for men.

Bouvard and Pécuchet are reproached with the misconduct of their pupils.—Also why did they adopt the children of a convict?

Theory of rehabilitation. They would dine sometime with Touache.

Foureau returns and reads, as a revenge on Bouvard, a petition from him to the municipal council in which he asks for the establishment of a brothel at Chavignolles.—(Rustic disputation.)

The meeting breaks up in the greatest disorder.

On the way home Bouvard and Pécuchet notice Foureau's man-servant galloping at full speed along the road to Falaise.

They go to bed very tired, without suspecting all the plots that are being hatched against them—explain the motives for ill-will towards them in the curé, the physician, the mayor, Marescot, the villagers, everybody.

Next day at lunch they discuss the meeting again.

Pécuchet sees the future of Humanity in dark colours.

Modern man has been whittled down and become a machine.

Eventual anarchy of the human race (Buchner, 1. 11).

Impossibility of Peace (*id.*).

Barbarity through excess of individualism and the extravagance of science.

Three possibilities: (1) a pantheistic radicalism will break every tie with the past, and an inhuman despotism will result; (2) if theistic absolutism triumphs, the liberalism with which humanity has been imbued since the Reformation succumbs, everything is overturned; (3) if the convulsions which have been going on since '89 continue, endlessly between two issues, these oscillations will sweep us away by their own force. There will no longer be ideals, religion, morality.

America will have conquered the earth.

Future of literature.

Universal vulgarity. All will be a workmen's orgy.

End of the world through cessation of heat.

Bouvard sees the future of Humanity in a cheerful light. Modern man is evolving.

Europe will be regenerated by Asia. The historical law being that civilisation goes from East to West—role of China—the two civilisations will at length be fused.

Future inventions: modes of travel. Balloons.—Submarines with windows, in a constant calm, the movement of the sea being only at its surface.—One will see fishes pass and the landscapes at the bottom of the ocean.—Animals tamed. All kinds of cultivation.

Future of literature (opposite of industrial literature). New sciences.—Control of magnetic force.

Paris will become a winter garden; fruit espaliers on the boulevard. The Seine filtered and warm—abundance of precious stones artificially made—prodigality of gilding—illumination of houses—light will be accumulated, for there are bodies possessing this property, such as sugar, the flesh

345

of certain molluscs and the phosphorus of Bologna. People will be ordered to paint the fronts of their houses with phosphoric substance, and its glow will light the streets.

Disappearance of evil with the disappearance of want. Philosophy will be a religion.

Alliance of all nations. Public festivals.

People will visit other earths—and when this globe is used up, Humanity will migrate to the stars.

Hardly has he finished when the police arrive.—Entrance of the police.

At sight of them the children are terrified as a result of their vague memories.

Marcel's despair.

Anxiety of Bouvard and Pécuchet.—Do they mean to arrest Victor?

The police display a warrant.

It is the fault of the lecture. They are accused of having attacked religion and order, having incited to revolt, etc.

Sudden arrival of M. and Mme Dumouchel with their luggage; they have come for the sea-bathing. Dumouchel is unchanged, Mme wears spectacles and composes fables.—Their bewilderment.

The mayor, knowing that the police are at Bouvard and Pécuchet's, arrives, encouraged by their presence.

Gorju, seeing that authority and public opinion are against them, has hoped to profit by it and accompanies Foureau. Supposing Bouvard the richer of the two, he accuses him of having once seduced Mélie.

'I, never!'

And Pécuchet trembles.

'And even of having given her a disease.'

Bouvard violently protests.

'At any rate he should pay an allowance for the child which is going to be born, for she is pregnant.'

This second accusation is based on Bouvard's familiarities at the café.

346

Little by little the public invade the house.

Barberou, called into the neighbourhood on private business, has just heard at the inn what is going on and arrives.

He believes Bouvard to be guilty, takes him aside, and advises him to yield, to pay the allowance.

Arrival of the doctor, the count, Reine, Mme Bordin, Mme Marescot under her sunshade, and other persons of importance. Outside the lattice, the village children yell, throw stones into the garden. (Now it is well kept, and the inhabitants are jealous.)

Foureau wants to drag Bouvard and Pécuchet to prison.

Barberou intervenes, and Marescot, the doctor, and the count also intervene with insulting pity.

Explain the warrant. The sub-prefect, on receipt of Foureau's letter, has issued a warrant so as to frighten them, with a letter to Marescot and Faverges, saying that they might be left alone if they show signs of repentance.

Vaucorbeil also seeks to defend them.

'A better place for them would be a lunatic asylum; they're maniacs.—I'll write to the prefect about it.'

Everything calms down.

Bouvard will pay an allowance to Mélie.

The custody of the children cannot be left in their hands.— They object; but since they have not legally adopted the orphans, the mayor takes them back.

The children display a revolting insensibility.—Bouvard and Pécuchet weep at it.

M. and Mme Dumouchel go off.

Thus everything has come to pieces in their hands.

They have no more interest in life.

A good idea cherished secretly by each of them. They

hide it from one another. From time to time they smile when it occurs to them, then at last communicate it simultaneously:

To copy as in the old days.

Manufacture of a two-seated desk.—(They seek the services of a joiner for this. Gorju, who has heard their invention spoken of, offers to make it.—Refer to the chest.)
Purchase of books and of utensils, sand-sprinklers, erasers, etc.

They set to work.

THE END

New Directions Paperbooks

Ilangô Adigal, *Shilappadikaram*. NDP162.
Corrado Alvaro, *Revolt in Aspromonte*. NDP119.
Guillaume Apollinaire, *Selected Writings.*† NDP310.
Djuna Barnes, *Nightwood*. NDP98.
Charles Baudelaire, *Flowers of Evil.*† NDP71.
Paris Spleen. NDP294.
Gottfried Benn, *Primal Vision*. NDP322.
Eric Bentley, *Bernard Shaw*. NDP59.
Wolfgang Borchert, *The Man Outside*. NDP319.
Jorge Luis Borges, *Labyrinths*. NDP186.
Jean-François Bory, *Once Again*. NDP256.
Paul Bowles, *The Sheltering Sky*. NDP158.
Kay Boyle, *Thirty Stories*. NDP62.
W. Bronk, *The World, the Wordless*. NDP157.
Buddha, *The Dhammapada*. NDP188.
Louis-Ferdinand Céline,
Death on the Installment Plan. NDP330.
Guignol's Band. NDP278.
Journey to the End of the Night. NDP84.
Blaise Cendrars, *Selected Writings.*† NDP203.
B-c. Chatterjee, *Krishnakanta's Will*. NDP120.
Jean Cocteau, *The Holy Terrors*. NDP212.
The Infernal Machine. NDP235.
Contemporary German Poetry.†
(Anthology) NDP148.
Hayden Carruth, *For You*. NDP298.
Cid Corman, *Livingdying*. NDP289.
Sun Rock Man. NDP318.
Gregory Corso, *Elegiac Feelings American*. NDP299.
Long Live Man. NDP127.
Happy Birthday of Death. NDP86.
Edward Dahlberg, *Reader*. NDP246.
Because I Was Flesh. NDP227.
David Daiches, *Virginia Woolf*.
(Revised) NDP96.
Osamu Dazai, *The Setting Sun*. NDP258.
Robert Duncan, *Roots and Branches*. NDP275.
Bending the Bow. NDP255.
Richard Eberhart, *Selected Poems*. NDP198.
Russell Edson, *The Very Thing That Happens*. NDP137.
Wm. Empson, *7 Types of Ambiguity*. NDP204.
Some Versions of Pastoral. NDP92.
Wm. Everson, *The Residual Years*. NDP263.
Lawrence Ferlinghetti, *Her*. NDP88.
Back Roads to Far Places. NDP312.
A Coney Island of the Mind. NDP74.
The Mexican Night. NDP300.
Routines. NDP187.
The Secret Meaning of Things. NDP268.
Starting from San Francisco. NDP 220.
Tyrannus Nix?. NDP288.
Unfair Arguments with Existence. NDP143.
Ronald Firbank, *Two Novels*. NDP128.
Dudley Fitts,
Poems from the Greek Anthology. NDP60.
F. Scott Fitzgerald, *The Crack-up*. NDP54.
Robert Fitzgerald, *Spring Shade: Poems 1931-1970*. NDP311.
Gustave Flaubert,
Bouvard and Pécuchet. NDP328.
The Dictionary of Accepted Ideas. NDP230.
M. K. Gandhi, *Gandhi on Non-Violence*.
(ed. Thomas Merton) NDP197.
André Gide, *Dostoevsky*. NDP100.

Goethe, *Faust*, Part I.
(MacIntyre translation) NDP70.
Albert J. Guerard, *Thomas Hardy*. NDP185.
Guillevic, *Selected Poems*. NDP279.
Henry Hatfield, *Goethe*. NDP136.
Thomas Mann. (Revised Edition) NDP101.
John Hawkes, *The Cannibal*. NDP123.
The Lime Twig. NDP95.
Second Skin. NDP146.
The Beetle Leg. NDP239.
The Innocent Party. NDP238.
Lunar Landscapes. NDP274.
Hermann Hesse, *Siddhartha*. NDP65.
Edwin Honig, *García Lorca*. (Rev.) NDP102.
Christopher Isherwood, *The Berlin Stories*. NDP134.
Gustav Janouch,
Conversations With Kafka. NDP313.
Alfred Jarry, *Ubu Roi*. NDP105.
Robinson Jeffers, *Cawdor and Medea*. NDP293.
James Joyce, *Stephen Hero*. NDP133.
Franz Kafka, *Amerika*. NDP117.
Bob Kaufman,
Solitudes Crowded with Loneliness. NDP199.
Hugh Kenner, *Wyndham Lewis*. NDP167.
Lincoln Kirstein,
Rhymes & More Rhymes of a Pfc. NDP202.
P. Lal, translator, *Great Sanskrit Plays*. NDP142.
Tommaso Landolfi,
Gogol's Wife and Other Stories. NDP155.
Lautréamont, *Maldoror*. NDP207.
Denise Levertov, *O Taste and See*. NDP149.
The Jacob's Ladder. NDP112.
Relearning the Alphabet. NDP290.
The Sorrow Dance. NDP222.
To Stay Alive. NDP325.
With Eyes at the Back of Our Heads. NDP229.
Harry Levin, *James Joyce*. NDP87.
García Lorca, *Selected Poems.*† NDP114.
Three Tragedies. NDP52.
Five Plays. NDP232.
Carson McCullers, *The Member of the Wedding*. (Playscript) NDP153.
Thomas Merton, *Selected Poems*. NDP85.
Cables to the Ace. NDP252.
Clement of Alexandria. Gift Ed. NDP173.
Emblems of a Season of Fury. NDP140.
Gandhi on Non-Violence. NDP197.
The Geography of Lograire. NDP283.
Raids on the Unspeakable. NDP213.
The Way of Chuang Tzu. NDP276.
The Wisdom of the Desert. NDP295.
Zen and the Birds of Appetite. NDP261.
Henri Michaux, *Selected Writings.*† NDP264.
Henry Miller, *The Air-Conditioned Nightmare*. NDP302.
Big Sur & The Oranges of Hieronymus Bosch. NDP161.
The Books in My Life. NDP280.
The Colossus of Maroussi. NDP75.
The Cosmological Eye. NDP109.
Henry Miller on Writing. NDP151.
The Henry Miller Reader. NDP269.
Remember to Remember. NDP111.
Stand Still Like the Hummingbird. NDP236.
The Time of the Assassins. NDP115.
The Wisdom of the Heart. NDP94.

Complete descriptive catalog available free on request from
New Directions, 333 Sixth Avenue, New York 10014.   2864   † Bilingual.